The Era of Herbalists

The Era of Herbalists

a Novel

Timothy W. Sparks

ISBN: 9798366238496

This book is dedicated to the late Professor Ernest Wettstein. His anthropology lectures stimulated my interest in the past. And to John Page who taught me about horticulture and medicinal plants. And as always, my thanks goes to my significant other, Terrie and to my editor, Max Van Zile. Plus cheers go to JD & J Book Cover Design along with the proofreaders and beta readers at Entrada Publishing

Table of Contents

CHAPTER 1

The Raid

STRONG HANDS SHOOK the boy awake.

"Get up, Pine. Go to the cave."

"Why?" Pine rubbed his eyes. "What's happening?"

"A raid. Gatherers are here. Go now," said his father, Chirp Nyte.

Pine sprang to his feet and slipped his moccasins on.

"Your mother is waiting at the tree line with your brother and sister."

"Why not wake me first?" asked Pine.

"Because they were not sleeping. Take this."

Chirp thrust a gray fox fur pouch into Pine's arms. Fifteen years old and already his son stood eye to eye with him. Pine clutched the bulky satchel with both hands.

"Are you not coming, Father?"

"No. I must protect the apothecary. Go."

Chirp held the door skin open, and in the light of a half-moon, Pine scampered away from the village and into the trees.

Once Pine passed the clearing, Gemma, Chirp's wife, poked her head out from the shrubs and waved a white feather to him before disappearing into the dark woods with Pine and the children.

A few moments later, barking dogs and the cries from the next hut alerted him. Chirp took hold of his battle club with both hands. The club, a hunk of oak the length of a man's arm, had a hefty river rock lashed to the working end.

As he gripped the bludgeon and braced himself, Chirp questioned the timing of the raid. This was late spring, not harvest time, so why had they come so far to Twin Oaks? The village was many days' walk from the prodon's realm.

Torchlight flared outside the hut, and he heard a clear voice call out, "Take the herbalist!"

Slick with bear grease and wearing only a loin skin, a bald, burly man rushed into the hut. By the glow of the oil lamp, Chirp saw strange symbols scarring his bronze skin. The second he cleared the entry, Chirp swung his bludgeon. The blow struck the man's tattooed head, and he landed at Chirp's feet.

The next intruders came through the door as a pair. Chirp jabbed the club like a spear. The basher rock struck the charging man in the mouth. Teeth, blood, and spittle sprayed from the blow. He landed on top of the first victim.

The other man tried to grapple the weapon away. Once Chirp felt the man's strain, he let go, and the gatherer flew against the wall of the hut with a thud. A sizable clay cooking pot toppled onto his head and broke into shards.

Unarmed, Chirp knew his fight was futile as four new men burst in and bowled him over. Realizing his fate, he relaxed and let them haul him to his feet. One of them, a stinky fellow, hefted him by his hair.

He was unable to resist as they wrapped his wrists in front of him with some sort of jute fiber. Chirp strained; rough as mastodon hair, the cord cut into his skin. A gatherer gripped his beard. He jerked Chirp's head down, and another rammed a long shaft between his elbows and spine, forcing his shoulders back. Gatherers took each side of him, and they marched him outside.

The other gatherers helped their injured comrades and began emptying the apothecary. Careful not to break the clay pots holding the herbs, spices, medicinal potions, and healing salves, they fitted them in individual fur pouches. By their orders, the raiders took all the tools and trappings. The gatherers stacked them together into tanned hides, forming two bundles.

The two men holding Chirp between them used the shaft to force him forward. A single man carried a torch, lighting the path ahead, while two others hauled the two bundles of his apothecary on a travois behind them.

At the south end of the village, dozens of torches were glowing. The men pressed Chirp toward the shimmering light. In a clearing, the gatherers shoved him to his knees as more of them led a column of tethered prisoners. The intense glare of the torch by him kept him from seeing anyone's face.

The Era of Herbalists

Spear tips herded the ten men into a tight group. Without warning, harsh hands pulled the rod from behind him. Chirp grimaced as the log burned his back and the crook of his arms. The raider yanked him to his feet by his hair and led him to the group of captives.

Another gatherer, with half a nose, grasped hold of his bindings and secured him to the end with the other hostages.

In this torchlight, Chirp recognized the hunters from his village. This was the second clutch. The hunt master, Falk Moon, and the first assembly were off after wandering elk. Many of these second group hunters were older boys, only a few moons older than his first son, Pine. Among them, Chirp spotted a fisherman he traded with from the village of Seaside Hill, the nearest other hamlet. It was Ute Augend's misfortune to be in Twin Oaks tonight.

More torches glowed in the distance. Another line of captives. As they neared, Chirp realized they were women: prisoners. He counted eleven. Most of them he identified. Sorrow for them pained him, so Chirp asked the gods to protect them. At the same time, he thanked them for shielding Gemma and his daughter Neva, of thirteen years. If they had been found, they would surely be among these terrified women.

The guard leader called to the captives, "Be silent or suffer!"

He ordered everyone up and in line on the trail, first the women and then the men. Chirp trailed as the last prisoner, and he endured the curses and swats from the disgruntled guards. The two men lugging his apothecary walked with the rear escorts.

After several hours, the gatherers ordered everyone to sit while they took turns drinking, pissing, and shitting in the bushes. The thought of them relieving their bodily functions gave Chirp an idea.

He knew that because of the prodon's well-known fear of illness, his instructions to the gatherers would be to bring back only healthy captives. But Chirp was unsure of what fate they would meet should they become sick. He considered the future horrors the women faced as slaves of the prodon; death would likely be preferable.

Near Chirp was a patch of locust plants as tall as a man, and while none of the minders were looking, he picked all the leaves he needed. While the herb had little effect on men, it worked well on women. As stealthily as possible, he convinced the captives near him to pass the leaves to the women and convey to each of them to eat three leaves apiece and to chew them when they got their water ration.

If he were using the herb for treatment, Chirp would boil the leaves in water and medicate as a liquid. But since that was impossible, he guessed at the dose that would yield the results needed. He figured two leaves, but for fear of that not being sufficient, for the larger women he decided on three. This might distress them, but they would come to no lasting harm.

During the next stretch of trail, one of the girls collapsed on her hands and knees. A gatherer guard rushed behind her and raised her up. Abruptly, her bowels emptied as a soupy spray that splattered his feet. The stink assaulted him, and he backed into another woman who was squatting down. The same thing happened to her.

The gatherer called for the group leader. By the time the man reached them, the other nine women were suffering the same. Unsure what was happening, one of the gatherers cried out that the women were possessed. But the leader struck him across the face and grabbed hold of the nearest woman, Marg, a friend of Gemma's. He held her chin and stared in her eyes. "I see no demons! These women are not possessed, they have a sickness!"

The leader brought out his obsidian blade. Chirp closed his eyes so as not to see, but he didn't hear any screams, so he looked. The man was sawing on Marg's bindings, and one at a time he freed the rest of the women and ordered them away so as not to make anyone else ill.

Because of the darkness, the women did not go far. They went to the stream they had crossed earlier and washed themselves. Without fire kits, they huddled together under a tree and waited for dawn.

Meanwhile, the gatherers led the male captives around the soiled area and, without the women in tow, they pressed the men to trudge harder. Once they reached an open meadow, the gatherers ordered everyone to sit. They passed around gourds of water and handed out helpings of tough, stringy meat.

Chirp chewed. Not deer nor bison, nor pig either. Certainly not bear, sloth, or mastodon. Camel, he guessed.

The Era of Herbalists

As Chirp chewed his morsel, a hunter named Sand Skeye whispered, "You have my thanks for saving my woman."

But the gatherer guarding them moved close, so Chirp didn't reply, only gave a slight nod and continued eating his ration. After feeding the prisoners, the gatherers made them lay on the ground. Exhausted, Chirp fell fast asleep along with the rest of the captives.

Eventually the first light from the sun shone on the eastern horizon, and as the sun rose higher, the gatherers rousted the captives. Each of them was given a ration of water. After they finished, the guards led them to the latrine before they continued their march south.

At midday, a group of four gatherers carrying an empty litter met the caravan of slaves. "By order of the Lord Prodon, we come for the herbalist and his wares."

The leader called for his men to round up Chirp and his apothecary.

Leaving Chirp's hands bound together, he was freed from the line of captives and loaded on top of the litter with the two bundles. The four gatherers raised the litter to their waists, then their chests and up to their shoulders. Once they had fitted the litter properly, they started to run.

Considering the landscape, the ride was reasonably comfortable. Mostly, the trails they took had been made by herds of deer. Occasionally, as the trees and brush thickened, they followed wider tracks made by mastodons. The litter jerked as they zigzagged around the massive piles of dung.

Traveling south, they came upon four gatherers who ran alongside them, and one by one, without missing a step, they took the places of the first four men. Rested, these men, all built the same as the last crew, hustled him through a wonderland of flowering plants. Pink bearpaw blossoms, strings of white wind shakers, orange cat mallow and, in the distance, a patch of yellow flowers that might be either widow's wort or spiny bindweed.

The afternoon sun and rhythm of the bouncing caused Chirp to fall asleep. When he eventually awoke, he gaped at the hill that loomed ahead. They started up the incline. The pace slowed only as long as it took to turn the curves of switchbacks. The gatherers' thick-soled sandals pounded the dirt as they forced themselves up the slope. So as not to tumble from the litter, Chirp clenched the rails and leaned forward.

At the crest, four more gatherers relieved the men carrying him, the same as those men they had replaced on the last leg. The vista ahead showed a green valley with a meandering creek. At the near edge, a spire of gray smoke rose into the sky.

This side of the hill dropped at a gentler rate, with fewer rocks on the trail. Still, they took it slower to keep from slipping.

By sunset, the gatherers had delivered Chirp to a camp at the bottom of the hill. Because no escorts came, Chirp overheard them say he was to stay overnight. They cut his bindings and moved him to an elevated cage. For him to enter, Chirp needed to climb five rungs on a ladder. Not quite tall enough to stand, he crawled to the back and sat on the bear skin.

The guard lashed the gate, and as soon as he left, Chirp took in his surroundings. From the structures, he figured this was a permanent camp, three or four times the size of Twin Oaks. He tried to count men, but they scurried about like ants. His best guess was three hundred, but there might be more inside the many huts. A flint quarry must be near, as much of the work involved stone carving and tool making.

In his pen, the bear skin they had left him was poorly tanned, and inside it stank of rot. No matter, Chirp would sleep in the fur.

The cage bars fascinated him; they were made of a wood Chirp had never seen. Yellow, spear-straight, round, smooth, and segmented. He could see from the cuts on top of the wood forming the gate that the segments were hollow. The guard turned away, and he tested its strength. Harder and stronger than oak.

The scent of cooked meat wafted to him and his stomach growled. A guard brought him a gourd filled with water and a hunk of pink meat.

"Tell me," said Chirp. "What wood is this?"

"I do not answer questions," the guard replied.

"Why not?" asked Chirp.

"Because it is forbidden."

"What wood is this?"

"I told you, I cannot answer questions."

"But you already answered one."

"I did not."

"Yes you did. I asked you why you could not answer questions. And you answered that it was forbidden."

"That is different," said the guard.

"How? All I want to know is, what kind of wood is this cage made from?"

The guard looked around. He whispered, "It is called bamboo."

"Where does it come from?"

"From the south. This is all I can say. I must go."

"Wait, tell me when I will see the prodon!"

Without turning his head, the guard muttered, "Two days." He joined his comrades at the fire. Tonight Chirp wished the gods well. He bore them no blame, for these were the actions of men. Soon the throng below began cheering on a fight.

To dampen the uproar, Chirp picked hair from the bear fur. He rolled some into a round shape and stuffed the thing in his ear. After he fitted the other, Chirp wrapped himself in the hairy but less smelly section of fur and set himself to sleep.

CHAPTER 2

Morning in Twin Oaks

GEMMA NYTE WAITED until the dawn before checking if the gatherers were still pillaging. Outside, the morning air had yet to warm. Leaving, she grasped a branch from a stiff shrub to assist her out from the narrow cave exit. Cold dewdrops sprinkled her. From the village, the acrid smell of smoldering fires soured the air, but she did not see anyone about. Caution had told her to return to the cave, and she had waited all through the night for Chirp, but he never came. Worse, thoughts of his death plagued her the whole time. Regardless of the danger, she needed to know.

Before breaking cover, she peeked once again through the trees. Spotting no one, Gemma swallowed the knot in her throat and dashed to the hut. Once she reached the far side, the first thing she noticed was the crooked door cover. Wary, she picked up a river rock. For a moment, she lingered close to the skins of the hut. She listened. Hearing nothing, she slipped in.

No Chirp, nor any piece of the apothecary. The gatherers had taken him. The rock fell from her hand. Heartbroken, Gemma started out the door. Across the village, a gatherer stumbled out of a hut. Gemma ducked back inside.

She peeked out. From her angle, the gatherer appeared to have wandered from the cloud speaker's hovel, a hairy-headed brute with dark tattoos from his neck down. He stretched and moseyed to the bushes to relieve himself. While his back was to her, Gemma ran to the trees by the rock cliff.

With the cover still ahead of her, she worried he would turn soon. Some shrubs presented themselves, and she ducked behind them before he might spot her. On her hands and knees, Gemma crawled the rest of the way to the safety of the trees.

The Era of Herbalists

Behind thick brambles, Gemma located the cave opening. Kneeling, she wriggled through the narrow entry, careful not to scrape herself. So as not to be crowned with clubs, she made her tongue clicks to announce her approach.

A single torch lit the cavern, and Gemma crawled toward the glow. The tunnel widened. Hands reached for her and she edged forward, and her son, Witt, helped her up. Besides him, Neva, Pine, and Chirp's father, Evon, were sheltering inside with some of the villagers.

Even before Gemma had completely risen to her feet, questions assaulted her.

"Are the gatherers still here?"

"Did they burn the village?"

"How many are there?"

"Did you see my son?"

"Why did they come?"

Of all the questions, one pierced her heart.

"Where is Father?" asked Witt.

Unable to hold back, Gemma cried out, "They took him!" and laid on the fur-covered ground, burying her face in her arms.

After a time, Gemma composed herself. She sat, rubbed away her tears, and stood.

"This is what I learned. The gatherers are still here. I saw but one, and he appeared to be newly awakened. I watched him come from cloud speaker's hut. None of the buildings seem damaged; only the pit fires are smoking. Other than the one gatherer, I saw no other person nor dogs about."

"They still may sack the village," said Elm Moon, the hunt master's wife.

"This raid makes no meaning," said Ona Hogg, a mat weaver.

"This was a slave raid," said Evon. Up until now he had kept silent.

"If this is so, we must be of good fortune having my husband Falk, our son Grand, and the first hunters, runners, and dogs away on the hunt," said Elm.

"But Gemma says Chirp is took, so we have no healer," said Ona.

Pine stepped forward, holding the bag. "Father gave this to me."

He opened the bag and showed the skins with the markings and drawings. Then he showed them the samples and identifiers for finding the makings, and the guide for how to process and treat.

Pine passed the bag to Neva. "My sister has been the herbalist helper since her seventh spring."

"We have a new herbalist until my son returns," announced Evon.

The positive statement from her father-in-law gave Gemma hope she would see her husband again.

The first of the gatherers woke, and he staggered to some bushes and pissed. The others were still asleep, having drunk their fill of the fermented berry nectar. As the group leader, he began rousting his men.

The prodon's orders were clear. Capture the herbalist, the whole of his stock, all the healthy tender young women fit to breed who could be caught, and ten sturdy men to serve as hunters. Also, as much salt and preserved meat as could be carried. The prodon's final demand surprised him. Certainly unusual for an offseason raid. Spare the village; harm nothing.

Last night they had fulfilled most of those instructions. Now he ordered his men to collect the salt and meat. Though he would never speak of it, the group leader questioned the sense of such a raid so far from the seat of the prodon's rule.

His men rounded up the salt and the preserved meat, and were ready to begin the return journey before midmorning. After dividing the weight among the bearers, he called for them to get into formation.

The men assembled into two columns. The group leader took the point, and the forward guards assumed the front of the lines with their long spears. Next, the meat bearers positioned themselves, and they were joined by the carriers hauling salt. Four men served as the rear guard; they bore leather vessels of water on their backs.

Once everyone had taken their positions, the group leader ordered them to move, and they trudged off. A day away, a relay team waited to carry the booty to the next relay team. This was the prodon's idea of efficiency.

Evon squirmed out of the cave and stood sentry at the forest edge. Like Gemma said, the village had been spared, and he witnessed the theft of their dried meats and salt.

The Era of Herbalists

But it worried Evon that he couldn't see any of the villagers. He wondered if the gatherers had taken them all as slaves or worse, slayed them. During his vigil he witnessed the gatherers organize and leave. To make sure they had truly departed, he trailed them to the forest. Once they disappeared over the rise, Evon dashed to the nearest hut.

Evon found the wood carver, Bo Rift, his wife Kare, and their small son, Bodo, alive but tethered together with jute. Immediately, he freed them with his flint blade and returned to the cave.

At the cave entrance, he gave the all-clear signal. As each of the villagers exited, he bade them to search their neighbors' huts and to free those tied up. Also, he gave them a notion that there should be an immediate assessment of any loss and damages wrought by the raid.

As an elder, Evon possessed some say, and he suggested a village fire meeting for everyone to declare their losses. Those assemblies traditionally started at sunset, and depending on the emergency that had brought the meeting together, they sometimes carried into the next day.

The Nyte family went to their hut. Evon pulled the door free so that the midmorning sun shone inside. The place was in shambles. Even though Gemma had already visited, now with her family she took more care to see the damages.

"Look," said Evon. He pointed to the floor skin, which was stained crimson. "This is blood." He squatted to look closer and picked something up: a bit of broken incisor. A few feet farther, a front tooth. "Somebody got some teeth broke."

"Chirp?" asked Gemma. She retrieved the rock she left and tossed it outside.

"No, these are green and rotted."

"Father's club is bloody," said Pine.

"So is my ruined cooking pot," said Gemma.

"The apothecary is empty," said Neva. Her shoulders sagged.

"You should check out back," said Witt. "The gatherers may have overlooked the plants."

"Nothing is left!" cried Neva.

Taking her daughter's hand, Gemma went outside. Witt and Evon followed. They checked behind the hut. "The garden still grows," said Neva. "All is not lost."

"Enough is lost," said Gemma. Tears formed in her eyes.

Evon hefted Chirp's battle club and said, "My son is resourceful. If it is in his power to escape, he will come back to us."

Even after he said it, he knew Chirp would not escape, because the prodon would send his army to destroy the village. No one would be spared this time.

CHAPTER 3

The Trail Home

AT SUNRISE, AFTER a wakeful night of stomach cramps and diarrhea, the eleven women, freed from the gatherers, assessed their situation. They had no weapons to defend themselves, no food, and they were half a day from home.

At the creek, they found a herd of elk drinking with a massive bull standing sentry. The women stayed downwind so as not to alert the protector. Once the herd moseyed off, the women took their turn upstream from where the elk were. After drinking first, they bathed and washed their smocks. Refreshed, the women went scrounging for anything they could use to defend themselves from the bears, boars, saber cats, and dire wolf packs.

Fortunately, the gatherer leader who cut their bindings had left their wrists wrapped with the jute fiber. After unravelling their bands, they had lashing material. River rocks and a fallen oak tree gave them some clubs and broken limbs to use as pokers.

Armed with their makeshift weapons, the women kept in a tight group to further discourage predators. As they trudged through the oak forest, birds chirped, squirrels barked, and insects droned. To their good fortune, no saber-tooth cats growled, nor did any bears roar, and no dire wolves howled. Still, they remained watchful and quiet as they trudged through the forest.

By their best guess, the women were soon halfway home. Voices and laughter broke the silence, so they rushed into the bushes and hid. From the safety of the undergrowth, they peered at the gatherers carrying the booty stolen from their village.

Two men from the rear, bearing spears, walked directly toward them. At the underbrush, the men propped their lances against the bushes. They lifted their loin hides and pissed into the shrubs.

Three feet away, opposite one of them, Nel Pyre, a fourteen-year-old girl, held her hand over her mouth and stared at the ground. A golden stream sprayed the leaves and splashed the ground near her.

Laughing about last night's raid, the two men took their spears, turned, and trotted after their companions. Fearing more raiders, the women lingered for a time before rising from their cover.

Once the path was clear, the women headed north to Twin Oaks. The freshly trampled pathway from the recent traffic guided their way. Having had their bowels evacuated, hunger encouraged their pace.

Hours later and near exhaustion, the raucous cawing of crows told the women they were close to the waste pit. They began calling out and dashing toward the village.

Hearing their cries, people collecting firewood for the meeting that night hurried to greet them. Dropping their burdens, the villagers helped the women home to be cared for. The hoots and whistles brought out the rest of the dwellers. Joyous cries filled the air as the women reunited with loved ones. Tonight they would tell their tales. Now they needed food, water, and rest.

That evening the fire blazed, and because he had suggested the meeting, Evon became the talker. He stood so all could see him. "Last night, demons descended on us. They took from us, and we suffer for their crimes. With the help of my son and the gods, our captured women are free. We should offer the gods something."

Thon Doone, another elder, made himself seen. His daughter, Whi, helped him up and, along with his walking stick, she supported him as he spoke. "The gods have our meat and salt. Why should we give them more for taking our second hunter band and herbalist?"

"I agree with Thon. The gods have payment enough," said Walmac Lukan, a clay pot maker.

The Era of Herbalists

"How can you say such a thing?" asked Jal Skeye, the honey finder. "The gods did not take my brother, our herbalist, hunters, meat, and salt. The gods received no tribute from us."

"Listen to Jal and Evon," said Reed Pyre, an amulet maker. "It was not the gods bestowed with what was ours and taken from us by force. Myself, I ask my kin be plentiful to the gods for my sister Nel's safe return."

The path keeper, Jonn, raised up and said, "This should be a choice. To offer to the gods or not."

"That sounds fair," said Walmac.

The consensus agreed. Including Evon, who removed his saber-tooth cat talisman from around his neck and threw it on the fire. Others followed suit, sacrificing a possession each.

Thon, having listened to his nephew Reed, took hold of Whi's arm and started to toss his walking stick into the blaze. Evon stopped him and threw a flint knife in the embers. Smoke curled around the staghorn handle. "Remember, old friend, I owed you a blade. The gods thank you for your gift."

Thon shook his head, laughed, and sat back down on the skin his daughter had brought for him.

A hide tanner, Lane Todd, announced his presence with a loud cough. Evon acknowledged him, and he rose.

"Among the hunters, the fisherman, Ute Augend from Seaside Hill, got took with the second hunt team. Had trading."

Evon asked, "Who will be the sunrise runner for the telling?"

As four hands raised, Evon looked over the volunteers. He knew the speed of his grandson, Pine, but he dared not show bias. The crippled boy, Ash Skeye, was among them. Born with a bent foot, the boy exhibited the spirit of a warrior with an elder's mind, but the gods and his parents had chosen to humble him.

Another hopeful volunteer, Micha Hogg, gave a chuckle and said, "By the time the lame one reached Seaside Hill, the village would wash to the sea."

"And you, Micha Hogg, would be the village idiot by then. I choose Nat Awell," said Evon. Micha turned a shade of red and hung his head.

After admonishing the boy, Evon asked, "Who has lost kin?"

From the show of hands, he counted losses from seven families. "By the practice of our ancestors, once the hunters return and the meat is cured, the village will suffer seven black feather days of mourning."

For each of the losses, the mourners would display a black feather in front of their huts. And each villager was obligated to leave an offering to each of them over the seven days of mourning. Any sort of gift counted. A pretty stone, a flint tool, a bird egg, or even a feather. Most offerings were anonymously left.

Without the comfort of her eldest son, Graygar, away on the hunt, the mention of the loss caused Maple Lukan to burst into tears and lurch to her feet. The theft of her husband, Chal, and her youngest son, Ander, overwhelmed her. Surrounded by her neighbors, sitting or squatting on their mats and hides, Maple stepped carefully over and around the people in her way. Clear of them, she ran to her hut.

To be polite, Evon waited for the woman to reach her destination before he spoke. "Who has other losses to charge?"

Over a dozen hands raised. Evon called the closest, Lane Todd.

"The entire three moons of spirit juice got drunk by gatherers. When the hunters return, they will need another means to celebrate their efforts."

Having already spoken to Lane, Evon said, "If they want, the hunters can trade with Seaside Hill. Hides for spirit juice."

The stolen preserved meat and salt made for all the other losses. The consensus: dig more salt and organize a new second hunt team. This news excited Pine, as this was his chance to compete as a hunter. But he owned no dog, and though other hunters worked without one, Pine did not want to be among them. Tomorrow he would speak to his grandfather.

Except for Marg, none of the other women wanted to speak of their ordeal. With Gemma's encouragement, Marg stepped to the fire and faced the people. "The gatherers made fun with their spear tips," she said, turning and showing where Gemma had stitched her sheath. Marg did not want anyone to see her gash, save her friend Gemma, who asked her daughter Neva for a cure. Neva had made a poultice with segments of shave grass and clay for Gemma to apply.

Marg continued, "They took more fun watching us at the latrine. On a water rest, our men passed leaves to us and said Chirp Nyte asked that we each chew three. They were bittersweet, and we were told to drink. In only the time it takes to start a fire from a flint kit, my belly wanted to cry. The diarrhea came with a stabbing pain, it burst from me like a broken vessel."

Before she continued, she swallowed and held her head down. "It was not myself who succumbed first to the treatment. Nel Pyre shit on a guard's sandals. Sickened by the stink, the gatherer backed into me, and I needed to squat and empty."

Wetness formed in her eyes, and she rubbed them with a forearm. "That guard called that we were possessed, but his leader smacked him and grabbed my face and looked in my eyes. He said to his men he saw no demons but we were sickly."

What sprang from her next came with tears. "He brought his blade to bear. It seemed to me then, from his growl at me, it was time for me to die by his hand. But instead he cut my binding and the rest free as well and bade us to go, so as not to sicken him and the others."

The woman was exhausted, and Gemma walked her to her hut. On the way Marg said, "This I said not to anyone, but a gatherer said to another that the raid was to bring the herbalist to the prodon."

"They came for Chirp?" asked Gemma.

"From the man's mouth, Chirp and his wares were the first cause, but we were second to be wanted. We were to be bred."

"Who would be the father?"

"That was not said. But our most fear was to be raped by the prodon."

"For your freedom I am glad, but I fear Chirp is lost to me."

"Perhaps he will escape."

"He would not try," said Gemma. "He knows the prodon would send his men to burn the village and worse."

CHAPTER 4

The Path to the Prodon

THREE LOUD BANGS on the bamboo pen woke Chirp. "Get awake!" hollered the gatherer guard.

Chirp pulled his head from the fur. He recognized one of the men that had brought him. From the cuts and bruises on the man's face, Chirp guessed him a loser from last night's brawls. That must have been the reason for the man's surly attitude.

"Your face must pain you," said Chirp.

"You should pay homage to the Lord Prodon," snarled the guard.

"For what? This bamboo box?"

"For sparing your life! If it be for me to say, I would stick you and carry you no farther."

"In that case, you would suffer the loss of the comfort I offer your wounds."

"What comfort do you speak of?"

"Yonder, near the creek, grows arnica. From here I see the yellow blossoms in the breeze. If you bring me a handful of flowers, and three fingers of clay, and the tools of my trade, I will make a salve to soothe and heal your injuries."

"Why would you do this?"

"Because I am a healer and I want for no one to wish me dead."

"Would you do this for others?"

"Surely, but with more mud and blossoms for each man."

"Then I will return with what you ask."

"What is your name?" asked Chirp.

"Gorg," replied the man.

Gorg spun around and started off.

"Wait."

Gorg turned his head.

"For the welts on your back, bring more flowers and mud."

Gorg grunted and trotted to where some of the gatherers had congregated around a fire. From Chirp's view it seemed Gorg spoke to three men. From a distance he was unable to tell their mindset.

With a bunch of flowers and a deerskin heap of mud, the guard returned with three comrades: Bru, Luca, and Werth. The three were bruised as much as Gorg.

"What tools do you seek?" asked Gorg.

"Of my two bundles, the heavier will be the one. Inside are two stones and a flint scraper."

The first choice found the grindstone. A granite slab, with a flat bottom and a working surface as smooth as plum skin that curved like the bend of a bow. Gorg passed it to Chirp, who set the stone on the bamboo cage floor.

Gorg brought out Chirp's rounded black piece of basalt. He hefted it to appraise the weight. The dull side maintained a texture like sand, while the other seemed glossy and slick.

"This stone is one to cause harm to an unwatchful head," said Gorg.

"Perhaps," said Chirp. "But not from my hand."

Satisfied with Chirp's response, Gorg handed him the rock.

"My scraper lives in a red fox hide sheath."

Among the other coverings and fur pouches inside the bundle, the red fox stood out. Gorg removed the stone from the swathe.

Gorg placed the scraper back in the pouch and handed it to Chirp. Using his own gourd of water, Chirp splashed some on his grindstone and filled the basin with the flowers. With the rough side of the basalt, he began pressing and grinding. Once the mash stuck to itself, Chirp rolled the smooth side over and over until the pulp turned to a paste. He counted drops of water and used a finger to mix a portion with some brown clay.

Once it was complete, Chirp applied the salve to the abrasions on his wrists.

"Herbalist?" asked Gorg. "If this cure is meant for us, why do you heal yourself first?"

"To test the herb's strength and to show you the safety of the salve."

"How be it?" asked Gorg.

"The arnica flowers are fresh and potent. Give me a moment to mix more, and I will give you each a measure to apply."

With the dull edge, Chirp divided the paste into four equal parts. Scooping the clay with his fingers, he split the mud evenly and mixed a part to each of the helpings of arnica flower paste. Pleased with the results, he gave each man a share.

"Since none of you can see all your own wounds, it may work best for you to apply the salve to each other."

Gorg smeared some on his upper arm; the bruise, a purple and red slash, bore the image of a baton strike. The others wiped the medicine on the places they saw or felt. They took turns spreading the salve on each other, those places unseen or hard to reach.

"Herbalist, it is as you speak," said Gorg. "For this, I vow to you, no harm shall befall you in my company."

"The hurt is no more," said Bru. "You have my liking."

Luca and Werth gave Chirp their thanks as well and brought him warm slices of roasted venison and a wild plum. While he ate, the escorts Aden and Sert took positions at the trailhead.

Recognizing the escort guards' impatience, Gorg opened the cage gate and said, "Herbalist, come forth. Finish your meal as we travel."

Bru and Werth loaded the bundles, and Chirp sat. The four men took their positions. Chirp braced himself and held his gourd of water close as the men raised the litter. Fitting the rails to their shoulders, they skirted the camp and followed the path. The scouts vanished in the distance.

The well-traveled trail meandered along the foot of rolling hills. Gray rock monoliths jutted up from the crests. As the sun moved overhead, the road straightened and the foliage changed from a lowland oak forest to a plain covered with sawgrass and low growing, broadleaf plants with clusters of tiny orange flowers. The sap found in the cradle plant root put restless babes to sleep with smiles, the dried leaves made for a calming tea, and fresh mashed flowers eased the pain of toothaches.

The Era of Herbalists

A field of boulders loomed ahead, and though he had met them both before in the camp, this was the first time on his journey that Chirp caught sight of the escorts. The path straightened and they gained on the guides. Suddenly Aden, the archer, leaped to the side and landed in the sawgrass. He writhed on his back, hugging his leg, grimacing, and cursing.

Holding his spear with both hands, Sert used his lance to part the brush. Spotting movement, he stabbed and raised the lance. A serpent, half the length of a man, squirmed in its death throes from the obsidian tip.

Once he got closer, Chirp recognized the serpent's pale-yellow body, arrow-shaped head, and the dried blood–colored blotches on its body. A dog-killer viper. Ordinarily non-lethal, although the agonizing bite often crippled.

Once they approached, Chirp leaned and asked, "Gorg, can you lower me so I can treat the man's pain? Hurry and take off his sandal before his foot fattens."

Aware of the herbalist's skill, the four men halted next to Aden, the wounded archer, and carefully lowered their burden. Sert heard Chirp and removed the shoe. Already, the site of the bite was inflamed and enlarged.

The moment they lay the litter down, Chirp climbed off and dug into the first bundle. He felt the pouches. His fingers found what he sought: the thick roots lived in a rabbit fur. He handed one to Gorg.

"Gorg, scrape off the brown and have him chew the root until no bitter remains. He should spit out the pulp."

"Will he die?" asked Gorg. He brought out his blade and shredded the bark.

"Not from the snakebite. He will have pain like ten red ant bites. The wolf root will help calm him. A healing wrap will draw away the poison and ease the suffering."

Sweating and shivering, Aden took the root and bit down. Squeezing his eyes closed, Aden chewed and sucked on the bitter stem.

"Will he walk?" asked Luca.

"No," said Chirp. "You must keep him still."

"But we must meet the barge," said Bru.

"So as not to push the poison into him, Aden should ride in my place and I should walk."

Gorg narrowed his face at Chirp. "This could be a place to run."

"Perhaps, but not by me," said Chirp.

Gorg grinned and slapped Chirp's back in jest.

Quickly, Chirp rummaged in his bundles. The dried, crying-widow seeds were the size of his thumbnail—he chose six. Along with the seeds, he smashed a stick of burnt spruce. The properties of the seeds combined with the charcoal would absorb the toxin. After setting his grindstone, he searched the other bundle for the all-heal herb. He found the plant in a deerskin bag. Of this he needed to be liberal.

First he mashed the seeds and the charcoal with the rolling motion of his crushing stone. Once he was satisfied with the texture, he brushed it aside and dumped a handful of all-heal herb, then pressed and rocked the stone with the smooth side. Once Chirp had mashed it to his approval, he added a few drops of water, used his scraper to bunch it together, and continued compressing.

After centering the all-heal powder, he wet a strip of deerskin and pressed it against the pile he had formed. Chirp picked the deerskin up and the herb bonded to the leather. He lay it upright across his knee and added the crushed charcoal and crying-widow seed on top of the all-heal. A few drops of water, and Chirp stirred the medicine into a thick gray paste.

"Wash the bite and wrap his leg, not too tight for the swelling. Be sure to press the paste against the fang marks. The best is to keep the dressing wet."

While they treated the archer, Chirp stored his herbs back in his bundles. A thought struck him. All the time he had performed his trade, his mind had allowed his heartache and the memory of his family to hide from his attention. But at this point it was clear that Chirp's only course was to acquiesce to his situation.

There were gods he could plead to, but which ones? The angry gods, lightning and thunder, could help, but it was never good to wish harm on anyone. The same with the wind gods and the rain gods. The healing gods seemed closest, but he would never hurt with those things the gods had taught him.

The Era of Herbalists

The archer continued to chew the wolf root, though Chirp thought it nothing but pulp. The tone of his skin warmed, but he glistened with sweat. Luca and Gorg carried him to the litter, and he lay where Chirp had traveled.

Once he had ensured his comrade's comfort, Sert asked, "Who will be the archer?"

Of the four, Bru possessed the skill, so Gorg asked Chirp, "Can you bear the weight as did Bru?"

"My strength will abide," answered Chirp. He took Bru's spot, the front left. Bru took the bow and quiver of arrows, and he trotted alongside Sert while the two men ran ahead on the path.

Chirp squatted with the others and took hold of the lift bar. Gorg gave a nod, and with slow, precise movement, they raised the litter to their waists, then onto their chests and then to their shoulders. Once all were secure, Gorg on the front right stepped with his right foot forward, and the others followed in step.

The juniper wood lift bar was padded with soft doeskin and curved where it rested on Chirp's shoulder. The pace was set by Gorg's chant of one, two, one, two, and he would increase the tempo on the straight clearings and slowed on the dips, rises, and curves. Once Chirp picked up the rhythm, Gorg quit counting.

Keeping his mind off his predicament, Chirp took notice of the plants around him. So far, everything he'd seen he had in his apothecary. Mostly he spotted walking root plants, a cure for blisters, and tale teller's leaf plants, a stimulant many hunters carried.

Among the wildflowers, Chirp spotted a patch of bear-breath—the gossamer flowers made a fine base for an insect repellent. Something he kept in abundance.

Up ahead, at the base of a rounded knoll, Bru and Sert lingered on the path alongside a thick growth of green foliage. A narrow creek skirted the edge of the hill, with a small herd of pigs near the water. Not wanting to drink after the pigs, Bru kept an arrow at hand while Sert cleared the brush to expose the spring. Water poured from a crack in the rocks.

On his knees, Sert reached up into the crevasse with a drinking gourd. He filled the vessel with the spring water bubbling from the rocks and passed it back to Bru.

The litter bearers did their best to avoid the piles of pig shit scattered along the path. They found a clear spot close to the escorts, and Gorg made them lower the litter. The movement caused Aden to rouse from his sleep. He pulled his foot back and removed the wrap. The leg was less swollen, and the wound appeared only slightly irritated.

Bru handed Aden the gourd and he started guzzling.

Seeing him, Chirp said, "Careful not to drink too much too quickly."

But Aden ignored him and drank the vessel dry. He handed Chirp the gourd, who passed the empty cup to Bru.

"More," said Aden. His eyes bulged, his cheeks swelled, and he heaved. Chirp dodged the burst of mostly clear vomit.

Bru busted out laughing and gave the empty gourd to Sert to fill. Suddenly, the bushes behind them cracked and snapped loudly. Bru readied an arrow, and Sert seized his spear. A massive wild sow and a string of piglets broke through the brush, heading directly to the stream. The back of the sow rose close to a grown man's chest. Ignoring the men, the piglets squealed and romped in the water while the sow drank.

Werth and Luca found rocks to throw should the sow decide to attack, while Gorg brandished a broken limb and put himself between Chirp, Aden, and the sow.

The piglets continued to wrestle and roll in the water, but having drunk her fill, the sow hustled them back into the brush. The piglets' noisy complaints continued until they were out of earshot.

Sert went back to filling gourds, and after a snack of dried bison they set up to continue the journey. Unable to walk yet, Aden still needed to be carried. To give their shoulders a rest, they switched sides.

The broad path descended gradually with an increase in vegetation. Up ahead, Sert and Bru came into view, but they turned to the right and vanished. At the bend, the sight of the river so soon surprised Chirp. Broader than a man should try to swim and darker green than the forest, the waterway where he walked was vast. In the distance, it flowed from the mountains in the east and meandered west toward them like a worried serpent.

"Where do we go from here?" asked Chirp.

"We are going to meet with Master Lewell," answered Gorg. "He will take you to the prodon on the barge."

"Who is he?" asked Chirp.

"He is the one who is the say of the prodon," said Gorg.

"For him to greet you is a great honor," said Luca, who carried his share of the litter behind Chirp.

Up ahead, Sert and Bru ran toward the river. By the time Chirp and the litter bearers reached the shore, the escorts had spilled the whole story of what had happened on the journey.

CHAPTER 5

The River to the Prodon

CHIRP AND THE litter bearers advanced, and he received his first view of the prodon's barge. The float was as long as the tallest of trees with a shape like a peapod. Unlike the wooden dugouts the fishermen in Seaside Hill made, the vessel had been constructed from animal skins. The light spots on the dark, slick hide were unknown to Chirp. Several men held the boat against the shore.

From a distance, Chirp regarded Lewell. He stood out among the sixteen paddlers and the tillerman. Those men were bare-chested, while Lewell wore a leather shirt decorated with feathers and bones. Besides that, he was an immense man. A hawklike nose protruded from his bronze face, and his brown eyes seemed too small for him. The man was bald, except for a single curl of dark hair that stuck out from the left side of his oblong head. The sight reminded Chirp of a squirrel's head poking out from a den.

Gorg told them to lower the lift to the ground.

"Greetings, herbalist!" said the large man. "I am Master Lewell, the sayer of the prodon, lord and master of all to be seen."

"Chirp Nyte is how I am called."

"Chirp Nyte, what deeds! Already the healer. These men pledge their allegiance to you. And you, the captive, carried the heft of a captor."

"The gods have wished this to be so," said Chirp. "Until the gods make things different, then I have no choice but to follow their will."

"The only god is the Lord Prodon. Remember this and speak of no others."

"Does the prodon make rain?"

"If rain falls, it is Lord Prodon's will."

The Era of Herbalists

From this, Chirp decided to keep silent. Something his father had told him growing up. Gods do not boast or make false claims.

"Bid your charges your leave and we shall be off," said Lewell.

Chirp clasped hands with each of the men. Standing, Aden embraced Chirp for saving his leg from the snake bite and bearing his weight.

Chirp and Lewell boarded the barge, and they took their seats beside each other in the center. The paddlers loaded the apothecary bundles and several baskets of flint tools behind them. The barge rocked with the weight changes, as well as when the rowers took their positions. After the last man boarded, the slim, dark-skinned man brandished a long spear and went to the bow. Floating free, with the help of the current, the barge drifted away from shore. Once all had their paddles, the tillerman called, "Stroke!"

The boat lurched with the force, and the tillerman directed them to the middle of the river, where the paddlers took advantage of the swifter current.

"Herbalist," said Lewell, "you must have questions. Perhaps you ask yourself why the prodon summons you to him."

"For his pleasure is my thinking."

"Indeed, but for more than joy. A sickness troubles a great many. For each ten inflicted, seven die."

"Tell me of the sickness."

"First are chills, then fever and the shakes. Some die quickly, and some are plagued with more chills and fever. For survivors, pain troubles all the muscles."

"Can this barge turn back?"

"Why? The prodon awaits us."

"The cure is behind us. The bark from quito trees."

"What trees do you speak of?"

"The stout ones with the rough red bark."

"We shall stay our course, as many more are ahead."

As Lewell said, before them on the right bank was an extensive grove of quito trees. Lewell gave orders to the tillerman, who directed the paddlers to a beach to moor the barge. Before the bow reached the sandy bank, several of the paddlers climbed into the shallows and helped tow the barge against the shore. The spearman searched the water with the lance poised to strike at any threat.

"What does the spearman hunt for?" asked Chirp.

"The river monster dwells near here."

"River monster?"

"A great beast comes from the depths with a mouth that swallows men."

"This beast I have not heard spoken of before," said Chirp.

"Few have seen the beast and lived to speak."

"Have you yourself seen the creature?"

"No, I have not. The prodon offers a reward for one's capture."

"Does the thing live on land as well as the depths?"

"Nothing is understood except that men disappear when they swim and the few people that were witness only talked of the vast mouth taking the swimmers without leaving any flesh, blood, or bone."

"Does the beast trouble the barges?"

"Never."

"If no one swims, then nothing is harmed."

"People bathe."

"If it were for me, I would bathe elsewhere."

Because of the mass of people infected, Chirp enlisted the paddlers to reap bark from the quito trees. He showed them how to harvest the bark without wounding the trees. A single three-finger-wide strip from a man's reach to the root. So not to offend the river god, Chirp instructed the paddlers to take the bark on the opposite side of the trees. But because of Lewell's declaration that the prodon was the only god, he told them that the reason was to obtain the strongest medicine.

While Chirp and the paddlers labored, Lewell paced and muttered to himself. As if another person was marching with him, he gestured and waved about with his hands. The spearman, apparently so as not to join in the labor, searched the shadows in the water, hunting in vain for river monsters.

Once they had sufficient bark, the paddlers returned to their places. For the bark's preparation, Chirp instructed Lewell how to brew the cure. Already behind pace, Lewell ordered them to resume paddling. Chirp took his seat and Lewell held out his hand. "You seem to me a man to be trusted, but I am not Lord Prodon, so pass me the flint blade you toiled with."

Chirp handed him the knife and said, "Throughout the land, the prodon's wrath is told. Should I cause him anger, then truly the prodon would take vengeance on my family or on the village from where I come. This I would not wish."

With a grin, Lewell held the flint to Chirp. But he kept his hands at rest and said, "For me, the tool has finished its purpose."

Laughing, Lewell set the blade aside and the barge continued its journey.

In the sky ahead a dark cloud was rising. Not a storm, but a fire. Before Chirp asked, Lewell said, "Yonder is the funeral pyre. The flames have grown since I passed only a few suns before. The cure is in need."

He urged the paddlers to push harder.

Later, they could see the flames. Lewell said, "Fortune smiles on us, since the wind carries the stench away from us."

To himself, Chirp thanked the wind god for bestowing the favor he had asked earlier.

The barge rounded a bend and, in the distance, Chirp glimpsed the prodon's tower. Like no structure he had ever imagined. Even at this expanse, from the yellow glow in the sunlight Chirp guessed the material to be bamboo.

If the structure were alive, it would be a beast. On top, a bamboo thing like a giant lily flower protruded from the tower. Chirp had no theory as to the purpose, except maybe to catch the wind. But he could not fathom a reason for holding wind prisoner.

Around that thing was an overwhelming spectacle. For as far as his vision allowed, he witnessed an immense human presence. And among the mass of humanity lay a wasteland.

The paddlers continued to a straight stretch of water. Another structure loomed ahead. This bamboo thing moved in slow circles. Baskets dipped into the river and emptied into other baskets on another moving thing. That device turned on a flat plane. Lines of men ferried the baskets on their heads out of view.

A foul whiff came his way, and Chirp considered the unwashed population he was about to encounter. "Master Lewell? The stink of the people is about to overcome us."

"Until we reach the cook fires, nothing can be done."

"But there is a cure."

"Then heal me, herbalist, before we reach the mooring."

"In my bundles, of which one I must guess. My salve stays."

"Hurry, as the place nears."

Chirp gave each bundle a sniff. To be sure of what his nose told him, he pulled a gray fox skin pouch out and breathed in the menthe paste.

"Here," he said as he held the clay pot out to the leader. "Dab your finger and take a measure to rub on under your nose."

The man narrowed his eyes. "Is this a trick on me?"

Chirp stuck his finger in the paste and rubbed it on his mustache. "No trick."

Once Lewell caught the pleasant scent, he did the same as Chirp. "It must be a powerful medicine to overwhelm the stench that is before us."

"More is not harmful," said Chirp. "If it pleases you, your paddlers are welcome to share."

"No, they will stay with the river. It is for them to return to the north and wait for others to ferry here."

On hearing that, Chirp guessed the men captured in Twin Oaks would be the ones Lewell spoke of.

A bamboo transport was waiting at the mooring to carry Lewell and the herbalist to the prodon. The thing, the length of a battle dugout, featured a bench in the center. Lewell and Chirp sat, eight men lifted them, and they advanced toward the tower.

"It is only a little farther, herbalist," said Lewell. The smoke thickened as they edged closer to the tower. On one side, cooks cranked levers and turned flanks of meat over the glowing coals in a field of a hundred fire pits. On the other side of the open path, men swarmed about. Baskets and bundles of all sizes and measures of weight passed about in seemingly endless streams. In the far distance, he spied sawtooth cliffs, the color of dried blood. The mountain was pocked with caves.

"Master Lewell?" asked Chirp. "What is this mass of men?"

"Those at the east make the ground smooth for the tower's path."

"The thing moves? How?"

"More than a hundred men lift the tower."

"Please tell me more."

"Do you see those who are the farthest?"

Chirp nodded.

"Those are the reapers who slay all the plants and creatures. The ones closer are diggers and fillers. It is they who smooth the ground with lash cords and drag rocks so the carriers walk easily and the tower does not tremble."

"Is it true that the prodon's feet never touch the loam?"

"Mats are laid before him, and if there are none, the slaves lay on the dirt for him to step."

A loud voice overwhelmed the buzz of the crowd. Chirp held his hands over his ears. "Is that him shouting?"

"Yes, he uses his great mouth so all can hear."

"It hurts my ears and his words warble. What is he saying?"

"He is declaring, 'I am the Lord Prodon! You are my keep! I shield you from spoil! My will is your being!'"

"What is that he bears on his head?"

"That, herbalist, is his hair."

"But Master Lewell, it is yellow! How can there be yellow hair?"

"A potion makes it so."

"It looks not true, but as dead locust plants and dried grass."

"Be careful, what you speak is blasphemy."

"As you wish. I will not speak of his hair again, but not saying so will not change how I view foolishness."

"Should you wish for your life to remain, you will learn to perceive all the prodon's foolishness to be wisdom."

Nothing more was said until the lift reached the tower. The litter lowered, and Lewell gestured for Chirp to climb down first.

"Prepare to meet Lord Prodon."

"How am I to address him?" asked Chirp.

"As Lord Prodon."

To rise to the top of the tower, Lewell led Chirp to a bamboo platform. As soon as they stepped on the bamboo floor, ten stout men picked up a thick, braided jute cord and tugged. The platform wobbled, and Lewell showed Chirp where to hold so as not to tumble out. The farther the men pulled away, the higher the platform rose. In only a few moments they were level with the floor of the tower.

Two guards with blue painted faces raised the tower railing and greeted Lewell with hand grasps, and they helped Lewell off the lift. After he was clear, the two brutes seized Chirp by the arms and dragged him in front of the prodon. The man sat on a throne made from mastodon tusks. From the prodon's elevated position he seemed an immense man with broad shoulders. A wide neck supported his square head, which sprouted a score of yellow spikes as long as a man's hand.

"Herbalist. Runners have brought word of your treachery. Only you could have given the women something to make them shit so. You cost me eleven maidens. How should you be punished? Should I blind you?"

"Lord Prodon, if you blind me, I will not be able to serve as your herbalist."

"Perhaps I should take away your tongue."

"How then, Lord Prodon, could I tell my patients of my medicines?"

"Very well. What if I should cause you to be without a hand?"

"Lord Prodon, you would suffer the loss of my skills to fashion medicines and administer the cures."

"Would you not still serve me with no feet?" asked the prodon.

"To gather my herbs and such it would be for me alone in the fields to know the identifying, time for harvesting, and the keeping pure."

"You must be punished. I demand it."

"For me, Lord Prodon, to have been taken from my life is a worse hurt than any other torture."

The Era of Herbalists

"For me I see not enough hurt for the loss of eleven women. Should I take away your manhood, you would still be a herbalist. Perhaps even a better one."

Lewell whispered to the prodon, who paused for a moment.

"Lewell tells me you claim a cure for the shaking sickness."

"Yes, Lord Prodon."

"Should the cure be true, then I will spare your punishment."

"Thank you, Lord Prodon."

"Should you not cure the sickness, then all those things I spoke of will be done to you before your death and I shall seek another herbalist elsewhere."

"Yes, Lord Prodon. From where should I work?"

"Master Lewell will show you."

CHAPTER 6

The Bitter Cure

THE GUARDS ESCORTED Chirp to the lift. Out of earshot from Chirp, Lewell chatted with the prodon. From his hand gestures, Chirp guessed Lewell was sharing the story of his capture, his earning comradery with his escorts, and of the quito trees and failure to spot the river monster.

Taking in his surroundings, Chirp looked about from his high position. To the north were the trees and hills he had come from. To the east, past rows on round-topped knolls, he spotted an endless ridge of snowcapped mountains. The view south held a meadow mixed with a thick forest of trees, and to the west over the trees he saw the sea.

Lewell rejoined him, and Chirp clasped hold of a cord. With a hand signal, Lewell ordered the men below to lower them to the ground.

"Master Lewell. For such a mass of medicine I will need some assistance."

"All you need will be provided," said Lewell. He led Chirp through a worker's area. Potters, weavers, tool makers, and wood carvers toiled in straight rows. None looked up as they passed by.

To Chirp's surprise, Lewell led him to a high bamboo fence. Lewell opened the gate, and Chirp stepped into a spacious enclosed area with two huts. A lengthy split log lined a wall. Chirp assumed the seat was for patients awaiting care. A fire blazed in the open stone hearth in the center of the space.

He entered the larger hut. Not a new place. All his apothecary was unpacked on shelves. Among his things, Chirp found additional grindstones and herbs he guessed the former herbalist had abandoned. As he took inventory he rearranged his herbs, potions, spices, and salves by their purpose. Later, he would assess those things left behind.

His grindstones rested on a waist-high granite table. Chirp regarded the flat, smooth surface and the basalt roller rock someone had added to his tools. The roller would be well used.

He peeked into the other hut. A simple sleep chamber. What he wanted was to climb into the cozy bed nest. But Lewell was pacing.

"Herbalist? When are you going to make the cure you promised?"

"The quito bark needs pulverizing. Four sturdy men with two heavy stones each would make the work go quickly."

"What else?"

Chirp studied the pile of bark strips. In his head he considered how much medicine the bark would yield for the many affected people. A cauldron of steaming water sat next to the hearth.

"Provide me with three more cauldrons half full of freshly boiled water to soak the pounded bark. Later, I will need as many assistants and gourds available to distribute the remedy to the afflicted."

With a wave of Lewell's hand, a gatherer rushed over, and Lewell passed him the instructions. The man took off at a run.

"The man is Patto," Lewell told Chirp. "He will answer to you. For me the day has been a trial. While I rest, I have assured Lord Prodon of *your* continued labor."

"Yes, Master Lewell. My rest will come after my task is accomplished."

Leaving the gate open, Lewell left Chirp to his assignment. First, Chirp divided the bark strips into four even stacks. He rolled each quito strip with the bark on the outside. He counted them as he worked. Forty-seven. He left eleven rolls in each pile, then cut the three extra strips into quarters and evened the stacks.

Patto returned with four hefty men carrying rocks. Chirp showed them where to work. After a time, two men entered bearing a wooden rack which held a simmering cauldron. Those men were followed by two other pairs of haulers. Chirp directed them where to set the vessels. Not all the men understood him; Patto spoke to those men in a different tongue.

Instead of giving Patto more instructions, Chirp asked, "Tell me, Patto. What became of the herbalist before me?"

"Lord Prodon punished him."

"Is he dead?"

"Yes, he died many times over."

"For what crime was he killed?"

"He failed to cure this sickness."

Chirp swallowed. Should the disease be the shaking sickness he knew, he was sure of the cure. However, if this ailment proved different, then rather than be tortured to death, he would choose to eat some snakeweed leaves. Not a pleasant death, but a quick one.

To concoct the cure, first, Chirp evened the water levels in the four cauldrons. Next, he assigned each man a cauldron to feed the pulverized bark. The men pounded one roll of quito bark at a time. As soon as Chirp approved, they dumped the leavings into the steeping water. To ease the bitter taste, Chirp stirred a measure of powdered bullfoot root into the mix with a wooden spoon the length of a man's leg.

After a time, the liquid cooled and turned milky. The medicine was potent. Each of the four robust men picked up a cauldron. Patto led them to the sick field, and Chirp followed. Mats on dirt covered the meadow. Chirp counted two hundred seventy-three stricken men and women. More than Lewell had first said.

By his calculation, there would not be a sufficient quantity to give all a dose from the first brew. He whispered to Patto, who then announced in a loud voice, "All who can, sit up and raise a hand."

Counting eighty-six sitting men and women with raised hands, Chirp asked for them to be separated. He told Patto to tell his twelve assistants to give the people unable to raise their hands a half gourd full of the most potent remedy. Others raised their hand but were unable to sit up. Chirp told Patto to tell the assistants to treat those people next.

Everyone able to both sit up and raise their hands would be getting their medicine from the second brew. Not as potent as the first batch, but Chirp reasoned that the people able to rise were the less ill.

The Era of Herbalists

Finally the medication ran out, and the burly gatherers carried the cauldrons with the soggy quito bark back to Chirp's work area. Already, Patto had ordered more water. With green wood tongs, the helpers added scorching stones to the fresh water. After the mixture heated to his satisfaction, Chirp used a piece of deerskin to skim the ash off the top. He added powdered bullfoot root, moved from one pot to the next, and stirred. Patto sent for more spoons.

With more hot stones and more help stirring, Chirp thought the medicine to be ready. When he tasted it, from the bitterness he could tell the second batch was more potent than he had expected. The milkiness of the solution confirmed the strength. Silently, Chirp thanked the goddess of trees.

The cauldrons cooled and the men carried them to the sick field. Already some of those he had treated appeared improved. The helpers started dosing those patients they had separated earlier.

With several helpers following, Chirp walked among those still bedridden. He checked their eyes, the glands under the chin, and their tongues. He pointed to the patients needing another dose.

Chirp worked through the sunrise, and soon he learned two men had died. He felt a failure until Patto indicated that the night before, the dead had numbered over twenty. As the final batch brewed, Chirp checked the patients once again. Some of the bedridden were up, and some well enough to return to their work.

"Herbalist," said Lewell. "The cure worked. You have spared yourself the prodon's punishments. He may reward you."

"Would he send me back to my village? To return to my family would be the only reward for me."

"No. In truth, you best forget them for all time."

"Yes, Master Lewell. To my family I am dead, and I must grieve for them as they mourn me."

CHAPTER 7

Mourning in Twin Oaks

FOR THE VILLAGE, the theft of the preserved meat and salt hit hard. But the loss of the hunters and the herbalist took a deeper, more lasting toll. More so for those who had lost loved ones.

Determined to mourn Chirp until her own death, Gemma vowed to do so no matter the traditions. In her own lifetime she had witnessed how others endured their losses. With some it was a long-lasting sorrow, and others, an eagerness to take a new husband or wife. For her, the loss of Chirp was the loss of her heart. Now she felt so much of a hurt that, if not for her children's urging, Gemma would have taken no food or drink.

Envisioning Chirp's fate in the clutches of the prodon, Gemma believed the black feather on her new, smaller hut to be appropriate. Besides, Neva and Witt had the apothecary. Next year or the year after, Pine would want a site for his own hut.

Each day from the rising of the sun to its setting, Gemma mined salt. Without care for the world around her, she dug, sifted, and strained. While her hands separated impurities, her thoughts drifted to memories of Chirp. In her mind Gemma sent him messages, hoping to receive one from him.

Every day of mourning, Neva and Witt collected the offerings. Today, on the last official time of grieving, they found a new stone oil lamp, a bone bear talisman, a sprig of menthe, a dove egg, and an assortment of stones and feathers. Since their father had been taken and Neva took his position, Witt became the assistant herbalist.

The Era of Herbalists

To Pine, grieving meant driving deeper into his goal to be a hunter. From his first memory, his focus never had wavered. His father and grandfather both recognized the spirit of the hunter in him and encouraged him. To him, the achievement of his goal of success as a hunter would be a tribute to his father.

Devastated as he was, the anger he felt toward the prodon and the gatherers became his fuel to run and toil. Still, not having his father left a bigger hole in his heart than he thought he could bear. Adding to his heartache, the talk at the council had been to not have a second hunt team. But his grandfather was steadfast in his visions of Pine as a hunter. Still, doubt plagued him.

The black feather stayed fixed to Gemma's hut long after the mourning period. Every day she tested the firmness to be sure the wind did not steal the misery from her. Having Witt with her kept her from shedding sorrow blood. Not many practiced the ancient ritual.

Only days after the official days of mourning ended, some single men strolled by her hut. And even after recognizing the black feather, they followed her around the village. To discourage them further, she began carrying a raven's tail feather any time she left her home. On one occasion a man grew bold and challenged her resolve in public. She shook the thing in the man's face to chase him away. Eventually, they gave up and sought other women.

The following spring, news spread through the village. The hunt master had picked his son, Grand, to lead the second hunt team. A competition was planned to join him. This was his chance to be a hunter, so Pine Nyte readied himself. Seven of the seventeen challengers would be selected. The problem was that he still owned no dog. Not having a dog ached. So he sought the wisdom of his grandfather. He found him squatting in front of his hut, feeding sticks to the morning fire.

"Blessings for the day, Grandfather."

"Be blessed, Pine. Sit by me. What question do you have that you wear?"

"Grandfather, why have I no dog for mine? How can I compete?"

The old man rubbed his hands together close to the fire. "Young Pine, a dog is a spirit animal and the spirit will find you when it is the time."

"But Grandfather, the testing is near."

"Be patient. A great spirit awaits you."

"How can you know this?"

The old man took a stick and stirred the embers. "Because a dream told me this was so."

"Am I to do nothing but wait?"

"No. You should keep to your skills and learn the signs of predator and prey. Watch the sky and care for the wind."

"Why is the wind to be cared for?"

"For the dog's nose. Now go. I will tell more later. Do your chores. Practice. Make your tools. Have you fashioned a blade?"

"Not yet, Grandfather."

The old man reached into his pouch and pulled out a carved piece of elk antler. He handed it to Pine. "Your father carved this handle for your hunting knife. He hid it from the gatherers."

Pine admired the carvings. A symbol of the sun on one side and a crescent moon on the other. "I will fill it with a worthy blade."

"Go. Do your chores before your mother needs to remind you."

"Yes, Grandfather, I will give tribute to the gods of the hunt first."

Every day after his chores, Pine ran. And each day he sprinted farther than the day before. On this day, one moon away from the competition, he tested his endurance up a steep hill. The hill, close to the sea, was the farthest he had sprinted so far. He pounded his legs up toward the top of the knoll. Between the trees, the sun glared in his face and he tripped on some loose stones.

To his surprise, he landed on his rear, hard. If not for the wet bit of deerskin in his mouth, he might have cracked his teeth. He spat out the strip of leather. As he pressed his hands on the ground beside him to gain his feet, something cut his finger. The milk white stone held a sharp edge. He sucked his finger until it stopped bleeding.

Pine found more of the white stones nearby, some larger than a man's head. He tested a broken piece against a strip of leather. The shard cut as well as black obsidian and seemed just as hard, if not harder than his grandfather's broad hunting spear points and knives. Pine had never seen such whiteness in rock anywhere in his village, nor among the other hunters.

The Era of Herbalists

He decided this to be his secret place and his secret stones, where he could also practice making the sharp arrowheads, spear points, knife blades, and hide scrapers. Those tools he would need when he ascended to become one of the hunters he knew he would one day become.

This place was farther from his village, and he had seen no other of the challengers he would face running the distances he ran. Spring was giving way to summer, and Pine's testing would come on the first day of the solstice celebration. He felt ready, but kept increasing his speed and distance and difficulty over inclines and obstacles. Pine knew the course changed each year, and that the trail to follow would only be revealed at the start of the race.

Selecting some stones to take home, a breeze brought what he thought he heard was singing. He could not make out the words, but the voice and melody shared gladness and some sorrow. He listened again but just heard the wind.

He slammed a hunk on a nearby boulder and broke off a large chunk. What could it be if he could shape the blade without changing the form? Possibly the shape of an axe. A voice behind him caused him to fumble the stone, and only with luck did he manage to keep hold of it and by some miracle, avoid cutting himself.

"What are you doing?"

He turned. A young girl in a red deerskin sheath with markings of flowers made from sea shells and feathers stood with pursed lips and balled fists.

Smiling, he said, "I am trying to make tools with the white stone I have found here. I thought this place a secret."

The girl crossed her arms in front of her and frowned. In a sharp voice she said, "It *is* a secret! My secret!"

Pine lowered his face and in a soft voice said, "I shall leave the secret for you and abandon the stones. My only wish is to know of the singing I heard before the wind carried the pleasure of the song away."

With that, the girl relaxed. She smiled and said, "My name is Lily and I am of the Sayed clan of the fisher people in the village Seaside Hill. It was my voice you heard. This is where my voice is free, and the place I sing brings the sound back to me."

Pine grinned. "I am Pine from the Nyte clan of the moccasin people in the village of Twin Oaks."

Lily asked, "Are you of the Nyte clan kin to the herbalist captured by the prodon's gatherers?"

"Yes, you speak of my father, Chirp Nyte. Now my sister, Neva, is the village herbalist."

Lily changed the subject. "This hill is a far distance from Twin Oaks."

"I am practicing for the hunter's competition."

She searched around them. "Where is your dog?"

"Sadly, all the dogs in my village are owned, so I must compete alone."

"In Seaside Hill there are many dogs. I will ask if one is for trade."

"Please do. The competition begins next moon."

"I must go," Lily said. "You may keep your stones, and this knoll is large enough for two to share as a secret."

If Pine could lift off the ground and fly, it would have been possible with how light he felt. "I thank you for sharing the secrets together and I really do like the stones, but I still wish to hear you sing."

Lily gazed at Pine and scrunched her lips. "My voice has not chosen me to share it—perhaps someday."

As Pine looked up at the sky, he saw the hour was past the distance to his afternoon chores. "I have a long run. Our secrets are safe; may we chance again." Pine ran off at high speed, as the girl he met had left him with a feeling of lightness. He looked ahead and realized he was coming to the valley. It seemed as if he had just left her minutes ago; not only that, but the sun was still high. He must have run like a deer.

CHAPTER 8

The Quest for a Dog

THE VILLAGE OF Seaside Hill—Lily's home, and where the fisher people dwelt—was nestled on the side of a gentle hill above the western seashore. There the villagers fished, hunted, farmed, and traded.

Like all villages, Seaside Hill had many dogs. Dogs hunted, hauled, protected the foodstuffs as they dried in the sun, and safeguarded the children as they played. A dog's value was considered high trade.

Today, Lily's mother had given her some weavings to barter for a dog to give to her friend. Lily held the door flap open to view the day. Smoke rose into a blue sky. Lily breathed in the aroma from the many fires curing the fish and clams. The sounds of barking dogs and children's laughter mixed with the sound of the sea as the sun rose off the mountains. The tide was coming in.

With her arms full of weavings, she went to a fisherman she knew, Hal Lago. Since he owned seven dogs, she hoped he would trade. Because he was sitting at his fire with his back to her, Lily called, "Fair day, Hal Lago."

"Lily Sayed. May the day be fair to you. Are you here for my clams? Some are near cooked."

"Not today. My quest is to offer trade for one of your dogs."

Eyeing Lily's burden, Hal said, "Your mother's weavings are cherished by all but, dear Lily, I have only seven dogs. When I owned but six before, I feared to leave only five to guard and worried with but one to fish with me. Someday I hope to have eight."

"Do you know of any who might be willing to trade?"

Hal scratched his chin. He said, "Visit the cloud watcher, as he has the ears from all those who seek his counsel."

Lily thanked the man and walked to the cloud watcher's hut.

Stem Bruk was a fourth-generation cloud watcher. The knowledge came from stories and ages of watching the sky. All combined to comprehend the nature of the wind, sun, and rain.

The thirty-two-year-old expert was showing his eldest daughter Essel what the morning clouds would bring today when Lily arrived. Since Essel had chosen to be the fifth-generation cloud watcher, Stem explained to her how he came to his forecast.

Lily passed a few of the local villagers returning from the cloud watcher's counsel, content with today's predictions for a fair day. "No snow today, young Lily, if that is what you are looking for," said Stem.

Lily smiled, knowing that Stem was making fun, so she replied, "If you could make it rain dogs so I might pick one for a friend, but no snow, please."

Stem looked at Essel, who saw no humor in dogs raining. Lily explained about Pine and how he needed a dog, and Essel mentioned that the tool maker kept a cluster of dogs about all the time. Lily thanked them and headed back down the trail to the village.

"Do you not wish to know the day?" asked Stem.

Lily replied, "The blue above me tells me enough and if a storm lingered, you would have more feathers flying."

"Young woman, you alone count my feathers; to others they only glimpse decoration or wind worship."

"My mother is the one who shared her learning."

"Give her my fair blessing."

"I shall, and fair blessings to you both."

Continuing her quest, Lily followed the sound of nonstop barking. The tool maker, Poe Rolf, was chipping a piece of obsidian. Her shadow passed him and he looked up. "The word is Lily Sayed searches for a dog."

"Yes, and I have weavings to trade."

"Of the words said, no one has spoken the purpose for you having a dog."

"A friend needs one to hunt."

Poe chuckled, pointed to the three dogs, and said, "You see my dogs? None are swift. They have legs like badgers and they haul my stones from the hills. None could hunt except for near-dying squirrels."

"Who would have dogs that hunt?"

"Hunters. But if a hunter traded one, it might mean the dog suffered a lameness of some sort. A guard dog might be learned to hunt."

"Someone must have a dog," said Lily.

"If the gods will. Good fortune to you, Lily Sayed."

"And you, Poe Rolf."

Unwilling to give up, Lily spotted the rainbow woman's hut with the staff-mounted seashells. Many colored feathers fluttered in the breeze that decorated the walk.

Only twenty-six years old, the woman possessed a full knowledge of the making of tints from the many plants and insects that could be gathered by clever seekers. This learning was not passed down as were so many jobs. Her knowledge had been acquired by watching and listening and experimenting since her earliest memories.

Ammer Wynn's hair hung long past her shoulders, and her hazel eyes and wide lips smiled at the same time. She hung blue and red feathers and small seashells on the left side of her hair and wore many necklaces and bracelets. She decorated her lightly tanned skirt and blouse with tinted floral patterns.

Two years ago, the rainbow woman's husband, Jal, had been killed horribly by hornets while picking wild plums. The gray feathers on the hut showed her to be still in mourning. But in truth, Ammer was content living without a man.

Lily came to the hut of the rainbow woman. Unintentionally, she surprised Ammer's son Val as he was carrying a collection of flowers. He spotted Lily, turned away quickly, and ducked into the hut. The boy's mother came from inside bearing a bouquet of flowers. She smiled at Lily.

"Lily, fair day to you."

"Fair day, Ammer," said Lily. "I did not intend to startle Val."

"My son is not so easy to shy but by the sight of a pretty girl. Have you come for more goldenrod flowers for your mother's weavings?"

"My mother always needs more of your tints, but I am seeking a dog for a friend and have been asking about the village for any for trade."

Ammer shook her head. "I have not caught story of any; have you asked the tool maker? He seems to always have some, they bark at nothing all the time."

"The tool maker's dogs will not hunt," said Lily, as she turned to leave. From within the hut, a small voice said, "There is a lost dog by the spoil pit."

Ammer beckoned her son to come out and he stood in front of her. Val, at nine years, was small for his age, and standing before his mother he seemed to shrink even smaller. "When did you go by the spoil pit? I do not like you near there."

Val squinted in the sun. "I go almost every day to pick the little blue flowers you use for the tints."

Embarrassed, Ammer had no words to apologize to Val. "Tell us then about this dog you have seen."

Val narrowed his eyes and raised a hand over his head. "He is big—dire wolf big—and he has gray eyes, and enormous pointy ears, and he is almost black with brown markings." He scrunched his nose. "As soon as he sees you, he shows his white teeth and they are big—panther big. The claw marks on his neck tell he lived through a fight and his ribs show. No other dogs go there anymore, he is there by himself. He lives there, I think."

He looked up at Lily, smiled brightly, and ducked back into the hut. Lily thanked Val and Ammer, and before she could turn to leave, Ammer cautioned Lily to not go looking for that dog alone. "I will just get close enough to look; it may not be a dog fit for my friend."

Val came from the hut and announced that he would take her to where she could see the dog safely. Ammer approved and the two set off.

Val led Lily behind the hut and down the hill following a small path lined with yellow flowers, and as the path descended it became rocky. Pointing here and there, Val showed Lily some of the plants and flowers he picked for his mother, and Lily could hear the pride in his voice as he showed her his many finds.

Once they reached the bottom of the trail, Val gestured to Lily to move to the right and stand behind some bushes, where they would be able to view the pit without being seen. The position of the bush was upwind of the pit, so Val and Lily were spared its stench.

The light was just bright enough for Lily and Val to see the dog's face looking directly at them. They were caught in a staring contest. The dog was large—not the largest in the village, but Lily could see from Val's small stature that the dog was truly sizable. However, no teeth were showing, and Lily took that as a good sign. Because he sensed a lack of fear from them, the dog's posture was relaxed. Still, he showed a feeling of wary curiosity, so he kept his distance from the onlookers.

It was Lily who decided to step out from behind the bush so that the dog could view her. Recognizing no change in the dog's posture, Val joined Lily in the clearing. The dog remained a calm statue.

Lily spoke loudly to the dog as if it could understand her.

"You seem ragged before me. I happen to know of one to cure you. Tomorrow I shall come again with meat to fatten the bones that show through your skin."

The dog cocked his head slightly as if to acknowledge her, and turned and trotted off into the brush. As if he had just seen some magic, Val looked up at Lily with his mouth hanging open.

The next morning, Lily sang on the side of the hill, a new song she made in her mind while thinking of Pine. On her way back to the village, she stopped by the spot she had first met him. On the ground she spotted the piece of leather that Pine had left. An idea came to her, and she took the piece of hide.

Following her chores, Lily made her way to the spoil pit with some dried elk meat. She walked the same path to where she and Val had stood before, and she saw the dog was in the same place as yesterday.

Facing the dog, Lily laid the strip of leather and the meat on the ground. Without looking back, she marched up the hill.

The next day she returned with more meat. The leather strip remained, but Lily could tell the dog had moved it. The day after she brought more treats, and she noticed the leather was gone from where she had last seen it, but then she spotted it on the ground near the bushes by the creek.

On the fourth day, careful to not make eye contact, she sat on a rock with her head down and held the morsel in her hand.

Wary, the dog stepped forward two strides and lay down as if to tell Lily he would not come closer.

The next move belonged to Lily. She stood, stepped forward two paces, and squatted down. There was a stalemate, as neither was going to move. Someone called from behind Lily. It was Val. He ran down the trail and Lily stood. The dog leaped to his feet and grabbed the meat from Lily's hand. She lost her balance and rolled into the spoil pit, while the dog ran off with the meat into the thicket, all in the snap of a twig.

Val hurried to Lily's aid. When he helped her stand, he realized how awful Lily smelled, and he pointed to the mess on her skirt. She looked down at herself and laughed. Val looked concerned, not really understanding just what had occurred, but he was thankful that Lily had not been injured. The two made it back to the hut. Ammer was quick to aid Lily with a thorough cleaning as Lily relayed the event.

"Did you count your fingers?" asked Ammer.

"The dog meant no harm, and it was my own surprise that caused me to tumble."

Since no one wanted the dog, Lily decided to keep trying. Others had seen him at the spoil pit and, even wounded, he defended his keep without challenge. His legs were long and it looked as if his ears were too big for his head. His not-so-thick coat was black with a smattering of brown lines and splotches, and a black mask that shaded his gray eyes.

The following day, after singing in her spot, Lily walked to the place Pine had made tools. On the ground she saw a bit of hide Pine had used to keep from cutting himself. Knowing he would have more, she took it to give the dog another taste of his future master's scent.

No one she asked remembered the first time the dog had been seen, and nobody knew where he had come from, but he gave them all a glower that made them always look away and not turn back. This time, when Lily came by the spoil pit, he offered her a different gaze. His manner was that of a pup in need of attention, and Lily was only too happy to leave him the piece of leather. Extending her hand, she held out a piece of venison.

Still shy, the dog feigned disinterest, and Lily laid the meat on a rock and backed away. The dog waited for her to reach the bushes before he dashed over and snatched the morsel. Keeping his eyes on her, he chewed.

While Lily peered at him, he sniffed the hide, gave her a brief glance, cocked his head and took the leather. With the prize in his mouth, he trotted into the brush.

The following day, near the spoil pit, Lily brought more meat and tore it into small pieces. She dropped it here and there as she walked about. The dog, less wary than before, followed her as he nibbled her leavings.

In the clearing Lily was able to get a better view of the dog, and it became apparent he was young, probably only a year or so. Also, what she had thought to be brown markings were really only splotches of mud. The dog was probably all black.

She needed to bring Pine, and he would determine if this dog would make a good hunter's companion. Lily came to the creek and took off her moccasins. She raised her skirt and waded through the cold water. As she crossed, the dog still trailed, so after she reached the opposite side, she set another morsel on a rock near the shore and walked farther on the trail.

The dog went to the creek and drank. He looked up at Lily and slurped some more before crossing. The water came up to the dog's shoulders. He went to the other bank and shook, revealing a shiny, medium-length black coat.

As Lily went along, the dog continued to follow her. Without taking his eyes off her, he took each scrap Lily set down. With only one piece of meat remaining, Lily turned. She faced the dog, knelt, and extended her open hand with the offering. The dog took a step and paused. His eyes met hers and they gazed at each other. The dog stepped closer and stopped. Without warning, his lips curled and he bared his white teeth. Val had not exaggerated their size.

Behind her, twigs cracked. She turned her head. A bear loomed over her. On all fours, the beast stood taller than any man. His rancid breath assailed her with his growl.

In a blur, the black mass of fury leaped over Lily. He landed on the bear's back. The bear staggered. In a snap, the dog jumped to the ground and attacked the bear's back leg. The bear's jaws reached for his tormenter, but he switched to the other leg. He gnawed, twisted, chomped, and pulled, leading the bear away from Lily.

Rearing to his full height, the bear danced in circles, frantically swiping his massive paws. Missing each time. The bear lashed out with his immense paw, but like lightning, the dog ducked and attacked him from behind. Facing the dog, the bear came down on all fours, but the dog darted out of reach.

Each time the bear confronted the opponent, he attacked somewhere else. The bear made a desperate sweep at the charging canine. The dog dodged the claws and jumped between the bear's legs. His hurtful teeth chomped down on the bear's genitals. The bear bellowed loudly. The dog jerked and twisted his head.

Unable to shake the dog free, the bear burst into the brush, rolled, and bucked. None of the bear's thrashing freed the dog's grasp.

Shoving his paws into the bear's belly, he ripped the genitals free with a spray of blood. The bear howled a seemingly endless wail as he ran into the woods. Dropping the meat, the dog gave chase.

Exhausted, the bear rolled on the ground while the dog harassed him with assaults until the bear's energy waned. The dog drove his fangs into the bear's throat and the bear gave a strangled bellow, huffed, and died.

CHAPTER 9

The Dog No One Wanted

COMING TO HER senses, Lily found herself sitting. She trembled as she grasped what had just occurred. In her quivering hand, she still held the treat she had offered the dog. With a bloody face, the dog approached Lily calmly, and before gently taking the treat from her hand, he gave her cheek a quick lick. Lily blinked and the dog scurried off, following the blood-splotched tracks left by the bear. She blinked again and he was gone.

Hearing the uproar, some villagers came running. Several of the men showed up with their long spears and went in pursuit of the bear while others rushed to Lily's side. Lily assured them that she was untouched; the streak of blood on her cheek belonged to the bear. And she told them the dog had saved her life.

A group of six men reached the bear. On top of the carcass, the dog showed his teeth and they backed away. No growl accompanied the display. The group realized the dog was grinning.

A Seaside Hill council member, Kase Smit, praised the dog, and the dog hopped off the bear and wagged his tail.

The six men took positions around the bear to lift the beast. As hard as they tried, the bear proved too weighty. Kase sent for more help.

Eventually three more men came, and they carried the bear back to the village. For a while, the dog kept pace with the group until they reached the first of the huts, then the dog simply vanished into the woods. The men laughed at how the scrawny dog had chased the bear far off over the hill, and how the bear had bled to death while on the run.

The skinner, Oster Dopt, was stroking the pelt on a lynx skin when they brought him the bear. Deaf in one ear, he had missed the commotion. The sight of the bear caused him to gasp.

"Gods give joy!" said Oster. "By what lance did this beast die?"

"No lance," said Kase. "A single dog defeated the bear defending Lily Sayed's life."

"Please tell me the girl is not harmed."

"True. She wears no blood," said Kase.

"Bless the gods. Who claims this bear?" asked Oster.

"By council rules," said Kase, "the meat and lamp fat are to be shared with all. The claws are yours for skinning and tanning the hide. The skull and pelt are to be part of the harvest prizes."

"The bear's leavings belong to me until harvest," Oster replied. "Someone should bring Leek Rhyne and his son to butcher this brute. They clean fish at the shore."

Several men ran off in that direction.

In celebration, a feast was held to honor the dog. Since the dog still had not shown himself, some of the town boys made an imitation dog from straw and sticks to represent the hero. A dancer donned a bear skin and danced around the dog statue to the beating of drums and seashell chimes.

The crowd taunted the bear dancer because he made a vulgar imitation of the faux dog eating his genitals. To make up for his offensive parody, he collapsed and bade a boy to put the stick dog on his back. His fake death gasps brought cheers from the crowd.

Lily felt a cold nose on her shoulder. She turned her face and the dog flicked her cheek with a wet tongue. Still unsure, Lily reached and let him smell her hand, and he gave her a quick flick of his tongue. She scratched the dog under the chin, and the dog responded by offering more for her to rub. His fur was rough and matted in places.

Finally someone spotted the dog. "Our hero has found his rescue. Now who shall be his master?"

Surprised at herself, Lily stood and said, "I claim this dog. I have spent six days making friends. You can see with your eyes the dog has chosen me."

The Era of Herbalists

Cayl Wonn, a hunter with three dogs already, stood and said, "This dog is too much the hunter for a girl to own."

"True," said Lily. "What Cayl says, this dog is too much the hunter for me. But I sought this dog not for myself, but for a friend."

"What friend? Have him show himself!" demanded Cayl.

"He is Pine Nyte from Twin Oaks."

"What is this? A gift for the son of the prodon's herbalist?"

"Yes. So he can compete for the hunt trials."

"Seaside Hill comes first!" said Cayl. "I claim this dog for mine!"

Arch Fogg, the council leader, listened to the banter. He said to Cayl, "Go and take him now." Then, having seen the dog in the fight with the bear, he muttered to himself, "If you can."

Cayl grinned and pulled a leather cord from his pouch, and he approached the dog. Before he made two steps, the dog moved in front of Lily and bared his teeth.

Holding the cord in a loop, Cayl came within reach of the dog. The dog's hackles raised and he stared Cayl in the eyes. Cayl shifted his weight forward, but the dog's growl froze him for a moment. Cayl braced himself to toss the loop over the dog's neck. But the dog lunged first and chomped on Cayl's loin skin. Though he did not bite down, the dog held him tight and growled.

Cayl searched the faces around the fire for someone to help. No one moved. The dog added pressure. Tears formed in Cayl's eyes, and then he yowled and dropped the cord. The dog let loose of Cayl's privates.

Lily said to the dog, "Good boy, come here." Without taking his eyes off Cayl, the dog backed up and sat at Lily's side.

But Cayl was not willing to give up. He called to his friends, "Come. Help me tame this beast."

No one stood. Arch said, "Sit down, Cayl, the dog has chosen."

"But the dog needs taming."

"True, but not by you. Sit before the dog feeds on your manhood."

Admonished, Cayl sat, but he was seething inside. Not so much for the failure to acquire the dog, but for the loss of Lily Sayed's regard to an outsider.

Knowing the young man's surly temper, Cayl stared him in the eyes as he spoke. "The gods and the dog's spirit have chosen."

The other council members kept their objection feathers down. The dog belonged to Lily, and soon to Pine Nyte. The thought made her heart flutter, and she felt a redness in her skin. While the fire burned, and gossip spread, Lily took her leave with the dog at her side.

Trying his best not to stare at Lily, Cayl glowered at the fire. Anger festered inside him. What he wanted was to follow her and take her to his bed. But the throbbing in his loins reminded him of the dog's grip. And then he recalled what he had seen as the men carried the bear to the skinner. Nothing of the bear's gender remained.

From the time of his becoming a man ceremony, in his mind, he had claimed Lily to be his. To his thinking, the man should be the one to pick a mate. Tomorrow he would make a talk with Lily's father, Ric Sayed the storyteller.

Getting up, the hunt master, Bogg Rez, called him. "The drums speak. Cayl, a herd of bison has been spotted north. Two days away. Be ready with your dogs at the sunrise."

The excitement of the hunt overruled his disappointment that he would have to wait for his courting talk with Ric Sayed. He would gift them a pelt and promise to keep the Sayed's rich in skins, and the family coffer full of meat.

CHAPTER 10

A Dog Finds Pine

THE HUNT AND runner's challenge was only three days away, and Pine was again on the knoll chipping his white stones when he heard a call.

"Go away! Why have you followed me?" Pine got up and saw Lily being trailed by a dog, black as obsidian, long-legged, big-eared, that looked to be young and lean as if malnourished.

Lily saw Pine and pointed to the dog. "I came to sing and this dog followed me through my village. No one would claim him, and he would not stop following me."

Aware she was joking, Pine looked the dog over and told Lily, "He looks in need of help and sees you as one who cares."

Lily pointed to the dog, who was standing in front of Pine, and said, "Now look at him, he regards only you and I am no longer his thought."

The dog sniffed Pine, sensing a familiar smell. He showed his neck where he had scratches, as if from a confrontation with a bear or big cat. Pine remembered what his grandfather had told him of his dream. How a dog would find him and he knew this to be so.

"If no one has claimed him, I will accept his charge and care for his sores should it be his will to follow me."

Pine handed Lily a heavy fur pouch. "I brought a gift for you; the sack has some gray clay from my creek. You still have yet to sing for me, not fair trade I think." Pine turned to walk off and the dog followed.

"Thank you for the clay," Lily said quietly as she gazed at Pine and the dog, fading into the distance. "The next time we meet I will sing for you." She ran to her place and practiced the song she had chosen.

On his way back to the village, Pine stopped and so did the dog. Pine set off, and each time he paused, the dog did as well. A fallen tree made for a bench and Pine rested on it. The dog sat facing him, just out of reach. Pine gazed in the dog's gray eyes and the dog looked back.

As if the dog understood, Pine said, "You are like a shadow, so that is what I am going to name you."

The dog cocked his head as if listening. Pine extended his hand palm up and the dog came to him.

"Good boy, Shadow," said Pine. He set off running at a leisurely pace and the dog trotted beside him.

"Let's go visit Grandfather," said Pine. As he trotted, he spoke to Shadow as if speaking to a person. "Grandfather will have salve for your wounds. Shadow, I have been waiting for you. You will sleep beside me; your bed is ready for you."

The dog did not comprehend, but he seemed to enjoy the conversation. So Pine continued, "Shadow, Lily thinks she fooled me. The talk was all about you, the dog who saved her from the bear. Grandfather told me how the Seaside Hill council ruled that you belonged to her."

The pair broke through the tree line near the tanner's boiling skins. They called to him, "Look, Pine has a dog."

Grinning, Pine waved to the tanners as the two trotted to his grandfather's hut. Sitting on a log, Evon was carving on an antler to fashion a new handle for the piece of obsidian he had chipped for the blade. He sensed someone approaching from behind. Turning, he saw the dog and said to Pine, "The gods heard you."

"I call him Shadow. Is he the one from your dreams?" asked Pine.

Studying the animal, Evon rubbed his whiskers and said, "He must be, since he is the one who found his way to you."

Evon set his carving down and stood. The dog trotted to him and sniffed the back of his hand. Evon reached down, and the dog raised his head for Evon to examine his wound. Spreading his fingers, Evon measured the gouges. From the healing, he judged the injury to be ten days old.

"A panther claw," said Evon. "A valiant symbol on a living dog. Pine, fetch my remedy bag and I will use Chirp's cure."

The hut door stood open, and Pine reached in and lifted the lynx fur pouch from the peg holding it.

After he handed Evon the bag, Evon said, "See how his belly sucks in? Shadow needs food. Bring him some dried elk and a gourd of water while I treat his hurt."

Pine ran off, and Evon reached into the sack for the clay pot wrapped in doeskin. Inside, the ointment formed a crust, and Evon used a finger to stir. The dog sniffed the lotion, and as if he understood, he showed his wound to Evon.

The healing salve covered the gashes, and the dog gave Evon's hand a flick of his tongue. Since the dog was letting him touch him, Evon lifted his gums and checked his teeth. Evon's touch was tender, and after his inspection, he scratched Shadow under his chin.

Pine returned with a gourd of water and dried meat. He set the fare in front of Shadow. Before eating, Shadow eyed Pine as if to ask, "Is this for me?"

"This dog is no more than a year from birth. A pup still."

"No one in Seaside Hill could say from where Shadow came."

"The spirits. They brought him."

"But why did Shadow not first come to me here in Twin Oaks?"

"Did your father not give you a mind?" asked Evon. "Pine Nyte, you should clean your eyes."

"I do not understand."

"The spirits pointed to Lily Sayed first. The spirits acted through her."

Hearing her name, something revived in Pine, and his mind drifted to the hillside, the white stones, and the enchanting singing.

"She is from another village, the fisher people."

"Your mother did not come from Twin Oaks. She belonged among the keen eye people. Her village was a place over the east hills, Forest Gorge."

"That place is far from here. How did she meet my father?"

"For that, you should ask your mother. Now comb him with your fingers. Find and kill the ticks, should he have them. That will add your smell to him."

"Why, Grandfather?"

"For the town dogs to sniff him as kindred. Show your dog the boundary of the village. Before you take him to your hut, call on your sister Neva and ask her for herbs to bathe him."

At bedtime, Pine asked Shadow to lay beside him inside the hut, but Shadow backed out and laid in front of the entry. Seeing how Shadow had decided to guard, Pine set a bowl of water beside him.

CHAPTER 11

The Hunter's Challenge

THE RULE HAD been that a boy needed to be the age of thirteen to compete as a runner and, to participate in the hunter's challenge, sixteen. Since Pine was only a moon shy of his sixteenth year, the elders voted he could compete in the hunter's challenge.

Like the others, Pine unwrapped and set out his scrapers, blades, spear tips, and arrows for the judges to examine. The judges gathered around him. No one had ever seen white stone points. They took turns cutting and scraping their sample skins. All Pine's tools passed.

"From where did the stone come?" asked the head judge and hunt master, Falk Moon. "Tell us. Many could benefit from such stones."

"There is only a small amount," said Pine. "For that reason, I will keep the secret to myself."

"Would not the gods wish the place known?" asked Falk.

"The gods have shown me and no one else. If the gods wish, then let others find the place."

With nothing else to say, Falk led the other judges to the next competitor.

Pine readied himself for the first contest: long-distance spear throwing. He grasped his atlatl and selected one of his spears. While he waited for his turn, he studied the competitors. One thing he noted when Talon Doone used the lever of his atlatl to throw was that he left his head up to see his spear land. His throw was short and outside of the rock-free lane. From the sound, his spear tip may have broken.

Pine's friend Roth Uhl's pitch was farther than Talon's, but the same thing happened as he watched his throw with his head up. The spear tip fragmented on the rock he hit. But when Berm Hogg made his fling, he kept his head down, and his was the furthest throw and inside the clear lane. And though his throw did not reach the winner's distance, Todd Pyre stayed low and his aim stayed true.

Pine's turn came, and he fit the butt of his spear inside the catch of the atlatl. He brought the spear to his shoulder, aimed, and flung the lance. He remembered to keep his head lowered, and his thrust sailed two spear lengths beyond Berm's mark and stuck deep into the center of the clear lane.

Nine more contestants gave their best throws. Syd Lukan's heave bested Pine's by half a spear length. But because Syd's spear tip chipped when it struck a rock at the edge of the clear lane, the judges declared a tie for first place.

The next tests left the same players remaining at the top of the heap. Pine, Syd, Roth, Todd, Talon, Berm, and Sharpe Awell, who defeated everyone in the archery contest.

Finished with the weapons tests, seventeen contestants readied their dogs for the hunter's run. Since his dog was so new to him, Pine worried Shadow would succumb to the distractions placed along the course.

The route started with a dash through an open plain and into thick shoulder-high brush to the top of the hill. Once they reached the peak, feathered staffs marked the rest of the course, a switchback up-and-down trail wrought with diversions and obstacles for both hunters and dogs.

A judge called the start, and they began to dash across the field. Some of the contestants held leads with their dogs pulling them along. Others had loose dogs that ran far ahead. Shadow ran free but kept his two-legged partner's pace a few lengths ahead of Pine.

According to his grandfather, dogs possessed senses beyond man, so based on that counsel, Pine followed Shadow into the scrub. With three spears, a bow, a quiver with three arrows, an axe, a blade, and his pouch of scrapers, moving through the thicket proved to be a challenge. Per the rules, all the contestants carried the same burdens and therefore all faced the same challenge.

Pine held his spears in front of him to force the branches aside. As he pushed through, he ignored the scratches. Shadow led him upward through the thinnest

The Era of Herbalists

of the brush. On his left a dog fight happened—not Shadow. He was just ahead, breaking through the cover.

The staff with three black feathers marked the course entrance. This was a target trail for running spear throws. Shadow waited for Pine under a canopy of oak trees. With two lances in his left hand, Pine gripped one, ready to fling. On the run, a scent turned Shadow's head. Off the trail, a hunk of raw bison was hanging on a pike. Without slowing, Shadow gaped at the meat, but scampered past the diversion. At a bend in the path, a judge held them back a few moments for the competitor in front to complete his trial. A toot from a bison horn gave them the okay to continue.

Further on, loose stones covered the ground on a downward path. Shadow danced amid the rocks while Pine stumbled. So as not to rush too far away from his master, Shadow paused. Pine caught up, and a boar hide target swung from an overhead tree branch in front of him. His throw was hasty but accurate. A judge caught hold of the target to rate the hit and retrieve the lance. Pine and Shadow continued, and Pine readied his second spear.

Behind him, he could hear others on the trail. Maintaining his pace, keeping his spear poised above his shoulder, Pine checked for movement. A bear hide target dropped from a limb, and he threw his spear on the run. A hit. The judge hauled the hide back up to remove the lance and drop for the next contestant.

Around a bend, a fallen oak blocked the path. Pine scrambled through the maze of twisted branches. In front, Shadow held his head up and growled. A saber cat target loomed above, and Pine thrust his final lance into the straw beast's chest. When he pulled his spear free he left it with the two other spears on the ground, proof that two contestants were ahead of him. Barking dogs told him more were coming from behind.

Past the tree, a staff with three white feathers marked the next challenges. Pine readied an arrow in his bow and rushed ahead. Shadow's nose caught the scent of the scraps of meat scattered alongside the trail, but Pine urged him on, and they passed by the lure. The two hurried on the trail. Suddenly, Shadow halted, his nose pointed up. Pine spotted the wild turkey target. He aimed while running, then let go, and his arrow sunk into the straw bird's chest. Another decoy replaced that one and the pair resumed the trek.

Timothy W. Sparks

At a fork in the course, a staff with one blue feather showed Pine to take a bypass trail to a stationary target station. The short path led them to a precipice overlooking the river. A red painted pole marked the place as a turnabout. A bull elk call brought his sight across the canyon to a full-sized elk hide target. Pine readied an arrow and took aim. He considered the distance and determined that the target was beyond the range of an arrow. Even raising his bow in as high an arc as could be made, he was sure his arrow would fall short. And when he considered the loss of such a hard-to-make thing, he relaxed his stance and returned the arrow to the quiver, and he and Shadow ran back to the main course.

Out of the oak forest, Pine and Shadow moved through a valley of giant boulders. With an arrow ready to draw, they moved from one rock to the next. Shadow lifted his head and sniffed the air, and Pine traced his focus. A doe target stood between two massive egg-shaped boulders. Before he released the shaft, Shadow gave a soft yip, and Pine spotted the fawn facsimile a distance away. He lowered his bow, replaced the arrow in the quiver, and he and Shadow dashed to the next feathered staff. This one marked the end of the contest.

The two who were ahead of him, Berm Hogg and Todd Lukan, were waiting by a fire pit. One thing he noted right off was that neither had any arrows left.

The leader for the new second hunt team had already been decided, and that was Grand Moon. Based on the decision of the judges, the second hunt team was formed: Pine Nyte, Syd Lukan, Roth Uhl, Todd Pyre, Talon Doone, Berm Hogg, and Sharpe Awell.

CHAPTER 12

Gaining Friends

EACH MORNING CHIRP notched the pole outside his sleep hut to mark the days. Today, while he sawed with his flint, he counted. Three hundred forty-seven days. He wondered whether Gemma was still mourning. Did she tally up the time without him as he did with her?

While he convinced himself to begin his day, the bones outside the fence rattled loudly, signaling an anxious patient. Standing, he straightened himself and unlatched the gate.

Using the wrapped bundle in his arms like a ram, a brute of a man pushed the gate in and stumbled past Chirp. The woman with him clung to his tunic.

"Our son! He will not wake!" cried the woman. She rushed to Chirp. "Will he live?"

Her husband pulled back the blanket, revealing a young, unconscious boy. Chirp felt the boy's chest rise and fall.

"He breathes," said Chirp. Grasping a pelt, he draped it on the bench. "Lay him here."

The boy, about six years old, lay still. Chirp felt the boy's skin. Cool and dry. He lifted his eyelids. They were rolled back. A greenish mucus coated his lips. Opening the boy's mouth, Chirp spotted a dark blue-gray bit stuck in his teeth. With a finger-length bamboo sliver, he scratched it free. A toad berry skin. For a child his size, one berry would heal coughing, two would produce drowsiness, and three would cause this for a day. If the child ate more than three, only the gods could cure him.

"Has the boy trembled?"

"No," said the father. "He is unmoving."

Chirp dashed away. Inside his apothecary, he found the herb he needed. He called for Patto, who came running. "Chirp, the line of sickly grows. What is your need?"

"Hurry and boil some water while I crush these goat's foot leaves."

Patto threw some more wood on the fire and heated some rocks. He checked the cauldron; it had enough water. Once the stones were glowing, he used his bamboo pincers to drop them in the cauldron. Splashing, they sizzled and steamed. Patto added more.

As soon as Chirp felt satisfied that the leaves were ground enough, he fetched a square of perforated goatskin. He draped it over a clay cup, made an indentation, and filled it with goat's foot leaf powder.

The water finally began to bubble, and Patto dipped a gourd and brought it to Chirp, who proceeded to drip the steaming liquid over the powder. While the medicine dripped into the cup, Chirp rolled a piece of grease bark into a funnel.

Seeing a sufficient amount of remedy, Chirp added cool water and stirred. Satisfied, he carried the funnel and cup to the boy.

The father stiffened when he saw Chirp, and he backed away for Chirp to administer the treatment. His wife stood beside him.

Facing the father, Chirp asked, "What is your name?"

As if he was unsure of the question, he blinked before he answered. "My name is Palawan, my wife is Arwon."

"Palawan, I need you to raise your son up and hold his mouth open."

The man hesitated, unsure of how to grip him. Chirp showed him.

Squeezing her talisman, Arwon said, "His name is Davan."

Chirp nodded to her and told Palawan, "Use your finger to hold his tongue down."

While the boy's mouth gaped wide, Chirp inserted the funnel and poured the medicine in. Once he had emptied the cup, he pulled the funnel free and replaced the father's hands with his own. Chirp closed the boy's jaws and pinched his nose closed.

Seeing his son turn blue, Palawan rushed up and tried to wrestle the boy from Chirp. "Wait!" shouted Chirp. He wrapped an arm around Davan, picked him up under his arms, and spun him away from Palawan. Abruptly, the boy's chest rocked. Chirp took his hand away from his face. Davan coughed and spewed a yellow mucus speckled with pieces of toad berry skins. For a moment, Davan's eyes snapped open. But he closed them and retched some more before he cried. Chirp gave the boy to his mother, who had been calmer than Palawan.

"Do not let Davan sleep until nighttime, otherwise he may not wake. I will give you some wake-me tea. Add honey to help the bitterness. Keep him active."

"What if he should sleep before night?" asked Palawan.

Checking, he glanced at Patto at the gate, calming patients. To be sure Patto could not hear his blasphemy, Chirp whispered, "Then pray to the gods, for there is nothing I can do."

The bigger man embraced Chirp. "My thanks. I am in your debt."

Chirp pulled himself away, went to the apothecary, and came back with a satchel which he gave to the woman. "Here are two doses of wake-me tea. Brew Davan a cup when you return to your hut, and another at midday. Keep him upright and moving, the danger is still with him. Do not allow him to rest."

Before Chirp saw the next patient, he went into his apothecary and silently prayed to the gods for the boy's recovery. By his count of toad berry stems in Davan's vomit, he had eaten five.

His next patient, a stone carver, had a sizable sliver in the palm of his right hand. The wound had become infected. After washing the sore, Chirp placed an obsidian blade in the fire. Patto held his hand down. Placing the blade on the infected hand, Chirp pressed and sliced. Blood and pus flowed from the gash. The patient jerked and howled in pain, but Patto held his hand firm. With a bamboo probe, Chirp lifted out the jagged piece of wood. With a patch of doeskin, he pressed a globule of ginger salve on the injury and held it until the bleeding stopped. He wrapped the wound with boiled pig intestine.

"Return tomorrow for a second treatment."

"What of my work?" asked the man.

"Rest today, and if there is no improvement tomorrow, then perhaps another day of rest will serve you. Keep the sore clean and covered."

"But Master Lewell said the Lord Prodon wishes his face to be carved."

"I will tell Master Lewell. A day or two cannot make such a great difference when so much time is needed to finish such a project."

"My thanks, herbalist."

"Chirp is how I am called."

"Then you may speak of me as Terral."

"Fair day, Terral."

"Good fortune to you, Chirp."

After Patto finished boiling more water, Chirp sent him to bring Master Lewell. To Chirp's luck, Master Lewell came seeking a headache cure.

"My head throbs like two rutting rams busting horns." He pointed to a spot above his temple.

"When did you first pain?"

"A while after my inspection of the barge."

"Where did you go from there?"

"The cook's area, and then through the weaver's space. I lingered to watch them weave. On the way to Lord Prodon's tower, my skull pained as I have spoken."

"Were the weavers dyeing fiber?"

"Yes, and the stench boiled my stomach."

"Be thankful, because I have a cure."

"Then heal me before another ram joins the two fighting."

Inside his apothecary, Chirp mixed menthe paste with arnica salve.

On the bench, Lewell sat with his head in his hands.

"Master Lewell, allow me to rub this under your nose."

For his treatment Chirp scooped a fingerful. He applied the remedy and told him of Terral's need for rest. Lewell inhaled a breath and sneezed a couple times. He looked up at Chirp with watery eyes.

"My head senses a ram surrendering. What of the stone carver?"

"The injury requires healing before he can perform his work."

"Can he do nothing?"

"Nothing with his right hand, Master Lewell."

"Very well. Treat him so he can make Lord Prodon's face live in stone."

When Lewell rose, he grabbed his head and sat down.

The Era of Herbalists

"The ram is back."

"Master Lewell, you need fresh air. If you are able, go to the knoll above the sea and breathe there."

"The Lord Prodon has fresh air in the tower. I will breathe with him." This time when Lewell stood, he moved more slowly.

Chirp called to him at the gate, "If you feel no cure, come back and I will give you another dose."

Though he did not tell Lewell, others came to him with similar complaints. Since he had never visited before, he decided to call on the weavers and find out what was causing the headaches. The tint man picked his own plants for the dye colors. Chirp wondered if perhaps some were noxious.

Finally, having treated the last patient, Chirp surveyed the weaver's area. The tint man had arranged the botanicals by the colors they produced. Even though the stench saturated the place, Chirp saw no harmful plants. Certainly nothing to cause headaches. He was about to leave when a man passed him carrying a bundle of firewood. The variegated red and yellow wood caught his attention.

Following him, Chirp waited for him to drop his load. The man scrunched his face when looked at Chirp. "Is there a reason you tracked me here?"

"The wood you bring; I have not seen before."

"For that I am not surprised, since it came as trade from a raid east."

Chirp picked up a scrap and sniffed. The odor caused his nostrils to burn.

"Tell me what trade you spent."

"Weavings. Some of our finest."

"Then my sorrow is for you, as I must say that you must abandon the wood and burn it no more."

Lifting his chin, the man said, "This wood is paid for and all we have."

"The smoke is foul and causes illness."

"Are you the herbalist?"

"Yes. Chirp Nyte is how I am called."

"Boss of the weavers is how I am known. And you have no say here."

"For myself that is true, but Master Lewell came to me with his head in pain from breathing the smoke here. It is for him that I say for you to stop burning the wood."

The man paled. He asked, "Are you sure the wood causes the illness? My weavers suffer not."

Chirp pointed. "See how the smoke hovers above them. Squatting as they do, they breathe less than a person standing." Touching the side of his head, Chirp gestured to the ground. "Let us sit. My own head begins to ache."

"If Master Lewell tells Lord Prodon, then my life is gone."

"Not so. When I sniffed the wood, it seemed to me to have a cure inside. From soaking the wood, I could craft a tincture for burns and rashes."

"But what of Master Lewell?"

"I will ask him to have the wood replaced with oak."

"My thanks, Chirp. Call me Oly."

"Oly, I will go to Master Lewell, and you will have good wood to burn."

On his way to find Lewell, Chirp spotted Patto. "Patto? Who has firewood in abundance?"

"The cooks."

Crossing his arms, Chirp said, "The weavers have a wood with a medicine inside I want. How can I have it and not leave the weavers wood-poor?"

But as soon as he spoke, Chirp realized the answer to his own question. Spices. Something he had not shared.

"Ask the head cook, he commands some woodsmen."

"My thanks. I will go speak with him."

Taking stock of his herbs, Chirp selected some baysweet leaves and wrapped them in a doeskin pouch. His spicy powder he added to a clay cup. Lastly, he crushed some ginger root and mixed it with some honey. This too he put in a cup.

The gate to the cook's hearth stood open, so Chirp entered. He waited while the cook mounted a rack of boar's ribs on a spit. He wiped his hands on his doeskin apron.

"Come back later," said the cook. "My meats are barely singed."

"It is for trade I seek, not to feed."

"What trade?"

Chirp laid out his herbs. "These are sample spices to flavor your meats. If it pleases you, I would trade for oak firewood."

"For spices I use salt. And of that, I have a full measure."

But Chirp opened his pouch and presented the man with a leaf. "Rub one of these baysweet leaves on a modest piece of pig to roast."

The cook broke the leaf and sniffed it. The aroma brought a smile to his face. "Having died before she shared her secret, the mystery of my mother's slim bread has been shown me."

"Slim bread is one of many ways to enjoy baysweet. Meats, soups, stews, as well as lentils benefit."

The cook offered his hand. "I am Sole."

Taking the cook's firm grip, Chirp said, "And I am the herbalist. Chirp is how I am called."

"What other tastes do you bring me?"

"For almost all meats, the ginger honey sauce is desirable. And for spoiled or unsavory meats, the spicy powder overwhelms the unpleasant tastes."

"How do I measure?"

"For this, there are no directions—only to taste and discover. It is best to use a small measure and add more when needed. With the spicy powder, this is truth. Only goat milk cures a sweltering mouth."

"For a fair amount of spices, my men will bring you oak wood. Tell me of your need, and I will have my men bring the fuel to you."

"The wood is for the weavers."

"What of the wood Oly traded?"

"Not good for burning, but the medicine inside will help me heal rashes and burns."

"I myself suffer so." Sole pulled back the sleeve of his tunic. Chirp studied the rash on his forearm. Red blotches with white pustules: poison leaf rash.

"I can fashion a cure in my apothecary. I will return."

On the way, Chirp considered the other herbs he could introduce to the cook. Sage and four-leaf herb would suit some meats. Both of these he had in abundance.

Inside his apothecary he mixed an ointment for the poison leaf rash and crushed a dozen ginger roots. He heated honey, mixed the two, and poured the sauce in a clay vessel. Then he amassed the rest of the herbs and called Patto.

"Please see that these bundles go to the cook."

Sniffing a bundle, Patto said, "The aroma stirs my hunger."

"Four-leaf herb is the flavor you sense. Perhaps Sole will use some tonight on his bison meat."

A pleasant fragrance led Chirp to the cook's area. Sole had basted a flank of elk with the ginger honey. To enter, Chirp needed to skirt between the many people enjoying the smells.

Seeing Chirp, Sole grinned. "Please tell me there is an abundance of honey and ginger, and my woodsmen will fill the weaver's needs."

Chirp handed the pot of sauce to him. "I will provide that and more." He had Sole pull his sleeve back. With a short bamboo stick, he applied the remedy. "Make sure you spread more on before you sleep and again when you wake."

"Already the cure stopped the itch."

"By the waning moon you should be healed."

Before the woodsmen brought the oak to the weaver, the men stacked the variegated wood along the fence in the apothecary yard. Chirp flayed some of it and soaked it in a pot of water. With his pincers he dropped a few hot rocks in. Immediately, he spotted a film forming on top. He added more shredded wood. For this first try, he decided to boil the water away, and tomorrow experiment with whatever remained.

The next day Chirp opened his apothecary. All the usual complaints but, fortunately, he possessed all the remedies needed. After seeing all his patients, Palawan and Arwon came with their son Davan. The boy fidgeted and stared at his feet.

"Fair day, Chirp. Our son thrives. We offer thanks," said Arwon. She handed Chirp a finely fashioned mixing spoon. "Perhaps this small gift will aid your craft."

Chirp admired the carving. "It is a fine tool and it will aid me. But any thanks for me is for Davan to never eat toad berries again."

Embarrassed, Davan faced the ground and shuffled his feet. In his small voice, he said, "I promised to only eat what my mama feeds me."

The Era of Herbalists

Stepping forward, Palawan said, "To you, I offer my skill as a hide tanner and pelt groomer."

Hearing the pride in Palawan's voice, Chirp said, "My bed nest needs freshening. For your skill, my sleep would benefit."

A smile spread across Palawan's face. "This I will perform now." He dashed off to Chirp's sleeping hut and brought out the furs. With them bundled under his arm, Palawan promised to bring them back before sunset, and he and his family left.

The sun hung low, so Chirp checked the pot. A fine reddish coating lined the bottom. With a fox hairbrush, he swept the residue into a pile. From the fragrance Chirp suspected the agent to be of a healing nature. With a sharp flint, he cut the back of his hand. He blotted the blood and on half the slash, he sprinkled the powder and rubbed it in. For a brief moment that part of the cut burned, but soon it numbed. He wrapped his hand with pig intestine and put away his herbs and ointments.

His shells shook and Chirp opened the gate. With his bed nest in her hands, Arwon stepped into the yard. With a brilliant smile, she said, "My husband has offered me to you along with your freshened bed."

Raising his eyebrows, Chirp said, "Please." He held his hands out for the pelts. "I have promised...promised to be true to my woman."

Pulling the furs back, Arwon spun in a circle. "What woman? I see none. A man needs a woman's vessel to please him. My husband sent me for that, but this to me is my pleasure."

"For your pleasure I am sorry, but you have a husband. My heart travels with my fulfillment, not my manhood."

Arwon handed Chirp the fresh pelts. "What can I say to my husband? He may wish to punish me for my failure."

"Thank him for the fresh bed nest and ask him to accept you back as a gift from me."

Bowing her head, Arwon turned on her heel and ambled to the exit. At the gate she turned and waited. He laid the pelts on his bench and followed her.

"The woodcarver's place is my work. Should you change the promise you made to yourself, wear a white feather." While she walked away, Chirp closed and latched the gate.

Immediately Chirp rushed into his apothecary. He lit an oil lamp and scanned his shelves for white feathers. He found three. Before he laid out his bed nest, he tossed them in the fire and prayed to the gods for strength.

CHAPTER 13

A New Cure

IN THE MORNING Patto shook Chirp awake. "Hurry! One of Lord Prodon's sons got burned!"

Slipping on his moccasins, Chirp rushed out. A guard held the boy to his chest. Chirp laid a pelt on his table, and the guard put the teary-eyed boy down. Judging from his size, Chirp guessed the boy to be around four.

Studying his blistered red legs, Chirp said, "Tell me what heat caused these burns."

"Boiling water. A pot spilled on him."

For scalding burns Chirp used bear grease, arnica, ginger, and honey. He dashed off to his apothecary. Inside he reached for a wolf root and noticed the back of his hand. He wiped the red residue off, and the cut was completely healed.

Out in the yard he checked inside the clay pot. With his brush he amassed a pile of the red dust. He took the vessel inside and mixed the powder with his other herbs and the bear grease.

Lewell was pacing near the boy, but froze when Chirp came from the hut. "This Lord Prodon proclaimed," said Lewell. "That you cure Junna or be disemboweled."

"Then stand aside and trouble me no more as I treat."

Without seeing Lewell's scowl, Chirp put a slice of wolf root in Junna's mouth. "Chew this," he said. "It will help with the pain. The medicine I am giving you will burn for a moment."

While Junna gnawed on the root, Chirp spread the medicine on the boy's painful blisters. A moment later Junna jerked his legs, spit the root from his mouth, and cried out. Lewell rushed up, but Chirp held his arm up. Then Junna relaxed. Chirp gave him a fresh hunk of wolf root.

"Take him to his bed, but do not cover him. Bring him back before sunset for another cure."

Before leaving, Lewell said, "Lord Prodon cherishes his sons. See to their care above all others."

"Tell me, Master Lewell. How many sons belong to Lord Prodon?"

"More than the number of men who carry him."

"Daughters?"

"He claims none."

"Are all the sons' names known?"

"All Lord Prodon's sons bear the name Junna."

"Does the name mean something?"

"In Lord Prodon's born tongue, it means son of a god."

Chirp nodded. To himself he admonished the prodon's narcissism.

As soon as Lewell left, Chirp called to Patto. "Today my need is for two stout men to shred...wood and boil water." He realized as he spoke, he had no name for the wood. He decided to call it weaver wood.

While the men labored with the weaver wood, Chirp saw patients. The stone carver, Terral, showed Chirp his hand, which was still festering. Chirp checked: he had enough of the weaver wood powder to treat him. He mixed the cure with honey and a pinch of arnica.

"This is a strong new remedy, but it will burn at first."

"Cannot hurt more than when you cut the sliver out."

Chirp spread a measure on his palm. Terral's eyes widened; he shook his hand and yelped. Thinking it would work, he blew on his palm. Soon it itched, and then the wound numbed. Terral flexed his fingers. Feeling no pain, he asked Chirp, "Must I still rest?"

"Until the swelling wanes."

"You have my thanks."

By midday the men had shredded all the weaver wood, and Chirp had boiled down half to a sludge. Both men bore blisters from their efforts. After explaining about the pain, he treated them with the slurry. Once the fire in their hands burned out, the men filled a cauldron with water and heated rocks.

By sunset, all the weaver wood had been boiled down, and the same guard brought Junna for his treatment. However, this time Junna could walk on his own. Chirp gestured for him to come to the firelight. He examined the boy's legs and was amazed. The redness had faded and the blisters dried.

"You made me better," said Junna. "I told my papa. He wants you."

The guard nodded. "Lord Prodon said to send you after Junna's cure."

Chirp rubbed Junna's legs with the medicated bear grease. Junna gritted his teeth for a while, then gave Chirp a slight smile.

"Come," said the guard. With the boy at his side, the guard led Chirp to the tower's lift. As the platform raised, Junna waved to Chirp.

At the top, two guards helped Chirp to the deck. In his throne, Lord Prodon gestured for Chirp to approach. "My stone carver lays about and my immortal face goes undone. For that offense, I wanted your manhood on a pole."

"Lord Prodon, the offender was an oak splinter left to fester."

"Master Lewell has said so. Yet every time I wish to punish you, you make a cure. Now my son says to me how you made him well."

"A new remedy, Lord Prodon." Chirp showed him the back of his hand. "Yesterday I used a flint and cut my hand. I tried the new medicine on half the slash, and in the morning my cut was healed. It is that treatment that cured Junna. Tonight I treated the stone cutter with that remedy; tomorrow the man can resume his labor."

"How can I reward you?"

"Many times I have asked you to send me back to my village, and as many times you have refused. So then I ask you to reward Patto in my place."

"Patto?"

"Yes, Lord Prodon. My craft for so many is only accomplished with his help."

"Herbalist, you behave like no other captive."

"My skills are my life and my fulfillment comes from my healing."

"Very well. Send Patto to me and I will give him the reward."

CHAPTER 14

The Proposals

THE SEASIDE HILL hunters returned carrying a winter's worth of meat. For Cayl, the bison hunt yielded him a substantial portion. After smoking his share and tanning the hide, he gathered his trade for his proposal to Ric Sayed. All the time he hunted with his clutch, he had been composing his speech in his head.

At the Sayed family hut, he jiggled the seashells strung by the door cover. The door opened a crack and Ric Sayed peered out.

"Cayl Wonn? What business brings you here?"

Not being invited in confused Cayl. He said, "I come for your daughter."

The door parted and Ric came outside. Crossing his arms in front of him, he asked, "By what manner do you seek my daughter?"

"I choose her for my mate. Here are my gifts for trade."

"Hear me and know this," said Ric. Sneering, he stepped close to the boy. "My daughter is not for trade. She has her own mind."

But Cayl said, "Bring her out for me to sway."

Having heard the exchange, Lily came out followed by her mother, Reba.

The commotion brought some bystanders out of their huts.

"Must we speak among the villagers?" asked Cayl.

Reba moved forward. "For this talk I wish all to listen." She shook her fist at him. "Since you were born, I have known you. You grew up to be a brute. You beat your dogs. You disrespect your parents, and this behavior to trade meat for Lily is offensive."

"But I bring a full bull bison pelt as well."

Lily scurried up to Cayl. "Please go. My heart cares not for you."

Cayl ignored her and said, "A man picks his wife. This is our way. Come with me now."

"No. Not now, not ever."

"But I choose you," said Cayl. He grabbed her arm. Lily wrenched free.

In a blur, the point of Ric's flint knife pressed against Cayl's loin skin. Cayl's eyes grew wide as he gaped at the blade poised to cut him.

"If you return, if you trouble Lily at all, what the dog spared, I will take." Ric pressed firmly to emphasize his resolve. Finally, he withdrew the blade. "Now go."

With nothing to say, Cayl picked up his bundle and hurried away.

Over the winter, in the village of Twin Oaks, Pine had carved the beads for a courting necklace. During the fall, while hunting with his team, he had found some of the makings. On his first elk hunt, he found a hunk of red soapstone. Days later on the trail home, he picked up a sizable piece of amber. On other quests he acquired two round crow nuts and some colorful sea shells.

The shiny russet crow nuts, twice the size of Pine's thumb, proved hard as elk antler. A searing crystal burnt holes through the shells on two sides, and with a porcupine quill he extracted the bitter nutmeat. Since the fleshy centers possessed a healing purpose, Pine saved it for his sister Neva.

Adorning the crow nuts, Pine took his time. He etched flower symbols in the shells with a pointed flint as best he could. He scratched the dark outside deep enough to reveal the bright yellow underneath.

From the soapstone Pine carved the symbol of a bear, and after piercing it, he split it in two. He lashed them so that on the necklace they faced each other.

He decided the amber should be the centerpiece. He shaped it to represent a waxing crescent moon and planned to string the bears on either side, along with the carved crow nuts and seashells.

In the first of spring Pine strung the necklace with a tanned deer thong. To be sure the necklace was fine enough to offer Lily, he decided to ask his mother to judge its worthiness.

Running helped Pine think; he needed to sort things out. What he found most difficult to grasp was how he would rather brandish his spear against an angry bear than bare his heart to the friend he had known for but a year and a half. Over that time, he and she had grown into full-fledged friends.

In the crisp early morning air, Pine could see the steam from his breath. The sun would make itself known to the knoll when it cleared the hill behind him, and with the brightness would come the warmth. Shadow scouted ahead and returned to race with Pine until the dog reached the border of his earlier search, then he dashed ahead to clear the way of any predators.

With the questions in his head, he went to the only person who could help him: his mother. To ease into his uncertainties, he sat next to her while she ground maize. Surprised by her son joining her, Gemma studied his face.

"Those eyes tell me you yearn for the girl you spend your free time with, but I also see doubt. Tell me your troubles."

"My head is filled with thoughts of Lily. Never have my lips touched hers, yet my heart now yearns for her in ways I had never thought before."

"My son is in love. And she feels how?"

"Since we have not spoken of this, I am unsure. Our friendship is true."

Pine opened the rabbit fur pouch and showed her the courting necklace.

"Ah, this is what you toiled on when no one watched."

"Will she like it?" asked Pine.

Gemma held the necklace and said, "This, she will, and wear it with pride. The way Lily Sayed looks at you, my guess is she would take a bare cord necklace from you as her greatest treasure."

Once Pine returned to his chores, Gemma reached under her top and fondled the bird amulet on the courting necklace Chirp had made for her. Tears filled her eyes, and she buried her head in her hands.

Spring arrived, and finally Pine decided to ask for permission to court Lily. On his way to Seaside Hill, Shadow trotted close beside him. Because of the gifts he carried for the Sayed family, he kept an easy pace. As they continued on the trail, troublesome thoughts filled Pine's head. *What if she is of a different heart? What if what I say of my heart casts no shadows on hers? When this*

The Era of Herbalists

is known to her, would she turn and run or worse, laugh? Would she no longer sing for me?

Pine entered the village; some dogs barked at him as he did. Even though he saw no one staring, he felt eyes on him. *Remember to breathe*, he told himself. At the door to the Sayed hut, he should have reminded himself of that twice. Something else he should have told himself was to shake the seashells, or to cough or speak and let himself be known. Instead, he stood in front of their door, hoping it would open on its own somehow. Ultimately, Shadow gave a woof.

Ric Sayed opened the door and Lily brushed past him. Reba followed.

Shadow barked, jumped up, and ran to Lily. He circled her with an I-am-happy-to-see-you yip.

"Mother? Father? Pine is here."

"I have eyes," said Ric. "Tell me, Pine Nyte, why have you come so far?"

"To ask Lily—um, to ask you for your permission to court Lily."

"What are you to ask Lily?" asked Reba.

Pine faced Lily. "Lily? Do you wish for me to court you?"

"Yes," said Lily. She turned to her father. "Father, Mother, show Pine inside. He brought gifts."

Pine kneeled by Shadow. He rubbed him under his chin. "Wait for me."

Shadow wagged his tail and sat. Reba walked up to him and extended the back of her hand for him to sniff. He did, then gave her hand a lick.

"This cannot be the scruffy dog that saved Lily from the bear," said Reba.

"Yes. This is Shadow."

"He is well groomed. If his manners are equal, he is welcome inside."

"Shadow is respectful, but he prefers the outdoors."

"Very well, he may stay," said Reba.

"Come inside," said Ric. "Let us talk."

Fur cushions lined the inside of the storyteller's spacious hut. Ric pointed to one for Pine to sit, and he sat opposite him. Lily helped her mother brew the berry leaf tea.

"Tell me again why you have come all the way from Twin Oaks," said Ric.

"I would ask permission to court your daughter, Lily."

Leaning back with his arms behind him, Ric said, "You are not the first to seek my daughter's company."

"I did not know this. Am I too late?"

"No, I decided against the first man." Ric straightened up and laid his hands on his knees. "The word told from Twin Oaks is that you have earned a place on the second hunt clutch. That is an impressive achievement."

"My thanks. I trained since I was small."

"Did you know your father once traded with me?"

"No, I did not. When?"

"Long ago when I courted Reba. Chirp Nyte traded me this blade." Ric showed Pine the flint knife.

"What did you trade to him?"

"He was seeking vision mushrooms. I shared the path to Forest Gorge where they grow."

"My mother is from that place."

"This is true. They met then."

Jerking his head back, Pine said, "It seems I owe my birth to you."

Ric chuckled. "If not me, your father would have found someone else to tell him the trail there. His determination led him to that place."

"Still, I am indebted to you."

"Maybe so. But I still have yet to give you permission to court Lily."

"If you give me consent, I swear to her, to you, to her mother, and all the gods to cherish Lily for always."

"Reba? Should we allow this courtship?"

"Tell me, Pine," said Reba. "Would you also cherish her by bringing her here to visit her family?"

"As often as you wish. Also, you would be welcome to come to Twin Oaks and visit us."

"Husband, I think our daughter is more anxious to hear our permission than Pine. Ric? I do not believe Pine is breathing; he is beginning to pale."

"Very well. We shall have the ceremony here," said Ric. "On the shore."

"When?" asked Lily. She sat on the fur on Pine's right side.

"Tomorrow is the full moon. You will wed on the full moon after."

The Era of Herbalists

Pine reached in his fur pouch and pulled out the necklace he had made for Lily. He held it open for her and she beamed.

"Oh, Pine, this is lovely," said Lily. She held the necklace in front of her with both hands and turned her head for Pine to attach the ends. Pine's fingers found the small bone he fashioned tied to one end. He slipped it through the loop on the other end, turned the peg, and tugged it tight.

The necklace hung just below her throat. Beaming, she showed her mother and father.

Pine handed Reba a leather satchel. She opened it and admired the cyani flowers. Perfect for making blue dye for her weavings and very hard to find.

To Ric, he handed a gray fox fur pouch. He reached inside and brought out the elkhorn-handled white stone knife. Ric's eyes widened. "Where did you find such a white stone?"

Pine and Lily answered as one. "At our secret place." Then they laughed.

But Ric grinned and asked, "Do you mean the hill you sing on?"

"How do you know?" asked Lily.

"Do you think I would let you off on your own with the predators?"

"I had my sling."

"Yes, and I had my bow," replied Ric.

"Where were you?" asked Lily. "I never saw you."

"He was in the thicket under the curled oak tree," said Pine.

Ric arched his eyebrows. "You saw me?"

"Not at first," said Pine. "But when Lily brought Shadow to me, he gave you away. After that I looked for you."

"Were you not worried?"

"No, I knew you were there for Lily."

CHAPTER 15

The Wedding

THE TWIN OAKS council of elders met to discuss the upcoming wedding of Pine Nyte and Lily Sayed from Seaside Hill.

"Many of us are too old to walk so far," said Thon Doone.

"If we could set stepping stones in the marsh, we could cut the trip to the seashore in half," said Ever Hogg, the youngest elder.

"In the fall when the rains come, the stones would sink," said Thom.

"Ever has a fine idea of making a path through the marsh. Why not make a trail of straw and maize stocks?" asked Evon.

"The rain would wash the straw away," answered Ever.

"Perhaps," said Evon. "But the trail would last until the wet season."

The men came to an agreement.

"The moon is waxing near half," said Thom. "The work needs to start soon."

"Today. I will tell Pine," said Evon. "All his hunt team can help. We can call a meeting for tonight and ask for more volunteers."

With his brother and sister assisting, Pine collected a dozen helpers. Most of his hunt teammates joined in. But not Grand.

Because Witt aided Neva, he showed Pine's crew where the tallest grasses grew.

"Do you think anyone from Seaside Hill would help from their end? For trading, a shorter trail would benefit them as well," said Berm.

"We could ask," said Pine.

"I will be the runner," said Micha, Berm's younger brother.

"Seek Ric Sayed, the storyteller," said Pine. "He is Lily's father."

The Era of Herbalists

The boy tightened the cord on his moccasins, untied his dog, picked up his short spear, and trotted off to the path that led to Seaside Hill.

From the village, Ash Skeye limped toward the group.

"Look. Here comes the lame one," said Todd.

Pine moved in front of Todd. "It is only my friend Ash's misfortune that allows you to best him at anything."

"How can you speak such a thing? It is said he does nothing but spread pig shit on the loam. His father and mother curse him all the day and nighttime."

"You should listen with your eyes and not your ears." Pine called Shadow to his side. "You admire the collar Shadow wears."

"Yes, you made a fine one."

"Not me. Ash. He carved the designs you say appear real."

"I did not realize he possessed such a gift."

"If you regard *him* and not his one birth flaw, you will find a true spirit."

Todd thought for a second. "Do you think he would make a collar for my dog?"

"Ask him. If he says yes, give him the skin to work. Trade him fresh meat."

The apology came out in pieces. A good-to-see-you greeting crowned with an earnest smile. Todd complimented Ash on his skill in creating Shadow's collar and then said, "The gods afflicted you, and yet you thrive despite your impediment. That is a high measure of a man. It shames me how I have treated you. For that I am sorry."

The surprise of Todd's apology caused Ash to simply nod. After clasping hands with Pine, he took out his long flint blade and started cutting straw.

With the additional help from Seaside Hill, they completed the shortcut trail in only five days. The consensus among the people of both villages was to keep the path open except for the rainy season.

The wedding ceremony began early evening with a feast. The village of Seaside Hill set the main fare of meat, seafood, and spirit juice. Most guests contributed with either fruit, greens, lentils, honey cakes, or goat's milk.

As the Twin Oaks herbalist, Neva Nyte assisted the cooks with the herbs and spices. She was joined by the Seaside Hill healer Ryne Willet. Older by five years, the woman scrutinized the girl closely. And after already having to prove herself to her entire village, Neva was unfazed by the woman's blatant gaze.

The full moon and the stars reigned over a cloudless night sky. Because the joining of Pine and Lily linked the two villages, the elders of Seaside Hill made a pageant of the affair. Singers sang, and dancers danced to the beat of drums in elaborate costumes.

Children fed the bonfire while the grownups cheered the joined couple with song and dance. Even the elder, Thon Doone, to the dismay of his daughter Whi, made his feet and arms move to the drumbeat. His walking stick kept him upright, but Whi stood close by in case the fermented berry juice he drank caused him to fall.

As an honored guest, Gemma sat with Reba and Ric Sayed. No one commented on the display of black mourning feathers adorning her hair. Nor did any single men approach her for a dance or a walk on the shore. All her dancing she did with her sons. For her stroll on the shore, she walked alone with Shadow as her escort.

On the beach, a secluded area gave her a place to sit and pray to the gods. Even on this joyous occasion, Gemma felt a looming dread. The anxiety of some impending calamity pressed on her stomach, and she retched in the sand.

By himself, under a tree and away from the glow of the bonfire, Cayl Wonn sat and gawked at the couple dancing alone. This was the marriage dance and, to his thinking, it should be him holding Lily. As he watched them, his mind put arrow after arrow through Pine Nyte's heart.

The dance finished, and a chill at the back of Cayl's neck changed his focus to the crowd. Even in the dim light he could feel Ric Sayed's watchful stare. And the dog. The dog seemed to foresee Cayl's dislike for his master. Each time Cayl set his eyes on Pine or Lily, he caught the dog's look at him. The way the dog glared, his eyes glowed fire.

Before a new song and dance began, Cayl took his anger back to his hut. Stomping up the hill, he cursed Pine, his dog, and Ric Sayed under his breath the whole way. With his head spinning from too little to eat and too much spirit juice, Cayl flopped on his bed nest and cursed himself to sleep.

Some of the guests chose to stay in the lean-to shelters the Seaside Hill villagers had made for them. Those same guests prolonged the celebration long after the wedding party departed. For their anticipated morning discomfort, Neva Nyte left them a generous amount of ginger root, menthe, and star flower tea.

Afterward, torch bearers led the wedding procession back to Twin Oaks. A few of Lily's kin followed for a short distance, wishing the couple well while pleading to the gods to bless them with children.

At the village, some of those who had stayed cheered and welcomed the couple home. Some of them joined the parade all the way to Pine's hut.

The commotion brought Grand Moon to the door. The first sight of her caused him to stare. A girl he had never met. Even in the torch and moonlight, she was the most beautiful young woman Grand had ever seen. And when he saw her take Pine Nyte's hand, he clenched his teeth, and the deer's leg bone he was clenching in his hands broke in half. He watched them walk away and swore in his mind that he would have her for his own someday.

The procession ended at Pine's hut. He held the door flap open for Lily. Somewhat embarrassed, she waved behind her as she ducked inside. As self-conscious as his bride, Pine slipped in behind her with the wedding party cheering and hooting outside.

Someone, Pine suspected Neva and Witt, had filled the hearth and stoked the fire, leaving the hut warm and lit by three lamps. Also, several sprigs of lavender scented the place. Possibly his mother's contribution.

The moon of waiting for this day had left them both eager and nervous. Alone for the first time as husband and wife, Pine led Lily to their wedding bed. Staring in Pine's eyes, Lily unfastened a tie on her shoulder and let her dress fall to the fur-lined floor. She helped Pine raise his tunic over his head. While he fumbled with the strap on his loin skin, Lily pulled Pine down to the bed pelts.

They laid together atop the fur and explored each other. Slowly at first, but soon instinct and passion took control.

Before the fire died, the two coupled several times in a row. Before they crawled under the furs, Lily said, "Inside me, from our last time, I think a child must have begun."

Pine hugged and kissed her neck. "If that is so, then the gods must truly approve our mating." Then he whispered, "But for our lovemaking we should keep trying as if each time would be our first."

Hearing that, Lily wrapped herself around Pine. He responded with kisses and caresses. With her tender hands, Lily guided him inside her. Pine took hold of her by her waist and rolled her on top of him. Smiling broadly, Lily gyrated while Pine raised and lowered his hips. The two climaxed together and when Lily climbed off, they embraced and fell fast asleep.

CHAPTER 16

The Skeye Family

UNDER A WILD plum tree, Ash Skeye scratched on a flat piece of slate with a pointed quartz crystal. Occasionally, he glanced at some flowers growing nearby.

"What are you doing, Ash?" yelled Mara, his mother, shaking a switch at him. "What is this nonsense?"

Ash held the slate for her to see. He said, "See, Mother? I made it look just like the flowers."

"Yes! And you have work in the field. Your sisters are as you see them now, only playing at picking berries. Your father already suffers in the field with so little help from you!"

The moment Ash rose to his feet, the switch found his rear, and he limped alongside his mother toward the field as she lectured. "You are but our poor tool to carry the farm. You are here for that! Not to scratch images on rocks for your pleasure."

Facing his mother's scowl, he said, "Mother, I am sorry, but why have I the skill to make the images? No one has taught me this. Do not the gods gift skills?"

Her reply came with another smack. "Your only skills are in the fields and spreading the shit that comes from the pigs! That is why the gods have given us a son! Even a lame one. This skill you say you have is no use to this family." She pointed to the field ahead of them. "The rains were thin this year and the crops are weak. At harvest when the gatherers come to the village, they will seek other ways to make up for their bounty—perhaps in our tools. Should that skill you claim be seen, then the gatherers would take one lame as you. This is so! So no more of this folly and go help your father—throw that stone away and no more of this."

At the sight of his father in the field, Ash readied himself for another strike. It did not come. He turned to see his mother marching home, then hurried to join his father in the sweet maize field. Ash gazed at the flower he had etched, sighed, and tossed the stone behind him.

On his way to the field, he passed his neighbor, Ona Hogg, who had been listening to Mara Skeye's scolding. He faced the ground as he passed by her so as not to see the spite she wore on her face. He did not look back to see her pick up the abandoned slate.

Finally, he entered the clearing. His father Denn's head poked through the field of maize. Ash's feet crunched the dead straw that crept toward the drought-stricken stalks.

Denn turned to the sound. "There you are, you burden on the loam and shame of foot! The gods cursed Skeye family with no runner for the challenge! Skeye family now only bargains for the meat and skins a runner would have, and then others would bargain with Skeye family for their meat and skins."

Denn shoved a digging staff to him and pointed to a basket of dried corn kernels. "When the toil begins, I see the slowness in you, yet when it pleases you, I have seen swiftness. I must see that swiftness now while we plant, or you shall feel the willow as it tempers your flesh. Start digging! Move! Now!"

As best he could, Ash shoved the sharp end of the stick into the crusty soil, leaned, and twisted. His father followed, planting the seeds. Ash dug another, a foot length away.

"Dig faster!"

Ash plunged the stick down and struck a rock. He squatted and scraped around the stone with his fingers. The stone came free and he tossed it aside. Before his father could scold him, he stood and thrust the pole into the next spot. After a time, the two acquired a rhythm, and labored without stopping.

Finally, sensing a change in the light, Denn glanced up. The sun hung low in the western sky. With four rows to go, he hollered at Ash. "Hurry, tool of mine! Lest you wish to finish by yourself tomorrow along with spreading the pig shit."

The Era of Herbalists

The planting staff seemed to gain weight as Ash struggled to pull the rod high enough to sink into the brittle ground. Only when he leaned on it did his muscles rest.

Just as the orange sun went down, Denn ran out of seeds. He tossed the basket at Ash. "Your sister failed to scrape enough kernels. Tomorrow I want you to scrape two more cobs and finish the row."

His father marched off and Ash picked up the basket. The weight of the thing seemed to have doubled, and it was the same with the planting staff. Besides the heaviness he carried, the ache in his foot cost him. By the time he washed himself, his mother had put away the leavings from the evening meal. So as not to starve him, she gave him a piece of underdone, slim bread.

To avoid any more reprimands, Ash took the morsel to his sleep nest. He climbed into the furs in slow increments. Every move he made hurt him some place. Once he settled on his back, the pain subsided. He nibbled on the bread, but after only a few bites, he fell asleep. While he dozed, a mouse ate the remnants of bread from his fingers.

In between the planting and harvest time, and morning and afternoon chores, Ash practiced alone in a grove of small scrub trees. There, no one could see his efforts. Like his other tries, he stumbled on his third attempt at a running start. From watching some of the boys practicing theirs, he knew all of them leaped off on their left feet. His left foot was turned out and twisted down, and he had little control over whether he bent his foot up or turned it in. So he was trying to leap from his right foot, but then the left foot caused him to trip. Then it occurred to him how he threw his sling. On his throw, he put his weight on his heel.

Once again, he planted his right foot. He bent down with his elbows at his side and balled his hands into fists. Keeping his eyes forward and his head straight, he took a leap. This time he landed on his left heel and his right leg followed, but rather than stumble, Ash found his left heel again, then his right foot, on and on.

If someone had witnessed his dash, it would have first appeared awkward. Yet if one were to look more carefully, they would observe a certain grace. Plus, no one could reject the speed Ash was achieving. But the pain he could feel in his heel caused the effort to end.

Through the pain, Ash thought that if he continued practicing, he might face the runner's challenge. It was true; Ash would never be a hunter, but runners always received a share of the game.

At fifteen years, Ash qualified to be a runner. Would it please his father that he would attempt the next competition? Did he have a chance at winning? Would he still be the burden his mother and father blamed him to be? A runner did more than chase out game. They skinned the animals, processed the meat, carried the kills, tended the fires, cooked the meals, and guarded the meat.

He sat on a rock, pulled off his moccasin, and looked at his heel. Only a little bruised, and the pain was already diminishing. He looked inside his moccasin and thought that if he could wrap his heel, he would dampen the pain.

Doing as he was told, Ash gathered wood from an oak tree. The tree he selected granted him an abundance of manageable branches. He gathered them and found a wedge-shaped broken piece from a knot. The part had a round depression, just about the shape and size of his heel.

Ash sat on a flat rock and removed his moccasin. He placed the wood to his foot and realized that, with a little scraping and maybe a deerskin pad inside his moccasin, the wood would soften the impacts while he ran. Fitting the wood bit inside his pouch, he gathered the branches and continued toward home.

In the village, Ash saw some of the town boys holding court with Grand Moon, the brawny son of the hunt master, Falk Moon. This was an unavoidable situation, and Ash resolved himself that he would just have to pass and the gods would be either with him or against him—or possibly both. Continuing by, and without looking at them, Ash towed the firewood behind him.

"Hey, Grand!" said Berm. "There is the broken foot one."

Grand blocked the path and said, "That's a lot of wood for such a small broken boy to slog. We should be your help. Come, friends, let's aid this poor suckling."

Grand and his three friends started picking branches out of the heap. As each walked off carrying their loot, Grand told Ash as he pointed, "Now here is a fitting amount for a small broken boy to burden."

The Era of Herbalists

Ash looked down to his now depleted stash of branches. Crossing his arms in front of him, he said, "Thank you for relieving me of so much load! Your kin must be poor and of great need! If this is so, I implore you, please take more, lest your hearths burn cold. It would pain me should this be so."

Grand's friends' faces sagged while Grand himself chuckled. They looked about and at each other, not quite grasping just what had occurred but somehow feeling foolish.

First, Talon dropped the wood that he had stolen, then Berm and Nat followed suit, save Grand. He walked off laughing, toting off his booty, which was substantial.

Ash waited to pick up his refunded wood and smiled as he continued on his way home.

CHAPTER 17

The Spotted Fever

ON HER THIRD spring as herbalist, Neva Nyte lifted the door flap when the shells shook outside her hut. Council member Atte Uhl stood slumped over and holding himself. As soon as Neva saw the man's spotted face, she came out and placed a mat in the shade outside the hut, where she told him to lay down.

"Atte? Tell me when you first felt ill."

"Last night my back was sore, but this morning when I woke, I thought a bison must have trampled me, and my head hurts like a hit with a battle club. Now, these eyes sting from behind like a panther scratching them."

Placing a hand on his head, she felt his fever. She asked, "Who stays in your hut?"

"My wife, Tiana, and her sister, Denia."

"Do they have symptoms?"

"Tiana, she hurts. Of Denia, I cannot say."

"I am going to brew a remedy. Rest here." Neva went inside, washed her hands, and shook them dry. For a few moments she paced. Both hunt teams were off, hunting, so Pine could not help. Plus, while Pine was away, her mother, Gemma, took Lily to visit her parents in Seaside Hill. Still, she had Witt.

Staring at her apothecary, she sat hard on her cushion and put her head in her hands. This was a fear she had, that the spotted fever would come to the village. All she could do was treat the symptoms. Anything else was up to the gods.

In her whole apothecary, only two plants would help bring down a fever. In the garden behind the hut, she dug some wild ginger roots and picked a handful of meadowsweet flowers. She returned to the apothecary and began chopping the two together until the mash proved fine enough. Filling a gourd with cool water, she stirred until the brew darkened.

Outside she heard Witt's voice.

"Witt. I need your help."

The boy burst into the hut. "What ails Atte?"

Avoiding the question, Neva said, "He needs a sweat. And I need to speak to Grandfather."

"What remedy are you crafting?"

"Atte has a fever."

"What are the blotches on his face?"

"Witt, make a fire and heat some stones for the sweat lodge. Atte needs his tea and I must talk to Grandfather."

Shrugging his shoulders, Witt went to heat more rocks and fetch water for the sweat lodge.

Crouching beside Atte, Neva lifted his head and offered the treatment. Unable to hold the gourd by himself, she brought the vessel to his open mouth and trickled some in. He drank all she gave him and lay his head down. Once she was sure of his well-being, she dashed off to speak to her grandfather.

Today, like every day in the afternoon, Evon was preparing bear fat for his lamp. He stirred his mix with some menthe to freshen the air. Seeing his granddaughter Neva striding toward him, he put the clay lamp down.

"What burdens you?" asked Evon.

Squatting before him, she said, "Atte Uhl and his wife might have the spotted fever."

"How sure are you?" asked Evon.

"The signs are the same. I need to check the kin in his hut."

"This is a hard thing, but before all are learned, you must be sure."

"I will know soon," said Neva.

"How is Atte?"

"Witt is making a sweat for him, and I gave him a remedy for fever."

"When you are certain, I will call the council together."

"Many thanks, Grandfather."

Without pausing, Neva marched to Atte Uhl's hut. About to shake the door shells, Neva heard crying. "Tiana? Denia?"

"Come," said a weak voice.

Tiana, Atte's wife, lay curled on top of her bed furs. Denia sat on a cushion.

Neva knelt by Tiana. The same blotches marked her face.

"My head, it pounds my skull like drums," said Tiana. "My hands. I squeeze my fingers and I cannot close them and when I do, I cannot open them again. Help me, please."

"Denia? Do you suffer?"

"Some," replied Denia. "Not like Atte or Tiana."

"Can you help me with your sister?"

"Yes. What do you need?"

"We need to go to the sweat lodge."

The two women helped Tiana stand. On either side of her, they walked her to the sweat lodge. Witt came out. "I have more stones to add."

Neva and Denia held Tiana, who began trembling.

With his wooden cradle of sizzling rocks, Witt rushed inside and dumped them with the rest. Quickly, he poured some water, and the steam hissed and caused a fog. The women came inside and Neva fixed places for them. They sat, and she picked up the gourd and dumped more water on the stones. Witt went to attend the fire and heat more rocks.

Leaving the sweat lodge, Neva went to her hut. At first, seeing him so still, Neva believed Atte to be sleeping. But closer to him, she saw his empty eyes staring at the sky. Atte Uhl had died. Pulling a fur over him, Neva ran to her grandfather's hut.

"Grandfather. Atte Uhl is dead. A meeting must be called."

He raised himself and Neva said, "Every hut must be checked. Anyone with symptoms must be found."

"Yes," said Evon. "And someone must tell Atte's kin."

"Later. First I must keep Tiana Uhl and her sister alive."

Without telling them about Atte's death, Neva brought gourds of the remedy to the sisters. She waited while they drank.

The Era of Herbalists

Outside, she went to her brother's side. She whispered the news, and for the time she asked him to keep the death a secret. While Neva went to check for more patients, Witt brought more scalding stones and water.

Her search for the fever-stricken started near Atte's hut. She asked each person the same question: "Do you ache anywhere?"

Several rows over, Bo Rift, his wife Kare, and their small son, Bodo, were beginning to suffer.

Even though they had yet to show spots, Neva urged them to go to the sweat lodge. There she had fever medicine, and sweating would help control their temperature. Of those others Neva found ill, none dwelled nearby Atte's hut. They, too, she bade to sweat and partake of the remedy which she had crafted.

Later, it fell to Neva to wash and prepare Atte Uhl's body for the burning. Pal Lukan and Yar Awell laid him on a litter while Neva mixed menthe with the herb water. As she requested, they left his loin skin on him.

Washing his partially bald head, she rinsed and brushed his hair and beard with a boar brush. With a sea sponge, she started cleansing his arms and his chest. From there, she started washing his feet. Spreading his toes apart, she found a tick lodged there. The bug was dark brown with light markings. The bite was dark and swollen.

She rushed to the sweat lodge.

"Who has ticks? Check yourselves and each other."

Raising her hand, Kare Rift said, "Got one under my arm. Bodo has two. One was eatin' him same place as me, the other was in his hair. Almost did not find that foul bug."

"Leave them till I can take them off. Witt will concoct a salve."

"What if I already picked them off?" asked Raden Awell.

"The salve will work. Just make sure you know where the bites were."

"They is all red and swelled, those places is easy to see."

They examined themselves and each other—everyone had ticks or bites.

Armed with this knowledge, Neva hurried to the council meeting. Fortunately, she caught them before the meeting ended.

Several council members asked questions at the same time. Evon held his hand up. "Tell us, Neva. What have you learned?"

"Ticks cause the sickness. Of this I am sure. The mystery is the source. All the inflicted are family groups, but the real puzzle is none dwell near one another. Of the ill, only the Rift family set their hut by any shrubs at the village edge. And only Raden and Rona Awell live under an oak tree."

"Can you guess who the ticks bit first?" asked Ever Hogg.

"Must have been Atte Uhl," answered Neva. "I am going to that hut first."

"I will go with you," said Ever.

Thon Doone leaned on his walking stick. "Myself as well."

To her grandfather and all the other council members, she said, "Make sure you search yourselves for ticks."

As was the custom, when entering an unoccupied home, Neva announced her purpose to the neighbors. Several came out of their dwellings to watch. After telling them about the fever and the death of Atte Uhl, they rushed back inside to hunt ticks.

Inside, the two men waited by the doorway, and Neva stood near the hearth. Coals were still burning. She scanned the room. Atte and Tiana's bed nests were on one side and Denia's on the opposite. The kitchen area was cluttered. Neva picked up some platters. Flies, but no ticks. Across from the kitchen were Tiana's basket weaving stock, along with several finished baskets and one newly started.

She picked some up and a tick jumped on her hand. Promptly, Neva brushed it off and ground it with her moccasin.

"That will not kill them bugs," said Ever. He picked the insect up and tossed it into the hearth. The tick blazed and popped. "Be best if we burn the hut."

"If you burn this house, then you must do the same with all them folks got the fever," said Thon. "It could be we just kill the ticks."

Ever scratched his chin whiskers and nodded.

Picking up a finished basket, Neva turned the weaving this way and that. No ticks, but the golden straw with purple striations she had not seen before. Maybe Witt would have seen some on his gathering expeditions.

The Era of Herbalists

With Tiana's basket in her hand, she asked all the afflicted if they had traded with her. All had, and recently. Tiana did not answer, and Neva could not wake her. The woman's skin flushed. She asked Denia where the straw came from, but she had no answer, only that Atte had brought it to her one day.

"Do you recall when?"

"On the night of no moon."

From that Neva guessed eight or nine days. Dipping a sponge in cold water, she wiped Tiana's fevered forehead. The woman stirred. "Tiana? Can you hear me?"

She fluttered her eyes and spread her lips, but did not speak. Using a fresh sponge, Neva soaked up some of the remedy and squeezed some in her mouth. Tiana swallowed and opened her mouth for more. Dipping the sponge, Neva wrung out another dose, and she gulped the liquid down.

The sweat lodge door opened and Witt entered with a load of scalding stones. After he placed them, Neva showed him the basket. "In your journeys, have you seen this straw growing?"

Taking the basket outside, Witt turned it over, studied the inside, and scrunched his face. "Not anywhere I have seen. Still, since there is only one place I have yet to forage, the straw must grow there."

"Where do you speak of?"

"The east end of the flat hill to the northeast," said Witt. "The straw must grow there, else he had to have been gone more than a day from Twin Oaks."

"Can I task you to go there and find where Atte Uhl reaped this straw?"

"If Ash Skeye can accompany me," answered Witt. "I will ask him today. Should he choose, we would leave at first light."

Neva suspected Witt had chosen his crippled friend to be his escort because of his skills. No one else, except for Pine herself, knew the boy's real worth. It was he who had taught both Pine and Witt how to use a sling. And the ones he made seemed to be better than any others.

"His kin, Jal Skeye, has tick bites," said Neva.

"How bad is Jal's fever?" asked Witt. Knowing his friend, Ash, the boy would be heartbroken should his uncle die. Jal was his father's elder brother and the only kin to treat him kindly.

"Not so bad. His wife, she must have suffered first. Opalla is near as grave as Tiana."

"For them," said Witt, "and all, I shall pray to the gods."

"Pray hard, but gods or no gods, I mean to keep these neighbors living best I can." She wiped her forehead. "Now, I must make more treatment. Should there be more sickly, I must learn of all who own baskets from Tiana Uhl. The council has chosen to hunt and kill the ticks. If you find the straw growing, they may choose to burn the place."

About to check for more patients, Neva asked, "Witt? Can you chop and smash some ginger root with an equal amount of honey for me? Use all the roots, I will dig more later."

"Is the salve for the bites?"

"Yes, and if I do not return when you finish mixing, tend the wounds."

"But…but most of the sick is women folk! Cannot someone else tend to them? Please."

"Ask Elm Moon. Make her check herself for ticks."

That afternoon, Neva found five more feverish, aching patients. Having learned of her father's death, Seema Pyre and her daughter Nel helped Witt, heating rocks, fetching water, and keeping the fire going. Her aunt and a cousin needed healing.

By nightfall, the sweat lodge had no more room, so Thon Doone asked for volunteers to make another lodge. Some villagers and council members worked until daylight to construct the second sweat lodge. By the afternoon the new place was half full.

Ash, the elder of the two boys, set the pace because of his twisted left foot. Chances were, should Witt travel by himself, his pace would be the same. There was too much to see, and Witt prided himself on his valuable finds. Not just for Neva; anything growing in abundance, like menthe, he gathered and traded with villagers. For his sister he found harder-to-find plants.

Closer, Witt pointed to the edge of the flat hill. A breeze rippled a tall golden grass.

"That straw might be what has the ticks," said Witt.

"Best we check to be sure," said Ash.

"When we get nearby, allow me to do the checking. I know the straw."

Ash motioned ahead of them. "Some animals been in there, best if I stay close with my sling."

"Careful of the ticks. If they come from that straw, they might be near."

Spotting some straw sticking up by itself, Witt headed that direction. A loud snort from behind startled them. Ready with his sling, Ash turned ready to fling a rock. Stiffening, Ash stood between Witt and a giant camel. Considering themselves and the immense beast, Ash prayed to the gods that the animal did not charge them. A stone against a camel had no purpose but to cause more anger.

Breathing in their scent, the camel yowled a garbled bay. Lowering his head, he stomped three steps toward them, spit white phlegm at the ground, and exhaled a blast of camel breath at the dirt, spraying red dust. The camel raised his head and sidestepped with his massive hooves. Snorting snot in all directions, he did a quarter turn and bolted away through the brush around the hill.

Breathing a sigh, Witt said, "That beast would have fed the village for a whole season."

"Last year, my father traded maize for camel meat. Tough as hide, one roast lasted half a season. Took near that long just to chew," said Ash.

Witt chuckled. "Let us find the straw that keeps the ticks."

"Go no further," said Ash. They stopped. He pointed to the tick crawling up Witt's leg.

He yelled and brushed it off, then backed away. "This whole place needs to be burned."

"Come," said Ash. "We should go. If I step too slow then leave me."

"We came here together and I see no hurry. At this place yesterday there were ticks, and tomorrow will be the same."

"True," agreed Ash. "We best check for ticks on us."

Brushing himself, Witt said, "Having one crawl on me, now my skin feels them all over."

"What god made such a tiny thing to kill a full-grown man?" asked Ash.

Peeking under his loin skin, Witt said, "One of the bad ones. Like the scorpion god."

"Do you think there is a tick god?"

"If there is, then he will be doing battle with the fire god tomorrow."

Satisfied they were free of ticks, the boys sauntered off to the village.

CHAPTER 18

A Change for Ash Skeye

THE SPRING BROUGHT only sprinkles of rain, and now a moon into summer, none fell at all. It fell to Ash to haul water from the stream and feed the maize stalks. The task began at the first light, and one goatskin barely doused four plants. He could only carry two filled sacks, and as he toiled, he tried to focus on the ground and not the endless rows ahead of him.

Midday found him in the center of the field. Glancing ahead, Ash guessed how much longer he needed to work and decided to take his meal. The gourd he filled from his mother's pot was half empty. He took a sip. From his pouch he bought out the dried elk strip, wild plums, and slim bread.

Once he was fed, Ash trekked to the creek to fill his goatskin. On the way he spotted a few ripe berries his sisters had missed. He stopped at the bush.

"Save some of those berries for me," said a familiar voice behind him. He turned and saw Pine. "Fair day, Pine. It surprises me to see you."

"Today is tribute day for the women folk. They congregate around Lily."

"Then these berries hang on the vine because Fern joined them. Be best to leave them for her."

Not seeing Pine's dog, Ash asked, "Where is Shadow?"

"With Grandfather. Today, he dries venison."

Ash dipped a sack in the stream. "Must be a lot to keep Shadow from your side." Dragging the sack against the current, he hefted the full goatskin out and it dripped on his moccasins.

"Give me one of those sacks and I will help your labor."

"Many thanks," said Ash. He handed an empty goatskin bag to his friend, who filled it. On the way to the field, Pine said, "Look, Ash, there is Todd."

Pine waved. Spotting them, Todd trotted over.

"Are you both hiding from the women?" asked Todd. "They have been chasing some men and scolding them. My sister Nel has words against me."

"I bear no reason for a scolding," said Pine. "But Lily is their new attraction."

"And you, Ash? Your mother is one of the chastisers."

"Any penalty for me will come from my father if I fail to water the field."

"Then let me fetch a goatskin, and I will help you avoid your father's wrath." He dashed off while Ash and Pine lugged the heavy skins to the maize field. As they watered, Pine said, "Considering the drought, your father's maize thrives well."

"Yes, and if I do not keep the roots wet, then the failure will be mine."

True to his word, Todd met them at the stream. A few moments later, Roth and Syd came with goatskins. Grinning broadly, Todd said, "I found more water spreaders."

Stepping forward, Ash greeted the newcomers. "Many thanks."

Roth raised his chin. "The rain god frowns on us all."

"Truth," said Syd. "While the stream still flows, then we should make our own rain. If we make the rain god envious enough, he could cry for us."

Pointing to a puffy cloud, Roth said, "Pray he does not become resentful and beckon his brothers, lightning and thunder."

"Thunder roams the village," said Todd. "My own sister hunts me."

"Before we met up with Todd, we watched the women let into Grand," said Syd. "They surrounded his hut. His mother led the badgering."

"For what offense?" asked Pine.

Roth let out a laugh. "For being lazy."

"Then let us not be blamed ourselves for laziness," said Pine. He filled his sack in the creek and marched toward the field. The others followed.

Later, Ash caught sight of the lengthening shadows and recognized the hour nearing mealtime, so he walked to the creek and washed up. No one paid him any attention when he returned to the hut. His sister Fern was tending the cook fire and his younger sister, Shy, was sorting berries. As if Ash were invisible, neither seemed aware of his presence. Fern turned to fetch more wood and bumped into him; instead of her normal, temper-ruled responses, she ignored Ash entirely.

The Era of Herbalists

Following the meal and his chores, Ash slipped into his bed nest. Deep in sleep, Ash woke with a smelly hand over his mouth. He tried to scream but only gurgled. A gatherer glared at Ash. Shaggy, sweaty, and covered with strange symbols carved into his skin, he pulled Ash from his sleeping nest as if he weighed nothing. Grinning, he spread his lips wide and showed Ash his broken teeth. Ash gagged from the man's foul breath. His last sight before the leather-wrapped club thumped his head was another gatherer dropping a freshly gutted stag in front of his family's hut.

Hours later, in his sleep, a strangler snake clutched him. The more he struggled, the tighter the snake grasped him. Ash roused, unable to rise, and he realized he was wrapped in an animal hide. The dream he woke from was not a dream, but a reality. Powerless and blind in total darkness, he lay on his back. From the rhythm of the bouncing, he presumed he was being carried, and from the warmth, he felt it was daytime.

Thirsty, he used his tongue to make saliva. The side of his head ached from the blow he had received. Thinking of his predicament, another worse hurt pierced his heart. That his parents had sold him to the prodon. His value? A single stag.

As the day wore on, Ash wondered: in the few moons that the stag would feed the Skeye family, would they then, when no more meat remained, mourn his loss? Or would his mother and father then trade his sisters for food if they should not wed hunters or men of worth?

Someone uncovered his wrap. With sunlight blinding him, four gatherers were hovering over him. One of them poured a gourd of water in Ash's face. Though he could not tell at the time, his mouth must have been open, since before they covered him he was able to swallow a mouthful.

The heat and the steady tempo of his captor's gallop put him back to sleep. Another face full of water woke him. This time he coughed. The four litter bearers laughed, and when Ash saw them, they were not the same men who had first carried him away.

"Up with you," said one of them.

Having been bound for so long, Ash's moves were slow, but the gatherers were impatient and jerked him to his feet. But his one foot caused him to stumble. He fell backwards. A gatherer snatched hold of his arm before he hit the ground and pulled him back up. The man held him until he was sure Ash could stand on his own.

"What misfortune caused your foot to be twisted so?" he asked.

Ash heard annoyance in the question. "If you asked my mother," he replied, "she would say the gods cursed her because she bedded with my father. And if you asked my father, he would claim my bent foot his burden for planting his seed inside of my mother while under a crooked moon. But for me, my slowness is not an affliction—it gives me time to see the things most pass by."

"We have no time for that," said the man. He brandished his spear. "Go now. Be swift or bleed."

Turning to the man, Ash balled his fists and said, "Spear me now and spare this journey, for my swiftness is naught."

The man growled and feigned to jab him, but Ash stood still.

Another man laughed. "Our lame charge has spoken like a warrior."

"Only because he sees his worth does he make challenge."

"My only worth was a stag at my parents' door," said Ash.

"If that were all, then Master Lewell would not have sent for you."

"Who is Master Lewell?"

"He is the voice of Lord Prodon."

"You say Master Lewell has sent for me? If that is so, then it must be the prodon who summoned me."

"This is so," answered the man.

Without saying, Ash limped back to the litter. He sat and folded his arms. "If the prodon sent for me, he must have commanded you to bring me."

All four of the litter bearers laughed. They took their positions, hefted the carriage to their shoulders, and began trotting.

The ride caused Ash to doze. He woke as the sun hung low over the western hills. Ahead of them, trails of smoke showed in the sky. Ash patted his pouch and felt his wooden foot wedge. They had not taken it from him. Still, he could never outrun these brutes.

The Era of Herbalists

In front and below, Ash viewed a vast compound on a plain. The steep trail twisted back and forth, and when they reached the bottom, they were greeted by a dozen gatherers. One of them was bigger than the others. The hulking figure's shoulders were covered with a shirt of fur and bones.

The man played with the single nub of hair sprouting from the side of his head and said, "Tell me, Ash Skeye, is this your work?" He passed Ash a piece of slate, the same one his mother had scolded him for etching. The one he had cast on the ground. He remembered seeing Ona Hogg. She must have picked the slate up after she passed him.

"Yes," said Ash. He handed the stone back. "I scratched the flowers with a pointed crystal."

"I welcome you on behalf of Lord Prodon. I am Master Lewell, the eyes, ears, arms, legs, and say of he who is the one and only god."

Ignoring the statement, Ash asked, "How did you come by the slate I tossed away?"

"A woman in your village traded you for her brother's son, a hunter who was taken with the herbalist."

"Why then did gatherers leave a stag at my parents' door?"

"The stag was from the woman as reparation for her sin of betrayal."

After hearing this, Ash was relieved. His parents had not sold him, but his mother's warning had come to be true. His skill had caused his capture. "If it is my skill the prodon desires, what then will be my task?"

"To etch the herbs, flowers, birds, and animals for the prodon."

"And when my task is complete, may I return home?"

"The task is boundless as new plants, birds, and animals are found. You will scratch images until you be too elderly to journey."

Changing the subject, Ash said, "Does Chirp Nyte still live?"

"Yes, and with his cures he has earned much favor."

"Will I see him?"

"You shall. It is Lord Prodon's will for you to work with the herbalist."

Ash gazed out over the encampment. "What is this place for?"

"A flint quarry resides nearby. Workers make tools. Blades, arrowheads, and spear tips to arm the prodon's legions."

"The scent of meat cooking has my stomach churning. It has been a long journey since I have eaten."

"Before we continue the trek, we shall give you your fill."

The gatherers bearing spears followed Lewell and Ash to the cook fires. Cooks turned wooden rotisseries with racks of meat over hot coals. The entourage moved through the different kinds. The group passed by one that displayed a boar's head and on another pike was a bear's head. Lewell stopped at the place where the antlers from a bull elk rested. The beast roasting seemed cooked, and the embers were only keeping the meat warm.

"We will take our meal here," said Lewell to Ash and his men. They took seats on the logs laid out.

The cook wiped his flint blade on his doeskin apron. "Master Lewell. You honor me with your choice of my offerings."

"Feed my young friend first, then myself, and my guards. See to our drinks and bring us whatever fruit you offer."

"As you wish. For fruit, my daughters have picked wild plums."

The man sawed a hunk of elk meat on a clay platter. Two girls came from inside the hut. The first carried a pitcher of fermented berry juice. She set it down and fetched gourds to drink from. The second girl held a bowl of purple plums. Lewell considered the girl's limp. Like Ash. Her twisted foot was her right one, the opposite side of Ash's.

"Behold, Ash Skeye, the girl has your similar affliction."

Ash gazed at her for a brief second, but he turned his face away when she looked back at him. She may have smiled, but Ash chose to ignore her. But Lewell wanted Ash to see her. He gestured for her to stand before him. "Tell me your name, girl," said Lewell.

"Master Lewell, my parents named me Song. And my family name is Newt."

"Song Newt, can you manage the chores of a woman?"

"What chores do you speak of, Master Lewell?"

"Can you cook? Make fire? Thrash grain? Chew hides? Fetch water? Dig clams? Skin rabbits? Those things that make a hut useful."

"Surely," said Song.

"Master Lewell?" asked the cook. "Why do you pose such questions to my daughter?"

"My charge, Ash Skeye, limps like your daughter, and he is in need of a woman to care for him."

"But Master Lewell, Song is too young to warm a bed."

"That will be their choice whether to bed or not. His needs are not that, but his toil requires a woman's role for him to complete his task."

"Song is useful. Should you take her, I will be left shorthanded."

"Fear not, I will find a replacement."

The cook nodded and carved hunks of elk for their meal.

Ash, who had listened dumbfounded, asked Lewell, "Have I no say?"

"No, there was always going to be a woman to keep your hut, and I have chosen. And since I have, then Lord Prodon picked her as well. When you greet him, you must thank him for his flawless choice."

With nothing he could say, Ash began chewing the meat the cook handed him. The girl with the pitcher started to hand Ash a gourd of fermented juice, but Lewell stretched his long arm out and blocked her. "Give him water."

"As you wish, Master Lewell," replied the girl. She gave the gourd to Lewell. Then she came back and handed Ash his water.

Song, who had heard her fate, stood in front of Ash with the plums. Because Lewell sat so close, Song tried not to scowl at Ash, but her upper lip twitched when he took his share.

Ash picked his portion of plums and felt her eyes glaring at him—he tried to not look back. Having been taken from his own family, he knew the girl could not place blame on Lewell, so Ash bore her resentment.

After the meal Lewell ordered his guards to find an unwanted young woman. He told them, "Listen for wailing or any thrashing."

"What of the man causing the crying?"

"Bound him and bring him," said Lewell. "We will have bait for the river monster when we reach the barge."

The guards spread out among the worker huts. They stopped by each one to hear any distress. As they searched, a loud cry came from a hut near the edge of the compound. Several of the guards converged on the place.

A loud smack caused a woman to cry out. The first guard burst through the doorway. In the hearth's light the guard beheld a girl not much older than Song, kneeling and tethered to a post. Fresh welts striped her bare ass and before the man's willow switch struck her rump to leave another, the guard beat the stick from the man's hand.

"Leave!" spat the brute. "This is between a man and his wife!"

"By order of Lord Prodon, you have relinquished your wife."

Before he could protest, two more of Master Lewell's guards rushed in. They rolled him face down and bound his hands behind his back while the first guard freed and covered the woman. Once they were all outside, the lead guard ordered so all around could hear, "This hut belongs to Lord Prodon!" To the woman he said, "You may gather your possessions tomorrow."

"What of my belongings?" asked the man.

"All you own, you wear," said the guard.

"Why? I do not understand," cried the man. "A husband has a right to beat his wife."

"Not tonight," said the guard. They took him by his arms and marched him to the elk roaster's place.

Lewell stood when his men returned. He called the cook to him. "By the order of Lord Prodon, this girl is your new daughter and you shall accept her as true kin."

"Yes, Master Lewell."

The woman wiped her eyes. The cook strode up to her and looked her over. "What is your name?"

"Layan of the family Soalls."

"Now you are family Newt. You need to clean up. Luna? Take your new sister to the creek and bathe her. Find Layan a shift to wear. We have more customers coming."

Inside the hut, Song gathered her belongings. She said her goodbyes to her older sister, Luna. And though she wanted to, she said nothing to her father. She dried her tears and turned her sadness back into anger.

Among her possessions was an obsidian blade. She promised that should Ash Skeye touch her, then she would use it and then take her own life. But she had witnessed his annoyance at Master Lewell's announcement. And she thought that maybe he would ignore her.

Ready, she stepped from the hut. Lewell beckoned her forward. "This you do not know, but this is a great honor for you and your family."

"What honor? Now, I hope to die."

"If that is your wish," said Lewell. "But then your father would not be a cook at his place near Lord Prodon, and you would not see your sisters."

"What do you say?" asked Song. "That you are sending for my family?"

"Yes. By the half moon."

"Master Lewell. I will be the woman you wish of me, and I shall maintain his hut."

"This is what I want to hear. Fear not, your life may not be so harsh. I have spent enough time with Ash Skeye to say he is not a brute."

"I will be grateful for that."

"By the fading light tomorrow you shall be in the presence of Lord Prodon."

This revelation struck hard, and suddenly she said, "But Master Lewell, I am not fit to be seen in Lord Prodon's presence."

"You will be when the time comes."

CHAPTER 19

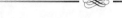

The Monster in the River

THE LIFT TO carry Lewell, Ash, and Song required eight carriers. They waited for the three to settle in their seats before raising the litter to their shoulders. All the passengers faced forward. Lewell sat in front with Ash and Song side by side behind him. The captive marched at the head with the torch bearers, while the guards divided themselves between the front and back of the transport.

Most of the night the passengers slept. When the sunrise came, they stopped at a stream for a break. The torch bearers changed vocations and became cooks. Before the men used the latrine, Lewell let the girl take her turn first, then Ash, and after himself his guards, lift bearers, and cooks took their turn.

Before midday they reached the river and the waiting barge.

To lure the river monster, the tillerman lashed a long bamboo pole to the side of the boat, and they tied the wife beater with woven cords under his arms to the end. The idea had sprung from Lewell, who had pondered a way to tempt and capture whatever beast plagued the river.

One of Lewell's guards kept him from dipping too deep by levering him. He did this because Lewell did not want to slow the oarsmen or drown the man before the river monster could grab him.

Lewell showed Ash and Song where to sit. Everyone stared at the river, searching for any disturbance. The guards stood ready with their spears. The tillerman gave the order to row, and the barge headed downstream.

After a time, several whirlpools appeared. One of them found the man's legs and he started spinning at the end of the cord. The other whirlpools joined that one. The cord knotted. The whirlpool grew, and soon the bamboo pole bent and the man was sucked to his waist. He yelled for help.

As the guard struggled to hold the pole, Lewell ordered another man to help him. But two guards could not pull the man free. Now the man was up to his neck in the turbulence. The thing continued to grow. Suddenly the man slipped from view, the pole bent, and the barge began dipping and spinning.

A horrific groan came from the side of the hull, and Lewell yelled for his men to cut the pole free before they were pulled down.

As they spun round and round, the side of the boat dipped into the river. A heap of water splashed inside. The guard with a flint blade sawed while the other held the pole still for him. Suddenly the pole came free with a bang and struck the man holding it. He landed on his back in the lap of an oarsman who rolled him away. Blood flowed from his broken nose. The pole vanished as soon as it struck the water.

The wounded guard stood. His hands covered his face and blood leaked between his fingers. Caught in the current, they continued to whirl. The tillerman fought with his lever to keep the boat from tipping, but the strain threatened to break the rudder, so he eased off. The boat jerked. The guard with the bloody nose lost his balance and went over the side into the twirling water. The whirlpool moved away and released the barge. The turbulence dissipated after swallowing the man.

Free from the whirlpool, the oarsmen came alert from their fright and started rowing away from the disturbance in the water. The tillerman, disoriented from spinning, held the tiller without regard. The barge aimed toward the jagged rocks on the opposite shore. Only with the help of the oarsmen did they avoid a collision.

To check for damage, Lewell ordered the tillerman to find a suitable shore to beach the craft. He was sure they would find teeth marks somewhere on the hull. A sandy beach presented itself and they paddled hard toward it.

With a slight scraping, the bow of the boat slid on the sand. The tillerman raised the tiller. The oarsmen and guards dismounted and towed the hull out of the water. Lewell stepped off, followed by the tillerman. Song and Ash stayed sitting as they were told.

Timothy W. Sparks

"Do you think that was a river monster?" asked Song. She clutched herself.

"No. Only a beast able to make a whirlpool, or not a beast at all."

"Not a beast?"

"In the sea, I have seen them when the tide goes in or out," said Ash. "They appear with the changes in the current. I did not grasp how vast they could become."

Hearing the word "sea," Song asked, "You have seen the sea?"

"Many times. The sea is only a half-day's walk from my village." As he said it, he glanced down at his twisted foot.

"What is the tide?"

"The times the sea rises and lowers."

"What is the cause of that?"

"If you asked my mother, she would say the sea lowers when all the fish eat and drink. And then she would tell you that the sea rises when they all shit and piss. But my father would say it is the sea breathing in and out."

"Is that what you believe?"

"No," said Ash. "I have witnessed that when the tide is lowest is when the moon rises and sets. The high tide happens when the moon is overhead. Somehow, the moon must be the cause."

But Song mumbled to herself, "Better a fool than a brute."

Lewell paced around the boat searching for some mark, some proof of the beast, but the only damage was from the creature bending the pole. Any blemishes he spotted on the seal skin hull, he felt with his hands. None were punctures or slits. Unsatisfied, he gathered all the men and ordered them to lift the barge. They strained raising the thing, but they held it long enough for Lewell to inspect the bottom.

He did not find any, so he cursed. Lewell could not understand how a creature could attack so violently without leaving teeth marks.

Before he ordered them to float the boat, Lewell commanded the men to empty the hull of river water. To accomplish this, he called Ash and Song to climb down. Ash climbed off first and when he turned to help her, Song crossed her arms and scowled at him. So he stepped aside for her, but her move was clumsy and she fell face first in the sand.

Again, Ash tried to aid her, but she refused.

Lewell had seen what happened. He stepped forward and said, "Pride has a place, but not here and not now."

He reached a massive hand to her. She took it, and he lifted her to her feet.

Embarrassed, she faced the river and brushed herself off.

This time when they boarded, Lewell had Ash sit in front, and he sat beside Song.

"Because you are still a child, there are many things to learn. When you are inside your own hut, how you act and speak to Ash Skeye is a private matter. Not so under Lord Prodon's eyes," said Lewell. He pointed to his own eyes and loud enough for Ash to hear, "Nor in the presence of any within the prodon's realm."

"Yes, Master Lewell," said Song. She kept her head bowed and her hands clasped together.

"For this time Lord Prodon's eyes are closed. However, when he opens them again, he will want to see a well-suited pair."

"Yes, Master Lewell."

Lewell reached in his pouch and handed Song the slate Ash had etched. She gazed at the flowers. "What magic is this?"

"What you see is the skillfulness of Ash Skeye."

Song studied the etching closer, and except for the flowers being stone, the petals seemed to be fluttering in the breeze. Lewell held out his hand.

"May I not keep this?"

"No. This one belongs to Lord Prodon. You have Ash Skeye himself. And if he wishes, he can scratch one for you."

Listening, Ash grinned. Maybe he would make one for her, but in truth, the idea of dwelling with a girl not his mother nor his sisters worried him. Unsure of what god to plead to for help, Ash regarded the sky. At midday, the moon was rising. He offered prayers to both the sun and moon.

CHAPTER 20

Preparing to Meet the Prodon

THE RIVER CONTINUED flowing west, and the dark clouds ahead of them were not clouds, but smoke from the prodon's encampment. The prodon's tower came into view. The tillerman called out, and the oarsmen picked up the pace.

Ahead, a file of staffs with feathers flying in the breeze marked a docking spot on the southern shore, and the tillerman steered the barge toward it. A guard in the bow picked up a bison horn, blowing a series of honks to announce Lewell's arrival.

Two of the nearby huts emptied. A man in tan leathers stepped out of one, and six women dressed in similar shifts came from the other. Like soldiers, they stood with their arms at their sides.

Once the tillerman secured the boat, Lewell and his guards climbed down. Lewell called for Ash and Song.

Ash scaled to the sand. This time when he held his hands for Song to step, she let him have her bent foot. He held her steady as she brought her good foot down to the ground.

Realizing her role, Song said, "My thanks."

Having never heard such a thing before said to him, Ash hurried his best to where Lewell was standing. Lewell instructed Ash to go with the man, and he directed Song to where the women awaited her. Lewell sent his fastest guard to act as courier and carry the news of Ash Skeye and Song Newt to the ears of the prodon.

The man tasked to care for Ash had more patience than the women. He let Ash come to him, but Song only limped a few steps before they all ran to her. Overpowered, all Song could do was let them haul her to the hut. Before entering, two of the women removed her moccasins and washed her feet. When the one holding her turned foot tried to straighten it, Song cried out, "Ouch! Do not try to fix my foot!"

"But it needs fixing," said the woman.

"No, it cannot be made right. I carry the burden from my birth."

The woman grunted and led Song inside. The substantial structure was filled with flowers and herbs. They led her to the center. First they stripped off her sheath. The slate floor felt cool on her bare feet. They made her sit and the coolness spread to her behind.

After unravelling Song's long braid, a woman soaked her hair. Another spread an herb-scented lotion in her locks and for a time, another woman massaged her scalp. They rinsed her hair and repeated the process.

The women pulled Song to her feet. One woman wrung the water from her hair while another smeared mashed seaweed on her skin, starting at her shoulders. More joined in, pasting her every surface. Once her entire body was covered, the women used boar brushes to scrub her. Finally, when Song's skin appeared pink, they stopped and rinsed her with a perfumed oil.

The oil burned with every touch. Song shrieked and yelped, but the women ignored her and rubbed in more. As soon as the oil soaked into Song's skin, the women dumped gourds of flowery water over her and began scrubbing her with sea sponges.

Finished with her body, they began drawing scallop shells through her hair, and while one woman held her forehead and chin firmly, a different woman cleaned her teeth with a licorice root. Song coughed and gagged from her efforts.

Finally, one of them brought Song her new fawnskin shift. The dress was decorated with symbols that Song did not recognize. But the attire was finer than anything she had ever worn.

The fit was loose but comfortable. And once she donned it, the women took turns fussing with her hair. They braided and twisted and pulled, and not gaining the result they wanted, they combed her hair out and started over.

The man assigned to prepare Ash guided him inside a sweat lodge. Ash undressed, and the man took his clothes and showed him where to sit. He chose his own place and splashed water on scalding rocks. Soon the space had filled with steam, and for a time the two sat and allowed the sweat to flow from their pores.

"What caused your foot to bend?" asked the man.

"If you ask my mother, she would say it is my punishment for kicking her in the womb. But my father claims I was *his* penalty for wedding my mother."

The man laughed. "Does it not bother you?"

"Not as much as it troubles others, and that bothers me."

Following the sweat, the man gave Ash a wrap and led him to the hut set for him. Inside the dwelling, the man showed Ash the bath water. He gave Ash a licorice root to brush his teeth. After he scrubbed his teeth, the man handed him a gourd and a sea sponge for him to wash his hair and bathe himself.

Done, the man fanned Ash dry with palm leaves and had him sit on a stump. With an obsidian blade against a sea sponge, the man trimmed his hair to an even length above his shoulders. Satisfied, he presented Ash a pair of soft leather leggings, loin cover, a matching tunic, and moccasins. The shirt bore symbols Ash had not seen. He dressed.

Reunited and properly outfitted, Ash and Song were overwhelmed by the magnitude of the pageantry. A flower-adorned litter carried them with Lewell through a mass of people. An army of gatherers with long spears led the parade toward the tower that loomed ahead.

The courier passed the message to the captain of the guards, who relayed the significance to the prodon's first sentry, who told the prodon the whole of the tales of Ash Skeye and Song Newt. Having the beforehand knowledge, the prodon formed an image of them.

Questions like bees in a busy hive assaulted the prodon. First off, he wondered: since their affliction had occurred at birth, why had they been allowed to live? Did the parents believe the feet would heal themselves? Were they so desperate for tools that even broken ones sufficed? Did they who rear them think their less-than-perfect children above their condition?

The prodon had always suspected such afflictions to be a curse. But these two flawed people somehow had survived the rigors of life. Through Lewell and some destiny, it was he, the prodon, who brought them together. And that fortune was bringing the two before him. To his tower. This was the revelation. Because Lewell chose his artist, he, the prodon, started the wheels of fate. And he, the prodon, sent his traveling mind, Lewell, to choose Song Newt to care for his artist, Ash Skeye. To him, this matching was his own perfect selection.

Feeling joyous, the prodon grasped the holder of his great mouth and proclaimed loudly, "I am the Lord Prodon! You are my keep! I shield you from spoil! My will is your being! I declare a celebration!"

Today Chirp Nyte was making batches of poultices for bruises and ointments for burns, but the announcement of a celebration brought his eyes away from his work. Rumors of the prodon's project had reached him days ago. Like him, someone had been sent for. From his hearing, the sufferer to complete the prodon's task was taken from Twin Oaks. If this proved to be true, then he would know them. Only three men he knew to be artisans. Erie Moon was too old to make the journey; therefore Choc Ness or Leed Uhl would be the one.

The parade advanced, and Chirp stepped outside the hut to glimpse the new artisan. When the litter neared, Chirp rubbed his eyes when he saw Ash Skeye and a girl his age with Lewell. Never had he suspected the boy would be the one.

Ahead of time, Lewell told his carriers to stop at the herbalist's place. They approached and Chirp came from behind the gate. Ash spotted him and raised an arm. The litter stopped and the carriers lowered them to the ground.

"Herbalist," said Lewell. "Come join us."

"Plead my leave, Master Lewell, the medicines I am crafting require my care until the sun touches the trees."

"We shall return after the sun has set."

"Good. Then I can speak to the friend of my sons. Then he can tell me of my family and the Twin Oaks gossip."

"Fair day, Chirp Nyte," said Ash. "There is much to say, so I will save all, except to tell the Nyte family fares well but still mourns your loss."

"Fair day, Ash. My thanks for the news."

Somehow, coming from Chirp, the thanks seemed less daunting. Still, having heard it for the first time twice in the same day made him uncomfortable.

Approaching the tower, Song trembled. In all her time she could never have imagined this moment. She tried to swallow, but her dry mouth prevented that. At the base of the tower, the litter bearers halted and lowered them to the ground. Lewell stepped off and held a hand out to Song.

Afraid to move, the girl stared at Lewell. Her lips quivered.

"Do not fear, child," said Lewell. "No harm will come to you. Lord Prodon has declared a celebration."

Blinking, Song gaped up to the tower and back to Lewell. He reached out his broad hand and Song grasped it. As if she weighed nothing, Lewell lifted her to the ground. With her feet on the land, she let go and turned halfway around.

The people stared at her until Lewell noticed. Those folks either looked away or down at their own feet.

Ash climbed down on his own and Lewell led them to the platform.

"Hold a cord so as not to tumble out." He signaled to the haulers, and they took hold of the lift lead.

Until now, Song had not guessed how they would reach the top of the tower. The platform shimmied and she yelped. She took hold of the cord with both hands and closed her eyes as the platform lifted. Ash, however, watched them rise higher, and when they reached the top he blurted out, "The sea!"

Song opened her eyes, and the sun blinded her. As her sight adjusted, she peered into the distance. Beyond the trees and rolling knolls, she saw the sparkle of the sea. As she and Ash gazed, Lewell said to them in a low but stern voice, "Turn and meet the Lord Prodon."

They spun and faced Lewell and he whispered, "Hold hands. Smile."

Ash, on the left, reached for Song's hand. Afraid of the movement of the suspended floor and the height, she grasped tightly. They attempted smiles.

The Era of Herbalists

Lewell moved away and the platform shimmied. One of the guards lifted the railing and offered a hand to him. He accepted the help and stepped off.

Ash let go of the cord first. He bent his knees when the thing wavered. Song released her grip on the cord, and the couple took careful steps. The floor shook, and they froze in place until the platform stopped wobbling. Song's smile waned. The couple hobbled a few more steps, and the guard caught them before they could fall. The hulking man helped them off the wobbly platform to the stable tower floor. Lewell gestured them forward.

The prodon stared at their feet, tracking their every move. Even when they stopped before him, he continued to gape at their crooked feet.

"What sort of child would the two of you make?" asked the prodon. "You shall make one for me."

Lewell answered for the bewildered couple. "Lord Prodon. The girl has yet to undergo her first bleed, and your artist has much work ahead."

The prodon looked up at Lewell. Unwilling yet to alter his command, he changed the subject. "As you have heard, I called for a celebration. See that Patto makes the suitable arrangements."

"Of course, Lord Prodon."

The prodon slapped his hands together. "The idea of a child with two lame feet unsettles me; therefore, you shall not make any."

Ash and Song both breathed a sigh of relief. The notion of creating a child frightened Ash. What if the child exhibited their affliction as the prodon feared? He pushed the thought aside.

As for Song, she had witnessed enough births to not want to suffer herself. Unstoppable bleeding at a birth she attended had killed a neighbor woman. For that reason alone, she vowed to never have a child. She promised herself, no matter what the prodon ordered, Ash Skeye would never touch her like that.

The prodon stood from his throne. He towered over the couple, and even Lewell, by half a head. He stepped over to the north railing and gestured for the couple to join him. "The hill is made with fine gray slate. You will begin your task there. A camp is being built to mine the stone."

"But Lord Prodon, I can only scratch a single stone a day," said Ash.

"This is true, I am sure, but we are going from this place and traveling east next year. You will need a lifetime's worth of slate before we leave."

The sun dipped into the sea and stars began to show in the sky. Chirp put away the remedies he had concocted and waited for Ash Skeye to visit. This would be the first he learned of his family in over two years. He doubted there would be time to share all that had happened during his absence.

If Gemma had taken another man, he told himself he would understand, but knowing would hurt. He prepared himself to be stabbed through the heart.

To speak to Chirp in private, Ash asked Lewell to mind Song.

"Tell me, young Ash," said Chirp. "How is my family?"

"Pine married a girl from Seaside Hill and won a place on the second clutch hunt team."

"Who leads the clutch?"

"Grand Moon," said Ash. He spoke the name as if dirt glazed his tongue.

"His father and I have had strong words over Grand's deeds."

"He is the same bully."

"Wait. Did you say Pine married? Who is she? Seaside Hill? What family?"

"Yes. She is Lily Sayed, daughter of Ric and Reba."

"Ric? He led me to Gemma. This pleases me."

"The wedding was on the shore. Almost everyone came."

"Did Pine compete in the challenge without a dog?"

"No. The same girl Pine married found him a dog. A wonderful beast, black as the night. He calls him Shadow. You would be proud of him."

"I am. What of Neva and Witt?"

"Neva has proven to be a sure herbalist and Witt, her assistant. The village suffered a fever, and Atte Uhl died. But Neva found that ticks caused the sickness and saved all the rest. She found the source was Tiana Uhl's basket fixings. I went with Witt, and he found where the straw grew. The council burned the place."

"And how is my father?"

"Older and wiser, and he still does his own chores."

"And Gemma?"

"Every day she digs salt and clay. A black feather still hangs on her hut."

This news hurt him. But not as much as if she had taken another man. Still, he did not want her to be unhappy. He hung his head.

"Tell me, young Ash. Who is the girl you brought with you?"

"My wife, not by choice. Master Lewell picked her to care for me when I toil. Her right foot is bent like my left. For that reason, she was chosen."

"You are lucky. She is a pretty girl."

"She is a pain I am joined to."

"In time, perhaps you will feel differently."

Changing the subject, Ash said, "Master Lewell is sending me to mine slate for the journey east."

"Is the prodon no longer traveling north?" asked Chirp.

"Next year," said Ash. "Master Lewell said the prodon grows restless. Five years here and he is weary of the valley. Master Lewell said scouts returned from the east and promised finer harvests to plunder."

Chirp realized Twin Oaks and the other northern hamlets were safe. A dozen questions rattled in his head. He asked, "How will the prodon cross the river? Does the tower swim?"

"No, but barges are being built to carry the tower."

"What of the mountains?" asked Chirp.

"I asked. The scouts located a pass."

"It will be for me to stock herbs. On my travels east, the plants vary."

A shout from outside the yard cut the conversation short.

"My thanks," said Chirp. "The news you shared warms my heart."

"It was told to me that my work will be to etch plants for you."

"Until then. Fare well."

Ash joined Lewell and his unwanted bride.

CHAPTER 21

The Newt Sisters

SILENTLY, ASH CURSED the prodon for picking the place for his hut. With his lame foot, the hike took too long to reach home from the slate mine. The sun disappeared over the trees as he limped to his home. It took every effort for him to lift his feet, and the weight of his arms seemed to tug at him. Blisters burned his hands and his fingers ached any time he flexed them.

Finally, Ash approached the hut. Song had tied the door flap open. From the smoke, he could tell a fire was burning in the hearth. Before Ash reached the entry, Song came out followed by her sisters.

"Look, husband, we have visitors. My sisters Luna and Layan. Master Lewell's promise proved true. My father builds his place to cook. Since we have so much room, until my sister's huts are finished, they will sleep here."

Ash's weary face showed no change as he continued toward the hut, but the sisters blocked him, so he halted.

"I have fresh blackberries," said Luna. She lifted the basket for him. "They are sweet and juicy."

Not wanting to be outdone, Layan held her pan for him to regard. "First you should have some of my slim bread. I spiced it with sage and bay leaves."

Song raised the platter for Ash to sniff. "Husband, slim bread would be dull but for my roasted boar meat."

Speechless, Ash sidestepped them and went into the hut. He climbed on his mat and pulled a bison hide over himself. Then he closed his eyes and fell fast asleep.

Outside, holding the servings of food, the sisters argued. They entered the hut and found Ash snoring.

"Is this how he is every night?" asked Luna.

"Most nights he eats first," answered Song.

Placing the slim bread platter on the hearth, Layan said, "Perhaps Luna and I should leave and watch the moon while you couple with him."

"Never. I vowed to never couple."

"But it is the burden of women to couple," said Layan.

"He knows," said Song. She raised her chin. "He cares not for me. Many times he has told me so."

"A man needs a woman," said Layan. "For you not yet, but someday you will need a man that way."

"I will not," said Song. "Never."

"What if he should couple with another?" asked Layan.

"I would not care," said Song. She stepped to the middle of the hut near the hearth and set the plate of meat next to the slim bread pan.

"But Song," said Luna. "Father wants a grandson. I heard him say."

This caused Song to chuckle. "Since you are old enough to bear children, sister, you should find a man to couple with and make him a grandson. The camp is full of men."

"Those men are slaves and brutes," said Luna.

"We are ourselves slaves," said Song, "and under the rule of the prodon."

Layan stood over Ash and said, "He is easy to watch when he sleeps. Look at his chin. He is sprouting whiskers."

"Allow him to sleep. You can make your beds over there," said Song. She pointed to the other side of the hut.

"I am hungry," said Luna. "If your husband will not eat, then we should."

"Leave enough for him," said Song. "Lest he complain to Master Lewell."

Finished with their meals, the sisters laid out their bed nests and Song added wood to the fire. Layan poked her head out the doorway. A three-quarter waning moon illuminated the camp, and torches lit the perimeter. She spotted the guards protecting them.

"Sisters," she said. "I bear dirt on my skin, so I am going to wash in the stream."

"Better take a fur," said Song. "The bath is a long way from the fire."

"Did you not bathe once already?" asked Luna.

"True, but I wish to feel cleaner," answered Layan.

At the stream, Layan laid the dire wolf fur on the dry rocks. She unfastened her deerskin shift, and it slipped off her to the ground. Naked, she stepped toward the middle where the water came to her knees. She squatted to her navel and used a sea sponge to wash herself, shivering as she scrubbed. As quickly as she could, she cleaned herself, and after soaking her face, she dashed to the shore and the fur she had left on the rocks.

Wrapped in the pelt, she strode back as fast as she could. Song had told her about the path, but the journey to the creek seemed shorter coming than the return trip to the hut. As soon as she entered, she rushed to the fire and huddled by the hearth. She rubbed herself until she dried and stopped quivering.

Bear fat burned in a stone lamp for her to find her bed.

"Sleep well, sisters," said Layan. She climbed in her bed nest.

No one answered, so she extinguished the lamp and lay on her back, staring up through the smoke hole at the few stars visible. Across from her in the flickering firelight, she watched Ash sleep.

Finally the fire died, and Layan slipped nude from her bed and creeped to Ash. Carefully, she lifted his bison covering and slid next to him. He stirred and she reached under his loin skin. His eyes flashed open, and before he could yell Layan covered his mouth with her hand.

"Shhh," she whispered, stroking his manhood. "Let me show you what a woman can do."

But Ash shoved her away hard and hollered, "Do not touch me!"

Layan yelped and rolled in the dirt. She landed on her back. Song and Luna woke from the commotion. In the darkness, Song put a log on the fire. But the log smoldered in the embers, so she used a twig to light the fat in the lamp. Luna sat up and rubbed her eyes.

In the glow she and Luna witnessed their sister unclothed on the ground, scrambling around the hearth on her hands and knees. She crawled into her bed nest and buried her face.

"Layan? What are you doing?" asked Song.

"She touched me!" cried Ash. "She...she fingered my man thing!"

Forgetting her bent foot, Song stomped to Layan, nearly tripping on the way. With balled fists she yelled, "Take your bed outside with you!"

Crying, Layan turned to face Song. "But you said you cared not if someone else coupled with him!"

"Not my sister! Not under the roof where I sleep!"

"But I am not your sister," she sobbed. "Not by blood."

Joining Song, Luna said, "Layan, the prodon made you kin. It is the same as by blood."

"All you!" called Ash. "Back to your beds! I demand silence!"

Layan pulled her fur cover over her head. Luna scampered to her place, but Song put her hands on her hips and stared at him. But before she could speak, Ash ordered, "Song! Go to your bed! Do not wake me until the sun rises!"

The tone of his voice drove her to her mat. With a flash, the log finally blazed, and Song gaped past the hearth at Ash. He glanced at her once and then, with a lurch, he turned away. Song smiled. Tomorrow she would make Layan stay with her father. And Ash would be hungry, so she would make something for him. Something with honey. She closed her eyes and slept.

The sun rose and Ash woke to the aroma of something appetizing. He rubbed his eyes. Both of Song's sisters' bed nests were gone.

Leaning over him, Song said, "Fair day, husband."

"Why do you call me that?" asked Ash. He slipped his moccasins on. "My name is Ash."

"I wish to remind myself of my standing."

"To me you are only someone who shares this hut. Nothing more."

"Master Lewell and Lord Prodon declared us to be more."

Ash stood, dipped a gourd in the water pot, and drank. He ambled to the hearth and warmed himself.

"Song? This joining was done *to* us. Neither of us wished for this. Please do not punish me for what I bear no fault."

Song handed him a platter of roasted pork and slim bread. "Ash is a bold name. From this day I will call you that."

"My thanks. Song, please keep your sisters from our hut."

"For Layan I am sorry. Luna is different."

"Song. I am uneasy even with you."

"As you wish...Ash."

CHAPTER 22

Song's Blessing

THANKS TO CHIRP'S soothing salve, Ash's fingers had healed from nearly a year of mining. Now he could hold crystals and etch the slate. For Ash's first project, Chirp chose arnica. Ash considered the plant and rummaged through his collection of crystals for a broad tip to scratch the stem. The one he picked was chipped. With a steady pressure he drew a downward stroke with a slight arc. Changing crystals, he scratched stem and leaf shapes.

At midday, having seen all his patients, Chirp and Patto went to dig up some ginger roots. They left Ash etching in the apothecary yard.

Once he was finished with the arnica plate, Ash brought the potted walking root plant for a model. After scratching the broad stems, he etched one of the distinctive, arrowhead-shaped leaves. Using a fine-tipped crystal, Ash had started scratching the jagged veins when someone pounded on the gate.

"Open!" hollered a desperate voice.

Ash unlatched the gate and two gatherers, holding a bleeding man between them, rushed past him to the waiting bench. They placed the man on his back.

Closing the gate, Ash faced them and said, "The herbalist is not here."

One of the men faced Ash and brandished his pointed flint. "Heal him."

Taking a breath, Ash moved to the prone man's side. The blood flowed from a lengthy gash across his thigh. Looking about, Ash went to the cauldron and tested the water. Tepid. Ash dipped a gourd and poured it into a basin.

Like he had seen Chirp do this morning before each patient, he scrubbed his hands. With another gourd of water Ash rinsed the man's wound. He yelped and tried to rise, but one of his companions held him down. Then Ash pinched the wound closed and held it until the bleeding stopped.

For a treatment, Ash rushed into the apothecary, stood at the work table, and allowed his eyes to adjust to the dimness. Thankfully, Chirp had organized the cures by sicknesses and hurts. From a covered platter Ash picked a strip of pig intestines saturated in bear grease and stretched it out on the stone work-table. Then he used a bamboo stick and spread the healing salve Chirp had concocted along the intestines.

So he could cover the cut and wrap the thing around his leg, he asked his friends to lift his limb and hold him. As best he could, Ash swathed the cure-infused bandage around his leg and across the injury.

The man howled and kicked the man holding his foot, who slammed against the wall with a crash. His friend went to his aid. The wounded man bounded off the bench, his face a red scowl. But as suddenly as the pain hit him, the wound numbed and his natural brown complexion returned.

He gaped at his leg and sat, lifting an end of the dressing to peer at the wound. He called his friends to see. The gash had already begun to heal. He pushed himself up and drew his obsidian knife. "Hold out your hand."

Obeying the command, Ash paled and his hand trembled, but the man turned it and handed it to Ash by the blade. "For your services, you have my thanks."

With his mouth hanging open, Ash stared at the knife. The three men waved and laughed on their way out the gate. Before the gate closed, the wounded man spoke to Chirp and Patto as they approached. "The healer is available."

With questions on their faces and their arms full of ginger root, Chirp and Patto came into the apothecary yard.

"Who were those men?" asked Chirp.

"Gatherers." Smiling, Ash held out the blade for them to see.

"What is this?"

"My worth for treating a leg wound." Grinning, Ash went back to his etching, leaving the two men with their mouths gaping open.

After hearing his story, Song made Ash a special dinner. Honey ginger fowl with roasted tubers and berries. After taking his fill, Ash yawned. Without asking, Song fluffed Ash's bed nest.

Surprised by the gesture, Ash thanked her and crawled inside. Fatigue caught up with him, and he closed his eyes and fell asleep.

The Era of Herbalists

Quarrying slate dominated Ash's dream. In a seemingly endless passage, someone or some creature was pursuing him. He searched for an escape. The gray stone surrounded him at every turn as he traveled inside a maze.

High up above, light shone, only enough to show him his way. The footfalls and scraping noises sounded closer. Deep in the mine, he reached a six-way junction. He entered one of the tunnels, where sparkling crystals lit his path. His own footsteps crushed broken bits of shale on the ground, and the crunching sound echoed ahead of him.

Tiring, Ash stopped and sat with his back against the quarry wall, and he listened. To him, his heartbeat resounded like a warning drum and his breathing a winter windstorm.

Closing his eyes, Ash recalled his run with the wedge of wood in his moccasin, how the wind had pushed his hair behind him. He opened them and felt the breeze striking his face. Using the rock wall to stand, he felt a vine hanging from above. Running his hand along its rough surface, he felt moisture, a root of some kind. He tugged and the root held tight.

Using the tiers of slate as steps, Ash climbed and the root's diameter increased, giving him a better grip. For the first time ever, his crooked foot gave him an advantage climbing. Him not seeing the sky gave him no reason to slow, because in his rapidly beating heart, he knew this was his getaway.

The cold told him he had reached freedom, and there on the top of the slate quarry, his bed nest was waiting. He crawled in and laid on his side. A sudden chill blew on his back and something cold embraced him. As the thing beside him snuggled against him, the heat against his back woke him in darkness.

Confused, he rolled over and gasped. "Song! What are you doing?"

"It is storming and I am frightened and I am cold. Please let me stay. You are so warm and I feel safe here next to you."

"But we talked about this," pleaded Ash.

"I will not bother you, I promise, but please do not make me sleep alone."

Too tired to protest, Ash grunted and said, "Very well. Then go to sleep and try not to wake me again."

"I promise...Ash."

Moons later, satisfied with the amount of slate he had mined, the prodon rewarded Ash by moving his hut to a knoll overlooking the sea.

Pleased with her view of the vast water, Song decided her marriage to Ash to be a blessing. Besides that, something had changed inside her. Her breasts swelled, and she became more aware of herself between her legs. Also, something caused her to want to be closer to Ash and for him to take notice of her. But he remained aloof and only looked at her when he had reason.

One evening after their meal, the two sat by the hearth. Ash thanked her for the food and complimented her cooking.

Facing him, Song asked, "Ash? Do you think I am pretty?"

In the hearth and lamp light, Ash gazed at her. "Your face is pleasing enough to see."

"And what of my body?" asked Song. She stood in front of him. "Is all of me pleasing for you to see?"

Bewildered, he blinked. "I am not sure what you are asking."

Song smiled and unfastened her dress. While Ash gawked with his mouth open, she let it fall to the floor. Naked, she held her arms out and slowly spun around. When she turned to face Ash, he had bolted out the door flap.

Surprised by what he had seen, Ash marched toward the sea. His lame foot failed him and, in his haste, he tripped several times. Out of sight, facing the water, he sat and stared at nothing. When he confronted what actually bothered him the most, it had been how he had been thinking of Song for the last few moons. Numerous times he had forced himself to look away when she bent over. Some of those times his thoughts of her caused his man thing to stiffen. In truth, he was angry at himself for running off.

Later, on the way back to the hut, Ash gathered some wood for the hearth. From the open door he peeked in. He saw Song sleeping. Quietly he limped inside and laid the wood in the pile.

The fire was still burning. Song must have added wood before going to sleep. This was the end of summer, and the nights were beginning to chill. He added some hefty sticks and watched them catch while he scrubbed his teeth with a licorice root. Before crawling in his own bed, he dipped a gourd in the water pot and took a long drink. He snuffed the oil lamp and crawled under his furs.

For what seemed like half of the night Ash squirmed, trying to find a comfortable position. Finally he buried his face in a fox pelt and drifted off to sleep.

Ash's snoring woke Song. She rose from her bedding, ambled to the hearth, and added wood to the fire. Instead of returning to her own bed, she crept to where Ash slept. She untied her sleeping shift and slipped it off.

Still snoring, she lifted his fur cover and slowly eased herself next to him. Even before her bare skin touched his, his heat warmed her. Next to him she pressed her breasts on his back and scooted her hips against his. Gently, she brushed his hair back and touched his neck with her lips. He stirred and she wrapped her arm around him.

Ash woke slowly. Something warm was heating him from behind. Song cuddled him. Instead of making her leave, he reached back and tenderly stroked the back of her legs. She pressed her hips and wrapped a leg around his. Slowly he rolled and faced her. In the firelight he saw her smile, and he inched his lips toward hers. They kissed.

Unsure of what to do next, Ash continued to kiss her. He recalled the time he had awoken and seen his father and mother. Although he had only watched for a few moments, the vision remained in his head.

Slowly, he pressed his lips along the side of her neck. Song responded with moans, and Ash caressed her with his tongue as if searching for a place to give more pleasure. His fingers brushed one of her nipples and his lips sucked gently on the other. Song's pleasurable moans intensified and she reached under his loin skin. Her fingers wrapped around his rigid shaft, and she softly tugged it toward her.

From this point, Ash was hesitant. Mercifully, Song's instinct guided him inside her, and with her hips, she defined the pace. Slow, yet firm. The rhythm intensified, as did her moaning.

For Ash, her gyrations caused him to pant. He buried his face in her hair and wiggled inside her. About to explode in her, Song screamed and he jerked himself out. He ejaculated in a steady pulse and splattered her belly with warm liquid.

"Did I hurt you?" asked Ash.

But Song did not answer. She clutched him tightly, trembled, and wept.

"Did I do something wrong?"

She shook her head and mumbled, "No."

"Then why are you crying?"

Song sniffled and said, "Because it felt so good and I...I am...sorry."

"Sorry for what?"

Her reply came with a burst of tears. "For not coupling sooner!"

Unable to respond, Ash held her until she stopped sobbing.

A while later she whispered in his ear, "Can we do it again?"

His answer pressed firmly against her.

One evening later, Ash and Song sat outside and watched the stars. The waning half-moon glowed in the sky.

"Ash? What do you think the moon tastes like?"

"What do you mean?"

"Half of the moon has been eaten," said Song. She pointed. "Can you not see with your eyes?"

"Song. The part of the moon you cannot see is in the shade."

"I do not believe you. My father said the gods build the moon and when it is finished, they devour it. Then they make a new one. Now the gods feast."

"Come with me," said Ash. He stood and offered his hand. Hesitantly, she took it and he helped her to her feet.

On the way back to the hut, Ash scooped up a roundish rock. Inside, two lamps were burning. Ash blew one out and picked up the other.

"Watch the stone as I move the light around," he said. He held the rock still in the palm of his hand, and with the other he moved the lamp beside the simulated moon.

"This is how the moon appears tonight. Now watch as I change the light." He moved the lamp behind the rock. Then to the other side and around to the front. Song took the lamp from Ash, lifted her chin, and said, "From the way the gods eat, the moon must taste like overcooked slim bread."

Song went to her own bed nest. She crawled in, blew out the lamp, and left Ash standing in the dark, holding his miniature moon.

CHAPTER 23

The Runaway

LIKE EVERY MORNING, the guards rousted the slaves. On this morning at the count, the tally came up short. One of the woodworkers.

Rushing up to another slave, Rooke, the lead guard, brought out his knife and pressed the tip under the man's chin. "Tell me! Where is your friend?"

"In the dark he went to the latrine! When I woke he had not come back."

Pressing the blade harder, Rooke asked, "Who among you sleeps by the door?"

Trembling, the man pointed to one of his coworkers. That man swiveled his head this way and that, but before he could run the guard was on him.

With the flint under the man's loin skin, the guard growled. "Tell me what you know about the missing man."

Gaping down at the blade poised to take his manhood, the man blurted out, "His name is Han Oma. He said he wanted to go home to Whispering Bay."

The blade pressed and tears formed in the man's eyes.

"When did he leave?" asked the guard. "He...he left at moonset."

"What direction?" growled Rooke. He pushed the flint.

"South! He went south."

"What did he take?"

"A share of dried bison and a...a goatskin of water."

"Weapons?"

"Of Han I cannot say. We have none."

"For your silence you will do his labor as well as your own."

"Yes, leader Rooke."

Rooke withdrew the blade and sent him off with the other workers.

The leader sent a man to report to Master Lewell.

On the run, the guard called out for someone to tell where he could find Lewell. A potter, coming his way, told him that Master Lewell had just been elevated to Lord Prodon's tower.

At the base, the guard hollered up, "Master Lewell!"

Lewell leaned over the railing and yelled down, "Speak!"

"A woodsman has run off to the south!"

Lewell stepped away for a moment. Then he came back and called down, "Track him down and slay him! Use archers."

"Yes, Master Lewell." He ran back to the leader.

The leader picked his best chaser and two bowmen. The tracker, a former citizen of Whispering Bay and a loyal prodon worshiper, chose a trail parallel to the escapee's. They began the chase at a jog. Behind the absconder by a half-day, the trio carried three days' rations of food and water.

At midday, the pursuers took a brief rest to nourish and hydrate. Afterwards, they spotted a knoll ahead and headed there for a lookout. On the way they came across the woodsman's footprints. The tracks headed southwest toward the muddy creek. The tracker led the archers along the coastal ridge. That way, they would spot him before he caught sight of them. Hopefully they would catch him before sunset.

Knowing the gatherers were pursuing him, Han found a murky stream heading for the sea. In the shallows he ran, and in the deep he swam. At nightfall, he heard a pack of dire wolves howling too close. With no weapon, he armed himself with river stones and took shelter in a sandbank.

From the top of the sea cliff an archer looked below him. So as not to be easily seen, the runaway was hugging the bluff wall, sprinting from one shadow to the next. But the bowman above him spied him. Unable to get a clear shot, he signaled his companions.

To get ahead of their prey, they all dashed through the tall grass on the crest. Along the way, they searched for an animal path to the bottom. At an overhang, the tracker waved the archers to continue ahead while he laid on the rock face and took a gander over the edge. Loose stones tumbled down and the absconder stared up. For a fleeting moment he and the tracker locked eyes. Then the fugitive rushed toward the breaking waves.

Finding a spot, one of the archers found a way down to the beach while the other fired arrows from the bluff. But the runner zigzagged and the projectiles missed. Racing to cut the escapee off, the bowman readied a shaft and hurried toward the man at an angle. Seeing the bowman, the man dashed to the surf and dove into the oncoming breaker.

Taking aim, the archer released an arrow, then launched another and another. His companion caught up, and he too let some projectiles fly. Uncertain whether their arrows had succeeded in hitting the swimmer, they continued their vigil, waiting for something to surface or a sign of blood in the water.

After failing to spot him, the three agreed to a tale. How they had dispatched the man painfully and left his carcass to the death eaters and dire wolves.

A month later, one of a dozen scouts from a caravan of travelers searching for a marauder named Yaotl and his army of destroyers discovered the partly dismembered and mostly decomposed skeletal remains of a man in a tidepool, being scavenged by seabirds. He chased them off and spotted the green and red feathered arrow lodged in the dead man's ribs. Without hesitating, he broke off the plumed end and headed toward the caravan.

Those travelers from the seven sacred cities were huddled in a lush valley eight days southeast from him. However, knowing the importance of the find, the scout endeavored to reach his high priestess sooner.

Five nights later, the scout hobbled to the sentry on guard. "Take me to the high priestess."

"She sleeps at this hour."

"For this, she will want to wake." The scout held out the feathered shaft. In the torchlight the guard studied the feathers. Recognizing them, he called for the captain.

The moment the captain saw the arrow, he had two men help the weary scout, and they paraded to the high priestess' tent.

The Era of Herbalists

The sentinel guarding the young priestess paced outside her door, debating to himself whether to wake her or tell her in the morning.

Finally he called out, "Your Highness! I have news of Yaotl!"

Moments later, lamp light lit the tent and her silhouette moved to the door. Abruptly, the door flap flipped open. Dressed in her robe, Zyanya, the high priestess, stepped outside. Gaping at the worn scout, Zyanya said, "Tell me of this news."

On his knees before her, the scout handed her the arrow. "Six days north of here, I found this buried in a dead man's chest."

Spinning the broken shaft in her hand, she asked, "A recent kill?"

"No, Your Highness," said the scout. He fell forward, catching himself on his elbows. One of the sentinels helped him to his feet and held him. The scout continued, "The man…dead…many…days."

"See to his comfort," ordered Zyanya. With the arrow in her hand, she returned to her tent. Inside she squatted on her bed mat and stared at the feathers. Under her breath she said, "Yaotl, I promise you the same death you gave my father."

CHAPTER 24

The Autumn Hunt

INSIDE THEIR HUT in Twin Oaks, Lily woke Pine with a kiss. Already, his trappings were waiting by the doorway. Outside, no light shone except on the other side of the hills. The aroma of baking filled the hut. Dressed, he slipped on his moccasins, and Lily handed him a gourd of wake-me tea and a warm slice of slim bread.

The door flap pushed in as Shadow poked his head in. He gave a muffled bark. Lily fed him a hunk of elk meat, and he took it outside.

From last year's autumn hunt, Pine knew that, at any moment, Grand would call with a blow of his bison horn. In the meantime, he cuddled with Lily. She placed his hand on her belly. From her swelling, the midwife guessed the child would be born near the beginning of spring in five moons.

A thump knocked on his palm. "Our child stirs this morning. If this is a man child, he is already showing strength."

"And if this babe is a she, what do you feel?"

"A singer and dancer, like her mother," answered Pine.

Playfully, Lily pinched his cheek.

The bison horn sounded. Hastily, Pine finished his breakfast, hugged Lily, shouldered his tool pouch, grasped his weapons, and left to join his hunt team.

From Twin Oaks, the hunters traveled east all day. On the flats they ran southeast. At the start of the gorge, Grand Moon split the clutch in half. They agreed to meet at the encampment when the sun touched the horizon. Here, the sandy bottom river was wide and shallow. The runners set a camp. He, Pine, Talon,

138

and Berm crossed the river. Instead of following the waterway, Grand chose to continue southeast between the hills. Sharpe, Syd, Todd, and Roth hunted south along the west bank of the river.

Heading downstream, the dogs picked up a scent and gave chase. The four hunters pursued them. Left behind by whatever they were hounding, the dogs returned. Knowing their masters' displeasure, they approached them with their heads down and their tails between their legs.

Finding fresh prints, the hunters followed them along a marsh. Upwind, a black-tailed buck with four antler tips on one side and five on the other wandered from a patch of cattails. Todd's arrow took the buck through the neck, and Syd's shot pierced its heart. To be sure it was dead, Todd cut its throat.

With an arrow set to draw, Roth stood guard. Behind Syd, Sharpe stood ready with his spear. The deer bled out as Todd held the buck up by the back legs and Syd gutted it.

Suddenly, a lone dire wolf burst from the foliage. Wild-eyed, the wolf bared his teeth and growled. Barking and snapping their teeth, the hunter's four dogs circled the beast. Each time they edged closer, the wolf slashed at them. Despite their effort to corral him, the wolf advanced.

Springing in front of his friends, Sharpe readied his spear. The wolf eyed the dead deer and glared at Sharpe as he paced back and forth, growling.

Roth, who had been guarding the rear, rushed over and flanked the wolf. Sharpe aimed his spear, but the dogs blocked his chance. Roth, on the other side, had the same difficulty. Todd called them, and when they cleared away, the dire wolf glared at Sharpe and charged. With both hands clutching the shaft of his lance, Sharpe thrust the spear into the charging wolf's chest. The wolf dropped with a brief yelp and a gasp. Pierced to the shaft, Sharp wiggled his spear free.

The dead wolf's legs twitched, and the dogs nipped at the carcass. Sharpe shooed the dogs away so as not to spoil the pelt. Todd and Syd grasped their spears, called their dogs to hunt, and did a search for more wolves. Roth helped Sharpe skin the wolf. They would leave the remains for the scavengers.

Fresh deer tracks led Grand and his group of hunters east against the flow of a stream. The dogs wanted to run ahead, but their masters kept them close. Every so often, Shadow would stand on his hind legs and sniff.

Three of the hunters readied arrows, but Pine held his spear. A saber-tooth cat was following the herd ahead of them. In a stretch of mud, the cat's right rear pawprint appeared fainter than the others. For some reason, the cat had not put its full weight on that leg. Pine guessed it might be injured. If so, that made the beast more dangerous. From the distance between the tracks, Pine determined the cat was trotting. The hunters quickened their pace.

At the first sight of the herd, the three archers spread out while Pine tracked the cat. Too late. Before Pine closed in, the cat absconded with a fawn. The lightning-quick assault scattered the deer.

Judging him as a threat, a graying stag stormed Berm. In his haste, Berm wasted his arrow. The projectile disappeared in the brush. The buck's massive rack of antlers came at him, but Berm rolled away at the last moment. The rack scraped the ground near his head.

Defending his master, Berm's dog nipped at the deer's back legs. The buck kicked him away, and the dog yelped once and rolled in the dirt. Regaining his feet, the dog harassed the buck with barks but kept clear.

A short distance away, Talon let an arrow fly. The shaft pierced the stag's shoulder, but he slowed only long enough to reverse direction. Targeting Berm, the deer assaulted him.

Close by, Grand released a shaft, and his arrow penetrated the creature's chest. The buck staggered a distance, landed on his chin, skidded, and collapsed. With his blade ready, Grand straddled the buck, took hold of his antlers, and with a swift motion slit his throat and pulled. A single spray of blood jetted out, then the stag's life spilled with it.

The doe with the lost fawn wandered aimlessly. Aiming, Berm let an arrow fly. A hit to her breast. She staggered and dropped.

Though Grand's arrow had killed the stag, he gave credit to Talon. To Pine, Grand only made the gesture to relieve himself of the whole burden.

The Era of Herbalists

After they gutted and bled the deer, Pine found a sturdy branch for them to tether and transport the buck. Berm elected to carry his kill over his shoulders. Once they were finished, Pine and the dogs escorted them to the encampment.

A distance from camp, the aroma of cooking meat drifted their way. Barking dogs from the camp met the hunters. Those dogs joined the escorts leading them in. The runners had already skinned the buck that Todd and Syd had killed and were cooking some of the meat over the fire.

While the runners went to work on Grand and Talon's buck and Berm's doe, Roth described the fresh elk tracks they had spotted near the great waterfall.

"The herd is led by Wisdom," said Roth.

"How did you figure that?" asked Grand.

"The size of the prints and the notch on the front left hoof."

Syd spoke up. "He must have over twenty cows with him, and even more calves."

In the firelight, Grand studied the group's faces. "Roth. You take first watch. Rouse Berm for second lookout. Pine, you can be last and wake us before the sunrise. In the morning we will track them. Now we eat."

CHAPTER 25

The Betrayal

ON NIGHT GUARD, Pine and Shadow had walked the perimeter of the camp a dozen times and Shadow had scared off a lioness, hungry for meat, twice. The second time, she tried to steal a haunch off the rack, but Shadow and the other hunters' dogs kept her back. Afraid for Shadow, at the front of the pack, Pine heaved a fist-sized stone and smacked the tawny cat in the ribs. She gave up and darted into the brush.

The ruckus brought some of the runners up to check the meat. Once they had ensured the racks were safe, they climbed back under their furs.

As instructed, Pine woke everyone ahead of sunrise. Some of the hunters chewed tale teller leaves with their venison and berries, but most, including Pine, just drank water with their meal. Pine fed Shadow first before he ate. At the first light they gathered their weapons and began the day's hunt. Pine left his bow and quiver with the runners, sticking his atlatl in his sash.

Grand told the runners to stay to guard, treat the skins, and dry the meat. Because of the distance, he had everyone trot to where they could pick up the tracks. He took the lead and set the pace. This stimulated the dogs, and that charged the hunters. To keep a reasonable steady rate, they stayed on the central animal trail along the river. Near where they could hear the roar of the falls, Grand stopped and stared at the ground. He squatted and spread his fingers against the hoofprint. "Has to be Wisdom. Spare your arrows for the weakest or any lame calves."

The hoof prints led them to an empty meadow. From the clipped grass and trampled ground, the herd had grazed and moved on. The tracks led them back to the river at the falls.

The Era of Herbalists

"They crossed not long ago," said Sharpe.

"Why?" asked Roth. "There is only sand and rock cliffs yonder."

"There must be something more," said Grand.

"Are we to follow?" asked Talon.

"We should split the group," said Grand. "Wisdom may be leading us. Some should wait here for the herd to double back."

Grand studied his crew's faces. "Pine and Sharpe will come with me. We will have our spears. The rest of you should be ready with arrows."

He almost reinforced the order, but they knew of the council's decision to spare Wisdom to breed.

The rumble of the falls prevented verbal communication. Rather than swim the river, Grand chose to cross the shallower section near the falls. The dogs swam alongside them. In some places, the fast-moving water came nearly up to their knees. The frigid runoff was coming from the last of the melting snow in the east mountains.

Grand led them from rock to rock, their legs beginning to numb. Since the stones were not completely stable, he planted each step carefully and used his lance to keep himself balanced. A fallen oak tree, trapped in the center of the river, made for handholds. The branches were thick with debris from the winter floods. The force of the flow caused them to slow, but the dogs continued to the sandy bank. Sharpe yelled to his dog, but his voice was lost in the roar of the waterfall.

Once they reached the shore, Grand waved once to the five hunters. The dogs sniffed and milled around the many hoof prints and piles of scat. The trio of hunters sat on the bank and wrung out their moccasins. A not-too-distant call from a bull elk hurried them along. They grabbed up their spears, listened again for the call, and pursued the herd of elk in the direction of the sound.

Facing the open ground along the wall rock, Shadow stood on his hind legs. The other dogs barked and scampered about.

"The dogs have the scent," said Pine.

The hunters quickened their pace, but the coarse sand swallowed their feet. They pumped their legs to keep momentum. Even the dogs' paws sank deep when they ran. None of the tracks were discernible, only hundreds of pocks with no direction.

Further on where the plain widened, they realized Talon had been wrong. There was more than sand and rock cliffs. Heavy brush stood between the sand and the rock walls. The bushes appeared lofty and thick enough to conceal Wisdom and his herd.

The dogs wove in and out of the scrub, sniffing where elk had rubbed, but there were no other signs. The elevation gained. Wind had sent the sand drifting, exposing solid ground. Pine kneeled and searched for scuff marks. None.

Abruptly, Wisdom called a lengthy, shrill cry, punctuated with three deep thumping sounds. The noise came from behind them. Somehow he had misled them. Grand turned them around.

They approached the river. Sharpe was behind Grand and Pine in back. Grand scuffed his foot and knelt.

"What is wrong?" asked Sharpe.

"Just a stone in my moccasin," said Grand. "Go on ahead."

Grand waited for Pine to pass, then stood and leaned close to him. As loud as he dared, Grand said, "Another man lusts for your woman."

Pine stopped and turned to him. "Only one?"

"Only one I am mindful of," he answered.

Pine laughed. "Should he try to sway her, Lily would turn him away."

Pine stepped into the river, and Shadow leaped in after him along with Grand's dog. Grand followed.

Ahead of them, Sharpe turned away. Once he was out of sight and earshot from him and Pine, Grand said, as he thrust his spear in Pine's back, "The man is me and I do not accept no from any woman!"

The obsidian point pierced Pine under his left shoulder and his foot slipped. He crashed forward into the tree branches. A limb broke free from his weight, and Pine Nyte plunged over the falls and into the boiling torrent below.

The only witness, Shadow, bared his teeth and snarled at Grand. Instead of attacking him, Shadow jumped after Pine. He disappeared in the foamy froth.

As loud as he could, Grand screamed, "Pine!" Then he rinsed the blood from his spear tip.

The Era of Herbalists

Sharpe, who had reached the end of the fallen tree, turned in time to glimpse Pine and Shadow below in the river. His heart froze when he saw the pink in the sudsy white before the two of them slipped away.

On the opposite shore, Roth had been watching for Pine and Grand to reappear around the tree and debris. He could not believe his eyes when he witnessed Pine fall, and a moment later, he beheld Shadow's brave leap after his master. Calling the others, Roth ran along the canyon rim to a rockslide and scrambled down the broken boulders to the river's edge. But Pine and Shadow had slipped away in the current. Roth hurried downstream as far as the canyon allowed, but he lost sight of them.

Heartbroken, Roth sat against a boulder and wept until his dog licked his salty cheek. Roth embraced his furry friend and dried his tears. Talon and Berm joined him. "What happened?" asked Talon.

"Pine is gone," said Roth. He wiped his eyes. "So is his dog. There was blood in the water."

"Did you see him fall?" asked Berm.

"Yes," said Roth. "And he took some of the dead tree with him. That damn dog of his just went after him. I think he hit the rocks, but I cannot be sure."

"Let us go talk to Sharpe and Grand. They were with him," said Talon.

On the way up to the canyon rim, Talon asked, "What did you see?"

"Sharpe was ahead," said Roth. "I did not see Grand behind the tree. But I caught sight of Pine falling. I saw him hit the water and the dog right after."

On the bank, Todd helped Sharpe out of the water, and Grand stomped out on his own. He asked, "Did anyone see what happened to Pine?"

"You was with him," said Sharpe.

"Yes, but I was searching the sky for death eaters. I heard the wood snap, I turned just as he went over the waterfall."

"Did you see what caused him to fall?" asked Talon.

"No, he must have slipped on the rocks. I think he tried to catch himself on the dead tree but the limb broke on him."

"We should try to find his body," said Syd.

"We need something of his for the dogs to scent," said Roth.

Timothy W. Sparks

"He left his quiver at the camp," said Todd. "Should have his smell."

"Yes," said Grand. "Two should go to the camp. Bring his quiver back with four of the runners and our bedding. We can set a camp here. We still have half a day to search."

"I will go," said Talon.

"Me as well," said Berm.

"Hurry back," said Grand. "We will meet here. Make sure the runners bring enough cooked meat for two nights. If we cannot find Pine's body by then, we will return home."

The two hunters trotted away.

They searched for Pine and his dog in the immediate area, paying particular attention to the debris trapped in the whitewater. Nothing was found. Todd and Berm returned with the four runners, and the two hunters joined in the search while the runners set up the camp.

In a wider, shallower section of water, the dogs took the opportunity to play in the river. Grand directed Syd and Talon to cross to the other side and search a tangle of branches. Even though they yelled, they found no sign of Pine or his dog. Grand insisted they pull the debris apart.

The sun ducked behind the hills and the searchers returned to the camp. The four runners greeted them with gourds of broth. The hunters, tired from searching, fed their dogs and took their places around the fire. The runners handed out slim bread, slices of roasted venison, and berries. The roar of the falls and the crackling fire were the only sounds as they ate.

Finished with the meal, Berm asked, "Why are the gods hiding Pine's body? How can they be so cruel?"

"Gods have reasons not fit for us to tell," said Sharpe.

"Was the water god took him," said Todd. "To get him back, we should pay homage to the river."

"Cannot blame a god without proof," said Syd. "Grand told he slipped on a rock and the dead tree broke on him. What god is them?"

Nobody answered. Then, Roth asked, "Grand? How many did you count?"

"What?"

"The death eaters you looked for," said Roth. "How many did you see?"

Grand paused for a moment. The sarcastic tone in Roth's voice gave him the idea the question was a trick, so he said, "I saw none."

"None?"

"That is what I said."

"You must be blind, because I counted nine."

Tossing a stick into the fire, Grand changed the subject. "What of Wisdom and his herd?"

Todd answered, "We could only witness them climb over the knoll."

"How long from when we crossed the river?"

"The herd must have been concealed nearby," said Syd, "because only a short time passed and they came, but Wisdom trailed after you and did not return until right before you reached the river. Talon wanted to chase after the herd, but we knew by the time we crossed the river and scaled the hill they would be gone."

"This hunt has cost us," said Roth.

"Pine's loss is great, but each of us stomachs risk every time we venture. Any one of us could suffer…an accident," said Grand.

Under his breath Roth muttered, "Nine death eaters. Not none."

CHAPTER 26

In Search of Pine

THE FOLLOWING MORNING, a scream from a bad dream woke Roth in a sweat. He sat up and listened. The roar of the falls dominated the forest sounds. He got up and stepped barefoot into the water, where the chill numbed his feet. He squatted and splashed his face with both hands.

While he washed, Roth gazed at the fallen tree and jumble of oak limbs in the rushing water. He relived the moment Pine had fallen and Shadow leaped after him. What had Grand been doing? Watching the sky as he said, or did he cause Pine to fall? How could he have not seen at least a few of the nine death eaters? The questions troubled him. The others came down to wash, and Roth went to the campfire.

No one spoke around the fire. They chewed their food, rubbed their muscles, slapped insects, and scratched their itches. Nobody mentioned the empty space between Roth and Sharpe. But they all looked there. And when they rose to stir the dogs and gather their weapons, no one stepped in that place.

Even though he bore no faith this would work, Berm showed Pine's quiver to the dogs to sniff. On land the dogs had proved themselves as trackers. But on the river? Taking in the smell, the dogs pranced about, but with no place to start, they meandered aimlessly, sniffing at nothing.

The searchers scampered to the place Roth had last spotted Pine and set off downstream from there. In the crystal-clear water, Todd spotted the shaft of Pine's spear lodged in some rocks. He signaled Sharpe, who waded in the shallows nearby and retrieved it. "No spear point remains," he said.

Grand said, "The stone probably shattered. I hear another waterfall ahead. We should check there."

"Not a waterfall," said Syd. "The noise is from a stream joining the river."

"How do you know?"

"This is where I had my manhood trial."

"What else lies ahead?" asked Grand.

"The ground here lowers to the bottom of the canyon where the river splits. The main channel goes west to the sea and the smaller, faster water flows south beyond where I traveled."

Sharpe called out, "Something dark is down near those boulders. Might be Pine's dog."

Since he was standing closest, Todd climbed down the embankment. Because of the steepness, Roth held his dog for him.

Trapped among the rocks, the black lump bobbed in the water. Closer, Todd gulped. Using the shaft of his lance, he turned the thing, then let out his breath.

"Not Shadow! A drowned pig!"

"Better fill your goatskins upstream," said Grand. "The water is fouled from here on down."

The group waited for Todd before they took water and resumed their search. At the place where the stream joined the river, they found another fallen tree. The debris, a mixture of uprooted plants and broken branches, gave the group hope of finding Pine. Everyone but Grand, who hoped Pine's body would not be discovered lest he have to explain Pine's stab wound.

Without success, they raked through the rubble. Grand said, "We should turn back here. The bodies must not have come this far, or else this wreckage would have snagged them."

"Not so," said Roth. He pointed. "On either side they could pass without being caught. We should keep going farther."

"If we do not find them on the way back," said Grand, "tomorrow we will start here."

"By tomorrow the sea would have them," said Roth.

"If the gods will," said Grand, "we shall either find them or naught."

"Then we should have our camp in this place," said Roth. "I will run to the waterfall and bring them here."

Grand thought for a moment. "Perhaps you are right. This is a drier spot to camp. Syd, go with Roth. The rest of us will wait. We can gather firewood."

Keeping an eye out for Pine and his dog along the way, the two hunters and their dogs trotted back toward the waterfall camp.

They reached the place ahead of Talon, Berm, and the runners. Haunted with the visions of Pine and Shadow, Roth glared at the place.

Barking brought Roth out of his trance. Ahead, the dogs, excited to see their friends, romped and sniffed each other. Berm called for his dog, the instigator. He cowered before his master, who gave him a friendly pat.

"Where is Grand and the rest?" asked Talon.

"Farther south. He wants to set camp there."

"Help lighten our burdens," said Berm.

Syd gathered some bedding from the runners, and Roth grabbed a hefty satchel of supplies from them.

The group plodded along, and after a while the light faded. Darkness came and the glow of a blazing fire led them to the campsite.

"Who bears the food?" asked Grand. He stood from his place by the fire.

"Roth has some," said a runner. "I got the roast." He patted his satchel.

"Give it," said Grand.

"The meat is cold," replied the runner.

Talon took out his flint and sharpened a stick to be a skewer. The runner stabbed the hunk of venison and hung it over the flames. Once the meat began steaming, the runner handed the spit to Grand. He used his flint to cleave helpings. Once the hunters took their share, Grand gave the remnant to the runners for their meal.

From the sack he carried, Roth handed out wild plums and squares of toasted slim bread. No one spoke until the meal was consumed.

In the morning the lookout, Talon, woke the runners first before the sun lit the sky. Once the fire was blazing and meat searing on the skewers, he woke the rest of his group.

The Era of Herbalists

The hunters fed their dogs, then ambled into the bushes to relieve themselves. After Roth pissed, he went to the river. The glow in the east gave off enough light to see.

Only Sharpe shouldered his bow and quiver. Everyone else carried spears. The search began. Since they had covered this area earlier, they did not linger. But because of the dimness of the dawn, initially they moved at a slow pace.

Near midday at a bend in the river, something spun circles in the water. Roth took off his moccasins and climbed into the frigid, knee-high water. He waded to it: an atlatl. He brought it to shore. The markings showed it had belonged to Pine.

"He must be close," said Syd.

"No," said Grand. "Only his atlatl. It was just tucked into his sash. He probably lost his tool on the fall."

"He and his dog could still be nearby," said Syd.

"We can see the bottom," said Grand. "If they're here, we will spot them."

The group skirted the shore.

"Talon? What is ahead?" asked Grand.

"The water gets faster for a spell. Lots of boulders and a couple small waterfalls. Farther, the canyon ends and the river splits how I told you."

The deer herds made a well-defined trail along the waterway and a multitude of paths down to the water. They used those paths to check around the boulders, but no trace could be found of Pine or his dog.

CHAPTER 27

The Return of the Hunters

BARKING DOGS ANNOUNCED the return of the second clutch of hunters. The people who were not in the fields harvesting their crops rushed out to meet the runners and hunters. As the figures appeared in the clearing, Lily could not spot Pine's red furred shoulders, nor the white spear point that only he owned.

The villagers stood to welcome the approaching runners and hunters. Those returning faces showed no enthusiasm. They carried meat and skins, but held their heads low and moved as if they were hauling great weight.

"I do not see Pine Nyte," said one of the villagers.

Lily Nyte ran toward the hunters yelling, "Where is Pine? Where is my husband? Where is he, Sharpe? Why is he not with you?"

"Oh, Lily!" cried Sharpe. "I am hurt to tell he was lost. The river god took him. His dog went after him."

"I do not understand. What happened?"

With his hands clasped, Grand said, "We crossed the river and he was swept away and over the falling waters. We looked, but we could not find him. I am sorry, Lily, but he is gone."

"No! No! He must be found! Go back! You must go back!"

"Lily, we looked until the darkness and again through the next light. He has joined the spirits. There is nil to be done," said Talon.

Lily fell to her knees and wept uncontrollably. Several of the villagers rushed to her side to offer comfort, and she convulsed with sobs so strong some later said they felt it under their bare feet.

Pulling Grand aside, Evon asked, "Grand, you were there—what happened? What happened to my grandson? And where is his dog?"

So as not to show his deceit, he stared at Evon's chin. Grand said, "It happened like the lightning flashes. He was afore me, and we had just reached a fallen oak. The rocks there were slippery. I looked away only for a minute, watching for death eaters up the canyon. I heard a loud crack and he went over the edge. The river god grabbed him. His dog leaped in after him and the river god ate him as well."

Roth added, "From the shore I saw him fall and his dog jump in, but I lost sight in the swift water."

Evon shrunk as if his life was sucked from his lungs. He ambled off to tell Gemma, Neva, and Witt.

Grand turned toward Lily and said, "Lily, we tried, we true tried, no man could fall so far and pass the quick water. I am crushed, it is hard to take the breaths that give life. He was as a brother to me."

Hearing the falsehood, Roth glared at Grand, turned on his heel, and trudged away.

Lily sobbed. She held her expanded belly. "What of our child?"

"It is not unheard of for a widow to take a new man," said Grand.

"I am not a widow! There is no true proof that my Pine is dead."

"Still. Your child should not be born without a father."

Clutching her necklace, she glared at Grand and said, "Whether my Pine returns to me or not, this child will only have him for a father. Never will there be another to take Pine's place. Never!"

Without another word, Lily balled her fists and hurried back to her hut. From a distance, Roth regarded the exchange. Even though he could not hear the conversation, Lily's manner and Grand's angry expression when she stomped away told him enough. The way Grand's face contorted as he stared at Lily marching away from him disturbed Roth.

He asked himself again: did Grand cause Pine to go over the waterfall? No one had witnessed what happened. He watched the three men enter the river. He saw Sharpe clearly coming around the fallen tree. But that same tree shrouded Pine and Grand. The death eaters were circling close by. Anyone looking at the sky would have seen them. If there had only been a few, maybe he would have missed them. But nine?

Roth closed his eyes and pictured what he had witnessed. First the movement in the falls caught his eyes. Pine falling. Roth froze the image in his mind. Moments later, in the foamy white waterfall, there had been a dark silhouette. He visualized how Shadow had appeared. Determined.

Next he recalled them in the river, how the two bodies were intertwined with the tree branch. Did Pine move? Did Shadow? He tried to envision the details in the scene, but he could not. The river's white froth had consumed them too quickly.

Concerned for Lily, Roth decided to share his doubts with her. After witnessing her encounter with Grand, he thought maybe she would believe him. When he caught up with her, she was talking with Witt. He spilled his suspicions about Grand to the siblings—his words came with a share of tears. His angst spread to her and she broke down once again.

Having mourned Chirp for three years, the news of the loss of her son crippled Gemma. If not for Evon catching her, she would have collapsed to the ground. With Witt's help, they brought Gemma to her hut. Worried for her, Neva traded her bed nest with Witt's, and she asked that he stay in her herbalist hut for a few nights.

CHAPTER 28

The Disappearance of Lily Nyte

THE CURE NEVA had concocted for Lily's morning sickness required two doses. Having already given her the first measure the day before, Neva brought the second treatment for her to drink the next morning. She shook the seashells outside Lily's hut. The tinkling brought no answer.

"Lily?" called Neva. "I have your medicine."

Again, no response. Worried for her, Neva opened the door flap, and she peered inside and gasped. Except for her cooking pots and cleaning tools, the hut stood empty. No bed nest, no clothes, and no Lily. Neva wondered if Lily had returned to her family in Seaside Hill as she had planned. But Lily had agreed to let her and Witt help her move.

Hoping to find a sound reason why Lily's hut was deserted, Neva called to the nearest hut, trusting that Clem Doone would have answers. "Clem?"

The flap of his door cover parted and Clem peered out. Rubbing his eyes, he tried to focus on the woman.

"Neva Nyte? What business do you have with me? I suffer no maladies."

"Your neighbor, Lily, is gone. Do you know what happened to her?"

"Perhaps she is visiting someone."

"Most of her belongings are missing."

"Then I have no answer for you," said Clem.

"Did you not hear anything?"

"Only what I listen to all nights. Dogs barking."

As quickly as she could, Neva ran to her grandfather's hut and called to him. Evon came out.

"Lily is missing," she said. "Are you sure?"

"Yes. She wanted her treatment, but when I checked, she and most of her belongings were gone."

After the runner Evon sent to Seaside Hill came back with no news of Lily, a search party was organized. Returning with the runner, Ric Sayed brought a group from Seaside Hill to join the quest.

Based on someone's guess that Lily might be hunting for Pine's body, the searchers headed for the river.

At midday, along the river bank, they found Lily's missing things bound in her bed nest. Worse, they discovered her courtship necklace on a rock and one of her moccasins wrapped around a fallen branch in the rapids. Those clues led the searchers downstream.

Climbing over a fallen tree, Roth asked, "Why would she go into the water? This makes no sense. Pine has been gone six days."

"It is not like her, going off by herself," said Ric. "Lily has more sense than that. Something else must have happened."

Behind them, Grand started to say something, but Todd called from the river. He had found her other moccasin. The group waited while Todd handed the wet moccasin to Ric. Without speaking, his shoulders slumped, and with his head sagged, he stumbled back toward the village.

With Lily's necklace and the other moccasin, Grand Moon ran to him.

"You should take these," said Grand.

Stopping, Ric gaped at the larger, younger man. For no logical reason, the urge to drive a flint through the man's heart crossed his mind. But he shook away the thought and held out his hand for Lily's possessions.

"My thanks," said Ric. He clutched the items, turned, and continued home. As his own heart ached, he grasped how Reba would be even more mournful. And for him to be the bearer of the tragic news crushed him.

From the trees, Roth witnessed the exchange between Grand and Ric Sayed. From his vantage point, it seemed to Roth that Grand had tried to earn Ric's favor. From Ric's expression, he could tell Grand had failed.

The Era of Herbalists

Because of his suspicion, Roth kept an eye on Grand. Considering Grand's manner, it seemed to Roth that he had searched as hard for Lily as anyone. Still, after what happened with Pine, Roth no longer trusted his team leader.

The day yielded no more clues as to what became of Lily Nyte. The sunset ended the search. Many of the hunters rallied around the council fire. For a brief time, Grand joined them. Mostly he listened for any hint of suspicion. Any talk of something other than a bereaved woman losing herself in a state of mourning.

At the fire someone uttered what no others had stones to say but believed. That Lily Nyte had taken her own life. When Evon Nyte heard it revealed, he stomped off with his fists clenched.

Giving a similar performance, Grand tramped away to his hut.

CHAPTER 29

The Prisoner

LILY WOKE WITH a splitting headache in total darkness. Pain caused her to touch the knot on the side of her head, and her hand came back moist with sticky blood. A chill came over her, and she hugged her swollen belly and assessed herself. The dress covered her, but she had no moccasins. She touched her throat: no necklace either.

She patted the ground. Soft dirt. She inhaled. Musty, stale air. A cave? Nearer, a more pleasant aroma. Burnt meat. Cautiously Lily stretched her hands, searching around her. She bumped a platter. Her fingers found a piece of something rough. She brought it to her face and sniffed. Pig. She bit through the brazed crust. The meat inside was juicy.

After several bites she searched more, and her fingers bumped an empty gourd. She picked it up and felt the rim. A drinking cup. Somewhere, she thought, there must be water.

Rolling over, she crawled on her knees, waving the gourd in front of her. The gourd clacked against a wall. She edged closer and probed with her hand. Rough rock, slightly damp. Reaching, she felt the wall. Keeping her arm above her, Lily tried to rise. At her shoulder height, she touched the ceiling. Farther away from the wall, the cave allowed her to stand.

Holding an arm above her head, she held the gourd in front of her and took a step. Not reaching anything, she took another and another. At five paces she came to the opposite side.

Lily turned and something gleamed to her left. Unsure of her surroundings, she bent down and inched her way toward the glimmer. Through a vertical gap in the darkness she could see the stars. She found the cave entry and scurried to the opening. An enormous boulder on the outside trapped her inside.

She pressed her face to the crack. The sparkle was only the sky. Scooting away, she placed her bare feet on the boulder and shoved with all her strength. The rock remained. Lily was only pushing herself away from the exit.

Because of the fresher air, Lily leaned by the gap and waited for sunrise. From the chill she suspected the time was near. She fell back asleep. Dreaming of a moment with Pine, a screeching noise woke her. A ferret hung in the gap, yelping and scrambling for a grip on the rocks inside.

A deep growl caused Lily to peek out. A dire wolf clenched his teeth on the end of the creature's tail. Clutching him, Lily ignored the ferret's claws and pulled the animal free from the wolf.

"Easy," said Lily, in a soft voice. "You are safe now."

The ferret buried his head in the crook of Lily's arm and quivered. She stroked the tiny creature until his trembling subsided.

Sensing Lily's wound, the dire wolf stuck his face into the crack, but the gap proved too narrow. Frustrated, he paced outside the cave, growling. After a futile attempt to dig into the cave, the wolf gave up and trotted away.

Releasing her hold of the ferret, she felt him sitting on her leg for an instant. Then he reared up and sniffed her mouth, chirped, and dashed away. When she looked to where he had gone, she realized the sun had risen, and she received her first view of her prison.

In a corner she spotted the goatskin bag. Water. She poured some in the gourd and drank. The ferret edged close to her. She added more water and offered the vessel to him. He drank, and she presented him some meat. He sniffed, gave her a chirp, and ran to the back of the cave.

After drinking more water and eating the rest of the pork, Lily searched for the ferret. Not finding him, she followed his tracks to a fist-sized hole in the rocks. Kneeling, she scooped a handful of dirt. The hole widened. She dug and dug more. She paused. Air. She dug with the gourd until she scraped rock. The opening seemed wide enough for her to fit through. With so little light, she could not tell how deep or how far away the air was coming from. She only knew it was drifting into her face.

She stuck her head in and listened. A distant sound. Running water, or just the wind? Or simply the sound heard from a seashell against an ear? Lily pushed the water-filled goatskin in front of her and wiggled her arms and shoulders through. Fortunately her belly had only begun to swell, so she managed to free her hips and squirm inside.

A fraction of light from where she had come gave her a sense of security.

But she needed to proceed into the darkness to break out. All she had was the gourd, a bag of water slung on her shoulder, and her determination to escape before Grand Moon returned.

Even though she had only seen his hands, she had smelled him when he hit her. Now she believed Roth. Pine was dead and Grand had killed him, now she was sure of it. The idea of Grand touching her and taking her caused her to shiver, and she felt herself to see if she had been violated. Sensing no intrusion, she stuck the gourd in front of her, rapping her path and crawling toward the breeze coming her way.

The lava tube she struggled into took her downward. With no other choice, she moved on. Tapping the gourd in front of her to find the boundaries, Lily kept scrambling forward. Ahead, she heard the ferret chatter and she followed him, hoping he would lead her out.

After what seemed to her a lifetime, she stopped and began to weep. Neither pain nor fear caused her to cry, even though she did hurt and felt more afraid than she had ever been. Her tears were angry, but the wetness on her cheeks sensed the air gently flowing, giving her a stronger direction to follow.

She finally cried out, energized by her rage. After taking a couple drinks, she resumed her efforts. Keeping the gourd in front, she probed with it as she crawled. Drumming out the borders. The tunnel leveled and Lily explored with the banging. On one hand and on her knees, singing an endless song, she pressed on. The pain in her toes and knees slowed her; she knew she was bleeding.

The gourd lost the path; everywhere in front of her, she clacked against solid rock. But the air still moved. Face down, she searched with her fingers and found the hole. Feeling around, Lily screamed. She would never fit through the narrow slit. So, she laid still and silently asked the gods for help before crying herself to sleep.

CHAPTER 30

The Cave

THE WAIT FOR darkness left Grand anxious. Having his hovel at the edge of the village helped him sneak out unnoticed by the village dogs. His own were asleep inside his hut.

The moonlight and stars helped Grand find his way to the hillside cave. For half the night, he hiked uphill. Far enough from anyone's sight, he took out his flint kit and sparked a flame for his torch. With the blaze in front, he approached the cave entrance and held the torch beside the boulder in front of the narrow opening.

"Lily? Come to the light," said Grand. "I brought food. It has been a whole day. I know you must be hungry."

No response came from the cave. Grand called again, "There is no use being stubborn. All the village and your father believe you dead."

Again, only silence.

"Lily? You should think of your child. You do not want to starve Pine's child. Pine's son. Lily? Do you hear me?"

The stillness angered him and he yelled, "There is nowhere for you to go! Get yourself here or be beaten!"

When she did not come, he jammed the shaft of the torch into the ground, retrieved his oak branch and levered the boulder away. He stood back in case she tried to attack him. But Lily did not show herself.

After waiting for a response, Grand held the torch in the cave entry and peered in. Not believing his eyes, Grand rushed into the cave with the torch in front of him. The gourd, goatskin bag, and meat he had left were missing, along with Lily. Holding the flame away from him, he turned a circle and spotted the hole.

On his knees, Grand poked the torch into the opening and peered in. Only his fat head and arm fit inside the gap. He yelled, "Lily! Come back! There is no way out!"

Then a breeze inside the lava tube blew the flame toward him and he panicked. There might be an exit. The flare only showed darkness.

Over and over, he hollered her name. He listened for a response, but his echo was the only sound. Desperate, he pleaded, "Lily! Please! Come back! I will not harm you, I promise."

Infuriated, Grand jerked himself up. His head smacked a low section of the roof with a resounding thud. As he staggered backwards, pain caused him to black out for a moment. He fell on his ass in the dirt and bit his tongue.

Angry with himself, he swore and rose to his knees. A wave of dizziness came over him. Rubbing his head, he found a knuckle-sized knot and blood soaking his hair.

Cursing, he crawled out of the cave. He tossed the satchel of food into space, planted the torch in the ground, and held the branch against the boulder to lever the rock across the entry. But the massive stone slipped away, leaving a man-sized opening. Grand picked up the torch and studied the ground. An animal had dug a ditch. From the tracks, Grand guessed a dire wolf.

A sudden wind extinguished the flame, a bright flash lit the sky, and a second later, a loud crack of thunder shattered the silence. Rain pelted him, the torch fell from his grasp, and he scrambled down the hill.

Slipping in the mud, Grand skidded into brambles. Painful thorns poked the whole right side of his head, and he cried out. Freeing himself, he stomped away. The tiny barbs stung his fingers. He let go and tried to focus on the trail.

Another flare of lightning blinded him, and in concert with the thunder, his foot caught on a root. Grand fell hard on his right knee.

Back on his feet, he clambered to the trail. If not for another flash of lightning, Grand might have collided with the enormous bull elk blocking his path. Grasping a nearby branch, he froze when the elk grunted and shuffled his feet. As it happened, for a brief moment, fear seized both their hearts.

The Era of Herbalists

If Wisdom would have known the man carried no weapon, then he might have charged instead of running off. When he did, Grand let out the breath he had been holding.

As he hobbled down the hill, Grand worried how he could explain his appearance. The burning pain from the thorns intensified, and he had no cure. Only Neva Nyte possessed the remedy. However, since Pine's death, the girl's stare concerned him.

He thought the gods had cursed him. But what gods? Wind blew out his fire, and rain caused him to slip, but lightning saved him from crashing into the elk. Perhaps he should seek council from the spirit talker.

Bleeding, he limped toward the village with rain splattering his agonized face. In front of him, another lightning bolt struck a tree, blinding him. Losing his footing, he slipped. Swinging his arms to keep his balance, he grasped for anything to keep him upright, but a thick limb slammed his forehead. White pain rolled his eyes back and everything turned black.

Inside the lava tube, the weight of her limbs pressing her abraded toes into the rough lava rock woke Lily. She bent her knees and lifted her feet. While she lay there wishing her circumstances were nothing but a bad dream, a faint puff of wind tickled her toes. Inching backwards, Lily reached above her head with the gourd and touched only air. She squatted and raised her arm higher. Still nothing. Lily used the side to rise. Carefully, she straightened up with her arm above her so as not to hit her head.

When she stood up, Lily felt the breeze to her left, so she probed that direction. Finding the boundaries, Lily located a shelf at her hips. On her knees, she climbed over and knocked the gourd about. A wide passage. Raising her arm above her, Lily stood slowly. The roof let her stand and, in the blackness, she took baby steps. Blind, she shuffled her feet with one hand above her while the other, waving the gourd, searched for obstacles. So as not to exhaust her, every so often she switched arms. Lily advanced; however, in absolute darkness, she dared not move too swiftly.

This passageway continued to decline. Here in the absolutely black, silent world, she could feel her heart beating louder and faster. Up ahead she swore she saw a glimmer, and her feet wanted her to race, but her mind tricked her and there was nothing there.

To keep her sanity, she sang songs she learned from her mother as she pressed on. Her voice strained, but as she shuffled forward through the labyrinth, she kept singing. Without stopping, she continued the trek, singing every song she knew, keeping the beat with the gourd.

Just when she ran out of verses, the solid rock under her feet turned to gritty dirt. Tired, she sat and drank all but a few swallows of her water.

With her hand above her, she rose and her fingers brushed the top of the tunnel while she whipped the gourd back and forth ahead of her without striking anything. A sudden bout of fear overcame Lily, and she sunk to the ground and embraced herself.

A horrible thought crossed her mind. That she would lose her direction and end up back in the cave. Before she forgot, she held her arm up and stood. She waited until the air moved against her and then stepped forward with the wind guiding her by blowing on her tears.

In this place of complete darkness, she had been straining her eyes to see, so she closed them and continued her journey until she lost the barrier and the wind. Instead, the air seemed as though it surrounded her. She stopped. With her arms out, she spun a circle. She laughed and the echo laughed with her. A cavern. From where she stood, she identified the dank scent of water.

A loose stone bumped her toes. She bent down, picked it up, and threw it in front of her as hard as she could. The rock landed a distance away with a dull thud. She found another and tossed it to her right side. That stone plopped in water, and from the splash, the water was not far.

Questions troubled her. First, was the water moving or stagnant? Would it help her escape or impede her? Blind as she was, she needed to find out. She shuffled her feet in the direction of the splash. Another step and the ground gave way, and Lily plunged into a gently flowing river. The cold surprise caused her to release the gourd and gulp underwater. She surfaced and coughed. Once she recovered, she relaxed.

The Era of Herbalists

A strong swimmer, Lily floated on her back. Ignoring the chill, she let the river take her. Still unsure of the cave, she kept a hand above her face, the other on her belly, closed her eyes, and prayed to the gods that when she opened them again, there would be sunlight.

CHAPTER 31

The Lie

BECAUSE OF LAST night's storm, many of the villagers ventured into the forest to forage for fallen fruit and nuts. Sisters Fern and Shy Skeye sought wild plums. Heading to the place they always found them, Shy spotted the man in the mud and screamed.

Fern, the elder girl, rushed to where Grand Moon lay. Cautiously, she checked him for breath. He was alive.

Hearing others nearby, Fern called to them. Madda Todd and Peta Hogg ran over. Recognizing Grand Moon, Peta ran off to fetch his father, Falk, while Madda checked his obvious injuries. Squatting, she examined the wounds on his head; when she pulled an eyelid back, his pupil constricted. Turning his face, she gasped. A dozen or more fire thorns jutted out from his forehead to his chin. Each prick swelled a dark red around the barb. Unwilling to touch them, Madda stood and waited for help.

Loud voices called out, and Madda whistled to be located. Falk dragged over a travois, and two members of his hunt team came to aid. Upon seeing his son, he asked, "How is he to be here in this place?"

Pointing to them, Madda said, "Fern and Shy found him here. No one knows anything."

Recognizing the many fire thorns, Falk said, "We need to take him to Neva Nyte. She will have a cure."

With the help of his friends, they loaded Grand on the travois and Falk towed him to Neva Nyte's hut.

Hearing a commotion outside her place, Neva came out. She looked over Grand's body. "What happened?"

"The Skeye sisters found him in the woods."

"Leave him on the travois."

"Should you not take him inside?"

"No," said Neva. "There is not enough light."

In honesty, Neva did not want the bully anywhere near her, but because he was here and in need, she would treat him and send him away after. One thing she thanked the gods for was that he was unconscious. Then again, if he were awake, he would feel the pain of her ministrations. A fair trade, she guessed.

Silently, she pleaded to the gods for some justice and answers to the questions about Pine and Lily that plagued her.

So as not to suffer pain from the thorns herself when she pulled them, she used her pincer shells. Taking hold of the one protruding from his ear, she tugged. The many barbs ripped the flesh coming out, and a putrid yellow pus flowed from the puncture. She deposited the sticker in a clam shell. Neva repeated the process sixteen more times.

Finally, while the puncture wounds drained, she returned to her apothecary and located the batch of healing salve. Kneeling, Neva used a soft leaf to spread the noxious-smelling balm on the fire thorn sores.

"What of his other wounds?" asked Falk. "Will he wake?"

"For his forehead I will concoct a poultice. All I can do for his head and knee is wash away the dirt. Cold water should revive him; if not, the stench of a death flower will bring him to his senses. But the closest are near Seaside Hill."

"How can it be known?"

"If you must have some, see the rainbow woman, Ammer Wynn. But you should delay."

"Why? If it is a sure fix?"

"If he breathes the stink to wake, his stomach will empty. Sometimes this happens for many days and nothing, not even water, will stay down."

"Then treat him as you say. Send your brother to fetch me when you finish your treatments."

"As you wish, but be aware Witt charges his own price."

"And you? What is your fee?"

Without hesitating she said, "A season of firewood and a deer haunch from your smoke oven."

Crossing his arms in front of him, Falk said, "Seems a steep price for such minor care."

With her chin raised she stepped up to the hulking man. She said, "The salve to cure fire thorn wounds uses nine herbs and takes five days to fashion. And your son used half of my stock. My fee is fair."

Blinking, Falk stepped back and eyed the girl. Seeing her resolve, he frowned and asked, "Can you wait for the wood?"

"Before the frost, no later."

"You shall have it. Send the boy." He turned and walked away.

Neva returned to the apothecary to make a poultice for the bruise on Grand's forehead. Considering the size of the thing, she needed a large measure of arnica. She crushed some of the yellow flowers in her mortar and threw in some shave grass. She ground it with her pestle, added a piece of honeycomb, and laid the mixture on a strip of leather.

Squatting by his head, she wrapped the poultice against his forehead. Then she washed the bump on the top of his head with a sea sponge. Rinsing it in a gourd, she swabbed his knee.

"What are you doing?" called Witt. "He may be responsible for Pine."

"His father brought him, and he is in need of healing."

"But you heard Roth."

"Yes, and if what he speaks of holds true, then the gods will punish him."

"To me, seeing him battered as death eater prey says the gods are already working now to penalize him."

"Perhaps so. But his care is done. Go tell Falk Moon to come fetch his son. Name your price."

"What worth did you call for?"

"A season of firewood and a smoked deer haunch."

"Thank you, sister. Collecting firewood is not an easy task, and Mother needs meat."

Meanwhile, trying to still appear unconscious, Grand kept his eyes closed while breathing slowly. As the two chatted, Grand Moon, aware of his pain and his present surroundings, listened closely.

The Era of Herbalists

So Roth had been spreading his death eater story. He would have to talk with him. Convince him Pine had fallen on his own. Otherwise, Roth would need to disappear.

Witt ran off and Neva went inside the hut. Whatever medicine she had used on the fire thorn pricks seemed to be working. The pain decreased there, but his knee ached, and as his heart throbbed, so did the agony in his skull. More misery when he opened his eyes into sunlight and snapped them shut. A brilliant orange beam glared in his brain along with the pounding headache.

After what seemed an eternity, Falk Moon came with Witt, who carried the smoked deer haunch on his shoulder. Wearing a new headband, grinning, the boy took the meat to his mother's hut.

"When will he wake?" asked Falk.

"Your son is awake now, and he has been for some time."

"Grand? Open your eyes."

Holding a hand over his face, Grand opened them only long enough to recognize his father.

"Can you walk?"

Grand grunted and groaned but said nothing, he only shook his head. Without thanking Neva, Falk picked up the end of the travois and hauled his son home for his wife Elm to care for him.

Elm Moon fixed her son a broth, and while he sipped the steaming soup, his father begged him to tell his tale.

The story Grand had concocted in his muted state flowed out of his mouth like water from a pitcher. Both Falk and Elm Moon drank their son's lie like drunkards guzzling spirit juice.

"A noise brought me from my hut and two gatherers clubbed me, and they must have dragged me away. In the storm I woke and struggled. I am sure I hurt them both, but one of them surprised me with a blow to my knee. That is when they forced me into the fire thorn bush."

"How did you get away?" asked Falk.

"The lightning god struck a tree, and when the thunder god hollered, something bashed my head and that is all I can recall."

Falk hurried to Evon Nyte's hut. "Gatherers were here!" he called. "They tried to take my son!"

The urgency of the matter brought the council together before the sunlight cleared the hill. More than half the village gathered around them. The anxiety level rose high, and Evon beat the drum until everyone settled.

Since Grand's injuries prevented him from attending, Falk relayed the account his son had told him. Once he finished, questions assaulted him.

"This makes no sense," said Lane Todd. "Why come here for one man?"

"Happened to Ash Skeye," said Falk. "Gatherers took him for trade."

"How sure is Grand that they was gatherers?" asked Evon.

"Said they had marks on their skin."

"Grand is a strapping young man," said Evon. "How did they get him?"

"My son told that a noise brought him out. A whistling sound."

"Did they come just for Grand or just happen on him?" asked Roth.

"Since they lured him from his hut, it must be they came for him."

"Were there more than two?" asked Walmac Lukan.

"Two were all he saw."

"Are more gatherers about, waiting to attack?" wondered Rex Awell.

Evon stood and spoke. "Falk asks that we search the woods, and I ask that the night sentries be reinforced."

Hands raised and names were shouted. Four groups of villagers secured weapons and went hunting for evidence of gatherers.

In the background Neva and Witt listened, and when the groups filed away, the two left on their own hunt. Though she held her tongue, both she and Witt, her assistant, knew that fire thorn bushes grew on the west side of the east hills—not the woods. But to be absolutely sure, they scoured the woods from the village past where Grand was found for a long part of the day. No fire thorn bushes.

With the knowledge of the lie, they sought Roth Uhl to share their discovery and pursue more evidence of Grand's deception.

CHAPTER 32

The Deserters

ANOTHER SUMMER ENDED, Chirp's third as a slave. Like every harvest, the prodon ordered his gatherers north. From the rumors, because of the move, these raids would be total, meaning the gatherers would take more than tribute. Much more, and any resistance would be met with blood.

Chirp watched the three assault teams with their weapons forming lines. He wondered which one was destined to attack Twin Oaks. It made no difference, he cursed them all. He had friends in Seaside Hill and River Shores.

Three barges lined the riverbank and Chirp gaped at them. Crowds cheered as they boarded the boats. Their joy equaled the villages' sorrow.

Maybe the river monster would take them. His curse tasted bitter in his mouth, but he continued cursing them until the oarsmen paddled them upriver and out of sight. In eight days, when the gatherers returned, he would resume his cursing.

Something he had never considered before was to taint their wake-me tea. For crippling belly cramps he could use man-fern leaves, but the bitter flavor might overwhelm the blood root and goldenrod taste unless he added honey. Then, when Lord Prodon's gatherers went to sack a village, their cramps would cause them to shit themselves. Surely then, Lord Prodon would seek a new herbalist, and he would suffer an agonizing death as did the herbalist before him. Still, should they harm his family, he would want retribution against them.

Today the prodon was making his men move his tower, all because the wind had changed directions and he inhaled an unpleasant odor. He instructed them with his great mouth. "Forward! Stop! To the right! Farther! Keep going! Stop! Back! Too far! No, no, to the left! Stop!"

After what seemed half of the day to the men hauling him, he finally found his perfect spot. But then he stared into a water-filled drinking vessel and gave orders to level the tower. That procedure took up the remainder of the day.

Proclaiming loudly, the prodon verified the rumor spread days ago when he declared he intended to move the camp east on the morning of the next full moon. To those working on the road, the move was common knowledge, but to those inside the encampment, little was shared.

Before Chirp could ready his apothecary, he needed to gather more herbs. From the scouts, he had learned the place they planned to travel differed from this coastal valley. The unidentified plants those people brought back proved to him that some of the plants he needed would not be available. At his request, Gorg, Bru, Werth, and Luca escorted him on foot. They headed north along the river.

"How is Aden?" asked Chirp. "Did his leg heal?"

"His leg mended, but Aden was killed on a bison hunt," said Gorg.

"The news saddens me."

"He died on his feet with a weapon in his hands," said Bru.

"I would rather die lying down with a kiss on my lips," said Chirp.

The men laughed at that, but Chirp was serious.

Near the river, Chirp spotted rounded white blossoms. Walking root plants. "We need to dig all these plants up," he said.

"Chirp?" asked Gorg. "What cure do they offer?"

"The sap in the stems is a remedy for blisters."

"Then should we not just take the stems?" asked Werth.

"Then the plant would die too quickly and the sap would lose potency."

Without another word, the men started digging. Chirp joined them. The light rain that had fallen the day before eased the task.

Once they were finished, they bundled the plants, left them beside the trail, and continued along the river. A low growing patch of dark green led Chirp to a clump of wolf root plants. His escorts recalled him giving Aden some for his snakebite. They dug them up and left the herbs next to the walking root plants.

Sighting some purple flowers on the slope of the hillside, Chirp led his group to harvest some verbena. On the way, he explained how the herb had many healing properties: it soothed sore throats, promoted sleep, healed anxiety, cured headaches, and settled upset stomachs.

For this plant, Chirp told them to cut them at the base of the stems, since the leaves and flowers kept their effectiveness when dried.

"Chirp?" said Bru. "We grow weary under the prodon's rule."

The others nodded their agreement.

"This I understand. If it were not for the fate of my village, this place would not keep me."

"Then we ask for your secrecy," said Gorg. "And for you to not ask for us, for fear that we be sought after before we escape the prodon's territory."

"Your secret is safe with me."

"To us, you have been a trusted friend," said Gorg, offering his hand.

Clasping him with two hands, Chirp said, "To me our friendship is as strong and enduring as the snowcapped mountains. On this, the day for our parting, there will be a lasting memory of our brotherly bond."

"It is the same for us," said Werth.

Embracing his comrades, Chirp said, "The prodon leaving this valley may benefit your flight."

"True," said Luca. "And since he travels east, then our journey to our villages to the south should not hinder our trek."

"Then I pray to the gods for them to give you fair weather, ample food, and fresh water along your way."

Without any more talk of this, they continued their tasks until they had delivered their load to the herbalist's apothecary. Inside, while Bru and his friends stacked plants in separate spaces, Chirp made medicine bags for them. All the remedies were made for teas. As he fashioned them, he explained what was what, the purpose, and the suitable dosages.

Having already bid their goodbyes, the four men walked past Chirp. He and they only nodded farewell.

The sun set, and the four runaways gathered their supplies and weapons. At full dark, having given the guards Chirp's sleepy tea, they passed by the sentries unnoticed.

All four of them agreed to travel south along the seashore. Werth's home would be the first destination. To his best guess, his village, Whisper Bay, was ten or more days away.

Wanting to gain distance from the prodon, the four friends ran along the surf. Their footprints glowed in the wet sand behind them. And like the fires in the prodon's encampment, the shine faded with their strides.

In the prodon's encampment, the sick lined up outside the herbalist's fence. Patto escorted the sickest inside the compound, where he made them wait on the bench. Before treating them, Chirp gave them a quick exam. Foul water disease, all of them.

Telling an ignorant people to boil the water before drinking made no sense to them. They trusted only what their eyes showed them. Even in their fits of fever, stomach cramps, retching, and diarrhea, they remained unwilling to accept the need for such an effort just to drink. Not when they witnessed animals drinking from the river every day without distress. Did they not also behold those same animals shit and piss where they stood?

For Chirp, this presented a constant need for sage and bullfoot root. In this valley, sage grew in abundance, but not bullfoot root. From here, the nearest he knew of grew a half-day upriver and a full day's walk to the far side of the round top hills.

Because of the closeness to Twin Oaks, Chirp's home, the prodon forbade him from going. Instead, Chirp trained four gatherers to recognize and harvest the plants. Now, five days had passed and the gatherers had not come back with the cure, and the line of patients kept extending. Until they returned, all Chirp could do was treat them with half measures. So far no one had died, but should the cure not come soon, some would.

Boiling water prevented this illness, that was a fact. Chirp decided to ask Lewell to ask the prodon to speak with his great mouth and proclaim a mandate for all to boil their drinking water.

The Era of Herbalists

Calling Patto, Chirp sent him to bring Lewell. Instead, the prodon's second guard came. "Where is Master Lewell?" asked Chirp.

"Master Lewell is inspecting the new barge."

"If I cannot speak to him, I must seek an audience with Lord Prodon."

"At this time, Lord Prodon breeds with maidens. Any hearing must delay until after his next proclamation."

Repulsed by the thought of the unfortunate girls suffering such an ordeal, Chirp dismissed the guard and returned to the apothecary hut.

Inside, the previous herbalist had left an unfamiliar plant on a shelf. Not a kind growing near Twin Oaks or the surrounding habitats. Here it grew in the sunny meadow along the river. Fuzzy, broad, wing-shaped grayish leaves, woody stems, and small yellowish flowers identified it. But having no knowledge of the plant's properties, Chirp needed to experiment. First he asked Patto what he recalled.

"The plant is called wormwood," said Patto. "I know not how the herbalist used it."

Crushing a dried leaf, Chirp added boiled water and let the blend brew. He sniffed the fragrance, but he had never inhaled anything to compare. Dipping a finger, he sampled some on his tongue. Bitter. He strained off the leaves and took a sip. Nothing tingled, burned, or numbed. After a time, he swallowed a mouthful and sensed the liquid traveling to his stomach. Soothing. He drank another swallow and, to be sure the drink presented no harm, he gulped more.

Still no ill effects. He brewed a full batch. Without further tests, he was reluctant to treat anyone, but this herb caused no harm and he had nothing else for a cure.

After treating those patients on the bench, Patto pointed to the gate. More ill lined the fence outside the apothecary. With Patto's assistance, Chirp administered the wormwood brew. Most kept the medicine down, but several spewed after drinking. With them he added honey to the brew and told them to drink slowly. Following his instructions, those people were able to cope.

Treating so many exhausted Chirp, and after cleaning up, he climbed into his sleeping nest. In the dark, sparkling lights danced in front of his eyes. He closed them and then opened them again. Bringing his hands to his face, the tiny lights glittered on his fingers. He focused on one on the tip of his thumbnail. Staring closer, the glow appeared to be hundreds of miniature flames combined into one. And that beam shone as a mass of colors too bright to stare at any longer.

He closed his eyes tightly, and the flame sprang from a spark until only light filled his vision. In a panic, Chirp opened his eyes and gaped into a blazing blue sun. Hoping for the blackness of the night, he shut them. For as long as he could remember, Chirp had believed blindness to be black, without light. But this was a worse sightlessness that plagued him. Gradually the light dimmed, darkness returned, and he slept.

The prodon's waking call freed Chirp from the dream. Shaking off the nightmare, fuzz and a sour flavor filled his mouth. No memory of the dreadful dream remained, yet he still felt mournful for some great loss. As if losing his freedom and his family had been nothing.

Chirp's head cleared and he slipped on his moccasins. From outside his hut, Patto called, "Chirp! The cure! It works! The sick suffer no longer!"

Having only begun to awake, Chirp grunted his reply.

From the previous night's intense visual experience, he realized he had ingested too much of the wormwood tea. Eager to find out if any of those he treated had similar experiences, Chirp hurried dressing.

Each of the previous night's patients heard Chirp ask them the same question. "Did sleep come easy?"

For most, there was no complaint. However, several men said they were blinded by the bright lights, and one woman claimed to hear the colors she saw in her mind. According to her, they sang to her. She asked if she might have more, but Chirp dismissed her.

Later, the four men he had sent after the bullfoot root returned with their load. He was about to question them as to the delay when Lewell burst into his yard.

"The barge failed," grumbled Lewell. "This is not news Lord Prodon will be pleased with. And since it is myself the bearer of such an outrage, I plead to you, Chirp Nyte, to concoct me a suitable cure for my upcoming headache."

"Of what on the barge failed?"

"The center of the keel collapsed and ripped the skin."

"Then who will Lord Prodon blame?" asked Chirp with a smirk. "To my thinking, Lord Prodon would charge others. Not yourself."

"Most assuredly those builders will be punished. But myself, I will face the first of his wrath. Though his discipline to me comes only from his tongue, for that, it will be the hurt of a hundred lashes."

"Wolf root and verbena tea with honey will put you at ease. Would you like some before your tongue lashing?"

"Only if I can keep my wits about me."

"Standing with your open eyes will keep you sharp, but closing them while laying down would make you wish for sleep."

"Then make me enough for tomorrow's suffering, for it will be my task to assign new boat builders."

"How long before we move east?"

"A moon and a half or never, if no one can make a proper barge."

Scratching his chin, Chirp said, "There is an ample supply of bamboo. Why not build a new tower on the other side of the river instead?"

For a moment Lewell's face wrinkled, then his eyes bulged. "Chirp Nyte, you may have saved me from my plight." He dashed off to tell the prodon.

After only a short while, a smiling Lewell greeted Chirp. "Lord Prodon is pleased."

"Do you not want the remedy I concocted?"

"Will it keep?" A drawn-out, spine-chilling scream interrupted the conversation.

"Lord Prodon punishes the boat builders," said Lewell.

Knowing there were more shrieks to come, Chirp excused himself and returned to his apothecary, where he stuffed pieces of sea sponge in his ears. The stuffing only dampened the sound of the men's agony. Sorting through the bullfoot plants, Chirp turned his thoughts to his friends and offered another prayer to the gods for their safe journey.

CHAPTER 33

The Discovery

In Twin Oaks, the hunt for the fire thorn bush started where the Skeye sisters had found Grand Moon. In the midmorning sunshine, Neva, Witt, and Roth trekked up the hill. The rainstorm had washed away most of the footprints, but not all of them. Armed with a short spear, Roth took the lead and helped Neva and Witt up the slippery spots.

"See those scrapes," said Witt. He tipped his head to a flat spot uphill above his head. "He must have slipped."

"He came down from there," said Roth.

The trio climbed to the animal trail running along the hill. Puddles showed prints. Witt squatted. "These are elk tracks."

"True, Witt. Only one bull makes tracks this size: Wisdom."

Studying the ground, Roth told the story left on the ground. "It must have been dark. Both Grand and Wisdom must have been surprised by each other. Wisdom ran left, and Grand went right and slipped."

"Where was he coming from?" asked Neva.

"We are going to find out," said Roth.

Farther, Roth pointed to some scuff marks near an exposed root.

"This might be where Grand hurt his knee."

Up the hill, Neva spotted a fire thorn bush. Witt clambered above it.

"Careful," warned Neva. "I do not have any cure with me."

"Sister, this is the offending plant. Many thorns are broken away."

"I will want to count the scars to be sure."

"Count them on the way down," said Roth. "Grand's trail continues up."

Continuing to climb, lava rock prevailed, and they spotted a pigskin pouch laying on the ground. Witt picked it up, empty and still wet. Partially hidden behind shrubs, Neva spotted a torch in the mud and a boulder partially hiding a cave entrance.

Afraid of what might be found in the cave, Roth pushed past the siblings. When he peered inside, he saw nothing obvious. Too dark to see inside clearly, he broke out his fixings and fire kit and struck sparks into the bundle of dry moss and pine needles. He blew until a flame grew.

Lighting the torch, he crawled inside. Panning the flame around, he saw an empty platter.

"Neva! Witt! Come in!"

The two creeped into the musty cave. Roth called them to the back.

"There is a hole back here. Looks like it was dug up."

Roth called for Lily over and over, but all he heard back was his own echo.

In the firelight, Witt's sharp eyes spied something reddish in the sand. He picked it up. A bead. Running his fingers in the dirt, he found three more.

"These came off Lily's dress," said Neva.

"She must have crawled in the hole," said Witt.

"We need to tell the council," said Roth.

"First let me count thorn scars," said Neva. "If I total seventeen, then we have true proof."

Concerned how Evon might respond to the news, the three went to Thon Doone instead.

"Thon," said Witt. "We have found evidence that Grand Moon lied and that he is responsible for Lily Nyte's disappearance."

"That is a serious accusation."

"We have proof," said Roth.

"Tell me."

They did, and they showed him the beads from Lily's dress. Unable to hike the hill himself, Thon rousted two men he trusted, Pal Lukan and Yar Awell. Both were council members. Roth led them to the cave. On the way he pointed out footprints, and the fire thorn bush with the seventeen scars where thorns had broken off. Each of the men counted to confirm what Neva Nyte had told Thon.

Without explaining why, Thon rounded up the council members, including Evon Nyte. Halfway through his explanation of why the meeting had been called, Evon climbed to his feet and drew his blade. Thon used his walking stick to block him.

"Let me pass!" yelled Evon.

"Sit down, Evon. Please, we need to make the charges official," said Thon.

"What of Lily?" asked Evon. "She could be alive in the tunnel."

"We called and heard no answer," said Pal Lukan.

"Someone needs to go to Seaside Hill and fetch Ric Sayed," said Evon.

"What benefit would that bring?" asked Thon.

"The thought that Lily took her own life must torment him," answered Evon.

"Yes. And when he finds Grand Moon, he will take revenge," said Thon.

"Good," spat Evon. He sat and crossed his arms.

The council members argued back and forth. Finally, they decided to have a trial before involving Seaside Hill. As a group they marched to his hut.

Hearing the commotion outside, Grand shoved the door flap aside and stomped out.

"Grand. Tell us your tale from your own lips," said Thon.

"I told my tale to my father. Nothing has changed."

"Many things have changed. You say gatherers took you. We found no proof of that. Tell us where the fire thorns poked you."

"That I cannot recall."

"How can that be?" asked Evon. "The pain is such as to not forget where and when a thorn stuck."

Thon leaned on his walking stick. "Tell us about the cave up the hill."

Grand's eyes flared. He stared at his father, hoping for help. "I know not what you speak of."

"We followed your trail," said Yar Awell, one of the men Roth had led to the cave. "We found the fire thorn bush."

Evon held a clay pot he was given for evidence. "These, my granddaughter Neva pulled from your face. Seventeen fire thorns. Too much pain to forget, me thinks."

"Pal Lukan and myself counted seventeen wounds on the fire thorn bush branches far up the hill," said Yar.

"Proves nothing," said Grand, folding his arms across his chest.

"What about these?" said Evon. He held the beads for Grand to see.

"Beads?"

"From Lily's dress. These were found in a cave above the fire thorn bush."

Grand laughed. He said, "You have no proof—"

Falk Moon smacked his son on the side of the face. His wounded side.

"Boy!" he screamed. "Tell the truth! Did you take Lily Nyte?"

Grand rubbed his face and glared at his father. His answer was his sneer. He turned to walk away, but Falk grasped hold of his arm.

Grand swung a fist, but Falk knocked his arm aside and slapped Grand's face again. Before Grand readied his own fist, Falk punched him in the gut.

Grand doubled over, and Falk grabbed him by his hair with both hands and kicked his already bruised forehead with his knee. With a thud, Grand fell to the dirt.

Elm, Grand's mother, rushed from her hut. She hammered Falk's back and screamed, "Falk! What are you doing? This is our son!"

Falk spun around and shoved his wife back. "Our son shows guilt!"

"Look at him, Falk! Gatherers took him! They beat him!"

"He lied! No gatherers came here!"

"Then who beat him?"

"The gods! It was they that punished him for taking Lily Nyte!"

"You heard Grand. There is no proof."

Ignoring his wife, he faced the men. "Take him for judgment!"

"No! Please, he is our only son."

Before they hauled him to the pit hold, Falk asked, "Pal? Will you take me to the places you found? I need to check for my own self."

Pal nodded his head. Falk dashed into the hut and came out with his short spear, a torch, and his tool pouch. The two headed to the hill.

Little was said. Pal Lukan showed him the scuff marks, the fire thorn bush, and the place where someone had slipped. Having hunted for so long, Falk recognized Wisdom's footprints, and as an expert tracker he read the story of the near collision in the drying mud.

At the cave, too many feet had trampled the ground to tell if any belonged to Grand. Striking sparks with his fire kit, Falk quickly ignited the torch. Inside, Pal showed Falk the hole they believed Lily had crawled into. As he approached the spot, the light of his torch showed something on the cave ceiling. Pal held the torch and Falk studied the place. Hair. He sniffed. Dried blood.

"This is where Grand hit his head," said Falk. "Proof enough for me."

"What of Lily?"

Falk stared at the hole in the back. "We should mourn her."

CHAPTER 34

The Trial

CONSIDERING THE SEVERITY of the charges, it was no surprise that most of the village attended Grand's trial. The witnesses sat closest to the council members, then the kinfolk. The observers surrounded them.

The kin was comprised of both the Moon and the Nyte families, including Evon. Since he was considered a victim, there was no place for him on the council.

The moment everyone settled, Thon Doone stood and said, "Three days past, we learned Lily Nyte went missing. Then we thought she went to the river searching for her husband, Pine. Now we know different."

A hand went up, and Thon recognized Nat Uhl. He asked, "What about all her things we found by the river?"

"Put there to lead us astray."

"Where was she then?"

"There is evidence she was kept in a cave up the hill."

"Why is Grand Moon being charged?"

"Found proof he lied about the gatherers. Roth Uhl, Neva, and Witt Nyte backtracked him to the cave. Inside they found a place dug out to a tunnel and uncovered beads from her dress in the dirt. Pal Lukan and Yar Awell said it looked like she squeezed herself through the hole."

"Did they find her body?"

"No, only an empty platter and a few beads."

"Maybe she is still alive."

"Nobody thinks so."

"Still," said Nat. "Cannot charge him with murder."

"Can charge him with snatching."

"What proof?"

"Falk Moon found the place Grand smacked his head," said Yar. "Was hair and blood on the roof of the cave near the hole Lily crawled in."

Neva raised her hand. Thon called on her, and she stood.

"The wound on his head was rough and unequal, like it hit rock. The bloody wound had some hair missing."

"Tell them about the fire thorns," whispered Witt.

"Um, I removed seventeen fire thorns from his head. Fire thorn bushes do not grow on the flats, only up the hill. From where he was found, we followed his footsteps up there. Found the bush, had seventeen scars on the branches where the thorns got broke off."

"Tell them how close the cave was," muttered Witt.

"Um, the cave was only a bit farther up. Could see a trail up from where he slipped into them thorns."

Neva sat, and Falk Moon held up his hand. Acknowledged, he rose and said, "My son claimed gatherers took him, but we found that to be false. In the cave we found proof he was inside and also that Lily Nyte's dress had lost some beads in the cave. With no body, no one knows what happened to the woman. Cannot charge my son with murder."

Waving his hand, Thon called on Roth. He took to his feet and said, "Me thinks Grand killed Pine to get to Lily."

Elm Moon jumped to her feet and shook a fist at Roth. "You got no proof to be saying such lies!"

"Was too! Grand lied!" hollered Roth. "He claimed to be watching for death eaters when Pine fell. Nine filled the sky, but I asked and he said he saw none."

"Not proof!" shouted Elm. She stood with a fist in the air.

To break up the conflict, Thon shook a warning feather at the arguers and they sat down.

At the bottom of the pit, Grand rubbed the side of his head where his father had smacked him. His anger focused on his father not backing him; that was his real pain. One comfort was that his mother had stood up for him.

Would the council banish him? Or would they stone him? Only once, when his grandfather was a boy, had anyone been stoned to death. A child killer. Surely he would be exiled and for him, it would be his own choice.

Not wanting to face the council, he yielded his own say. For his defense, his claim would come from his father's mouth. The thought made him smile. There was no real proof of him taking Lily. With no body to show, there could be no charge of murder—only his lie about the gatherers.

Another thought popped into his head. This one brought a chill. As soon as Ric Sayed learned of this, he would want revenge. No matter if he be banished, the whole population of Seaside Hill would hunt him. He needed to escape. He wondered who was guarding him.

"Who is up top?" called Grand.

Clem Doone leaned over the hole. "What do you want?"

"Is the judgment finished?"

"No one has said, but the council fire still blazes."

"Why have I no water?" asked Grand. "Is this my punishment before I have been judged?"

"No one has told me to give you comfort."

"Water is all I ask," said Grand.

Shrugging, Clem fitted a gourd to a knotted leather cord. He dipped the vessel in the water jar.

Leaning over the hole, he lowered the gourd. "Got me a club you try any—"

The moment the gourd came within reach, Grand jumped. With both hands he grabbed the cord wrapped around Clem's wrist. Clem tumbled face first into the hole. Grand moved against the wall in time. The man landed on his head. Without pausing, Grand grabbed the club from Clem's twitching fingers. He tied the club to the cord and undid the end from Clem Doone's dead wrist.

Three throws and the club wedged in the rocks. Tugging, he tested the strength. The cord held, so he climbed over the top. So as not to be seen in the light, he crept along the shrubs.

The Era of Herbalists

In the shadows, he rushed to his hut. Everyone seemed to be at the judgment fire. After he retrieved his weapons, he raided a few huts for dried meat, slim bread, and spirit juice. He wrapped it all up in his bed roll and strapped the bundle to his back. Without looking back, Grand Moon dashed south into the three-quarter moonlit night.

The vote came after the discussions ended. Six votes for banishment and two votes to turn Grand over to Ric Sayed for retribution. Elm Moon pleaded, "Please, do not send my son away. He is a good man."

On hearing her claim, those that heard hooted loudly.

The eight council members marched to the hold with torches. Approaching, they did not see the guard.

"Where is Clem?" asked Yar.

They rushed over to the hole. At the bottom, Clem Doone lay with his neck bent at an impossible angle. Grand had escaped.

Staring down, Thon Doone said, "Now we see murder. My cousin Clem."

"Cannot have gone far," said Pal.

"I change my vote," said Rallo. "Give him to Ric Sayed."

"Same here. Retribution."

All the votes changed. In the morning, a runner would do the telling.

"Once the village learns of this, a hunt will be started," said Thon.

A voice spoke from behind them. "And I will lead the pack," said Evon.

Storming to the hole, Evon glared at the body. Pointing, he said, "Is there doubt now that my grandson Pine was murdered? Is there doubt among you that Grand took Lily? When we catch Grand, Ric Sayed can have what I leave of him."

Because the judgment council had broken up, people meandered back to their huts. Then Roth came running through, shouting, "Clem Doone is dead! Grand has escaped!"

Hearing the horrific news, some of the men rushed to their huts and gathered their weapons. Clem Doone was a friend to most. His murder demanded justice. And now that they knew Pine had been murdered too, his friends from the hunt team assembled.

Evon learned of the nighttime avengers and seized a spear. Jos Doone, Clem's younger brother, tracked Grand to the south trail. The group numbered seventeen.

To find out what Grand had taken with him, Roth checked his hut. Tied up, the dogs greeted him with friendly barks and tail wags. The murderer had left them no food or water. From what Roth could tell, Grand had taken his whole weapons stash, his tool pouch, and his bed nest.

Joining the group, Roth told them, "He took all his weapons, but he left his dogs. We could use them to track him."

"Those dogs would just give us away," said Jal Lukan. "The way he stomps, following his marks cannot be troublesome."

"Curse him," said Ned Awell. "Stole my spirit juice."

"Took a hunk of my winter meat," said Erle Hogg. "Fetching it back gives me reason to go after him."

To not make themselves known, they stayed silent and jogged single file behind Jos Doone. He followed Grand's tracks and fixed the pace.

CHAPTER 35

The Raiders

Taking the main trail, Grand trotted to gain as much distance from Twin Oaks as he could. He was confident no one would chase him at night, but by morning when they set out, he would be far from them.

Finally, secure with the distance he had covered, Grand decided to rest. Taking a drink of spirit juice, he stared at the moonlit trail ahead of him. Another gulp warmed his throat, and he was lifting the vessel to his lips for a third swallow when a glow caught his eye. Torchlight. Off the trail, Grand hid in a patch of bushes. He watched the line of gatherers heading toward Twin Oaks. He counted: twenty-five. Seeing this gave him more reason to move.

At the pace the gatherers were traveling, the village was sure to be asleep when they attacked. He hoped his mother and his dogs stayed safe. As for his father, he had lost his caring.

A wild thought passed briefly through his head. That he should join the gatherers and slay the whole council. If he had the gods' favor, the gatherers would fulfill his notion. If not that, then what if he trailed them to watch the gatherers sack the village? No. He needed to get away, because Ric Sayed and all the men he could roster would chase after him as soon as the news spread.

The avengers chasing after Grand Moon spotted torches in the distance. Jos Doone ran ahead to see more clearly. Recognizing the gatherers, Jos came back and warned them. They took positions in the brush on both sides of the trail. The nine archers spread apart on one side and readied their bows. On the opposite side, the eight men armed with spears hunkered down in the bushes.

Closing in on the village, the gatherers extinguished the torches. Continuing on the trail, they marched two abreast. The leader ordered silence.

Hearing them coming, Jos Doone set an arrow. The others readied theirs. They waited until the gatherers were before them, and Jos released a shaft. The arrow penetrated the front man's side above his waist. He staggered several steps and collapsed to the dirt.

The one man down caused the formation to break apart. The other archers released their projectiles. Six additional men dropped to the ground, and before the gatherers could defend themselves, another spray of arrows came, taking down five more men. The leader ordered his men back, and they retreated into the brush.

Hiding behind a bush, Evon sprang up in front of the leader with his spear. He thrust his short lance into the charging brute's belly. Taking the hit, the leader pushed his own longer spear in front of him and into Evon's throat. Both men crumpled to the ground.

While Evon lay choking on his blood, the rest of the villagers revealed themselves with spearpoints and seven more gatherers fell, bleeding. Dropping their weapons, the five remaining gatherers surrendered.

Roth rushed to Evon. He sat and held him to his chest. Evon clutched Roth's wrist, blinked several times, gasped and died. Crying, Roth screamed for help. Talon and Sharpe came to him. They offered their hands. Shaking his head, Roth stood on his own. He glared at the man who had killed Evon.

On his back, with Evon's spear poking his gut, the gatherer tried to sit up. Roth dashed to him and grasped the shaft. Covered in Evon's blood, with his weight behind him, Roth ground the spear into the killer's stomach and twisted the lance. The man's shrieking encouraged Roth to wrench the spearpoint in and out of his abdomen. He kept jabbing even after the man became silent and his life escaped him.

Some of the bodies had leather satchels strapped to their backs; Roth tugged one off and dumped the contents on the ground. Dozens of jute strips and a capped goatskin vessel. He opened the end and sniffed. Lamp oil. A pouch with gray powder. He showed Yar.

Forcing the captives to their knees, Yar held his flint against the throat of the closest one. "What were your orders?"

The man sneered at him and he shouted, "I say nothing!"

Without hesitating, Yar sliced across his neck and pulled his head up. He twisted his face toward his comrades. The pulses of blood squirted at the other gatherers. He let him fall face first in the dirt.

Before he questioned the next man, Sharpe lit a torch. Berm and Talon grasped hold of that man by his arms. With the torch in his hand, Sharpe stepped in front of Yar and faced the man.

From behind Sharpe, Yar hollered, "Tell us your orders!"

The man spit at Sharpe, but Sharpe wiped the spittle off with the back of his arm and grinned at him. Abruptly, he held the torch under the captive's loin skin. Screaming, the man begged, "I will tell! I will tell!"

But Sharpe raised the torch to the man's face and shoved it against his open mouth. His beard and hair burst into flames, and Berm and Talon let him free. He ran away blazing, but Jos placed an arrow through his back.

The next three men started jabbering. Picking one, Yar held some of the jute up in his face. "What are these straps for?"

"To bind the slaves. The women."

"And the lamp oil?"

"To burn the huts."

"What is this powder?"

"Poison. The prodon ordered that we taint the drinking pots."

In only a few moments, the villagers learned that all the nearby villages were targeted. Also, they discovered the attack on Twin Oaks was to occur at first light. The big news was the prodon's army planned to move east on the morning of the full moon. They would no longer need to fear them.

After learning all the gatherers had to share, Yar picked up one of their battle clubs, and one at a time he crushed their skulls.

The villagers took the weapons from the dead and anything else they found useful. Some of the archers reclaimed their arrows from the corpses. One man thought himself clever, playing dead. Yar walked among them, prodding the bodies with his spear. Closing in on the trickster, the man tried to scramble away. Yar pierced him between the shoulder blades.

The consensus among them was that Grand Moon no longer seemed important. In truth, once Ric Sayed learned of the treachery, Grand was a dead man. The storyteller was so much more than a talker—his skill as a tracker and warrior had few equals.

"Another group is headed to Seaside Hill," said Sharpe. "Someone needs to warn them."

"Why do not we go from here?" asked Roth. "We can get behind them."

"No," said Yar. "We need more men. Let us go back to the village. When we near Seaside Hill, we can warn them with drums."

"The gatherers will hear the warning."

"Perhaps," said Yar. "But the villagers will gather arms and we will be ready for battle."

Roth and Talon carried Evon's body. The rest of the dead they left for the dire wolves and death eaters.

CHAPTER 36

Defending Seaside Hill

To raise some help to protect Seaside Hill, Yar Awell woke the whole village.

He yelled as he passed between the huts. "Gatherers tried to sack our village! Evon Nyte is dead! Who will defend Seaside Hill?"

Falk Moon dashed from his hut. He stopped Yar. "What of my son?"

"Gone. In our chase we interrupted an attack by gatherers. We vanquished all twenty-five, but Evon Nyte died in battle. I questioned some first. There are raiders heading to Seaside Hill and River Shore. The attacks are planned for first light. The prodon moves east. He ordered his gatherers to take all the harvest and kill any who resist."

"You can warn Seaside Hill in time, but River Shore is too far."

"Will you come?" asked Yar.

Falk nodded, dashed into his hut, and returned with his bow and arrow-filled quiver.

At the assembly near the trailhead, twelve-year-old Witt burst among the volunteers. In his hands, he held his grandfather's battle club.

"What do you think you are doing?" asked Roth.

"I claim vengeance against the gatherers!" demanded Witt.

"Go home," said Roth. "Comfort your mother and sister. Leave us to avenge Evon."

Sneering, Witt said, "You have no say over me! Having no father, no grandfather, and no older brother makes this my birthright."

"Very well. You best be true with Evon's bludgeon, lest there be no more to carry the Nyte family name in Twin Oaks."

This Witt had not thought of before. Should he die, then no other men in the village would bear the Nyte name. Gripping the club, he said to himself, "So be it."

Council member Pal Lukan led the thirty-eight volunteers to Seaside Hill. The bright moonlight gave them visibility. Two of the men near the front of the column carried drums.

Earlier, when Yar Awell had questioned the gatherers, they told him the attack would come from the seashore. With that in mind, they chose to warn the village from the hillside.

Nearing the village, the drummers beat the danger warning. Three-one-three-one, over and over. Yar blew a drawn-out toot on his bison horn.

Some men came from their huts. To the first of the villagers, Yar yelled, "Gatherers! They come from the seashore! Assemble defenders!"

Pal led them through the center of Seaside Hill. The drumbeat brought some men from their huts.

Recognizing the men from Twin Oaks, Ric Sayed shouldered his bow and quiver and ran to them.

"Yar Awell? What brings you and these men here armed?"

"At daybreak, gatherers are set to attack Seaside Hill from the shore."

"How do you know this?"

"We stopped an attack on Twin Oaks. Before I crushed their heads, several gatherers told of this assault and of another at River Shores."

"How many were there?" asked Ric.

"Twenty-five." Tipping his chin toward the east, Yar said, "The sun rises soon."

Ric hollered, "To the battlements!"

Five years previously, following the first gatherer raid, Ric Sayed had begged the council to construct defensive places around the village. The council considered the suggestion, but decided such a venture would bring the wrath of the prodon on them. During those years, Ric accomplished the task himself by gradually altering the landscape. He had cleared some areas and left groups of strategically positioned heavy shrubs. The sites he made concealed several men, and no one could approach through the open areas surrounding the village unseen.

Ready for battle, the Twin Oaks villagers charged to the foliage at the boundaries and took positions. The archers readied their arrows. The Seaside Hill townsfolk filled in the gaps and waited.

In the dim dawn light, the head gatherer spread his men out. Armed with battle axes, clubs, and spears, they slunk from tree to tree. When no more cover concealed them, they crawled. At the outskirts of the village, the leader expected a sentry. There were none. The wind was right, so no dogs were barking. He raised a hand and waved forward. Before his men charged, the thunderous whoop from a hundred voices brought the gatherers to their feet.

"Disarm yourselves or die!" hollered Ric.

The leader hooted, and along with a score of his men they stormed toward the village. Fifty-eight archers released arrows. The wind of the feathered shafts streaming through the air resounded like an angry bee swarm. Striking their targets, the projectiles thudded as they hit. In a breath, multiple shafts pierced each of them. They fell, their bodies twitching, to the ground. Confused, the remaining men froze in place.

The archers readied a second volley. Again Ric yelled, "Disarm or die!"

Seeing their leader and comrades so full of arrows, the survivors tossed their weapons, slumped to their knees, and raised their hands.

The Seaside Hill villagers converged on the gatherers; several elders joined them. Shaking a fist, council leader Arch Fogg said, "Now the prodon will sack our village!"

Grabbing a satchel off a gatherer's back, Ric faced the elders. He showed them the jute, the lamp oil, and the poison.

"These men did not come for tribute but for women slaves, all our bounty, to burn our homes, and poison the rest."

"Ric speaks true," said Pal Lukan. "We go to River Shores."

"If the gatherers attacked there now, then we can do little to save them."

"Agreed, but we cannot allow any gatherers to return to the prodon."

"Then make haste to River Shores," said Arch. He called out, "Someone fetch Oster! Have him bring cords to truss these men."

Smoke guided them to River Shores, too late to save the village. Closer, the whooping, screaming, and yelping dogs could be heard. The Seaside Hill and Twin Oaks archers spread out and approached from the edge of the woods.

Spotting a gatherer about to club a kneeling prisoner, Roth let an arrow loose. The shaft plowed into his ribs. He dropped the club and fell backwards. With a few saws on the prisoner's bindings, Roth freed him. The man, Sal Jamon, a hunter, took the dead gatherer's club and chased after one of the raiders.

Surprised by the sudden attack, the gatherer leader grabbed a pregnant woman by her hair and held a blade against her throat. He pushed her in front of him as a shield. Taller than her, he squatted to the bawling woman's level.

"Cease or this woman dies!" called the man.

At the edge of the camp, with a view of half of the man's face, Sharpe Awell held the tension of his bow and waited for a lull in the breeze. He aimed and released his arrow. The projectile vaulted through the smoke-filled air. The arrow struck the leader's right eye, penetrating his skull. His body failed to realize his death as he crouched holding the woman to his chest. Finally, his legs failed and the woman collapsed on top of him.

With his grandfather's battle club over his head, Witt charged a gatherer brandishing a war axe. Behind him, Roth trotted with an arrow strung. Having lost his friend Pine, he vowed to himself to protect Witt.

Running at the brute, Witt screamed, "For my grandfather!"

His fling caused the club to tumble, and when it struck the gatherer flat on, it drove the man's war axe into his throat. Blood spewed with his strangled cry.

At the edge of the village, movement to his side jerked Todd around. He spotted a gatherer carrying a woman over his shoulder, trekking toward the woods. Another raider bearing plunder ran behind him.

Too far for a sure shot, Todd chased after them. Several defenders from Seaside Hill pursued the gatherers as well. About to lose them in the spruce forest, Cayl Wonn let his arrow go. The shaft drove into the ass cheek of the man carting the woman. The man staggered, dropped the woman, and hobbled into the trees.

The other gatherer caught a shaft in the middle of his back. The shock caused him to straighten and toss his booty. He twirled in an awkward dance and fell flat on his face.

Determined to catch the wounded gatherer, Cayl dropped his bow, scooped up an abandoned war axe, and dashed after him. Because of the breeze, smoke overwhelmed the fir and spruce trees. The sunlight only clouded vision.

Todd and another defender followed Cayl while a third attended the woman. When the man squatted by her, the woman squeezed her eyes shut. "Be safe, woman. I am Kase Smit from Seaside Hill. Can you move?"

The woman opened her eyes. She blinked. "My son? Where is my son?"

"Let me help you." He offered his hand. "Can you tell me your name?"

"I am Etta Rhue."

"We will find your son together."

Etta took his hand and pointed to her ruined hut. Keeping her back, Kase used a stick to lift some of the smoldering skins that had been her roof. Taking a breath, he raised a piece covering a lump. Only empty bedding.

The hearth collapsed, and Kase scoured the area. None of the pottery had survived, but neither was her son's body anywhere in the hut. "Is this where you last saw your son?"

"Ludden was here, but gatherers were everywhere."

"How old is he?"

"Nine winters."

"Come. We will keep searching."

In the place where they were laying the bodies, Kase blocked Etta.

"I will look for you."

"No, these are my clan." Etta wiped her eyes with her forearm. "If my son is among the dead, it is for me to know."

Nodding, he let her pass. She stared at each body—all five elders had been killed, and eleven more husbands and fathers lay with their skulls split. Among them, the healer. Then her heart broke. Two young mothers and their infants. Killed because they would not give up their babies. No other children lay among the dead.

Nearby, they searched amongst the injured. Etta's heart raced. Trembling on a mat, a boy her son's size faced away. However, when she reached him, she recognized Ludden's friend Wyle. Milky blisters pocked his reddened back and swollen leg. Unable to aid the boy, with Kase's help she continued her hunt.

Out of arrows, Roth abandoned his bow and reached for a battle axe near a dead gatherer. The man came alive with a blade. Roth jerked from the movement, but the knife caught him in the side. He backpedaled, and before the gatherer made it to his feet, Roth had the axe over his shoulder. With the blade aimed at Roth's groin, the gatherer lunged—too slow, Roth's swing caught the man in the face. He rolled on his back and Roth stomped on his neck, holding his weight on him until he stopped twitching.

Grasping his injury, Roth held his side. Blood oozed from the wound. Staggering, he went to a nearby tree and leaned against it. Slowly, Roth bent his knees and slid until his butt hit the ground. He held his side and closed his eyes.

Finally the mêlée ended. After freeing the tethered villagers and assembling their wounded, the defenders made a count of dead gatherers. Twenty-three. Two were missing. One, they learned, was being pursued by Cayl Wonn and some others. The whereabouts of the last man were a mystery. Ric Sayed and Pal Lukan organized a search.

In the woods, leaning against a tree, the gatherer bit on a hunk of bark. He clutched the shaft with both hands. Grimacing, he tugged the shaft from his buttock. The arrowhead remained lodged in his hip. The pain kept him propped against the tree. The smoke choked him; his deep breathing interfered with his ability to listen for the men following him. He took a breath and held it. Not sensing anyone, he let out the air.

Moving from tree to tree, Cayl mostly studied the ground, following the dark dribbles of blood. Clutching the axe, he treaded cautiously. Every so often he stopped and stared at the smoke.

Sidestepping, Cayl moved right and peered around the thick trunk of a spruce. When he spotted the man, he tossed a stone opposite himself. The gatherer faced the sound and Cayl charged. At the last moment, the gatherer turned. Cayl swung the axe from his shoulder at a downward angle. The flint bit into the man's belly and he slid to the ground. Shoving first, Cayl jerked his blade free and the man's eyes widened. A burst of blood and spittle gushed from his mouth as he gasped and coughed. The tipless arrow fell from his hand. For a moment his fingers flexed as if trying to retrieve it. Then they stopped.

Hearing the others, Cayl called to them. His friend, the butcher's son Lek Ryne, and Todd Pyre from Twin Oaks rushed to the sound of his voice. Seeing the slain gatherer, they helped Cayl drag the man to the pile of dead.

On their way back to what had been Etta's home, a cry turned her and Kase around.

"Mamma!"

"Ludden?"

When she did not spot him, Ludden called from above. "Up here! In the tree!"

Tears welled in Etta's eyes as she held her arms open for her son. Dirty and bleeding from a scraped knee, he climbed down and ran to her. They embraced. Satisfied the two had reunited, Kase headed to where the Seaside Hill villagers were congregating. He was halfway there when a savage howl spun his head.

With his axe overhead and a war cry from his mouth, the gatherer rushed toward the mother and son. Ludden saw the brute coming at them. With all his strength, Ludden shoved his mother away and rolled backwards. The axe whizzed between them and struck the ground. The attacker stumbled. He lost his grip on the weapon and landed on his chest in the dirt.

Recovering, on his knees, the gatherer groped for the handle of his axe. Behind him, the woman whisked it away. With a fist on the ground, he began to gain his feet. Her swing was wild, but the edge of the axe sliced a red line diagonally across his back. Growling, he spun. He leaped at her, but she backpedaled and the gatherer landed face down. Huffing, Kase rushed up with his battle club over his shoulder. The gatherer raised his head only to meet Kase's bludgeon. The blow came down on the gatherer's skull with a wet thud.

Climbing to her feet, Etta said, "For saving our lives, we are your servants."

"Have you no man?"

"No. My man drowned three years past. And you, Kase Smit, are you without a woman?"

Gaping at the smoldering ruins, Kase said, "It is so that I have no woman and that has been my choice. To be indebted to serve for saving a life is said to be our way, but I will not hold you to that practice."

"To serve is a willing thing for me, and to not attend to the one whose life I owe would trouble me until my death."

"Very well. Since this is your choice, it will be for you to make the talk to my village and kin."

"What is your trade?"

"I am a wood carver."

"Would you teach Ludden?"

"If he is of mind to learn."

"His mind will fare."

CHAPTER 37

The Aftermath

SINCE THE RIVER Shores herbalist had been killed and his hut burned, Witt sought supplies from the gatherers' booty. Of the things he needed, honey was all he found. That and some unbroken clay bowls.

After fetching water from the river, he heated rocks and boiled it. Then he warmed the honey and cut skins for bandages. As best he could, he treated their injuries. Many needed true healers, but he offered comfort anyway.

Relief came near midday when the Seaside Hill herbalist and Witt's sister, Neva, came with several helpers.

"Witt? I brought Ryne Willet from Seaside Hill."

He had met the woman at Pine and Lily's wedding. Witt nodded to her.

"Your brother has proved himself," said Ryne.

"Not so," said Witt. Tears welled in his eyes. "Honey stops bleeding and soothes some. With nothing else for treatment, I cured no one."

Neva placed a hand on her brother's shoulder. "Curing takes time. All your care did comfort. With me, I have all-heal herb, mashed ginger root, shave grass powder, crushed arnica flowers, and wolf roots."

Holding out his hands, he said, "Let me have some arnica flowers and some wolf roots and I will tend to the burned folks."

"For the worst of them, Ryne has skill with snakeweed."

"There are some need some soon, else they might pain to death."

Already keen on who hurt the worst, Witt pointed them out to Ryne. Taking measure of their injuries, Ryne counted snakeweed seeds and asked those that were able to swallow them with water.

In the smoke, stunned villagers staggered about, searching for loved ones and neighbors or simply lost in shock. Among them, Neva looked for any injured. She spotted a man's legs splayed on the ground with his back against a tree. Her heart seemed to stop when she saw Roth's pale face. He was still alive, and Neva held him. She recognized Syd and Talon and called to them for help. Seeing their friend, they rushed over and carried Roth to the clearing Neva had set up for care. Examining the injury, she found it wider than deep—no organs, only flesh. While Roth stayed unconscious, Neva used a porcupine quill and squirrel tendons to close the cut.

Alone with him, Neva said, "Roth Uhl, you'd better not die." On his back with his feet raised, Roth's color improved. She brushed the hair away from his face. "Do not think I have not noticed how you watch me when you think no one sees you? I grow impatient for your asking me to court."

Roth's eyes fluttered open. "Neva?" His voice sounded raspy.

She helped him sit up and gave him a drink of water from a gourd. He swallowed some and said, "Your mother told me no."

"When did you ask her?"

"At the end of spring."

"After you heal, we will ask her together."

As well as he could, Roth grinned. "But you say yes?"

"Yes." She pushed his head down. "Now rest while I tend to others."

On the path to the river, a tethered group of women called for help. Rescuers untied them and they joined the others hunting for family, friends, and any remnant of their lives.

While the Twin Oaks and Seaside Hill warriors stacked enemy bodies for cremation, the River Shores survivors assembled and tallied their casualties. Twenty dead and sixteen wounded. Five of those folks still faced death. A third of the village, leaving a score of widows and several orphan children to be cared for. No huts remained, but the boats moored in the river were spared any damage.

The Era of Herbalists

The Seaside Hill elders had decided. Until the fourteen captives could prove their worth, they would serve as slaves. The skinner, Oster Dopt, secured their ankles so the men could walk but not run. With spear tips poised and archers at the ready, the captives piled their comrades' corpses atop one another. So as to make the captives witness their friends' end, the people made them place the bodies face up.

Under watchful eyes, the captives collected firewood. Once they had amassed enough fuel, the villagers poured the oil the raiders brought to burn the huts over the dead as well as the wood. While the captives faced their former companions, a villager lit the funeral pyre. The flames enveloped the dead gatherers. All day long, the captives fed the fire until the bodies became ash.

Runners spread the word to Seaside Hill and Twin Oaks of the devastating attack at River Shores. The villagers all contributed something, mostly food, hut skins, and bedding. One generous villager from Seaside Hill supplied a nanny goat.

At midday, the parade of helpers carrying supplies descended on River Shores.

Knowing about the poisoned water, the helpers dumped the drinking pots. Then the helpers went to boil fresh water.

On the walk back to Seaside Hill, Ric asked Yar, "Tell me. How did you interrupt the raid on your village?"

"We were a band in pursuit of Grand Moon. He killed Clem Doone."

"Clem? Why?"

"Because Clem guarded him in the pit and Grand killed him to escape."

"Why was he in the pit?"

"He was facing trial for snatching Lily."

Ric whipped around and grabbed Yar by the arm. "What do you speak? That Lily did not drown herself?"

Pulling himself free, Yar said, "Some found proof Grand held Lily in a cave up the east hill."

"Where is she? Did he kill her?"

"Signs showed she crawled in a hole inside the cave. We called her but got no answer. Hole was too small for a man to crawl."

"What cave? Show me."

With the sun low in the sky, Yar guided Ric up the hill, pointing to the places where they found evidence of Grand's trek to the cave. Because of the late hour, they each carried torch makings.

"This hill is known to me," said Ric. "When I was a boy, my father brought me here to listen to the gods sing."

"Same with me. But I heard no gods singing, only the whistling of the north wind."

The two men stopped at the fire thorn bush. "This is where Grand fell into the fire thorns. Seventeen pricked his face."

"Seventeen summers ago, Lily was born."

"Gives a man thought when signs show. Got poked by one once, hurt like being burned."

The men continued up the hill to the cave entrance. Already Ric could visualize how Grand had used the boulder to block Lily inside. They fashioned torches and lit them.

Inside, Ric went directly to the hole at the back of the cave. On his knees, he reached inside with the flaming light. Peering in, the glow only allowed him to see so far. Suddenly a rush of wind blew the flames at him. The blaze scorched his fingers and he dropped the torch. It rolled the length of a man stretching, and the breeze blew it out. But not before Ric saw the expanse of the place.

"This hole is a tunnel," said Ric. He crouched and followed Yar outside. The sun hung just above the horizon.

"Somewhere there is another cave or some other way out."

"Tomorrow we will do a search," said Yar. The two men ambled down the hill. On the way, Ric asked, "Where do you think Grand Moon will run?"

"His trail points him south."

"The prodon's territory? Do you think he would join them?"

"Perhaps. He sees himself as above others, but has no forethinking."

The Era of Herbalists

At sunrise the next day, Ric rallied some friends as well as some of the Twin Oaks folks. Beginning at the cave where they could see the hole, they spread apart and began scouring the hill. Everyone agreed the hole Lily had crawled into had an exit; they all felt the wind. No one was sure what to search for, only a place for her to escape.

The gap his daughter had crawled into pointed north, but Ric knew the tunnel would not keep a straight path. With Yar with him, Ric scaled the hill. On top he turned a circle and peered out at the distant landscapes. To the east, a cascade of hills butted against this one, all the way to the white capped mountains. West, Twin Oaks, and past the marsh, the sea. North from there, a patch of rolling hills leading to his village and further on, the blue river and the smoking remnants of River Shores. South, more hills and a seemingly endless prairie leading to the green river and the prodon. For a moment Ric searched for a sign of Grand. Death eaters circled the sky in that direction. Ric guessed they were there for the raiders killed by the band pursuing Grand.

Without a clue, Ric prayed to the gods to give him a direction. If the gods answered, Ric did not hear them, and if they touched him, what he felt was what had touched him all along, the wind.

CHAPTER 38

Lost in a Nameless Gorge

DREAMING WHILE DRIFTING inside the cavern river, Lily lay on cool green grass with sunshine warming her face. The dream ended and she woke abruptly. A raven was perched on her arm. She screamed and dunked herself underwater. The nasty bird flew into the sky squawking. Lily surfaced, coughing. Calming herself, she spotted cattails and the shore, so she swam to the shallows and walked to a sandy beach. She surveyed her surroundings, and studied the steep walls of the canyon on both sides of the river. This place was nowhere she had ever been or heard spoken of. From the position of the sun, she guessed this was midday, and soon she would be in shade. Lily struggled out of her soaked dress, wrung it out, and draped it along with the empty goatskin bag across some cattails.

While her garment dried, Lily foraged. She gathered some cattail stalks and a handful of blackberries. A tree above dropped a few black shell nuts. She collected them and some curly dock leaves. Hungry, she bashed the nuts with a river rock. A bit green, but she ignored the bitter taste and ate them anyway. Same with the blackberries, they too needed more days to ripen. But sour or not, Lily consumed them along with the sweeter cattail stalk and dock leaves.

Along the canyon wall, Lily found a hunk of obsidian and smashed it against a boulder. The second strike yielded a sharp wedge. First she unraveled the lacing and split the thong and the goatskin in half. She laid a foot in the fur side and folded what she had to form a crude moccasin. Identifying the waste, she laid the skin on a flat rock and cut off what she did not need. She did the same with the other half. Then she broke another piece of obsidian and formed a poker.

She made four holes on each side: two in the back and three in the front. With the leather lace, she strung them and tied the skins to her feet.

Examining her dress, she noticed some of her beads were missing. Probably in the cave or the lava tubes. The garment was still damp, and Lily trimmed the bottom. As she struggled with the material, the sun ducked past the gorge. Naked, she shivered and climbed into the clammy garment as soon as she had finished.

Next, Lily wanted a weapon. Among the broken pieces of obsidian she had collected, the slender pointed piece made for a spear tip. She kept the wedge that she cut the goatskin with and another wide slice that she might use as a scraper. Searching the flotsam, she found a suitable shaft.

Using the scraps from the goatskin, she secured the point to the shaft. Lily was armed. Now she needed to make a fire kit. Whacking different rocks together, Lily found two small enough to carry that made plentiful sparks. Scavenging around some plants, she found dry grass and leaves. She formed a nest and added it to the kit. In the last of the sunlight, Lily gathered firewood.

As she collected, the aroma of menthe permeated the air. A healthy patch covered the ground near a cluster of boulders. Lily decided this would be her sleeping area. The menthe would hide her scent from predators.

Before the sky darkened, Lily made a fire. Once the blaze flared, she made a torch to hunt the frogs croaking in the grass. Considering the size of the frogs, one would be all she needed. Two legs would feed her twice.

Holding the torch in front, she readied the rock and approached the grass. The croaking stopped, but she spotted the eyeshine reflecting the flame. Closing in, the frog froze, staring into the light. Looming over her prey, she pretended the frog was Grand Moon and slammed the rock on his head. Lily took her dinner back to the fire.

Hungrier than she thought, Lily ate both legs after they cooled. A storm had left puddles and Lily drank from one, lapping water like a dog. Then for a while she sat silently in front of the fire. After several kicks from the child inside her, Lily sang and rubbed her belly. "Be strong, child of mine…face your worries… be brave, child of mine…find your spirit…be not forlorn, child of Pine…his spirit travels with you…be not afraid…you are never alone…"

After the song, Lily made her bed in the menthe patch. For a few moments she laid her head back and gazed at the stars above her. Breathing in the pleasing aroma, she squirmed in the sand to form her shape. She disregarded the lumpy ground and drifted off to sleep.

A mournful howl caused Lily to wake and sit up. In the darkness, she grasped hold of her makeshift spear and listened for another dire wolf call. Just as she believed the sound only the remnant of a dream, a wolf howled from the cliff above her. The reply came from the opposite side. More whine than howl. Lovers separated? Like she and Pine.

A peek at the waxing moon told her this was the fourth night since waking in the cave. Anxious for the daylight, Lily closed her eyes and returned to her dreaming.

CHAPTER 39

Lost and Found

TIRED AFTER HIKING all day, Grand found a suitable rock on a hillside, shed his pack, and sat. The vista overlooked the remnants of a village. Hut skeletons covered the flats along with deserted firepits. By the time he reached the stream that ran through the place, the sun had vanished below the horizon.

Flint shards littered the ground. Grand guessed this place had been the prodon's weapons quarry. But why was it abandoned?

Scrounging, Grand assembled a shelter and laid out his bedroll. Confident none of the Twin Oaks villagers were near, he started a fire. No matter what the outcome, the gatherer attack overruled any concerns for him.

Spreading out his booty, he took some smoked elk strips and dried plums for his meal. As he chewed his meat, the sight of the spirit juice caused him to abandon his food and he drank several swallows.

A vision of his father striking him passed through his mind, and Grand cursed to the sky for the gods to punish his father until tears streaked his cheeks. Then another image came to him of bludgeons breaking his father's head open. Grand laughed at the thought and drank more spirit juice.

Howling from the west shattered the silence: a pack of dire wolves. From the ruckus, a considerable horde. Grand put more wood on the fire and propped his spear within reach. Concerned for his meat, he clutched the bundle to his chest. As suddenly as the uproar began, silence returned and Grand relaxed.

Finishing his meal, Grand threw some more wood on. He stashed his pack of booty in the back of his makeshift hut. Before he crawled in his bed nest, he took another drink of spirit juice. Snug inside, he closed his eyes and drifted off to sleep.

A crack of thunder woke him. He raised up and peeked outside. In the east, a flash of white light streaked down from the sky, and a few moments later, a roar rumbled. Checking the roof of his hut, he set some more skin scraps. Satisfied, he wriggled into his furs and tried to go back to sleep.

Soon the roaring became steady with increasing intensity. The ground under him vibrated. Confused, Grand scooted out of his bed and checked outside. East of him, in the three-quarter moonlight, he saw a wall of dust. Bison. A stampede heading right for him. A short distance away, he spotted a gnarled dead tree. The beasts were coming closer. With the bison nearly on top of him, Grand grabbed hold of a branch and pulled himself up. Hundreds of fleeing animals charged around the tree. With Grand holding on, the tree shook with the pounding hoofs to the point where he thought they would topple it. The wind from their breathing brought their musky breath to Grand, and he struggled to keep from retching.

Finally, the beasts passed and when he hopped down, he found that nothing remained of the camp. He surveyed the damage. His bow and quiver of arrows, crushed to pieces. The same with his spears. The obsidian tips, mashed to flakes. No sign of the bundle of food, and he found the pigskin vessel of spirit juice trampled into a muddy splotch. Even his bedroll was battered to shreds.

Frustrated and angry, Grand shook his fist and cursed the gods in the sky. However, when the gods answered, he received a steady rain in his face.

In the morning light, Grand stumbled on the pitted ground, searching for anything useful. So far, he had found a fractured spear tip. What he needed was a fire starter kit, a blade, a shaft for the spear, jute, any kind of vessel, and something to drink. The bison had trampled the stream, but ahead Grand spotted some rock formations. He headed there hoping for puddles.

Along the way, Grand discovered something else the bison had stomped away: the trail. On this flat plain, only the sun and the hills around him gave him any sense of direction.

The Era of Herbalists

Approaching the formation, Grand spotted some long yellow sticks poking up. Closer, at a niche in the rocks, he saw where goats had been kept. Tugging a shaft out of the soil, he untied the jute cords linking them and gaped at the smooth, segmented surface. He hefted it and jammed it in the dirt. Light, but sturdy. Wanting the longest, he yanked them all out. The one he chose made for a short spear. Until he found something better, this one would do.

On top of the boulders, Grand found plenty of puddles, but all he could do was lap the water like a dog. He needed a vessel. Scouting around the rocks, he walked to the area the bison had spared. Among the many plants, he found a vine with several gourds. The driest one was also the smallest of them. Carefully, he broke off the stem and shook out the seeds.

Combing the ground, Grand found a flint wedge someone had tried to fashion but never finished. As crude as it was, the flint would do for a blade. Then he dipped the gourd into the deepest puddle, filled it, and drank it dry. He filled it again, seized his spear, and set off in search of food.

Wandering about, Grand searched for signs of prey. Around a black nut tree, he found a well-traveled trail pointing south. That path led Grand to a three-way fork. He could see the right trail went up a steep hill with switchbacks. The middle road seemed to skirt the hill, and the one on the left went down to a ravine. Even though the middle trail seemed less traveled, the path seemed easier to walk, and he followed it. More forks offered choices, and Grand followed the ones with more prey prints. At sunset he found only insects and lizards. As hungry as he was, those things were nothing he would choose to eat.

With nightfall approaching, Grand searched for a place to sleep. Holding no fire kit, he worried predators would find him. A slide on the side of the hill gave him a place. He cleared some of the shale and squirmed into a sleeping position. Listening to the sounds of the night, he closed his eyes. The droning insects seemed his only sentries. Each time they silenced, he listened and braced for footfalls sneaking up on him. Laying his lance across his belly, he shivered and embraced himself and eventually, he fell asleep.

The chill of the morning woke Grand before the sun's first glow. To warm himself, he did a sort of dance as he rubbed himself. Thirst and hunger drove him back to the trail. Gradually the sky brightened and Grand quickened his pace.

Pig tracks crossed the path. Kneeling, he studied the ground. Grand determined the prints were recent: a sow and five piglets. He followed them into the brush. The pigs meandered, taking him deeper into the scrub.

Squealing gave Grand a direction, and he cut through the foliage toward the ruckus. The sound grew louder as he pushed through the bushes, careful not to spill his water. He used the spear to shove branches aside. One broke with a loud crack, and the sow shrieked noisily and she and her brood bolted. Thick brush forced him to go around. Once he broke through to the sow's route, the piglets' cries faded in the distance. Grand gave up his chase.

The thicket gave him no course to cut through to the trail. He backtracked and followed that to where the pigs crossed his footpath.

In the sky in front of him, Grand spotted death eaters circling. He quickened his pace. Without warning, the trail ended at a sheer precipice. Below, a mass of people were gathered on the shore by a green river. Downstream, Grand saw a barge heading toward them. From his view, the oarsmen were paddling against the current.

Above him, far off to his right, he spotted the path down. With the sun high in the sky, he finished his water and climbed the rocks to the trail. At the top, Grand watched some of the people board the barge. From the count, it seemed to him that four more barges were needed to bring everyone along. Too far to tell, but to Grand it seemed that most of the people were slaves. A dozen or so armed gatherers corralled them into a group.

It worried him that, should the gatherers see him, he would be made a slave, or worse, killed. For that reason, he chose to wait until dark.

Down below, torches were lit. Grand started down the track. The moon had yet to rise, so he depended on the stars to place his feet. Closer, he watched another barge arrive. Some of the gatherers caught lines thrown to them, and they towed the barge behind the one being boarded.

While all were focused on the boats, Grand hustled down the path. At the bottom, the gatherer guards faced the river. Creeping toward the group, Grand tripped on a loose pile of bamboo. He landed on his knees. As he picked up his spear and rose, a lance point poked his back.

"Poe! Look what I caught."

A bald gatherer rushed up and kicked Grand's stomach, and he went down on his ass. The other man stomped on his wrist and Grand let go of his makeshift weapon. A spear tip jabbed him behind his ear. Another prodded his side, and a hand pulled his blade from his sash. A torch flashed in front of Grand's face.

"What should we do with this pillager?"

"Bait for the river monster!" said Poe. "Alton! Ragger! Bring me some cords. Long ones to tease the monster."

Panicked, Grand looked for somewhere to run. Sensing Grand's change of posture, the guard moved the spear from behind his ear to his neck.

"Bloody bait may lure the river monster faster."

Two men manhandled Grand to his feet and tied his hands in front of him with jute cord. The lance prodded his back and he moved to the barge.

"What are you bringing on my boat?" asked a burly man at the ramp.

"Not for you, tillerman, he is bait for the river monster," said Poe.

"He is a stout brute and I need another oarsman. Unless you wish the work yourself, you should let me have him row."

Not wanting to become an oarsman, Poe said, "Take him, but keep him tethered. Caught him sneaking around, armed."

"Up the ramp with you," said the tillerman. He led Grand to a bench with an oar. "Sit." He pointed.

Grand scooted on the bench, and the tillerman pushed the oar to him. "Do what the man in front of you does. If you do it right, you will keep your fingers from getting mashed."

Staring at the man in front of him, Grand grasped the oar.

"Relax," said the tillerman. "A bison horn will call you to row."

"I need food and water," said Grand.

"Water you can have," said the tillerman. He dipped a gourd in a water pot and handed it to Grand. "Food comes with work."

Taking the gourd, Grand drank. Afterwards he returned the vessel to the tillerman.

More slaves climbed aboard, and the tillerman ordered them to sit and be silent. The stench of them gagged Grand and he locked his jaws to keep from retching. A voice behind him said, "Make sure you heave over the side, elsewise old Eval will make you clean the whole barge."

"My nose wishes to die."

"Cannot smell them when we go on the river."

The boat drifted away from the shore. The bison horn blew and the oarsmen grasped their oars. A drummer pounded a single beat on a drum and, like all of them, Grand dipped his oar in the water. The tillerman called, "Stroke!" The drum beat a cadence and Grand pulled back in time with the man in front, and when that man lifted his oar, so did Grand. Barely avoiding smashing his fingers, Grand got into the rhythm.

The current made the rowing less demanding. Still, the constant effort strained Grand's muscles. The promise of food drove him, but his hunger weighed on him. With nothing to eat, he swallowed his own spit and rowed.

CHAPTER 40

The Caravan

THE ROAD MAKERS stopped at the head of the storm. Behind them, the travelers secured their tents and hunkered down while the rain and wind gods battled with the lightning and thunder gods. For this the people were prepared. All through the mêlée the people ate and drank, told stories, sang songs, and did what all people did to tame the struggles life brings.

In the morning the road makers resumed their tasks, and the people dried what had gotten wet. Expecting only a half-day of travel, the people gathered berries the wind had shaken to the ground. While the grownups toiled, the children were allowed to play, but only after their chores.

Before Maita, a boy of nine years, could join his friends, his mother charged him with fetching water from the river. To bring the most, he carried three pigskin vessels. Yesterday's storm had left debris on the shore, and Maita began clearing the limbs away. He pulled on a leafy branch and yelped. At first sight he thought both the man and the dog dead. But the man's chest was rising and falling, and when he brushed leaves off the dog, he too breathed. Maita ran back to his group of travelers.

The boy returned with his father, Khuno, and his uncle, Huanca. The two men studied what Maita had found. Tangled in branches, the man held his arm around the dog that wore a decorated strap around his neck. The sign of a companion. Among his people, dogs were not unheard of; many of the people cared for them, but this beast was closer to the size of a dire wolf. Even in slumber, fear of the dog's teeth caused Huanca to wrap a leather strap around his muzzle.

Maita dashed back to the caravan for more help. Two men brought a travois, and they hauled the dog and his barely breathing master to the transient camp.

Axel the healer came from his tent. He placed his hands on the man. The skin felt colder than how a living man should be.

"Bring him inside," said Axel. He turned around and entered his tent. The men laid the stranger on a mat.

"What of the dog?" asked Khuno.

"See to his care and cage him, lest he wake frightened or angry."

Inside the tent, Axel stripped the stranger and assessed the injuries. No broken bones except for a rib or two. The bruises on his chest, arms, and legs bore a greenish tone. A sign of healing. Rolling him over, Axel gaped at the festering wound under the right shoulder blade. Upward and wider than an arrow strike, Axel guessed a spear tip had jabbed him. The stranger's skin was fairer than his people. He lifted the man's eyelids and gasped. They were gray, not brown.

Axel peered at the stranger's teeth. From the lack of wear, he surmised his life to be seventeen or eighteen years. The dryness and looseness of his skin told Axel he was starved and dehydrated. Axel wrapped the stranger in fur and prepared a poultice for the wound.

Among the stranger's garments Axel found a heavy fur pouch. Inside he took out a milk-white blade affixed to a finely decorated elk antler handle. Also, he took a spear point and a dozen arrowheads made from the same white stone. Axel admired the expertly carved black soapstone panther icon, wrapped in red fox fur. From these trappings, Axel supposed the man to be a hunter.

The medicine Axel made came from a plant he carried from his home, and so far on the journey he had not seen the purple and yellow blossoms anywhere. Next year, in the spring, plants would grow here from the seeds he sowed.

He laid his hand on the stranger's forehead. He seemed warmer, but still the man slept. The shallow breaths did not concern Axel, but the occasional wheeze did. Before he applied the poultice, he washed the gash and cut away some dead flesh. The man stayed unconscious through the process.

Khuno took the responsibility to make a cage for the dog. Knowing the dog would need to be carried, he built the cage on the back of the travois where the dog rested. Khuno lashed bamboo strips back and forth above the dog that never stirred. To give the dog room when he woke, he used most of the travois.

Khuno's son, Maita, volunteered to care for the dog until the stranger revived. Maita declared out loud that death would not find the man and the dog he had rescued.

While Maita rubbed the dog warm, Khuno insisted the strap on the dog's muzzle remain until the cage was finished and the dog was secure inside. Maita dipped a sea sponge in a pot of warmed water and herbs. He started washing at the dog's nose and worked his way to the tail. The dog never budged.

Before the travelers broke camp and resumed the trek, Zyanya, the high priestess, satisfied her curiosity by visiting Axel, the healer. Dressed in her traveling garb, she left her guards outside the tent. One of her protectors opened the healer's door cover and she entered.

Axel bowed to her, and after acknowledging the healer, she studied the stranger's oblong face. Without her asking, Axel held the stranger's eyelids open for Zyanya to see his gray eyes for herself. Zyanya stared into them. Until now she had only been told stories of different-colored eyes.

Axel showed her the contents of his hunt pouch. The moment her eyes beheld the white blade, she seized it and held it to the light. Admiring the pureness of the stone, she turned it on edge and considered the sharpness.

"The maker took much care. The blade sits firm." She examined the carvings. Gripping the elk handle, she said, "This knife fits my hand as if made for me." She slashed the air in front of her as if defending herself.

"This will be the blade for me to bleed the life from Yaotl," said Zyanya.

"The knife belongs to the stranger."

"And a paltry price for him to pay for the life we are giving him."

"Truth from your lips, Your Highness."

"See that I am told when he awakens and call for the linguists. His foggy-colored eyes and long face tell me he speaks another tongue."

"Yes, Your Highness. Forgive me, Your Highness, but the stranger is more than I can pull."

"Two of my guards will bring the stranger with us."

"My thanks, Your Highness."

With her prize safe in her own pouch, Zyanya went to see the immense dog that was the talk of the caravan.

Reaching through the bamboo bars, Maita groomed the dog with a brush that had once been among his mother Runtu's kitchen tools. The enthusiasm in her son's eyes to care for the stranger's dog impressed Runtu, so she gave Maita the brush and told him the tool needed replacing but was still good to clean with. He combed down the dog's back, and the bristles snagged. His fingers found bits of leaves and twigs tangled in the dog's black coat. After he freed them, he resumed grooming.

So far the dog's only responses had been sighs and gasps of air, like attempts to bark. Also, the dog's paws twitched from dreams. Since the dog no longer wore the strap to bind his teeth, Khuno told Maita to take extra care. But Maita daydreamed as he continued his brushing.

"Are you not afraid of the beast?" asked a voice behind him. Maita jerked. The tool dropped from his hand and he withdrew his arm from the cage. He turned and faced Zyanya. Immediately Maita dropped to his knees and stared at the dirt. "The dog sleeps, Your Highness."

"Raise yourself. How are you called?"

"Maita Tupac, Your Highness," he said. He found his feet but continued to gape at the ground.

"Are you the one who discovered the beast and the stranger?"

"Yes. Your Highness."

"Face away from me," said Zyanya.

Maita spun around, unsure of why. However, the tone of her voice gave him no fear other than the dread of having the high priestess addressing him.

Zyanya removed one of her beaded necklaces and placed it around the boy's neck. "Now all will know Maita Tupac has my favor."

For a moment, Maita stared at the turquoise beads. He fondled them. Cool and smooth. He turned around, and the priestess had gone.

From the tent, Runtu had witnessed the exchange. So as not to embarrass her son, she closed the flap and prepared for the day's journey.

CHAPTER 41

The Rest Camp Builders

UNABLE TO SEE their direction, Grand noticed a flickering glow on the back of the man in front. He turned his head enough to see torches ahead on both sides of the river. The beat doubled, and again Grand nearly smashed his hand.

Further downstream, the drummer beat a series of steady, rapid thumps. The tillerman yelled, "Stop!"

The paddlers held their oars deep in the water. The barge slowed along a torchlit shore. The tillerman edged the boat in, and men threw lines to watchers along the shore. The tillerman ordered the oars up, and those men tugged the barge against the muddy bank.

A ramp was fixed and the tillerman ordered the passengers off. Grand watched a group of gatherers at the end separating the slaves. The men were hustled off to different work groups by gatherers bearing clubs and spears.

Without being told, the oarsmen began going ashore. Grand was about to rise when a hand clamped on his shoulder. "You are to be last, pillager."

Grand recognized Poe's voice. Looking around, he saw the torches of camps on both sides of the river. More barges lined the opposite shore. As the boat emptied, a spear point nudged him. "Up and off."

At the bottom, the men made a display of prodding and poking him.

"What burden shall we bless him with?" asked a guard.

Poe slapped Grand's arm. "He can fill a place hauling barges."

"From the look of him, he can fill two places."

"Here comes the last barge. Let us see him haul it to shore."

"Come, pillager," said Poe. "Show us your worth."

The boat cruised up and a man tossed Grand a line. Grand wrapped the cord around his wrist and pulled hard. The barge passed by and Grand's feet slid. He could not stop, and suddenly he splashed in the water. The boat hauled him along with it. Four men waited farther along and lines were tossed to them. They towed the barge to the bank. The men on shore, as well as those on the boat, laughed.

Reaching out, Poe helped Grand out of the river. "Come, pillager."

"Grand is how I am called."

"Tell me why you were creeping behind us."

"For food," said Grand. "It has been two days since I have eaten."

"Your fortune is with you tonight. Follow me," said Poe. They headed for the fires.

"Must I stay bound?" asked Grand.

They stopped and Poe pulled his blade, slashing the jute holding Grand's hands together. "My thanks."

"Let us get to a fire and dry you off."

As they walked toward the scattered blazes, Grand untied his wrists. In the smoke, the aroma of cooking meat caused Grand to drool. Counting a half dozen cookfires, Grand asked, "Is there a choice of meat?"

"Surely. What is your taste?"

"Bison." He said it with spite in his voice.

Pointing, Poe led Grand to where a side of bison roasted over coals. He held two fingers to the cook, and the cook gestured to the benches.

Cutting slabs of sizzling meat, the cook signaled his helper, who brought two platters with portions of boiled turnips and red lentils. The cook placed a steak on each and served them.

Having no blade, Grand brought the whole thing to his mouth and chomped and chewed. Closing his eyes, he savored the unusual flavor. To the cook, he asked, "What taste is added?"

"Something I once traded wood for, ginger and honey. A gift from our herbalist."

Without thinking, Grand blurted, "Chirp Nyte?"

Both the cook and Poe reacted. "You know Chirp?"

Grand thought about it. He did not want Chirp to know of his presence. But he wanted these men to know his familiarity. "Personally, no. But his skill is well spoken of among my people."

"How did you come to be at the river?" asked Poe.

"In the nighttime during a storm, a bison stampede killed my hunting party," lied Grand. "If not for a tree limb, my life would have ended with them. Everything was destroyed and I sought food. The gods led me to you."

"Speak not of gods here," said Poe. "Lord Prodon is the only god."

Grand nodded and continued eating, and the cook brought gourds of spirit juice. With his in hand, Grand tipped his cup to Poe and took a sip and swallowed. Abruptly, his eyes widened and he gasped as a fire scorched his throat. Poe laughed. "The Lord Prodon's spirit juice bites back. To cure the tang, take another swallow and a third. Then you will not care."

Two of Poe's men joined them. The one who first found Grand asked, "How can you feed this pillager?"

"He is called Grand, and for me, he has proven himself worthy."

"How will he serve?" asked the other.

"With us. And be kindly, for he has just lost comrades."

"Our sympathy. I am Aric and he is Ragger."

"How did your friends die?" asked Ragger.

"Lightning frightened a herd of bison. They stormed us as we slept."

"How did you survive?"

"A nearby tree saved me."

"How many were lost?" asked Aric.

"Five."

"Let us drink for the five," said Poe. Waving to the cook, he said, "Bring us more nectar and feed my friends."

The cook bowed and returned with a full vessel. He poured them all drinks and left the container, then came back with plates for Aric and Ragger.

Fed, the four men finished the spirit juice, and the cook and his helper cleaned up around them. All at once, Grand began crying. "My dogs! I miss my dogs."

"You lost dogs as well as friends?"

Sobering enough to continue his lie, he cried out the names of his dogs and all the men in his clutch except Pine. With a promise to leave afterwards, Poe convinced the cook for one more full gourd for the dogs.

Holding onto one another, the four staggered to the guard's hut. Since Grand had no bed nest, he curled up on the dirt floor and passed out.

At sunrise, a loud but unintelligible voice woke Grand. He sat up. Throbbing in his head laid him back. He spit dirt from his mouth.

"Everyone up!" called Poe. "Lord Prodon speaks!"

Seeing his new soldier struggling, Poe offered his hand to Grand. Gaining his feet, he followed Poe and the others outside. They faced the river. Wiping his eyes, Grand gawked at the structure on the opposite shore. Try as he might, Grand did not understand Lord Prodon. He asked, "What is being said?"

"Our orders for the day," said Poe. "We are tasked to herd the slaves." Looking Grand over, he said, "Aric? Can you find a tunic for Lord Prodon's new soldier? He cannot be dressed like a slave."

Aric ducked into the hut and came out with a woven shirt. The symbols were the same as what the others wore. Grand took off his leather shirt and tossed it in a firepit.

"Might have to cut it some." He handed the shirt to Grand, who pulled it on. A tight fit, but the material stretched. Poe passed him a spear.

"Ragger, take Grand with you. Show him what to do."

"Come," said Ragger. "Let us rouse some slaves." He led Grand toward a series of lean-tos. "First, we wake them and remind them Lord Prodon provides for them. After they feed, we are tasked to herd them to the first place for the overnight camp."

"The first place?" asked Grand.

"Rest camps. We make all the odd number rests, and another group follows us, making even number camps. We do this until Lord Prodon makes a permanent camp."

"The Lord Prodon leaves the basin?"

The Era of Herbalists

"Yes, to a new valley in the east. Roadbuilders have already reached the pass between the white mountains. Lord Prodon's advance army is halfway there already."

Nobody Grand knew had ventured that far, but stories of the ancestors spoke of vast plains and healing waters. And most assuredly, beyond Ric Sayed's reach. He smiled as he kicked a slave awake.

Gains and Losses

THE EARLY DAWN chill woke Lily. Deep in the gorge, the sun would be a long time before shining on her. But the dim glow gave her enough light to see. With the trimmings from her dress, she fashioned a carry pouch. Adding the obsidian wedge and scraper to the pack, she gathered some berries and a handful of menthe. Singing a blessing song, she slung the makeshift pack on her shoulder. With the river on her right, she grasped her spear and started hiking.

Having no other choice, Lily followed the river through the narrow canyon, and it came to her that this path was not unlike her struggle through the lava tube, the difference being she had sight. However, looking ahead gave her no bearing. The river meandered, and the steep canyon walls seemed to end only to snake this way or that.

Birds kept her company with their songs, and her singing back to them lifted the weight of her plight. Also, their constant presence assured her no predators threatened her and her pace gave the birds no reason to fly away, only to flit ahead to another limb to sing from.

Further down the gorge, the puddles had dried and thirst motivated her to drink from the river. She rationalized that she had already swallowed a fair amount yesterday, and nothing troubled her today. At a suitable spot, she squatted and scooped with her hands cupped. The water tasted fresh, and she took several drinks before continuing her trek.

As she wandered, she studied the ground around her, searching for anything to aid her. Some sticks and twigs from the land above were strewn about, nothing she needed now. Her continued vigilance paid off when she found a gourd plant. Three seemed dry enough, and she chose the smaller of them and fashioned a cup.

At what must have been midday, the sun shone on the canyon floor. Taking advantage of the heat, Lily slipped off her makeshift moccasins, stripped off her dress, waded into the river, and washed herself. She let the sun dry her and took advantage of the fruit in the berry bushes along the gorge wall. Eating berries as she dried, Lily found a three-prong staghorn. Another useful tool for her journey.

Refreshed and dressed, Lily resumed her hike. Around the next bend, a section of cliff had collapsed. Probably during the recent storm. The landslide settled all the way to the river and Lily stopped. The river here ran fast and waist high. She scaled the rocks, and at the peak she stopped to take in the view ahead. A distance from here, the canyon widened but the cliffs seemed taller.

Hunger claimed her, and finding an abundance of plants, Lily began to forage. More cattails, blackberries, and a gnarled wild plum tree. Animals had eaten all the low-hanging fruit and anything on the ground. None of the plums were ripe, but Lily eyed the ones with the most color and collected them as she climbed. Reaching for another one, she spotted a nest. The robin flew away when Lily neared. The nest held six eggs. Lily prayed to the goddess of small creatures and thanked her for the bounty. She took two of them and climbed down.

When the robin mother flew home, she warbled a mournful call. Lily hugged her belly and sang a song to the robin, apologizing and thanking her for the sacrifice that would sustain the baby she carried inside her. Pine's child.

Avoiding the thorns, Lily picked a few of the darkest blackberries and found a place to sit and eat while she enjoyed the view. Studying the eggs, she tapped one with a stone. The shell cracked open, and she poured the contents into her mouth and swallowed. The second egg followed and she thanked the goddess again for leading her to the ones recently laid.

The wild plums tasted sour and not yet ripe. Same with the blackberries, but they were only a bit sweeter than those she had eaten the day before, so she consumed them all. As for the plums, she put three in her pouch, picked up her spear, and set off.

The shadows cast from the sun overhead showed Lily her direction: southwest, and she was on the south side of the river. Up until now, she had felt as if she was walking in circles. Turning about, she wondered where Seaside Hill and Twin Oaks were from here. How far? Without an answer, she trudged on.

Daydreaming, Lily happened to glance at the sky. Far ahead, a dozen or more death eaters were circling. Clutching her lance with both hands, she advanced toward the source of the gathering.

Using boulders for cover, Lily closed in and spotted three dire wolves feeding on a kill. Some death eaters hoping for a share of meat surrounded them.

Keeping downwind like Pine taught her, she snuck past. A three-boulder rock fort gave her a place to hide, and she planned her movements.

Gathering dry grass and some seasoned pine cones, Lily made a nest for a torch. Switching the obsidian with the antler, and knowing the tool might need to serve as a prod, she secured it firmly before she fitted the nest inside the prongs. Then she struck one rock against the other, over and over, until a decent spark started the bundle smoking. Blowing, she started a flame.

Peeking around the rock, one of the wolves seemed curious from the sharp pounding. He stared in her direction. At the peak of the blaze, Lily showed herself and rushed forward with a yell.

Surprised, two of the wolves scattered, but a she-wolf jerked her head from the doe's belly and glared at Lily. With her muzzle dripping blood, she stood over the dead doe and growled, displaying her impressive gore-covered teeth. But Lily needed meat and kept rushing, screaming, with the flaming torch low and in front of her.

At the last second, the wolf abandoned the kill. She remained close enough to attack Lily. Appraising the carcass, Lily brandished the torch at the wolf. A back leg nearly severed at the hip became her goal. Keeping her eyes on the wolf, Lily grasped the leg near the hoof and backpedaled. The tendons held the leg, and Lily began dragging the deer along with her. Unwilling to lose the kill, the she-wolf gripped the deer's neck, shook, and tugged. Taking advantage, Lily jerked the leg free.

Movement to her right caused her to swing the torch that way. The dire wolf cried out when the flame singed his face. He scampered off. From the left, another wolf attempted to seize the leg from Lily. He snapped his teeth; they clacked together when she whisked the meat away. By reflex, she thrust the torch at him at the same time she retreated with her prize.

She was halfway to her boulder fort when the flames died. The wolf trailing her attacked, and Lily jabbed with the prongs. In a fury, the wolf bit the smoldering antler. Promptly, he released the thing and fled away yelping. Lily passed by the fort and hurried off, constantly turning, to be sure none of the wolves were trailing her. None did, but knowing their nature she remained leery.

The sun moved past the cliffs and Lily walked on in the shade, bearing the weight of the leg on her shoulder. Behind her, in the distance, the death eaters still flew above the kill. Anxious to gain some distance, she increased her pace. As she traveled along, the soil became sandy, tiring her legs.

Satisfied the wolves were beyond caring about her, she rested, massaged her ankles, ate her plums, and drank a gourd of river water. Discarding the burnt antler, Lily reattached the pointed piece of obsidian to the shaft.

Inside her, the child kicked a few times, and she reassured her baby they were safe by caressing her belly and singing as she set off again in search of a suitable place to camp before the sunset.

Around another bend, Lily found an abundance of firewood scattered on the canyon floor, remains from the trees on top. Plus, she located a secure place to camp by the cliff. Tonight she needed a cookfire. In the waning light, she collected a sizable stack of wood, including a hefty oak branch. With a supreme effort, she hauled the hefty limb over the center of the fire pit.

The third time Lily clacked the rocks together, a glowing spark landed in the coil of dried grass. She puffed on the ember, a flame ignited, and she thanked her father for teaching her at a young age. As the fire grew, she showed gratitude to the gods for her blessings, of which she had many.

The skill she showed on her next task, she owed her mother. With the obsidian wedge, she cut through the hide. The wolves had already peeled a good section back, and she trimmed some strips of flesh away and laid them on the oak branch. Flames licked at the meat while she continued to cut through the tough hide and rip it away.

The venison strips smoked and sizzled. Lily used a stick to recover them, and the second they were cool enough, she devoured them. Savoring the taste, Lily leaned her head back. Her child shifted, and she held her belly and sang the first song she had shared with Pine.

Her strength renewed, Lily scraped the meat from the bones and laid the strips on the flat rocks she had placed around the fire to dry. Eager to eat the marrow inside, she separated and laid the bones on the glowing coals. After they steamed and before they burned, she used sticks to take them off.

Cool to the touch, Lily bashed them with a rock until she exposed the inside. With a twig she scraped the heated marrow a scoop at a time, ate, and drank from her gourd.

Filled, she found a place by the fire and leaned against the cliff. Soon sorrow overtook her. Not her own, but for her mother and father's pain at what they must be believing.

Lily began to weep, but soon anger replaced her tears and she focused her rage on the cause of it all, Grand Moon, promising herself revenge.

Cried out, she prepared the camp. To protect the meat, she covered it with more shale. The fire had burned the oak branch in two, so she shoved both ends into the flaming coals. The fuel caught and Lily gathered more wood. A rumble in her stomach caused her to find a place for a latrine. Cramps gave her some worry, but they subsided after she defecated. Burying her waste, Lily stepped into the river, lifted her dress, and washed herself.

Nestled between the shale cliff and the campfire, Lily stomped the grass down and made her bed for the night. Before she settled, she jammed the back of the spear into the ground within her reach.

Gazing at the stars, she brought her knees up and prayed to the gods. The shooting star streaking across the sky answered her, and she drew an arrow in the sand to where the gods pointed. Lily let her imagination define the shapes of the clouds drifting above her. A turtle with three legs, a flower basket, a herd of bison, and a bear paw that turned into a mushroom. Tired, she tossed more wood on the fire, closed her eyes, and fell asleep.

The Era of Herbalists

In the morning, Lily laid some twigs on the coals, blew on them, and restarted the fire. She checked the meat. It was cooked and dry enough, so she ate some.

Standing, Lily checked the length of her dress. For a large enough pack to carry her food, she would have to trim to her knees.

She stripped and laid her dress on a boulder, then took the wedge of obsidian and, cutting a piece at a time, she severed a suitable section of doeskin. Replacing her dress, she gazed down at her new style. If her mother were to see her, she would scream. Lily thought of her mother as she spent time making her new shoulder pack.

Carrying her new pouch, she studied the arrow she had drawn in the sand. For now, the river traveled the same direction. It seemed to her the gods confirmed her correct path. So with her food, tools, and spear, she trekked.

Farther along, the canyon walls on the opposite side of the river remained a constant height. However, on her side, the cliffs diminished and soon Lily beheld a vast shrub-strewn plain. Within sight she spotted a few trees, a herd of elk, and a giant sloth grazing on some bushes.

In this part of the gorge, the river turned south. Not the direction the gods pointed. Frustrated, she found a flat boulder and sat facing the west. She took advantage of the daylight by fixing one of her shoes that had been coming unraveled.

A swirl of dust in the distance caught Lily's attention. Replacing her goatskin moccasin, she stood on the rock. Bison. Too far to clearly determine the size of the herd.

But they were heading toward the river, and she did not want to be caught in the open. She decided to head from one tree to the next. As long as she kept a respectful pace, she was in no danger.

White puffy clouds covered the sun at midday. From her vantage point, the bison numbered less than twenty. As she followed their progress, the plain opened and the herd forded the river. Lily noted how shallow the river was there.

While Lily ate some dried venison and sipped some water, the herd lingered. They drank, wandered to the opposite shore, and grazed in the sparsely vegetated area.

Since the bison had so little to feed on, Lily guessed they would move on soon. Massaging her belly, she sang a song her mother had sung to her when she was a child. Halfway through the melody, the bison moved off, so she finished the lullaby strolling to the river.

The clamor of squawking caught her attention. A vast flock of sea birds was flying overhead. The arrow formation headed southwest. To follow them, Lily needed to cross the river.

With her foot covers in one hand and her spear in the other, Lily waded in the sometimes knee-deep water to the opposite shore. Rockier here, she followed an animal trail in the direction the seabirds flew. She drank from the river above where the bison crossed and filled the gourd.

Here, the gentle hills rose and fell, making it impossible to see over the next rise. On the following knoll, Lily walked the crest. She searched both directions, wary of predators that might be lurking in the shrub-filled ravine that ran parallel to her or the scattered trees and bushes on her left. None showed themselves.

Ground birds scattered in her path. They played a repetitive game of waiting further up for her and scattering again when she neared. Picking a clearing, Lily drank half of the water in the gourd, and ate some dried meat and one of her remaining plums.

As she continued on, the terrain flattened with more trees. Oaks, maple, and ash. Herd animals trampled or grazed the grass, making her path passable and clearing her line of sight.

Facing the setting sun, Lily traveled toward a partially downed black nut tree. Nowhere else did she spot a better place to camp, at least not one with as much wood to burn.

As she approached the place, several rodents scurried away. Lily hung her meat satchel in the tallest dead branch that she could reach and hauled fallen branches to build a fire.

The blazing fire warmed the autumn evening, and Lily retrieved her satchel and took the last two plums and a few strips of venison before replacing the bag in the tree.

The Era of Herbalists

Facing the flames, she ate and talked sweetly to the child she carried. She promised she would somehow return to Seaside Hill. At home, once she told her father and the council of her ordeal, they would go to Twin Oaks and bring justice to Grand Moon.

With those thoughts, Lily piled as much wood on the fire as she could, made her grass bed, and fell asleep.

When she awoke, Lily touched the grass around her. Damp. The dawn sky was a pastel orange, with some purple clouds.

Something nearby crunched. Reflexes caused her fingers to extend. She wanted her spear, but whatever it was, the thing was close and coming from her right. Concentrating, Lily played dead. With closed eyes she listened. More than one. A footstep, then another by her left leg, caused her heart to race.

Behind her, she heard a huffing sound, and then sniffing. A musky scent filled her nostrils. A hot breath whooshed over the top of her head. The thing sounded enormous. When it exhaled, the foul breath blew her hair like a gust of wind. She held her breath to keep from gagging.

Keeping her eyes shut, she recalled a wonderful time with Pine and emptied the fear from her mind. Controlling her breathing, thinking of her child, she slowed her pulse.

One of the beasts sniffed her face. As the thing inhaled her scent, the creature's hot saliva dribbled down her neck and on her shoulder. In her mind she wanted to scream.

A furry paw pressed against her left arm. At the same time, a hot snort blew on her crotch. Like her father had taught her, she turned her mind away, and after a moment, the animals lost interest in her and wandered off.

Unsure of how far away the creatures had gone, Lily waited until full daylight before she raised her head. Footprints in the sand beside her told her saber cats had visited her. Glancing up at the dead tree, her heart sank. The cats had taken her satchel of meat. Worse, they crushed her gourd, and she had no water nor any vessel to hold some.

Standing, she spotted the bag a stone's throw away. She retrieved it. As she suspected, nothing remained.

While she still had her strength, Lily assembled her belongings, and with the spear in her hand, she went hunting for food and water.

CHAPTER 43

The Stranger Awakens

UNDER THE NIGHT sky, Pine woke in confusion. Besides unfamiliar bedding, the garments he wore were not his. And not skins either. He looked closely. They were woven like baskets, but with thin fibers. Lying on his back, something else puzzled Pine: the moon shone almost three-quarters full. He recalled his last view of the moon. Only a crescent waxing glow. He tried to sit up, but pain in his chest laid him back down. Turning his head, he tried to take in his surroundings.

Where was Shadow? Did he live? He wanted to call for his dog, but since no one stirred, Pine thought it the middle of the night. Until daylight, Pine endured the torture of not knowing the fate of his friend.

In the moonlight Pine saw tents, though not any kind he recognized. His bed was a litter of some sort. He focused on his clothing. The symbols on the garment seemed similar to what he had glimpsed on the tattooed skin of the gatherers he had seen during the harvest raids. He feared then that he was in the grips of the prodon.

A faint yellow glow came from the east, and some people emerged from inside their tents. Not gatherers, but not like his people either. Darker skin, blacker hair, shorter, and stouter.

By his side he found a gourd of water and a basket with a fruit he had never seen: smooth, yellow, and oblong. Also some dried meat. He took a drink and sampled the fruit. Orange inside, sweet, and juicy. His stomach rumbled. He drank more water, ate more fruit, and chewed the meat. Venison.

A man saw Pine stir. He called in a language Pine had not heard.

"Bring the linguists, the stranger has awakened!" he said in his people's tongue. A man poked his head out from a hut.

"Ihop, help him up. Bring him inside."

With the help of the man, Pine gritted his teeth and forced himself to his feet. Standing, Pine clutched the man's arm until he steadied, and he led Pine into the hut.

He pointed to himself and said, "I am Axel Reyna." The stranger put his hand on his chest.

"Pine Nyte," Pine replied. He looked about and asked, "Where is my dog?"

Axel evidently could not understand Pine, so he shook his head. Three men in tan robes entered the hut. One of them said, in Pine's tongue, "Your dog is safe. I am called Wile Hai."

"I am called Pine Nyte. How am I to be with your people?"

"A boy gathering water found you and your dog five days ago on the river-bank after a storm."

Pine tried to think. How many days from the waxing crescent moon to this phase? Had he been in the river for four days? Then a horrible thought occurred to him. All the village would believe him to be dead. As for Lily, he was unsure. Without his body, she might hold on to hope. And what of Grand? The toxic words he had spoken as he speared Pine gave him chills.

Emptying his hunt pouch, Pine said, "My trappings are all here except for my knife."

"I claimed the blade for my own," said a woman's voice in his tongue behind him. Pine turned toward her. Like the man, the woman's skin was darker than his. Also the woman had a shorter but broader build.

"An insignificant payment for the lives we have given you and your dog."

"Your Highness," said Wile. He and the others bowed to the woman.

"Leave us. I wish to speak to the stranger alone."

"Yes, Your Highness," said Wile. He and the others left.

"I am Zyanya. High Priestess of the Second Sacred City and leader of this journey. Pardon my poor attempt to speak your tongue. The language was taught me at a young age and I rarely practice."

"You speak clearly. I am Pine Nyte, a hunter from Twin Oaks."

"I do not know that place," Zyanya replied.

"My village is to the north. From this view of the white top mountains, it must be far from here."

"Tell me, Pine Nyte, of this faraway land you come from."

"Twin Oaks rests on green fields a half-day walk from the sea. A stream meanders through the village and gives us water. All about the village, a thousand trees give us shade, shelter, firewood, fruit, and those other things that live in and about them."

"Do your people fear someone?" asked Zyanya. "A ruler of sorts?"

"Yes. The prodon and his gatherers. For five harvests, like ants his gatherers have pillaged our village and all the settlements within his reach. It was his order for his gatherers to steal my father. The village herbalist."

"What does this prodon look like?" asked Zyanya.

"I have never seen him or spoken to anyone who has," replied Pine. "But once I was shown symbols the gatherers bore on their skin to be like the ones your people wear on their coverings."

"Tell me, Pine Nyte, where is this place to find the prodon?"

"I do not know from here, but if you follow the river that brought me to you, then I would find his encampment from the place I was familiar."

Zyanya asked, "From the prodon's realm, where does your village stay?"

"Twin Oaks is two or three days true north of his realm."

Zyanya called her people back. Once everyone had gathered, she chatted to them in her tongue.

The eldest, Cualli, asked Wile, who asked Pine, "Can you find your way there?"

"By following the river's shore north to where I was betrayed, I would know."

They turned to one another. After a discussion in their language, Wile turned to Pine and asked, "Can you find your village from the sea?"

"Yes. There are many recognizable landmarks."

The elders conversed. Even though Pine could not understand them, from their expressions he felt their excitement.

After much discussion with Zyanya and the elders, Wile said, "The river is crooked. We would be better to head west two days to the sea and north from there."

Zyanya faced Pine and said, "Now, Pine Nyte, you should tend to your beast. He hungers and yearns for his master."

She faced Wile. "You shall speak for Pine. Take him to his dog."

Turning away, she called for two runners. As they kneeled before her, she explained their assignment.

Obeying her orders, one darted off to redirect the scouts and the other ran to give the roadbuilders new instructions.

Pine followed Wile until he spotted his dog. Since the people feared Shadow, they had made a cage for him. Catching Pine's scent, Shadow whined. Because Shadow still ached, Pine thought his keeping best for now. Once his dog fully recovered, Pine would be sure to convince the people of Shadow's loyalty.

Happy to see his master, Shadow's tail wagged against the bars and struck a drumbeat, attracting Maita's attention. He burst from his tent. At the sight of Wile and Pine, he stood with his head lowered and his arms at his sides.

"Maita. This is Pine Nyte. A stranger no more," said Wile. To Pine he said, "Maita is the boy who found you and your dog. He has been the one to tend to him."

Pine reached through the bars. Wagging his tail, Shadow licked his hand. To Maita, for Wile to interpret, he said, "I owe much to you. My life and the life of my friend."

"The high priestess rewarded me," said Maita. He fondled his necklace.

"Even so, you have my thanks and eternal friendship."

Somewhat embarrassed by the praise, Maita asked, "Does he have a name?"

"I call him Shadow."

"He seems fierce."

"He is well-mannered. You have nothing to fear."

"At night he paces and howls like a dire wolf."

"He longs for his freedom. By pacing, he is healing himself. Making himself stronger. Go ahead. Offer your hand."

The Era of Herbalists

The boy reached through the bars, and Shadow gave his hand the flick of his tongue.

"Shadow knows you have been caring for him. His kiss is his thanks."

Smiling, Maita reached through the bars again and scratched his neck. Shadow responded by lifting his chin, revealing more throat to scratch. A trusting posture to reveal such a vital and vulnerable place.

Alone in her tent, Zyanya clutched the milk-white knife and closed her eyes. She recalled her last sight of her father's face and the black blade in Yaotl's hand poised at his throat. Before the blade bit into his flesh, her father smiled at her. A farewell grin. In Zyanya's eyes she had conveyed to him a vow of revenge. As the edge drew a red line on his neck, she understood the plea in his final expression for her to escape. She turned away. His men had chased her, but she evaded Yaotl and his marauders. Today, ten years later, she had grown to be the high priestess, as had been her destiny from birth.

In her mind, Zyanya replaced her father's face with Yaotl's, and Yaotl's with hers. In her hand the obsidian blade turned white, but Yaotl's blood spurting from the jagged gash she gave him across his throat remained red.

CHAPTER 44

Allies

THE SCOUT RAN to reach the road builders. After catching his breath, he said, "Four strangers are ahead! They come this way!"

"How far are they?"

"A half-day over the rise and north on the beach."

"Are they armed?"

"Yes. Three have spears and one carries a bow."

The head roadbuilder called for the leader of the guards. "Take ten men and bring the strangers to us. The high priestess will want to question them. Try not to harm them."

Knowing they would reach them after nightfall, the guards brought torches, along with extra rations of food and water.

On this third day since their escape, the four friends stopped to watch the sun slip into the sea. Already they had gathered firewood and finished their evening meal.

Deciding to camp here, they laid out their bed nests and built up the fire.

"Was the man trying to hide from us, a scout for the prodon?" asked Luca.

"Not the prodon, but his dress is like what my people wore," said Bru.

"Your people?" asked Gorg. "I thought your people were a whole season away from here."

"Yes, but I am sure of his clothes."

"Do you think he was alone?" asked Werth.

"What I believe is he will come back with others," said Bru.

"Then we should be ready," said Luca.

"We will be," said Gorg.

The Era of Herbalists

Before they bedded down, they piled wood on the fire. Enough to last the night and into the morning.

When the moon hovered over the sea, the guards approached the fire. Seeing the beds, they surrounded them, and the leader ordered, "Wake and be seen!"

None of the beds stirred, but a spear tip pressed hard against the leader's back. In his people's tongue, Bru said, "Lay down your weapons or bleed!"

With their weapons poised to attack, Luca, Gorg, and Werth materialized from their holes in the sand behind some of the guards.

Hesitating, the guards stared at the leader. Bru pressed his shaft harder, and the leader dropped his battle axe. The others followed suit.

"You speak our tongue," said the guard leader.

"Seven years ago," said Bru, "I was taken prisoner from the Fifth Sacred City by the prodon and made a slave. My friends were taken from other places at other times, and they cannot speak this tongue. But we have declared ourselves free men and will die before we slave for any others."

"If the man you call the prodon is the man we seek revenge upon, then our high priestess will wish to know all that you can say."

Bru called to his friends, "These people seek revenge against the prodon. They wish for us to tell of him to their high priestess."

The men spoke to one another and Werth said, "We will return with them to speak to their high priestess, but not as prisoners."

Bru took the lance away from its provocative position against the leader's back. Lowering their weapons, Luca, Gorg, and Werth gestured for the guards to share the fire.

Offering his hand, the lead guard said, "I am Elia Koa from the Second Sacred City."

"My name is Bru," he said, clasping the man's hand. "My friends are Luca, Gorg, and Werth."

Beside the fire, Bru acted as interpreter. Several men brought out drinking sacks with spiced cactus nectar. Elia offered Bru some first. Smiling, Bru squirted some in his mouth. He savored it for a moment before swallowing the nectar.

"Ah, seven years is too long to have not enjoyed such flavor."

Bru explained to his friends the process for making the beverage, and he cautioned them to partake slowly, telling them that the juice burned going down one's throat but was somehow pleasant at the same time.

By their second swallow, they agreed and asked for more. After several more drinks the campfire fascinated them. Luca followed a spark until it fell to the sand. In an emotional outburst, he cried when the glow died. Gorg gave him another sip, and he grinned contentedly.

Later, the men from the caravan told jests, and even though they did not understand a word spoken, the three outsiders laughed along with them.

One after the other, they either found their bed nests or simply bedded in the sand where they fell.

Daybreak rousted them. Some lay moaning, holding their heads in their hands, while others stumbled off to retch. While his men suffered, Elia boasted how he had drunk more, and how childlike they were after drinking such an insignificant amount of cactus nectar.

With sand coating the side of his face, Luca sat up. Everything swirled around him and he fell backwards. Standing, Gorg and Bru seemed normal but both of them wobbled when they walked.

Surprising them all, Werth ran into the sea and disappeared in the waves. Everyone stayed watching for him, but nothing surfaced. To them he must have drowned. But then, a mammoth-sized wave broke, and Werth came to the surface holding a giant lobster in each hand. He tossed them to his friends. The lobsters landed in the sand in front of them. Having never seen the creatures before, Luka and Gorg yelped and leaped away from them. However, the guards knew how to clean and cook them, so they retrieved them.

Without a word he jumped back into the sea, staying underwater longer than anyone else could hold their breath. Werth finally surfaced with two more lobsters even larger than the last two. Again he dived in.

His fourth and final dive yielded a single crab with fist-size claws and legs the length of a man's forearm.

The cooks insisted Werth have the first taste. After his share, everyone broke into the steaming shells.

CHAPTER 45

The Sickness

THROUGH THE DAY'S trek, Lily had found no food or water, and she knew the sun would set soon. Most of the plants she had encountered she found too woody to suck out any moisture. Even so, her child remained at peace with whatever nutrients Lily's body could share.

Over another rise Lily spotted a patch of lush green at the bottom of the hill. Because of the thick underbrush, she tossed a rock into the bushes and readied with the spear for any predators. None showed, so she scrambled down to the foliage.

On her knees, she parted the plants and found water. She pressed her face to it. Kissing the somewhat unpleasant liquid, she slurped some, using her teeth to strain the tiny bits of decomposed shrubbery. She swallowed and drank more.

Refreshed, Lily pressed on. Behind her, the three-quarter moon rose ahead of the sunset. Setting her sights on the tallest hill, she continued forward. Without realizing it, night had arrived and she had not found a sleeping place. Too tired to build a fire or care where she lay, Lily curled up on the ground between some bushes and fell asleep.

In the early morning a piercing stomach pain woke Lily. She woke retching. A burning behind her eyes caused them to water, blurring her vision. Raising herself, another sharp pain stabbed her lower in her bowels, and she raised her dress and squatted. The diarrhea came with an agony like nothing she had experienced. But when she finished, the discomfort diminished.

Chastising herself for drinking the tainted water, Lily, determined to return home, put one foot in front of the other and continued her journey.

At the top of the last knoll, she thought she saw blue smoke along the entire horizon, but the sight dissipated and she believed it to be an illusion caused by her watery eyes. Still, she headed toward the direction of the vision.

At midday, the terrain had changed to a knee-high plain of green grass. By then, Lily's guts soured inside her. Having heaved all she had in her, the retching yielded only stomach bile.

With the sun still high in the sky, dizziness overcame her. She staggered and dropped her spear. Taking a dozen uncoordinated steps, she lurched, wobbled, and finally collapsed to the ground. Unable to rise, Lily slipped into unconsciousness.

Concealed under deerskins, the seven hunters from the travelers column crawled toward the grazing deer with their arrows ready. Hearing something, the buck protecting the herd lowered his head and snorted. He was about to warn his harem when a long shaft penetrated his chest and a second pierced his throat. The buck dropped, and before the dozens of skittish does fled, the hunters killed three of them with well-placed arrows.

Claiming a kill, a hunter tripped on something in the grass. Jerking himself upright, he stared down. A woman lay curled on the ground.

"Baptta! Come here! Hurry!" called the man.

The leader gazed down at the woman, and asked, "Is she alive?"

"Yes, she breathes."

Baptta sent some men to the day camp for some travois to haul the woman and the deer to the caravan. The woman's lips were cracked, so Baptta soaked a piece of hide in water and stuck it partially in her mouth. Even when he lifted her eyelids, she remained unconscious. He wondered if the sickness had caused her eyes to turn gray.

While those men ran off, the rest bled and gutted the deer.

At the caravan, they brought the woman to Baptta's mother, Gonda Mora, who served as an herbalist and midwife. While others prepared for the day's journey, Gonda set a place inside her tent to treat the woman. She greeted the men towing the woman at the doorway.

The Era of Herbalists

To the two men she said, "Put her in the tent, and quit gawking." She went to the woman's side. Since she wore skins instead of cloth, Gonda worried that the woman belonged somewhere close by, and that her people may be looking for her. But her son explained there were no villages anywhere nearby.

Meanwhile, she sent word to the high priestess. An ill, pregnant woman wearing animal skins had been found. From their position on the caravan, she guessed ten relays. The message would take almost half a day to reach Zyanya.

The woman felt feverish, so Gonda stripped and washed her. Pinching and pulling her skin, she determined her to be dehydrated. She laid a blanket over her. Gently, Gonda lifted her eyelids. Gray with pinprick pupils that grew in the dim light. The message she sent Zyanya would be incomplete.

Checking her mouth, she found bits of decomposed plants lining her gums, also between her teeth. Evidence of foul water disease.

Knowing the cure, Gonda gathered her dried chili peppers. She broke open three green chilies, one fat yellow chili, and two skinny red ones. Carefully, she removed the seeds. With a mortar and pestle, she mashed the peppers into a powder. Next she poured the powder in a clay vessel and mixed in a portion of lime juice and a splash of cactus nectar. Covering it with a cloth, Gonda checked the woman. Still asleep. She would look in on her later. Now, with her medicine satchel on her back, she made her rounds.

When Lily's eyes opened, she thought she was still dreaming. Herbs and red and green feathers hung over her. Still dizzy, she tried to focus, but her eyes burned and watered. The herbs gave off a pleasant aroma, and as she breathed, sleep took her.

Returning to her patient, Gonda found her still sleeping. The woman had had a rough time. Her blistered hands, and the scabs on her elbows, knees, and feet, told Gonda the woman had crawled a distance. Nothing to do except clean the wounds and let them heal naturally. She checked her medicine and scraped off the top residue with a stick. Because the woman was asleep, she would need to use her bamboo tube. Knowing how the cure would wake her, Gonda sought a neighbor to help administer the remedy. Also, she made sure a swallow of goatmilk stood ready to put out the fire from the spicy tonic sure to burn the

243

woman's mouth. For that reason, she readied two doses of the medicine. One she would vomit and one she would keep down.

The neighbor, Pella, held the woman's head and pulled down her chin.

Gonda set an end of the skinny bamboo tube on her tongue and let the syrupy concoction flow into her. Once the first dose filled her mouth, Gonda pulled out the tube, pressed the woman's jaws together, and pinched her nose closed.

Instinctively, the woman swallowed and her face reddened. Her eyes flew open and she rolled to the side, retched, and coughed. Without waiting, Gonda laid her head back, stuck the tube back between her lips, and poured the second dose.

Awake, Lily stared at the two women hovering over her. A fire scorched the inside of her mouth and burning sweat clouded her eyes. The woman forced the stick in her mouth again, but this time milk quenched the heat. Lily let the liquid settle before she swallowed.

Relaxing, Lily realized the women were caring for her. They spoke to her, but the words had no meaning and she shook her head in response.

"This I suspected," said Gonda. "The woman has no understanding of our tongue. With the will of the gods, Zyanya will send a linguist."

Gonda placed a cool wet cloth on her forehead and patted Lily's stomach gently. She smiled and said, "Your child thrives."

Though Lily did not recognize the words, she understood the message. Her child was alright and she was safe. Whatever the woman had given her, the cure made her sleep.

Sunlight and movement woke Lily. She was being pulled in a travois. The blanket under her arms kept her from sliding off. Behind her the people towing their own burdens called to someone in a foreign tongue.

"Gonda! The woman has awakened!"

One of the women treating her walked alongside. She leaned over and offered her a gourd of water. Lily took the vessel with both hands and sipped. The water contained a remedy of sorts, and a sour taste filled her mouth. The woman used hand signs to urge Lily to drink more. She finished it, and the woman smiled when she gave the gourd back. Lily tried to smile, but she could tell from the woman's response she had failed.

Opening her mouth, Lily struggled to speak. Her attempted thank-you came out as a rough wind. Once she closed her eyes, sleep snuck up on her.

CHAPTER 46

The Message

ONCE THE SUN hung low in the sky, the caravan stopped for the night. The people erected tents, dug fire pits, and made beds.

The ninth relay messenger arrived and kneeled before the high priestess. She gestured for him to rise.

"Your Highness," he said. "At the seventh column, Gonda Mora cares for a found woman. She sleeps with fever and carries a child inside her; she wears deerskin clothing."

"What color are her eyes?"

"No one has said," replied the runner.

"I will send a linguist. Rest and take food and drink with my guards."

"Many thanks, Your Highness."

The priestess was about to seek Pine Nyte when a file of guards stopped at her tent. Four tattooed strangers stood with them.

"Your Highness," said the guard, Elia Koa. "These men have escaped the prodon's encampment."

Studying them, Zyanya said, "Prove to me you are not spies."

Bru stepped in front of his friends. "Your Highness," said Bru, in her language. "My name is Bru Tupac. Seven years past, the prodon raided the Fifth Sacred City and took me as a slave."

"And these others with you?" asked Zyanya.

"My friends," said Bru, pointing to his comrades. "The prodon captured them from other places and they do not talk our tongue."

Gesturing to her sentry, Zyanya said, "See to their comfort." She escorted Bru into her tent. Directing him to sit, she began to pace in front of him. "Have you seen this prodon?"

"Many times, Your Highness," answered Bru.

"Describe him."

"The prodon colors his hair yellow and uses beeswax to make spikes that poke toward the sky. Each time I have seen him, he sits in his throne, but he seems taller than myself," said Bru, holding his hand flat above his head.

"Tell me of the nose on his face."

"Your Highness, his nose is bent like a hawk's beak."

Zyanya pictured Yaotl. The size and the nose fit, but he must have grown hair. But it would be like him, a narcissist, to make his hair yellow.

"Tell me of his army."

"Made of mostly slaves like us. Now his legions are scattered, raiding any villages for supplies. He leaves the valley by the sea to plunder east."

"How many? How are they armed?"

"More than three thousand archers and as many spearmen. Nearly all carry blades and battle clubs."

"When is this move?"

"We were told on the morning of the full moon, two days from now."

"In what direction does he travel?"

"East to the pass between the tall white mountain and the round one."

"This new knowledge gives me a decision whether to pursue or head off."

"Your Highness, if the prodon is your quarry then you will find him neither in front nor the rear, but the center."

"My thanks. For this my general will offer thanks as well."

"Then I wish you good fortune, Your Highness."

"Tell me of your friends. Where do you travel?"

"All of us are traveling homeward. Myself, to the Fifth Sacred City, but first we take my friend Werth to his village, Whispering Bay. Then Luca goes to Bison Roam Here, and Gorg to West Fields of Gold Flowers."

"Those villages have been sacked years past. Each place we came, the survivors told us of the raids. In some of the columns are the refugees from those places. Many displaced people from numerous hamlets travel with us."

"This is a hard thing to hear. From my friends' talk, those villages were prosperous."

"Little remains. Most settlements we encountered suffered by this prodon."

"What of the Fifth Sacred City?"

"Sacked twice."

"Does anything remain?"

"The sun temple stands, the marketplace, and some homes."

"Your Highness? What of the people?"

"Many died in the raids, and others were taken as slaves, same as you," said Zyanya. "Some who lived travel with us, and more stayed to rebuild. The caravan is made of people from all seven sacred cities. Did you say your family name was Tupac?"

"Yes, Your Highness."

"There is a family bearing that name near here."

"Are they from the Fifth Sacred City?"

"Of this, I have no knowledge."

A shortage of tents brought the four friends to the one Pine Nyte had been given. He welcomed them and showed them where to lay their beds.

While those men readied their places, Pine rubbed his chest and winced. Gorg asked, "Are you injured?"

"I am healing, but my ribs are still sore."

Gorg opened his medicine pouch and, in the lamp light, Pine's chin fell.

"Where did you get these medicines?"

"Our friend made them for us for our journey."

"These bear the knots made by my father."

"Are you Pine? Pine Nyte? Chirp Nyte's son?" asked Bru.

"Yes. You know my father?"

"He is our friend," said Luca.

Werth rushed over and studied Pine's face. "You have your father's eyes, but you must take after your mother since you are so pretty."

Everyone laughed.

"How does my father look?"

"Since our first meeting three years ago, gray hairs invade his beard, and the sun has browned him and wrinkled his skin some," said Werth.

"Tell me, how is my father's life?" asked Pine.

Gorg answered, "Our friend Chirp lives as well as anyone under the fist of the prodon. Many times the prodon has threatened to take your father's manhood, yet Chirp always wins back the prodon's favor with cures."

"With the help of these people, I plan to free my father."

The four men gazed at each other. "Four days ago," said Gorg, "we deserted the prodon's rule and swore to never return. Now, having learned of the destruction of our homes, we wish to join with you and these people."

"Chirp has been a friend to us from the start," said Werth.

"Tell me, Pine. How is it we find you here?" asked Bru. "From your father's mouth, your village is far to the north."

"The leader of my hunt team betrayed me with a spear tip in my back and a tumble over a waterfall," Pine replied. "These people found me and my dog in a river. The fool must think me dead."

"For what reason did he harm you?" asked Bru.

As he spoke, Pine squeezed his fists. "He lusts for my wife and swore to me at his deed he would take her no matter her say."

"What will you do?"

"My tale to the village council will settle his fate."

"If it be me he harmed," said Luca, "my spear would pierce his belly."

"For his offense, a spear to the belly might be his decided fate. More likely he would be banished."

"Then I would hunt him down and feed him his manhood," said Gorg.

"If he has harmed Lily or our child she bears," said Pine, "then I will do more than that."

CHAPTER 47

A New Tower

THE MORNING OF the full moon, Lord Prodon ordered his men to carry his overlook to the edge of the river for him to supervise the building of his new tower. The base and two levels up had been erected, and the workers were only now reinforcing the structure.

With his great mouth he called across the river, "Taller! Make my tower higher than the staff Patto holds!"

His voice warbled and the river swallowed his words. All the builders knew was that the prodon was preaching. Since Lewell had already ordered so, the tower would be taller, and because of that, more men would need to carry Lord Prodon's conveyance.

Because of the plans to move, Chirp made extra batches of blister salve. All day he pounded walking root stems and cooked them down to a mush. Blending boiled bear fat and melted beeswax, he wrapped each dose in a sycamore leaf.

So far, Chirp had not been questioned regarding his four friends. Perhaps their absence had gone unnoticed. For this he would be grateful. However, if it came to be that Lewell should ask why he had not requested their help, he would tell him they were no longer friends. And should Lewell press him for a reason, he would tell him how he grew tired of arguing with them. As for his own fate, Chirp had resolved to suffer as the herbalist to the Lord Prodon.

From his upbringing, he had been raised to believe in the gods. And many times he had seen them work their miracles. However, since he had been taken from his family, Chirp no longer trusted them. To his thinking they had betrayed him. Only his apothecary and his knowledge gave him any solace at all.

The Era of Herbalists

Chirp caught Lewell pacing in front of his apothecary. "Master Lewell? Is there a cure you need?"

"Only if you can concoct something to bring the raiders back. They were due yesterday, and none of the three teams has returned. Can you think of a reason for them to be delayed?"

"Perhaps the storm hindered them."

"Those were seasoned men and unafraid of foul weather."

"Storms bring other troubles besides wind and rain. Perhaps lightning struck them or they were consumed in a mudslide."

"Some perhaps, but all, never."

"Will the prodon send more?"

"No. He is anxious to leave here."

"If you need no remedy, then I must resume preparing my apothecary."

"This, Lord Prodon told to me—for this journey, you must take care to stay close. Also, to say to you his reach has no boundaries."

"Master Lewell, this is my life now. Where would I go?"

"There is nowhere," said Lewell. He lifted his chin and ambled away.

With another day remaining for the builders to complete the tower's construction, Chirp had more time to fashion necessary remedies. Having been here so long, he could almost anticipate the daily complaints and illnesses facing him.

Out of this territory, there would still be the same muscle aches, foot traumas, and stomach complaints. But he expected to encounter different snakes, toxic plants, and stinging insects. For those, he had weaver wood powder. It was Chirp's wish to find the trees that were the origin.

This change would test his knowledge of herbs when he found unusual plants. To learn the properties, he would need to test them. Sometimes that posed problems. For him, a healer, to harm anyone was unforgivable. So Chirp often tested himself first when he was unsure of a remedy. So far, other than a few headaches, some sleepless nights, rashes, and belly pains, he had not harmed himself.

While Ash stood watch, the prodon's men that Master Lewell had picked loaded slats on travoises. Once they loaded a stack, they tested to make sure it would not slip, and after three stacks they tested to see if a man could tow it. In the morning, those same men would be hauling them. When the entire lot was loaded, there would be six dragging the loads.

While those men toiled, Ash's mind drifted to Master Lewell's river monster. The whirlpool. A sudden thought came to him. The moment the men finished the task, Ash ran off to the potter's place.

The potter piled all of the broken pottery behind the kilns. Ash rummaged, searching for one large enough. After moving some chipped plates, he found a suitable piece with a broken handle. Leaning around a kiln, Ash called to the potter. When the man came, Ash pointed to the bowl he wanted. "What would you take for trade?"

"Why do you want one of my broken bowls?" asked the potter. "Look, over in the front, those are fine and sturdy."

"The bowl is only used once and discarded."

"Then take it."

"My thanks," said Ash.

But the potter turned and returned to his pots.

Inside the apothecary yard, Ash laid the bowl across two pieces of firewood. He held a sturdy crystal in the center and pounded it once with Chirp's mallet. The quartz broke through the pot. He placed a patch of leather over the hole and carried the bowl to the cauldron, then balanced it on the rim, dipped a gourd in water, and dumped it into the bowl. The bowl took seven more gourds to fill.

He called Chirp, who came from inside the apothecary. Ash waved him over. "Chirp, I think I have an idea about Master Lewell's river monster."

"You said it was a whirlpool."

"Yes, but then I did not know how the whirlpools formed. Watch."

Ash reached in the water and pulled the skin away, and water began draining into the cauldron. Soon a whirlpool had formed.

"Chirp," he said, "I believe there is a cavern under the river in the area where I witnessed the two men drown. The place must be the source of an underground river."

The Era of Herbalists

Nodding, Chirp said, "You are probably right, but do not tell Master Lewell. He wants to believe in river monsters."

At sunrise the following day, a loud call came from the prodon's great mouth. "I am the Lord Prodon! You are my keep! I shield you from spoil! My will is your being! Today it is my will that my new tower be completed by the sunset!"

Knowing the punishment for failure, the workers scrambled to the tower. Already the frame reached its full height. What remained was for Lord Prodon's comfort and rigging for the lift.

As the workers toiled, an advance group of soldiers formed columns. They waited near the new tower for the barges to bring the first group of laborers. Those hands would be responsible to make the camp stops, fashion the fire pits, and stock firewood. According to the runners, the road makers had reached the mountain pass. To Lewell's thinking, the journey there would be ten days. From the stories told to him by the runners, Lewell was eager to visit the white-capped mountains.

A day late, the morning after the full moon, Lord Prodon gazed at the mass of people before the tower. He circled the railing, congratulating himself on the accumulation of slaves and worshipers. All of them contributed to him, even the ones he used for examples. Of this he was sure, to see another man hanging with his intestines protruding from his belly quelled dissenters and rulebreakers.

Satisfied, he called over to the field of soldiers and slaves. "Carriers! Lift me!"

The tower raised and the prodon yelled, "All advance!"

A line of drummers beat the pace, and more than three thousand people and one god moved out, following the road toward the gap between the distant snowcapped peaks. Besides the prodon's carriers, nearly everyone pulled or bore weight. Even the children able to walk hefted their own rations and belongings.

As for Chirp, he towed his possessions and tools with a travois. Patto assigned four men to haul the whole of his apothecary.

Eight stout men carried the lift holding Lewell, Patto, Ash, and Song. The flattering portrait Ash had etched of the prodon earned him and Song transport. It seemed to Song that because of their affliction, Lord Prodon would have wished them carriage regardless of the gift so as not to leave them behind.

As the mass moved, the column stretched. From the top of the tower, the prodon barked orders with his great mouth. For those beyond hearing, runners carried the commands.

Chirp traveled behind the tower. Anticipating complaints, he kept the remedies and wraps close. His work lay ahead at the nighttime rest spot. The pains would be numerous.

They reached the first rest camp before sunset. The odd number setup team left to outfit the third camp. The prodon charged Lewell to survey and rate the camp. First he studied the tower site. True to size and properly leveled. He signaled the carriers to place the structure. Once the tower had settled, the prodon called with his great mouth. "I am the Lord Prodon! You are my keep! I shield you from spoil! My will is your being! Kneel before me!"

Like a gust of wind on tall grass, the people stooped. His guards surveyed the crowd for anyone standing, but no one did.

The guard huts were all made. Next he counted firepits and firewood bundles. Because the prodon ordered, Lewell inspected the cleared hut sites. Sufficient. Lastly, Lewell surveyed the latrines. Adequate for one night.

The line of moaners extended past where Chirp could see. Inspecting them, Patto collected the worst and brought them to the front. Bleeders came first, then burns, sprains, toe breaks, and blisters.

After putting up their hut, Ash and Song climbed into their bed nest. Song whispered, "Couple with me."

"We cannot," said Ash.

"We must," murmured Song.

Whispering back, he asked, "How can we couple with others so close?"

"No one will notice. Besides, you have been rubbing me all day."

The Era of Herbalists

"What? It has been you doing the rubbing."

"If you did not wish to couple, why wash with lavender water?"

"Because the drinking water is not for bathing."

"Still, you tempt me." She reached for him, but Ash rolled on his belly.

"Do you no longer like coupling with me?"

"Song," he said. "I love coupling with you."

Frowning, she asked, "Then why will you not tonight?"

"Because you cannot keep quiet," hissed Ash.

"But I promise…I will be silent."

"Can you keep the promise when you reach your peak?"

Brushing his hair back, she put her lips by his ear and said, "I can try."

CHAPTER 48

The Assembly

SURVEYING THE LANDSCAPE, Zyanya decided this open grassy plain to be the place to group the columns together. It had been more than a year since the last census. The river nearby, washing to the sea, promised water and possibly fish. Considering the day and a half to assemble everyone, a rest was needed. Once all had settled, to lift the people's spirits she would offer an additional three days of rest here.

Checking the soil, Zyanya scooped a handful of the dark brown dirt. Still moist from the rain. She inhaled its fertile aroma; she could tell the loam was rich in nutrients. The planters would be eager to sow chili pepper seeds, mangosteen sprouts, guava starts, and coco palms. Here in this humid coastal environment, with full sunlight, the plants would thrive.

Zyanya sent runners to recall the roadbuilders and tell them to turn the front of the column into the field to camp. The other columns would follow until tents covered the entire meadow.

At nightfall the columns continued filling the massive field. A full moon, bonfires, and torches lit their way. Column leaders directed them to campsites. The people already established helped the newcomers set up. As the people settled, Zyanya toured their camps, offering advice and giving blessings.

That night, Pine walked with Shadow among the tents. The people were leery at first sight of the dog. However, seeing Wile Hai accompanying them, they relaxed. He acted as interpreter and explained the two were healing and needed exercise. On the outskirts of the encampment, Wile Hai found a place for Pine and Shadow to run. Watching them, he could not figure whether

Pine's pace kept with the dog's, or if the dog stayed slow to be beside his master.

On the way back to their space, Wile led them through the middle of the encampment. Everyone they encountered wanted to meet Shadow, especially the children. And Shadow, happy for the attention, wagged his tail and offered his neck for them to scratch and pet.

As the three moved from one tent group to another, Shadow caught a scent in the wind and raised his head. Catching his dog's sudden focus, Pine turned in time to see two men carrying a litter of roasted meats. He pulled Shadow away. As they journeyed on, Shadow kept turning his head, but the wind changed and the trace vanished.

The seventh column set up their camps in the middle of the great meadow. Baptta Mora helped move the woman into his mother's tent.

The woman's fever came back and she slept. Gonda wiped her tender feet with cool water. The scabs peeled off, and she spread a glob of honey and mashed ginger root on the sores. The salve would help heal her wounds. Her biggest worry was the child inside the woman. She placed both of her hands on the woman's swollen belly. At first when she pressed, she felt no response. Then a kick, and another. The child lived.

So far the woman had only said a few words, but no one understood the meaning. The linguist had come, but lost his patience waiting for her to speak.

Word spread; this place made for a three-day rest. Just what this woman needed. Thinking of herself, a respite was long overdue. With those thoughts she checked her patient once more, blew out her oil lamp, crawled on her bed, and went to sleep.

Morning birds sounded, and Gonda rose. Wiping the sleep from her eyes, she checked the woman. Still feverish, she washed the woman's face. To aid her breathing, she placed crushed menthe around her nose. The child inside her shifted. Gonda rubbed a salve of soothing herbs on her swollen belly and covered her in another blanket.

Pine stirred and sat up. His pain had diminished, but he had yet to regain his stamina. Of that, he knew the cure: more exercise. After stretching, he went to get Shadow.

Today, instead of Wile Hai, Bru served as Pine's interpreter. Mostly because Pine wanted to run and so did Bru. As for Shadow, he pranced at the end of his lead, ready for his chance to dash. For now, they strolled through the tent area. The open field lay past the edge and from there, Shadow could run free.

"My spirit lifts with these people," said Bru. "Even as they labor, there is joy here." He gestured to some children running about. "Under the prodon, children toil. Here they play."

Those youngsters spotted Shadow and lined along their path to pet him. They all had questions and through Bru, Pine answered them.

Further on, Shadow stopped, turned his head, and sniffed. His ears laid back and he bolted. The leash whipped from Pine's grip.

Looking ahead, Pine saw Shadow rushing toward the same two men with another litter of roasted meat. They gabbed with each other, unaware of the dog charging. But Shadow shot under the litter without pausing. The man in the rear stumbled and several roasts hopped up into the air. Fortunately, the man regained his balance and managed to keep the meat from landing on the ground.

Pine yelled, "Shadow!" The dog paid no heed and kept dashing. Both Pine and Bru ran after him.

At the woman's side, Gonda checked her again. The fever had broken, but still the woman slept. Using a sea sponge, Gonda washed the woman's feet. Should she wake, the wounds were healed enough for her to walk. A neighbor had given a pair of sandals for her to wear when she recovered.

Again, Gonda placed her hands—she sensed the child. A ruckus outside spun her toward the entry. A black thing burst inside. She yelped.

Gonda thought the beast a dire wolf, but then she saw the collar and how he centered on the woman. The dog squealed and shrieked, lapping at the young woman's face as he wiggled and squirmed. His tail battered back and forth, fanning the air.

Suddenly, the woman's eyes flashed open. She coughed and in a raspy voice she said, "Shadow?"

The dog barked and danced, and two men peered into the tent. Seeing Shadow, Pine called, "Shadow, come here!"

The dog's head swiveled toward his master. He barked and turned back to the prone woman. Hearing the familiar voice, she sat up abruptly and stared. When she saw Pine, she said, "Am I in the spirit world?"

"Lily? Oh, Lily!" He rushed to her side and held her face. Tears streamed down Pine's cheeks. "I cannot believe my eyes!"

"Pine? You are alive! I knew it with my heart!"

"How are you here?" asked Pine.

"Whatever this place is, the gods brought me close and led these people to find me."

Taking her hand in his, Pine said, "It must be the same for myself and Shadow. These gracious people have found and healed us."

A bit confused, Gonda stood with her eyes wide. Bru explained to her and interpreted for the couple. Once Gonda heard the tale, she ran off to find the high priestess. The prophecy of the lost lovers had come to pass.

After listening to Gonda, Zyanya searched through the few sacred scrolls she had rescued and pulled out the appropriate one. She studied the symbols and the drawings.

A stranger from the north, drowned in a river only to be revitalized by the people. This part of the scroll was ruined, but somehow the woman had set off on a quest to find her lover. Hardships accompanied the woman to death's door until the people healed her and brought the lovers together.

This next section had been damaged as well, but to her understanding, when the two lovers become reunited with blood kin, peace and prosperity would reign over the people for millennia. Nothing in the scroll told of the dog or of the woman bearing a child. Still, the prophecy seemed true. Would this quest interfere with her hunt for Yaotl? Of this she chose not to question the wisdom of the gods.

Having met Pine, Zyanya wanted to meet his wife and hear from her lips her plight here. With Gonda and her sentries, Zyanya went to visit. On the way, Gonda described the woman's many scrapes and bruises.

Inside the tent, Zyanya listened as Lily told her story. Afterwards, Zyanya brought out the scroll and explained the symbols. The recounting assured the priestess of the parallel to the prophecy. With that, Zyanya promised to return them both to their kin.

CHAPTER 49

The Strategy and the New Plan

THE GENERALS AND Zyanya listened to Bru as he explained how much of the prodon's army had already advanced five days ahead of the prodon. They aimed for a pass between two mountains, and others would have camps ready for his arrival each sunset. The estimate for the prodon to reach the pass was ten days. "That is how long the roadbuilders said."

"What else did they speak of?" asked Zyanya.

"To be ahead of the prodon," said Bru, "the skillful thinkers judge that we go to the seventh camp. A three-day journey from here is their guess."

One of Zyanya's generals asked, "How guarded are the advance camps?"

"Between twenty and thirty soldiers will be guarding fifty or sixty slaves."

"Will the slaves fight us?"

"They will have no weapons."

"How will our army advance without warning them?" asked a general.

"Twenty men should go. Your army can wait a half-day away."

"How will twenty men defeat what may be thirty?"

"Myself and my three friends will advance on the road as if we were the prodon's men. We have the dress and know the signs. We will signal you."

Crossing her arms, Zyanya stared at Bru. "It will be myself to lead my twenty soldiers."

"Your Highness," said Bru. "The prodon's tower and his many guards will only be a day from there."

"It is for that reason I wish to be waiting."

Suddenly Bru slapped his leg. "Your Highness! The prodon's reputation with women is well-known. If it pleases you, my friends and I will carry you on a litter to the camp and tell the soldiers you are for Lord Prodon."

Zyanya put her hands together. She pressed her fingers against her lips.

Bowing his head, Bru said, "Forgive me, Your Highness, your beauty as a distraction would aid us to overwhelm them."

"For your flattery, you are forgiven."

Reluctantly, Lily bade Pine farewell as he joined with the high priestess' army. He left Shadow with Lily for her protection and his safety. This was his mission to free his father. The priestess, Zyanya, had promised Lily would be safe.

Bru, Gorg, Luca, and Werth carried Zyanya toward the seventh rest camp. The guards formed a line as they approached. As they closed in, Poe stepped forward. He recognized the four lift carriers and signaled his men. The archers lowered their bows and the spearmen relaxed.

"Gorg, my friend, word was you and your friends ran off."

"Lies," said Gorg. "In secret, Lord Prodon tasked us with finding the most beautiful woman for his pleasure. She is the one."

"Let us see her," said Poe.

The men kept the litter on their shoulders. Covered in colored scarves, Zyanya stood so all could see her. The soldiers, including Grand, surrounded them. With her face covered, slowly she began unwrapping them one at a time. First the red one tied around her waist. With slow but deliberate moves, she unwrapped it and held it over her head. The breeze lifted it, and it waved in the air. With a flick of her wrist, she let the wind take it away. The men hollered, "More! Take off more!"

The next one, a short yellow scarf, came away from her neck, then she teased a lengthy blue one off her shoulder to hoots and whistles. Grand caught a slave gawking. To set an example, Grand rushed to him and knocked him off his feet and into the dirt. "Back to work!" yelled Grand. The slave crawled away and stood, then ran to where huts were being erected. The other slaves looked away, and Grand resumed his own staring in time to see her take another red scarf away, this one from her face. She spun a slow circle so all could see. The soldiers moved in for a better look. Zyanya began unraveling the indigo scarf covering her breasts. All were focused and did not notice the armed men moving behind them.

The captain prodded Poe with his lance. "Relinquish your weapon or bleed! Order your men to obey!" He pushed the tip against Poe's spine to emphasize his resolve.

"I yield," said Poe. He dropped his spear and called to his men. They too had weapons poised against them. "Do as they say. Toss your weapons!"

With her men in control, Zyanya stopped her stripping and called, "I am Zyanya! High Priestess from the Seventh Sacred City! We are a free people! We own no slaves! Who will join us?"

"His army advances," said Poe. "Your small clutch will be no match."

"My army progresses as we speak and will be here by midday."

Unseen at the latrine, Ragger listened to the woman. Using shrubs for cover, he snuck to the gully running parallel with the road, crawling on his belly to avoid detection. The fading of the woman's voice helped Ragger to judge his distance. Once it diminished, he continued to slither on the ground. Ahead of him, he spotted some heavy brush. He broke cover and dashed to the nearest bush, then used his flint to cut branches. So he would blend in with the foliage, he strapped them over himself. He moved in short sprints until he was sure to be unnoticed, then ran to warn Lord Prodon.

In her plea, Zyanya rattled off the names of a dozen villages and cities. She explained, "Having been sacked by the prodon, many of the survivors travel with us." Watching their faces, Zyanya saw hope in their eyes. She continued, "How many of you chose to serve the prodon willingly?" No hands raised.

"What if we choose not to serve you, what then?" asked Poe.

"You would be bound until after the battle, and then you would be freed."

Interrupting, Bru said, "She speaks true."

"Tells a liar," said Poe.

"A needed story. Now there is no reason."

Poe nodded to Bru and asked Zyanya, "May I talk to my men?"

"Assemble them," said Zyanya. She sat and said, "Let me down."

The man guarding Poe lowered his spear, and Poe moved into the open.

"Gather up, men, there is a choice to be made."

Weapons withdrew and the men amassed. Poe took count. Looking around, he did not see his number two man. Poe asked Aric, "Where is Ragger?"

"Last I saw of him he went to the latrine."

Poe faced the bamboo fence. "Ragger?"

There was no answer. Poe checked inside. Empty. Searching outside, Poe spotted a place where the grass had been flattened. Zyanya's sentry followed Poe. "Is a man missing?" he asked.

"My second man. Seems he ran off. Probably to warn Lord Prodon."

The sentry said, "Back to your men." He rushed up to Zyanya. "Your Highness. One of the guards is missing. His leader tells he may have gone to warn the prodon."

Clenching her fists, she called her prime sentry. Zyanya told him, "Send a runner to the generals. Tell them the plan is thwarted and to assemble at the return encampment."

Without speaking, Zyanya took her bag of clothing and ducked into the nearest hut. Moments later she reappeared in her battle dress: a protective leather headdress and breastplate with covered sandals laced to her knees.

She called a lead man. "Inform the slaves of their freedom and bid them to help us leave the prodon with nothing of comfort."

"Yes, Your Highness."

Marching up to Poe and his men, she said, "Since your man spoiled our strategy, all who remain loyal to the prodon, go to him now. Upon my word, no one will harm you."

With her arms folded in front of her, she turned her back and waited. Hearing no footfalls, she turned and faced them. Poe held his hands out. "What is your wish, Your Highness?"

"You and your men, as well as the freed men and women, will be escorted to our caravan."

"How far are we to walk?" asked one of Poe's men.

Not wanting to give too much away, she said, "Until we reach our people. Fear not, you will be fed well along the way."

"Are we to be trussed?" asked another.

"No, but you will remain weaponless." Examining their faces, she repeated, "Any who wish to leave may still do so. Once we begin our journey, I will not allow it."

"What if I want to return to my village?" one of the men asked.

"What place is your home?"

"River Shores."

Hearing the name of a village near Twin Oaks, Grand searched for familiar faces. Seeing none, he relaxed.

"I have not heard of this place," said Zyanya.

"The village is four or five days northwest from here."

With a nod, one of her sentries moved in front of her. Pointing to the recently freed slaves, Zyanya said, "Bring them all here so that they may hear me and make choices."

Stepping on top of the litter, she sat and signaled to Bru for him and his friends to raise her. They lifted her, and once the litter was resting on their shoulders, Zyanya stood. Everyone formed a circle around her.

"How many of you wish to return to your homes?"

More than a dozen hands raised.

"Of what villages remain north, I cannot say. Only that the prodon leaves little when he moves on. Those places south have been plundered completely. The refugees from them are part of the caravan I lead." She watched hope vanish from their faces. "This man," said Zyanya, gesturing to the man wanting to go north, "wants to journey to his village, River Shores. What awaits him I cannot say, only that he has my blessing and whatever provisions he requires. Does anyone wish to join him?"

No one did.

"Go then. Take whatever necessities you require," said Zyanya.

The man bowed his head and went to gather his supplies. She announced, "Any others wishing to journey home may do so with my blessing."

Several of Poe's men stepped forward. One man said, "Your Highness, my village is Valley of Plenty, and from here I cannot know where to trek."

Zyanya turned toward what she believed to be the correct direction. "Southwest, but little remains from the prodon's final raid. Some families from there travel with us, as do many from those ruined villages we happened on."

Hearing the news, those men decided to go with the priestess. She made another proclamation for anyone to leave or stay for the journey.

Standing in the back, Grand weighed his choices. This was an opportunity to go on his own. He would be provisioned and free. His other option was to stay with this lot and be fed. Studying all the faces, he saw none of the Twin Oaks captives, nor anyone he recognized from Seaside Hill.

Regarding Zyanya's face, Grand was captivated by her tanned skin and dark eyes. Poking out the back of her helmet, her shiny black braid swung this way and that as she talked. The breastplate she wore concealed her femininity, but her short skirt offered promise. Grand shifted positions so he could view her legs. He edged closer.

Admiring her muscular thighs, Grand gasped when she spun as he saw the white stone blade and memorable carved elk handle strapped to her side. Pine's knife. How had she gained Pine's blade? His body. She or her men must have found Pine's corpse. Picturing Pine's putrefied carcass, Grand smiled and continued ogling Zyanya. Catching her gaze, he swore to himself to have her.

Lord Prodon's second man brought Ragger to the tower. From his throne, the prodon commanded he speak. "Lord Prodon, raiders overran camp seven."

"Raiders? What raiders do you speak of? From what village?"

"Lord Prodon, I saw them naught. What I know, I heard with my ears. A woman led them."

"A woman?"

"I heard her name. Zyanya."

The color washed from the prodon's face. "Who else knows of this?"

"No one, Lord Prodon."

Without hesitating, the prodon stood from his throne, whipped his blade from his sash, and sliced the man's throat. With wide eyes, Ragger grabbed his neck as the blood poured from the wound. He choked and coughed. "Her…her arm…" Unable to finish, the man fell to the decking. The prodon ordered his guard to remove the bleeding man.

Awaiting her army, Zyanya considered a new plan. Because of a lack of trust, at the rendezvous, Zyanya separated the prodon's guards and former slaves and split her sentries to escort them independently to the caravan. Concerned for her safety, Bru asked, "Your Highness? Is it wise to send your guards away before your army arrives?"

"The gods look after me and my army will be here by sunset. Until that time, you and your friends can protect me."

"Yes, Your Highness. With our lives."

"You speak for your friends?"

"Our allegiance to you is chosen by us all."

"That pleases me, yet I grow hungry. Does your loyalty allow you to make a meal for us?"

"Yes, Your Highness." Bru dashed off to enlist his friends, and they began gathering helpings of dried elk strips, greens, and plums. While they fixed a midday dinner, Zyanya poured gourds of cactus juice. Carefully, she sprinkled a gray powder in theirs. The brews fizzed until the residue dissipated.

In the shade of a plum tree, Zyanya set the litter up as a table. She put their drinks out while Gorg spread mats to sit. Picking her spot, Zyanya sat cross-legged, and Luca served her. Once all were seated, Zyanya raised her gourd, uttered a quick prayer to the gods, and swallowed the nectar. The others raised their cups and saluted the gods before sipping their share. They ate as Zyanya asked them questions. "What will the prodon's response be?"

Bru answered, "If the man heard and told how your army was a half-day away, then the prodon would first send scouts to assess your forces."

"How many of these scouts?"

"Three or possibly four."

"What next?"

"He would know of your forces and send his army ahead and, should he think you unbeatable, he would send runners to bring back the advance army."

After finishing his meal, Werth began smacking his thighs. "My legs have lost feeling."

Experiencing the same sensation, Bru said, "I cannot move mine. It is as if I no longer have feet." He began thrashing. The others complained of their similar predicament.

Standing, Zyanya said, "Be still, or all your motion will freeze."

"What did you do?" asked Bru.

"Nothing to harm. A surgeon's powder to still a patient."

"Are we not to be trusted?"

"This battle with the prodon belongs to me alone." She set a rolled weaving on Bru's lap and put a hand on his shoulder. Her touch was tender. "Give this to my generals."

"Do not go, Your Highness! Please!" said Bru. "Wait for your army."

"The gods will protect me." She strapped her sack across her shoulder and, with unwavering resolve and her white stone blade, she trotted off to kill the man who had murdered her father. Yaotl, the prodon.

At the meeting place, a scout for the generals hurried to the four men laying on the ground. "Where is Her Highness? And where have the sentries gone?" Unable yet to move, Bru said in his native tongue, "Before she put a medicine in our drinks to still us, she sent her men back to the caravan. Your priestess left this weaving for the generals." Bru gestured with his chin.

The runner took the cloth and scampered off to tell the generals. On the ground beside Bru, Luca moved a leg. "Pricks tingle my limbs."

"As do mine," said Werth.

Gorg tried to stand, only to roll on his stomach. With the side of his face in the dirt, he began laughing.

"What do you find amusing?" asked Bru.

"Your beloved has bested us all."

"My beloved? What do you speak?"

"Since she first looked at you, she bears the signs of a wanting lover."

"He speaks true," said Luca. "It is only you she calls."

"Because I talk her tongue. Besides, she knows I am only a potter."

The Era of Herbalists

"Me thinks she cares not. When you are not seeing her, she gazes at you," said Werth. "This I have witnessed many times."

Ignoring them, Bru flexed his prickling fingers. Sensation was returning. He strained and lifted his right arm, then the left. The others worked the numbness away in their own manner. When sense returned to his back and arms, Werth beat on his legs until feeling returned.

With the help of the plum tree, Luca raised himself. Leaning on the trunk, he spotted some men in the distance trotting toward them. "Some sentries are coming."

"Do you see the army?"

"No. Only a few men."

By the time the sentries reached them, all four were on their feet. They recognized Baptta Mora. His mother, Gonda, cared for Pine Nyte's wife.

Speaking the language, Bru translated to his friends.

"We have come for you. Can you walk?" asked Baptta.

"Yes, but slowly," Bru replied.

"Where is the attack to be?"

"Her Highness ordered us back to the caravan."

"What of she? Are you not planning to help Her Highness?" asked Bru.

"Our orders are to leave her."

"How can you obey such orders?"

"Her Highness placed herself in the care of the gods."

"But she does not know how well the prodon is protected."

"The gods will show her. Come with us."

"No. Not myself, I will help your priestess." Bru interpreted for his friends and explained their reply to the sentry. "They choose to aid Zyanya with me."

"But you have no weapons."

"We have our flints and our wits."

The army turned away from the prodon's camp with orders to return to the caravan. Joining with the army, Pine had been set on freeing his father. On the way back to the caravan, he learned how the priestess had gone after the prodon on her own, and that his four new friends went after her. A half-day behind them, Pine decided to follow.

Her Highness' orders worried the captain of the sentries with her command to leave her with the four escaped slaves. But she had insisted and reaffirmed her faith in the gods, and promised the army to join her by sunset. Still, the captain fretted not knowing.

Following his orders, he and eleven of his men led the prodon's former guards on the trail to the caravan. A short distance behind them, his other team guided the former slaves. Since these men had served the prodon with arms, they could not be trusted yet. Three of his men led the group, two archers flanked each side, and he and the remaining four covered the rear.

Over the three nights the groups would camp separately, and considering the uneven pace, the second group mixed with women and children would fall a half-day behind by the time they reached the caravan.

Because of Grand's size, the captain chose him to haul the travois of supplies. At first he chastised himself for not setting off on his own. However, the pledge that his effort had earned him more rations quelled his rage some. Plus, he had no other chores to trouble him, and he would be served. Those thoughts fueled him along.

Realizing their freedom, the former slaves joyfully strode on the trail. The loads they hauled or carried were no longer burdensome. A new life waited for them, and if the truth had been told, a better existence. The armed sentries ushering them served as their protectors.

Many of these refugees were kin to some who traveled with the caravan. Already some had names of friends and relatives traveling with the group.

The Encounter

As Bru had told her, Zyanya found the prodon's tower in the middle of the assembly. Until the moon set, she hunkered down. The anguished screams erupting from the top told her of Yaotl's unspeakable cruelty. Unable to see, she guessed from the length and intensity of the shrieking, and with her imagination, she visualized the punishments. Having witnessed Yaotl's brutality as a child, she speculated blades and fire.

Finally there was silence from the tower. No more wailing. After a time, the torches on top of the tower extinguished. Once the moon disappeared, Zyanya used the darkness to sneak up toward the structure. From watching the night guards, she picked her chance and dashed to the base. Before their return pass, she climbed the first section. The bamboo creaked and she froze. The guards walked below her without looking up. She waited for them to go before scaling the next section.

Reaching for a support on the fourth section, she came face to face with a dead man. She threw a hand over her mouth to keep from gagging. In the starlight she saw more hanging. Entrails cascaded from their bellies.

On the fifth tier, she spotted a woven cord to aid her over the railing. She grasped it with both hands and when her weight strained, bamboo poles covered in netting slammed down on either side of her. Trapping her.

Torches were lit and guards quickly came to haul Zyanya to the top deck. Four guards pinned her and one of them relieved her of her white blade. They removed her head cover, stripped her breastplate off, and took her sandals. Forcing her to her feet, they shoved her arms behind her and tethered her to a pole facing an empty throne. She struggled and the jute cut into her wrists. She heard the lift shimmy and someone lowered them. Sensing someone behind her, she called, "Yaotl?"

"No. Not Yaotl."

Hearing him, her heart thumped. The voice echoed from her past and she had been sure to never hear it again. "Father?"

He moved in front of her. "Zyanya, you have grown into a fine example of womanhood."

"Father. With my own eyes I saw Yaotl cut your throat. Did the gods save you?"

"A clever play. And only when we are alone like now shall you call me father. In everyone's presence, I am Lord Prodon."

"Father? How could you, a sayer for the gods, be this person? This Lord Prodon?"

"Gods?" He stuck his face in hers. "I, Lord Prodon, am the only god!"

"Blasphemy!" yelled Zyanya.

Taking his place on his throne, he laughed a hysterical cackle. Calming, he said, "You senseless child. There are no gods."

"But you taught them to me."

"Yes. What I taught you had been schooled to myself."

"Why then teach me?"

"Nothing less was expected of me."

"Tell me, then. How did you lose faith?"

"Faith? My only faith is my will."

"But your sermons? The passion in your lessons brought the people to tears. You gave hope."

"Those tears gave me riches. The hope you say I provided gave me a mass of worshipers. And, daughter, with that same made-up passion, I raised an army of soldiers willing to die for me."

"Made up? I do not understand."

He walked up to her and lifted her chin. "Zyanya, the zeal you witnessed was only my skill at pretending."

"How can you say such? Only such fervor could come from a pure heart."

"A heart?" The prodon laughed. "Pure or not, a heart is but meat."

"Then how did you learn to be cruel, Father?"

"Am I? Look around you. For these people, I am their hope. With my guidance, they are provided for. With their labor, they reap rewards."

"And those disemboweled people hanging from this tower, did you provide for them? Reward them?"

"Generously, until Master Lewell's blade did my bidding. Examples must be made."

"For what offense?"

"Dissension, gluttony, thieving, and all things that offend me."

"Do you not care anything for those people?"

"Nothing I cause gives me pain."

"What of the others?"

"Others? What others?"

"Those villages you pillage?"

"Tribute to feed my army," said the prodon.

"Have you no feelings?"

"Only joy and pleasure for myself."

"Your hair? Why do you color it yellow?"

"A god needs immediate identity and there are no others as me."

Lifting her chin, Zyanya asked, "What will you do with me? Kill me? Torture me?"

"Zyanya. You are my daughter. I would never kill you."

"Then what? Leave me tied to this pole?"

"No, to be Master Lewell's wife. Bear his children. According to the ancient scroll, you are destined to have three. They may as well be Lewell's."

"Who?"

"You remember him as Yaotl."

"Him! Never!"

"Daughter, it will not be your choice."

"Of that we will see." Picturing the brute in her mind, she asked, "Why do you call Yaotl by that name?"

"The feeble people here cannot speak his name properly. He grew tired of lopping heads over their defective tongues."

"And you, Father? The Lord Prodon?"

"In this people's tongue, 'prodon' means all gods. And I am he."

But Zyanya knew his definition to be incomplete. In truth, the word meant all gods of regretful deeds. To that, she believed he had picked a proper title, since all his deeds were shameful.

A creaking sound turned Zyanya's head. The lift raised with two guards on the deck holding an empty bamboo cage. The brutes carried it on the tower and sat the cage in front of her. One of them lifted the gate while the other freed her from the pole, only to shove her up to the cage.

"Climb in, Zyanya."

She stared at him.

"I suggest you do as I have told you. Otherwise, these men will shove you inside."

Zyanya climbed in. With no room to sit, she curled on her side, and the guard closed the lid and tied it shut. Then he secured a heavy cord to the top brace. The other guard raised a panel in the tower floor. With a signal from her father, the two men lifted the cage and held her over the opening. Peering down, she saw the ground far below. The prodon faced her. "I grow weary at this late hour. Perhaps this will give you a proper sense of your future duties." He gestured to the guards, and they dropped the cage through the opening. The cage reached the end of the cord with a loud snap and Zyanya crashed into the bars.

The panel above closed, and the stench of the dead men surrounding her caused Zyanya to vomit. After exhausting the contents of her stomach, she continued to retch. After a time, sleep overcame her.

The four rescuers reached the prodon's camp in the dark morning. To help conceal themselves, they blackened their faces with charcoal. A space between the cooking area and the weaver's place gave them a view. They studied the tower. Something had happened. The guards had doubled. Worse, some patrolled while others stood sentry.

Gorg whispered, "It must be her in that cage, hanging. We need a distraction."

Looking around, Luca pointed to the weavings draped over rails. "The cook will have oil. A fire should draw them away."

They agreed. Careful not to wake the cook, Werth snuck up to the roasting pits. Near the firewood he spotted a clay vessel. He sniffed. Pig fat oil. Taking it, he stood and turned around. Poised to strike Werth with a bludgeon, the cook glared at him. After his unsuccessful swing at Werth's head, Gorg tackled the cook. Behind Gorg, Bru jumped on top of the cook and grasped hold of his jaws. He held his mouth closed and pressed a flint against his throat.

"Be silent or die," whispered Bru. When he felt the cook relax, Bru released his hold. With his head facing the ground, Gorg tied the cook's arms behind him with cords and bound his legs. Stuffing his mouth, they left him staring at dirt.

Werth doused the weavings, and Luca struck flint together over dry moss. A spark made a glow and Luca puffed. A flame flared and he lit the weavings. While the blaze spread, the four rescuers took positions, ready to take advantage of the chaos. Adding to the confusion, they dumped all the nearby water pots and broke several.

Flames lit the weaver's space. Unsure of what to do, the guards stood frozen. With an empty vessel, Bru ran to one and thrust a pot at him.

"Save Lord Prodon's weavings! Get water! Hurry!" To another he yelled, "You! Move! Get water!"

The other guards joined them and, like good soldiers, they obeyed the authority Bru portrayed. While they rushed about searching for water, the four men scaled the tower. In the brilliant gleam, Zyanya saw them coming for her. She braced herself when Bru reached her. With a grin, he sawed on the cage lashings. After he freed her, Bru helped her down.

With the fire still blazing, Luca, Gorg, and Werth worked their way to the bottom. As they climbed down, they slashed the bands binding the bamboo structure. Some they cut through, others they scored deeply.

On the ground, the three shoved on the base. The tower moved. Slowly at first, it began to come apart, then the thing toppled. Running for their lives, they followed Bru and Zyanya to Chirp's place.

Focused on the blaze, none of the guards noticed the saboteurs scurrying off. Then the tower collapsed. Those men fighting the fire barely escaped being crushed when the massive structure crashed to the ground.

Having heard the commotion, Chirp rose and put on his moccasins. The tower had fallen. He smelled smoke. Outside his sleep hut, he heard someone. With his mouth hanging open, he gazed at his friends and the woman.

"Chirp," said Bru. "This is Zyanya. She leads a caravan of free people. Lord Prodon may be dead. Come with us."

"I cannot," Chirp replied. "The prodon would sack my village."

"He will not. Come. Your son and his wife wait at the caravan."

"My son?"

"Pine, his wife, and his dog," said Werth.

"We must go now," said Bru.

Glancing at the woman's bare feet, Chirp said, "The extra moccasins I have are too large, but later you can adjust them." He fetched them for her. She tied them on as tightly as she could.

"You must go and I must stay," said Chirp. They scampered off before the fire was extinguished.

Dreaming, Lord Prodon watched the mountain pass grow closer as his carriers transported him in his tower at a full run. He felt the vibration of their effort. Suddenly he woke. His tower shook and began to collapse. He grabbed a rail, and without warning the tower fell and everything turned black.

Agonizing pain brought him to consciousness. Tangled in his bed nest and pinned under bamboo poles and mastodon tusks, he stared in Patto's face. The prodon blinked and Patto called, "Lord Prodon lives!"

Men began lifting the weights off him. It seemed as if the whole tower had landed on him, not just the roof. Finally they raised the last pole off. Unable to feel his legs, in the torchlight he stared down at them. His legs were no longer limbs, just two flattened, bloody lengths of meat infused with jagged protruding bone fragments. However, his feet, other than the deep purple color, were untouched.

A man reached under his arms to pull him up and the prodon screamed a seemingly endless wail. His right arm dangled uselessly. As the man lifted, Lord Prodon's left leg, mashed to a section of broken deck, separated at his knee. With a shriek, he lost consciousness.

The Era of Herbalists

From his station near the front of the assembly, Lewell hurried toward the flames. In the firelight he watched in horror as Lord Prodon's tower came down.

Nearing the collapsed tower, Lewell saw Patto escorting two men carrying the Lord Prodon to the herbalist's place. Patto stood gaping at Lord Prodon's smashed legs, and Lewell pushed past him.

Worried, Lewell hovered over Chirp, who held a lamp above the prodon. Whatever pulverized his legs had pinched off his arteries, and little blood flowed. Feeling his legs, Chirp cursed. Both legs were pulverized to his loin skin. Nothing solid remained, only chunks, bits, and crumbs.

Chirp rushed to the travois, dug into his apothecary, and came out with his flint saw. He placed the blade in the coals. Adding more wood, Patto fanned the fire, and once the blade glowed, Chirp used a leather wrap to grasp it. Holding back the prodon's loin hide, he gasped. Half of the prodon's penis was pinched off. Ignoring that injury, he placed the edge on Lord Prodon's skin. The flesh sizzled. Chirp made a dozen swift back and forth cuts and amputated the ruined left leg. Without asking, Patto handed Chirp a flaming stick, and he held the fire against the wound.

Chirp then repeated heating the saw. The right leg, crushed to pulp, only needed three cuts, and the scorching blade itself cauterized the wound. Chirp washed his bloody hands and used a sea sponge to clean Lord Prodon's stumps. Since he remained unaware, Chirp spread a liberal amount of weaver's wood salve directly on the wounds.

"Will he live?" asked Lewell.

"He breathes."

"What happened?"

"Ask your guards, I was sleeping. Now I must attend to his arm."

Sneering, Lewell stormed off in search of answers.

Cautiously, Chirp lifted the prodon's right arm. Running a hand along the limb, he felt two breaks. He called to Patto, "I need four short slats of wood for splints and some jute!"

When Patto returned with the splint makings, Chirp said, "Hold his shoulder."

Patto was unsure of how, so Chirp showed him. Once he had a grip, Chirp held the prodon's elbow, and he tugged and twisted until the bone set into place. Then Chirp pinned the upper arm between the boards and wrapped the jute, leaving enough room for the swelling. Then Patto held the splinted arm while Chirp turned and pulled on the prodon's wrist. Satisfied, Chirp strapped the wood to his forearm.

Signaling the guards who had carried the prodon, he said, "Put Lord Prodon in my sleep hut. When he wakes, he will feel pain, so I must mix a wolf root and all-heal herb remedy."

Standing in front of the tumbled tower, Lewell ordered the loitering guards to stand before him. With a blade in his hand, he stepped in front of the first man. "Tell me what happened here. Every detail."

"A fire, Master Lewell," one guard said. "It started in the weaver's place. Someone commanded we save Lord Prodon's weavings."

Without changing his blank expression, Lewell slashed the man's throat. In the dirt, he clutched his neck, desperately trying to stop his bleeding. Blood flowed between his fingers and he died. Lewell stepped to the next man. "Tell me! Who caused this?"

The guard dropped to his knees. "Master Lewell, we tried to put out the fire, but there was no water and some pots were broken. We saw no one."

Grabbing him by his hair, Lewell lifted his head and kneed his face. He collapsed on the ground. Stomping the man's neck, he hollered at the remaining three men. "Tell me who caused the tower to fall!"

Before any of them answered, an abrupt grunt turned Lewell's head toward the cooking area. He stepped inside the fence. The cook's hut stood empty. Another groan took him to the roasting pits. He found the cook gagged and trussed.

Harshly, he ripped the gag from his mouth. "Who bound you?"

Coughing, the cook uttered, "Water...please..."

Scanning the area, Lewell saw a drinking gourd. Half full, he picked it up with both hands. Instead of offering the cook a drink, Lewell crushed the gourd in his face. Water and blood ran down the cook's cheeks.

"Who bound you?" yelled Lewell.

"Three men," choked the cook. "I challenged one man stealing my cooking oil but two men beat me, tied me up, and stuffed my mouth."

"Who were they? Tell me!"

"Strangers. The one man I saw had black skin from charcoal."

Lewell smacked his face. "You said there were three men!"

"Yes, Master Lewell, but the other two men came from behind and forced my face into the dirt."

Angered, Lewell kicked the cook's bound legs and trudged off. The cook was about to ask for Lewell to free him before he decided keeping silent would spare his life. His helpers would untie him when they came at sunrise.

Demanding answers, Lewell assembled all Lord Prodon's guards in front of the rubble. In the middle of the mound of mostly bamboo, Patto ordered slaves to salvage the prodon's throne.

A slave, rummaging in the debris, found a white stone knife. He held it to a torch and stared at the carvings on the handle. He wanted the blade for his own, but here, a death decree waited for a slave possessing a weapon.

Raising the blade over his bowed head, he called Patto. But Lewell snatched it from his grip.

"Where did you find this?" asked Lewell. Examining the tool, he turned it in his hand. This blade belonged to a hunter. But who?

"Master Lewell, the knife came from Lord Prodon's bed nest."

"Show me."

The slave took a few steps, gazed down, and pointed. Carrying a torch, Lewell stepped over the bamboo poles, careful not to slip. Beside the dire wolf fur bed nest, Lewell gasped when he saw Lord Prodon's smashed leg and blackened left foot. Quickly, he turned away.

Aiming a finger at a guard, he yelled, "Bury this!"

While that man approached, two slaves lifted a section of the top deck and uncovered the five men he himself had slain. Lewell saw the crushed cage.

Facing the prodon's guards, Lewell said, "Last night's sentinels, show yourselves."

Five of the men moved.

"Enlighten me on the night's events. Leave nothing out." He pointed to the first man.

"Master Lewell, after the moon set, a woman sprung the trap. She had a white blade and she wore battle dress. Lord Prodon took the knife."

"Describe her and her dress to me."

"She came about to here," said the guard. He brought a hand up to just below his shoulder. "She had long black hair made into a braid. Thing poked out the back of her leather head shell. Wore a breast cover. Me and Zac took it off her, had little teats. Also, she had sandals laced up her legs."

"What did she wear under the leather?"

"Only a plain weaving. Covered her shoulders and came to her knees."

"What did you do next?"

"Lord Prodon commanded we tie her to the center post. Then he ordered us away and for Rocca and Fenn to come back with a cage."

"Is that the last?"

"Only that Lord Prodon whispered his orders to us so that the woman did not recognize his voice."

Turning to Rocca, Lewell said, "Tell your tale."

"Myself and Fenn brought the cage," Rocca replied. "Lord Prodon ordered the woman inside and she obeyed. He called her Zyanya."

Lewell shuddered when he heard her name spoken. "What next?"

"Then Lord Prodon bade us to hang the cage among the dead."

"Is there more to tell?"

"From the lift we heard Lord Prodon tell her she was to be your own bride and bear your three children."

"What did she say to that?"

"That the marriage would not happen, but Lord Prodon promised her it would be as he said."

"What else?"

"Master Lewell, she called Lord Prodon father."

"Find her!" demanded Lewell. "Spread the word! She travels with three men! Bring them to me alive! Go now!"

CHAPTER 51

The Reckoning

HIDING OFF THE trail, Werth used his flint to trim off the excess doeskin and shortened Zyanya's moccasins. Since leaving Chirp, her face had held a scowl.

"Your Highness, do not anger at us," said Bru.

"I hold no ire at you. All of you have my thanks. My rage is at my father."

"Your father? Is he not the subject of your revenge?"

"A lie. My father did not die, he is the prodon. The man I sought revenge against staged his false death, Yaotl, and is known by Master Lewell."

"If the prodon is not dead, he will be sure to pain."

"I must know," said Zyanya.

"The finding may be difficult," said Gorg.

"Werth?" asked Bru. "Did the cook recognize you?"

"Nothing showed in his face. The charcoal disguised me."

"Then we can go back," said Bru.

"How?" asked Luca. "They think we deserted."

"With cures. Much mandrake root grows here. Chirp always complains he can find none."

"Also there is cramp weed and turtlebloom," said Luca.

Far enough away, heavy brush and a black nut tree gave Zyanya a safe place to wait. Bru had promised to return in the morning.

Carrying the litter full of cures below their waist, the four friends approached the three sentries at the rear of the column. The four men were strangers to them. Brandishing their spears, the guards challenged them.

Grinning, Gorg said, "I cannot believe we finally caught up to you."

"Who are you and what is your business here?"

"We aid Chirp Nyte, the herbalist. We bring him cures."

The lead sentry rummaged through the plants. He picked up some turtle-bloom and sniffed. "What is this for?" Bru answered, "An aid for stomachs."

He picked up a mandrake root. "And this?"

"For the diarrhea."

Wrinkling his nose, he said, "Peral. Escort them to the herbalist."

"Where is he to be found?" asked Peral.

"We will show you," said Gorg. "He will be near Lord Prodon's tower."

"Look with your eyes," said the leader. "Do you see a tower?"

"No," said Gorg. "He must be far ahead."

"No, not far. In the middle of the night, someone toppled the structure."

"Someone?"

"Master Lewell has orders to find the three men and a woman who caused the tower to collapse."

"What of Lord Prodon?" asked Bru.

"Alive, is all I am told."

"Will he build a new tower?"

"Of that I cannot say."

"Fair day," said Bru. They ambled off.

On the way several people recognized them, but no one challenged them. At the herbalist's area they had to wait while Chirp treated the prodon. Surprise lit his face when he saw his four friends. Catching the eye of the guard escorting them, Chirp played along. "I nearly gave up on you. What did you bring me?"

"Mandrake root, turtlebloom herb, and cramp weed," said Luca.

"Good, but that does not fill my apothecary. Tomorrow, bring me more."

Hearing the banter, the guard wandered back to his post. After he left Bru asked, "Tell me, is the prodon going to live?"

"Yes, but with no legs, a broken right arm, and only half his manhood, he will no longer be the god he pretended to be."

"How will he rule?"

"He may not," said Chirp. "Now, Master Lewell reigns. He spent the day punishing guards for not finding those responsible."

"How many know of the prodon's injuries?" asked Gorg.

"By now, most should grasp."

"Where is he?"

"Here. In my hut."

"Is he awake?"

"No. The skullcap essence keeps him slumbering."

"Seeing him in such a state would show the people their god is naught."

"Master Lewell promised the people his legs would grow back."

"How? He is no god."

"Master Lewell brought Terral, the wood carver, to size the prodon. He ordered him to fashion legs and make him taller."

"What of his manhood?" asked Luca. "Did Master Lewell summon the stone sculptor?"

Once the laughter ceased, Chirp said, "No, but Lewell commanded me to fit the thing in a doeskin sheath."

More hilarity erupted. An anguished cry from the hut brought quiet. The prodon had awakened. Chirp rushed to him. At the entry, Chirp gagged and backed away. Lord Prodon had shit himself.

The prodon hollered in an unfamiliar tongue. Away from the stench, Chirp called to Patto, "Lord Prodon requires care!"

Without hesitating, Patto darted to the hut and stuck his head inside. After a single breath, Patto heaved his morning meal in the prodon's face. Patto then jumped to his feet, wiped his lips with his forearm, and grumbled, "No god dwells here!" He stomped off.

From the hut, the prodon coughed and choked. "Tend me! I am Lord Prodon, god of all gods!" he cried. "Tend me!"

His shrieking brought the cook, his daughters, some workers, and several guards. With his arms folded across his chest, Chirp gestured to the hut. "The one and only god has shit himself. Who will clean him?"

As they milled about, Chirp kicked off the stones pinning the hut skin and pulled the cover off. The sudden stench backed people away. In the bright morning sunlight, the prodon scrunched his eyes closed.

Holding their hands over their mouths, the people gawked at him. Curious about the gathering crowd, more people assembled. The few who pitied the unfortunate creature slipped away, while others joked and teased him. The unrestrained levity brought Master Lewell. He forced his way through the throng of onlookers.

Waving his blade in the air, he screamed. "Dare you blaspheme against Lord Prodon!" He caught Chirp's eye. "You! You did this!" He charged Chirp. But Bru threw a rock and hit Lewell in the knee. Lewell staggered. Gorg took his shot with a fist-sized stone and hit him square in the loin skin. Lewell stumbled and landed on his elbows. Gulping for air, he dropped the milk-white blade.

More people picked up rocks, and they began to hurl them. Writhing on the ground, Lewell held his arms over his face. But the stones kept coming as more people pelted him. Hefting a substantial rock from the roasting pit, the cook flung the thing on top of Lewell's bald head. The rock bounced off with a thud.

Still alive, Lewell tried to crawl away, but one of the guards he had punished earlier ran his lance into Lewell's anus, causing a short but earsplitting shriek. The guard continued prodding him until Lewell stopped twitching. He abandoned his spear.

With a lance in his hand, Werth readied to impale the prodon, but Chirp stopped him. "Leave him to the death eaters. They have much to dine on." Chirp faced the people and yelled as loudly as he could, "You are free! The prodon and his heavy hand are no more. Let us have a celebration! Spread the word!"

Clasping Chirp's hand, Bru said, "Keep the death eaters away until I return with Zyanya."

"Here," said Chirp. He handed Bru Zyanya's sandals he had recovered.

With a wave of his hand, Bru took off at a run. He only hoped he returned with Zyanya in time for her to witness the death of her father.

Rolling Lewell's body over, Chirp stared at the elk handle of the white blade on the ground. The very handle he had carved and left with his father to give to Pine.

Bru reached Zyanya at midday. On the trek back to the prodon's camp, he told her the tale. Eager to face her father, she quickened the pace. Bru trailed close behind her, admiring her form.

"Slow down, Your Highness. Take some water."

Stopping, she said, "Bru, you may call me Zyanya."

The Era of Herbalists

"But Your Highness, you are a priestess." He passed her a goatskin vessel.

"Yes, and you are my champion. So speak my name." She drank and handed the bag to him, then trotted off.

"As you wish…Zyanya." Keeping her pace, he grinned the rest of the way to the prodon's former encampment.

Someone had dragged Lewell's body into the brush, and death eaters were feasting. Sensing another imminent death, several crowded out of the meal flew at the prodon, but Werth and Luca kept them away with rocks.

Thirsty, the prodon begged for water. To keep the man alive and wash the vomit off his face, Gorg dumped a half cauldron on him. Rather than clean him, they covered the prodon with sand to his belly.

With the sun still high in the sky, Zyanya gaped at the thing that had been her father. A murderous charlatan. The prodon's eyes fluttered, trying to focus on her. So much she wanted to say to him, but knowing it would be lost on him, she kept those thoughts to herself. Without a word she walked away, and with her, the others followed, leaving the prodon alone. Moments later, a death eater landed on his splinted arm. Too weak to defend himself, the bird pecked at his eyes. He threw his good arm up, and the scavenger took three of his fingers.

With his remaining strength, he yelled, "Zyanya!" At that moment, a second death eater swooped down and jammed his beak in the prodon's open mouth. Gouging with its beak, the bird thrust his head down the prodon's throat. Choking, the once one and only god drowned in his own blood.

Considering the prophecy, Zyanya asked Bru to take her to Chirp. To Chirp she shared the scroll and explained how Pine and Lily had come to them. Also, she promised to bring them ceremoniously to Twin Oaks and establish trade between the two peoples.

For their part in the festivities, the cook, Jos Newt, his new wife Dyna Rae, and his daughters, Luna and Layan, built a second and third fire pit. All would eat well tonight. To each of the diners, he told them this would be the last meal that he would fix here.

In addition, the distiller brought out the spirit nectar, and those freed people having musical talent brought out drums, and dancers pranced to the tunes they played.

Smoke guided Pine to the encampment. When he got closer he heard music. Listening to the song, Pine wondered if he had reached the prodon's camp. He saw no tower, and from what his four friends had spoken, music was not something heard there. Also, no sentries guarded the camp. Seeing no threats, Pine strolled toward the music and laughter.

The scent of cooking meat steered Pine. A familiar ginger and honey aroma. Searching faces, Pine spotted Gorg spinning a laughing child in circles. On a turn, Gorg recognized Pine. He stopped whirling and raised the boy to his shoulder and called, "Chirp! Your son has come!"

Standing, Chirp panned the crowd and saw Pine. They locked eyes and with face-splitting grins rushed to each other. Embracing, tears of joy leaked down their cheeks. Holding Pine's forearms, he backed away and gazed up to his taller son. "Never did I think I would see you again," said Chirp.

"Father. My joy is indescribable."

A familiar voice sounded behind Pine. "Where is Shadow?"

Turning around, he hugged his friend: it was Ash. Pine said, "Ash, I am happy to see you. Shadow cares for Lily at the caravan south of here."

Hobbling to Ash, Song wrapped her arm around his. Ash embraced her. "This is my wife, Song."

"Blessings to you both," said Pine. Seeing the two smiling at each other just as bold as he and Lily, Pine thanked the spirits for matching them.

"Along with Song, I bring her family to Twin Oaks. Her father cooks."

"Your family grieves the loss of you. I cannot imagine what joy your return will cause."

"The joy will soon fall when I tell of my choice to be an artisan instead of one who works the loam," said Ash.

"Perhaps," said Pine, "but your sister Fern married Luc Hogg. He works the land with your father."

"Was him got traded for me," said Ash. "Still, that makes me happy."

"More delight awaits Twin Oaks when we return with the other hunters taken with me," said Chirp. "Plus, Seaside Hill will rejoice when Ute Augend comes home to them. We begin the journey in the morning."

"As will I," said Pine. "Before I return to Twin Oaks, I must go to the caravan for Lily and Shadow. So be sure to say to Ric and Reba Sayed that Lily and our child she carries thrive."

The next morning at first light, Chirp hugged Pine. "How many days away is the caravan?"

"Three or four is my guess."

"Twin Oaks is that many days from here. I shall tell your mother to expect you twelve days from now. Should you come sooner, the better for all."

"It will be my effort, but Lily is with child and she shall set the pace."

Nodding, Chirp said, "Travel well, son of mine."

"And you as well, Father. Send my love to our family and tell the council of Grand Moon's crimes."

Since Patto had been Chirp's helper, he sought him before heading home. Spotting him, Chirp called, "Patto?"

The man turned. "Chirp, this is an overdue parting."

"Many thanks for your unwavering aid."

Clasping Chirp's hand, Patto said, "My thanks to you, for my head is full of cures to share."

"What will happen to the prodon's many sons?" asked Chirp.

"No one has seen them or the minders for days. Perhaps he sent them ahead with his advance army."

"What will become of the army?"

"With no orders except to wait, they will send a runner. And when that man returns to tell he found no one, then the army will fold."

Nodding, Chirp said, "Farewell, friend."

"And you as well. Go home to your family."

The men parted and neither looked back.

CHAPTER 52

The Refugees

THE CONGREGATION AT the caravan welcomed the newcomers. Halfway through the census among the new arrivals, the assessors chronicled their townships and family names. Crosschecking the people's lists, some relatives were identified. Even before that, some folks recognized friends and loved ones by sight, adding to the joyous atmosphere.

After a second trip to the latrine, Lily laid on a mat for Gonda to examine her. With his back turned, Wile Hai interpreted. Gonda put the wide end of a cone-shaped basket against Lily's belly and the small end to her ear. As she listened, her eyes grew wide. "Two hearts thump inside you."

"Mine and my child's."

"No, a second child. Twins." Gonda showed the cone to Lily and placed it on her stomach. "Listen."

Lily put her ear against the end. Hearing the thumps, Lily chuckled. "It is true. Two different hearts. Why is one fainter?"

"That child is farther away. Move the basket to the other side."

Lily did as Gonda asked. "Yes. Now the beat is stronger."

The seashells outside the hut shook.

"Who calls?" asked Gonda.

"Maita Tupac!" came a voice. "I come to care for Shadow."

"Enter and be quick," said Gonda.

Shadow came to Maita with his tail swishing. Maita tied the lead to his collar and took him outside. Maita walked him to the boundary, and the two ran back and forth along the east perimeter of the encampment.

The Era of Herbalists

After the run, like Pine had showed him, Maita started feeling around Shadow's ears and peered inside. No ticks. He recalled the command Pine had used. He spoke the words, "Down, Shadow." Immediately, Shadow laid down. Then he said, "Roll over." Shadow turned and showed his chest. Maita checked under his neck, between his legs by his chest, and then around Shadow's belly. Lastly, one at a time, he spread Shadow's toes apart. Tick-free, he fed him a portion of the elk strips Pine had left. By his count, he had four more days' worth.

Before Maita brought Shadow inside to Lily, he brushed him. Then he used his hands to spread the flower-scented oil Gonda made on Shadow's coat. He started at Shadow's tail and worked his way up to his head. Careful to not get the oil in his eyes, he used one finger to apply it around his face. Suddenly, Shadow shook his head violently and broke into a sneezing fit.

Hearing the disturbance, Gonda stepped from the hut. The scent of chu-lue flowers permeated the air. Chu-lue flowers made up the base for the hair cleaner the people used. But for dogs, the oil must cause distress to the nose. With a wet doeskin, she wiped the dog's face. He sneezed a few more times, then drank half a bowl of water.

Inside the hut, Shadow curled up next to Lily, near the head of her mat. Still awake, Lily petted Shadow, and he flicked her cheek with his tongue. Secure, knowing her protector watched over her, she rubbed her belly, comforted her children, and whispered prayers to the gods to bring Pine back to her.

Twenty times the size of Twin Oaks, the clusters of tents stretched farther than Grand could see. From the chatter on the trail, he had learned there were over a dozen hunt teams and he would easily find one to join. Now his stomach was churning and he no longer towed the travois. He headed to the cook smoke.

Nearer, the pleasant aroma of roasting elk brought him to a circle filled with diners. A man scooted aside and gestured for Grand to join them. Seeing the newcomer, the cook brought Grand a thick steak and tubers on a platter. When he noticed Grand had no blade, the cook loaned Grand his.

While Grand fed, the talk spoke of some staying here and starting a village. Some others wanted to go back to a place they had left days ago, but the majority wanted to keep moving north. A direction Grand would not go. If anything, he would go east over the mountains or south along the shore.

Finishing his meal, Grand heard his name called. He spotted Poe and stood. Before Grand left, the cook held out his hand for his blade. He wiped the edge with his sleeve, and Grand passed the knife back.

Poe waved him over. "Come, we have a hut."

"The sun has yet to set."

"True, but if you do not find the place now, after dark you would sleep in the grass. So come."

They walked across the recently trampled grass to a row of palm branch–covered overhangs. Pointing, Poe directed Grand. "Those four are ours, and that one has space for you."

"Why are we separated from the other people?" asked Grand.

"When I asked the captain the question, he answered it was his orders."

"What will be your plan from this place?" asked Grand. "Will you stay with these people?"

"Some say here is a fruitful place for a town."

"For me, I yearn for a new place, untouched by others."

"The word is the east is mostly unseen."

"The mountain pass had been my goal," said Grand. "Now, maybe over the southeast hills."

"Until then, we will eat well, drink, and be lazy," said Poe.

CHAPTER 53

The Returning

THE RUNNER ZYANYA had sent reported to the camp sentries, and word spread: the high priestess and more than a thousand of the prodon's former slaves and soldiers were coming. In expectation, more brush was cleared, firepits dug, and palm huts erected.

Eager to see her again, Grand stood along the path with the other onlookers. On foot, today she wore a new outfit that left her left shoulder bare. Grand stared as she stepped closer. Then his eyes saw the profile of the man's face to Zyanya's right. Pine Nyte. Grand backed away and headed to his hut.

Meanwhile, out of the corner of his eye, Pine caught sight of a man in the crowd. Pine rubbed his eyes. Had he just seen Grand Moon? How could it be him? He needed to go to Lily and Shadow.

On his way to his hut, it appeared to Grand that the air had grown thin. As he scurried along, it also seemed his heart beat louder than his footfalls. Each time he glanced behind him, he expected Pine to be following. But he did not see him, so Grand wondered if Pine recognized him. Regardless, Pine was alive and as long as he breathed, Grand's life was at risk. Without even a flint to defend himself, the danger doubled.

There was no time to waste. He needed to leave. Then he looked around. Thousands dwelled here and now even more were coming. There was time. Time to plan and arm himself. Besides, if Pine recognized him, would he not have followed? To be sure, Grand decided he should stay inside until dark.

Was this a trick on him by the gods? How could Pine have survived the fall? Thinking back, when he shoved with his lance, he had felt the flint tip glance off

Pine's ribs. Plus, Pine had slipped and brought the branch with him. Then the dog. Grand recalled the hateful glare before he leaped after Pine. Did the dog survive? Crawling in his bed nest, Grand buried his face in the fur.

The cheering outside signaled that Zyanya had returned, but Gonda barely noticed. Her focus was on the woman with her legs spread in front of her, huffing and shrieking while pushing with her hips. Wiping her with a soaking sea sponge, Gonda saw a crest of wet black curls poking from the woman's widening slit. Gonda slicked her hands with soothing cactus lotion and waited for the woman's ultimate thrust.

After a series of contractions a few moments apart, one powerful spasm spurred a heroic push. The boy child slithered into Gonda's hands. Placing the boy in a cloth wrap, Gonda massaged him, and he exhaled and cried loud and long. Handing the child to his mother, she moved the cord aside. After a while, she would cut it and add it to the afterbirth. Now, she scooped the placenta into a clay pot. Later, the mother would plant the gifts with a tree.

As Pine strode toward the healer's hut, the sudden wail of a newborn stopped him. Not Lily—she had nearly a season left. Still, the crying brought a smile to his lips. He quickened his pace.

Even if he were struck blind, he would have found Lily by following her honey-sweet singing. Careful to not interrupt the song, Pine listened away from the tent opening. Finally, she finished the tune and Pine stepped inside. Abruptly Shadow burst from Lily's side and rushed Pine with his teeth snapping.

"Shadow!" hollered Pine. He threw his hands in front of him. Recognizing his friend, Shadow dropped to the floor. Pine reached down for Shadow to sniff him, but he did not. Instead, he sneezed.

"Pine? Are you alright?" asked Lily. She got up and embraced him.

"Yes, I am fine. Is something wrong with Shadow?"

"His nose is troubled by chu-lue flower oil. Gonda said it would pass."

"Chu-lue flowers?"

"Something these people use to clean their hair."

"Has the news spread? The prodon is no more."

"Yes. And your father? Is he well?"

"When I saw him, he was. If his trail home proved true, then he should be holding my mother now as I hold you."

"And what of my mother and father?"

"By sunset they would have the joy of knowing."

"And us? When will we be going home?"

"In three days. Zyanya is leading us."

Holding her belly, Lily said, "I have news."

"Tell me."

Lily showed Pine how the cone listener worked, and she placed her end on her stomach. At first he heard gurgling, then thump-thud-thumping. And in between, an overlapping, lighter, slightly faster–sounding thump-thud-thump. Lily moved the cone to the side. Clearly two heartbeats.

"How can there be two?"

"My mother's sister bore two girls, one grew tall and the other is like me."

"This I think will make our mothers joyful."

"And you? How do you feel?" asked Lily.

"I am joyful, but now I must sleep in peace."

Up north, on the third night, Chirp's group discovered the remnants of a battle. The bones had been picked clean and scattered. From the trappings, Chirp guessed them to be the group of missing raiders set to attack Twin Oaks.

Too close to Twin Oaks to camp for the night, Chirp and his group pressed on into the early morning. The fastest of them ran and, by the time Chirp, Ash, and Song arrived, half the village was up and waiting.

Someone started a bonfire and in the glow, Gemma wiped her teary eyes. Not believing, she stood frozen, staring at Chirp's face. With a broad smile, Chirp came to her. He touched her cheek, and Gemma threw her arms around him and squeezed.

Neva and Witt joined them. Crying, Chirp embraced them.

"Chirp," cried Gemma. "Our Pine is lost to us."

"Not true. Pine is only four or five days behind us. He is coming with Lily, who is with child, and I am told a wondrous dog travels with them."

"How?"

"A gracious people set on revenge against the prodon rescued them both at different places and times. Pine told me his and Lily's tales."

Searching faces, Chirp asked, "Where is my father?"

"We mourn Evon," said Gemma, her eyes welling with tears. "He died in battle against the gatherers set to sack Twin Oaks."

"I saw the bones from the fight. Did anyone else suffer?"

"Roth got knifed in the battle up at River Shores," said Witt. "Neva fixed him, but before that, Grand Moon killed Clem Doone. Chasing after him was what kept Twin Oaks and Seaside Hill from getting ruined. River Shores is no more. The raiders killed nearly half the men. What folks lived is living here now and Seaside Hill."

"What happened to Grand?"

"Got away. Nobody knows where."

"At first light, someone needs to take the news to Ric and Reba Sayed."

"I will run there," said Witt. "Straw still lays on the marsh path."

"We should all go," said Gemma. "First let me cook a meal for us."

Not seeing any of his kin, Ash brought Song and her family with him to his parents' hut. Still sleeping; he shook the shells.

"Who wakes us in the dark of night?" asked his father, Denn.

"Up with you all," said Ash. "You have visitors."

"Ash?" called Denn.

"It is me, Ash Skeye, and I have my wife Song and her kin with me."

"Your wife? Give us time to wake."

"We have traveled far without sleep. We are hungry, and if you do not open the door, I will kick it open. Make haste!"

Scowling, Denn opened the door flap. With his arms swinging, Ash strode up to him. Denn gaped at his son. The boy, now a full-grown man and fit from mining slate, stuck his face in his father's. Denn's lips quivered. "Welcome my family, Father."

The Era of Herbalists

Rubbing his eyes, Denn stepped aside and bade the visitors inside. From her bed nest, Mara shouted, "Go away and come back at a decent hour!"

Not waiting, Ash lifted a curtain. His mother reached for her switch but Ash snagged it first. He shook it at her and she cowered. Then he broke the thing and threw it in the hearth. It caught flame on the coals.

"Your whip no longer rules here. Come greet my wife and her family."

"My son has changed."

"Yes, and when I am hungry and tired, I am even more changed."

"Have you lost respect?"

"No, Mother, I have lost fear." Then he whispered to her, "If you speak unkindly to my wife because of her twisted foot, I will break yours."

Mara's mouth hung open.

"Be nice to Song, Mother, and she will teach you how to cook."

Slipping on her moccasins, Mara climbed from her bed.

"Come. Meet the family Newt."

"From where do they come?"

"Whispering Bay, many days south."

"Why did they not go to their place?"

"Because Whispering Bay is no more. Hurry, you have six more to feed."

"Six?"

"Do not fret, Jos cooks for hundreds. He will help you."

"Hundreds?"

"Jos? This is Mara, my mother. Can you help her make slim bread?"

"Fair day to you, Mara," said Jos. "Kindly show me your pantry."

Mara lifted a tanned skin and revealed a shelf with maize and acorn flour, salt, cured meats, fat, and dried fruits and vegetables.

Checking the hearth, Jos said, "Luna? Layan? Help Ash's mother build a proper cook fire. Denn? Can you show these girls your firewood pile?"

Nodding, Denn led them outside and pointed. The girls filled their arms and the other partition opened. Shy Skeye plodded out and gawked.

"Who are these people?"

Turning for her to see him, Ash said, "Little sister Shy. Greet my wife, Song Newt, and her family."

Song stepped forward. With wide eyes, Shy gaped at Song. "You? You married my brother? How could one so pretty marry a cripple?"

Song hobbled closer; Shy saw her bent foot. "Ah! You are as lame as he!"

But Song laughed. "For me, this is from my birth and of no fault of my own. But you, girl, you choose to be ugly inside, and that unsightliness sits on your face for all to see."

Suddenly, Shy's face crinkled, and she burst into tears and ran outside. Song shrugged her shoulder and sat on a fur mat. Smiling, Ash sat next to her.

"My sister learned a lesson," said Ash.

"If not, her bitter face might attract a brute," replied Song.

Mara called everyone to the morning meal, and Shy came back inside. Her head was bowed and she cupped a handful of ripe berries. Without speaking, Shy knelt beside Song, smiled, and placed some of the berries on Song's platter and the rest on her brother's.

"Now I see the prettiness in you," said Song. "Do you see how easy it is to make yourself so?"

Embarrassed, Shy nodded and took her place. Before eating, Denn blessed the gods for the bounty.

CHAPTER 54

The Chase

On a walk to the cooking area, Grand spied some soldiers collecting weapons from a tent. He had found one of the armories. Two guards. One was stationary, and the other was walking a patrol. A single entrance. He would need to cut an opening in the rear.

Hearing the sound of tool making, Grand followed the tap-tap-tapping. Beside a hut, a boy, too young yet to hunt, was chipping away on a piece of obsidian. Careful not to startle him, Grand coughed in his hand. The boy looked up.

"What tool do you fashion?"

"A blade, but I broke the tip, so now I make a scraper."

"For whom do you make your tools?"

"No one. I only practice."

"I am in need of a tool such as that one. Would you trade?" Grand held out a soapstone bear talisman suspended on a leather thong. He had taken the amulet from a slave.

"Yes," said the boy. He handed Grand the tool, and Grand looped the cord over the boy's head. He fondled the charm. The boy said, "My thanks." But Grand had already hurried off.

As soon as Pine described Grand, Werth recalled seeing him at the prodon's rest camp. "He will be where the prodon's guards are being lodged."

"Show me," said Pine. "Shadow's nose is working again. If he is here, we will find him."

Werth led the way and Gorg, Bru, and Luca came along. Near a group of palm-covered huts, Shadow sniffed a bush, his hackles rose, and he growled.

"Grand pissed here."

Shadow trotted to the hut and someone yelled, "A wolf!"

Dashing to the entry, Pine called Shadow back.

"I am looking for Grand, the brawny fellow you travel with."

"He is not here. Try the cooking place. He eats more than the rest of us."

Circling the area, Shadow picked up Grand's trail. They followed him to a large tent. Someone moaned. At the rear, a man on his back tried to sit up. Bru helped him. Recognizing him as from his people, Bru asked him in his tongue what had happened.

"I caught a big fellow cutting the tent and he clubbed me."

Gorg peeked inside. "This is the armory."

"Can you tell if any weapons are missing?" asked Pine. Bru interpreted and the man crawled inside. He scanned the stacks, and soon spotted bows on the ground. He counted the quivers. "Took a bow and quiver of arrows. I do not see any other places he rummaged."

"How long ago?" asked Bru.

"I cannot say," said the man. He rubbed his head. "For a while I slept."

"Bru? Ask if we can borrow some weapons to go after him."

Gorg, Luca, and Werth armed themselves with spears, and Pine and Bru with bows and quivers. They trailed after Shadow, who headed for the hills to the southeast. Though the sky above was clear and blue, thunder rumbled from that direction. Crossing the creek, Shadow lost the scent and the five men split up.

Spread out, they studied the terrain for traces of Grand. With his nose to the ground, Shadow whined and pawed the dirt. Soon he picked up a trace. Pine signaled Bru and Gorg on his left, and to Werth and Luca on his far right.

Running hard uphill, Shadow breathed in Grand's scent with Pine trailing. Halfway up the hill at a fork in the path, a deerskin pouch lay in the dirt. Pacing, Shadow waited for Pine to show him his find. Reaching his dog, Pine picked up the pouch. He peered inside. Empty. A twang caused Pine to glance over to a tree.

Aiming at Pine, Grand released the bowstring. The shaft arced toward Pine's chest. A black shape leaped in front of Pine. The arrow pierced

The Era of Herbalists

Shadow's shoulder. He hit the ground on his side, yelping. Kneeling, Pine held him.

From his perch in the tree, Grand strung another shaft, but the clamor of the pursuers sounded too close, so he climbed down. As fast as he could, he dashed up the hill. Behind him, Grand could hear the pursuers. Two of them on the left side of the ditch. Out of sight, he slipped into the narrow ravine and continued rushing up the twisty clay gully.

In the deep slot, he moved unseen. More distant thunder rumbled, but no lights flashed. A tree root gave him a hold to climb a steep section.

Farther up, a trickle of muddy water washed toward him. Then more swept over his feet. Then, before he took another step, he found the rushing water up to his knees. At the place he stood, he had no way up the ravine walls. Both sides were nearly sheer. Then the sound gained volume like a thousand bison charging. Before Grand could realize, a wall of murky water rushed him. Instinctively, he turned away and braced himself. The force tore the bow from his hand. Panicking, he slipped, and the flash flood took him.

Flailing in the deluge, he found the root he had used before and wrapped his arms around it. Holding on, tree branches scraped him as the flood rose. Abruptly, a broken limb gored his back. Grand shrieked. He reacted by jerking sideways. The intense water pressure ripped the jagged limb out of his flesh. Grand passed out from the pain. He lost his grip. The force pulled him under and the current spirited him away.

Believing Grand to be hiding in the ditch, Luca and Werth searched above with their spears ready. Taking their time, they studied every alcove. From their vantage point, they watched the flood water flowing through the gully. The flow cascaded through the ditch, stopping an arm's length from the top.

Branches whipped by and Luca and Werth backed away from the rim. Staring into the brown turmoil, a hand reached out and for a brief moment Grand's terrified face appeared, but then he submerged. Werth and Luca ran along the gully, but the water was swifter. They searched but saw no other sign of him. The current had swept Grand away with the debris. Eventually, his body would be left in a marsh and devoured by swamp creatures.

Having more experience, Gorg studied Shadow's injury. The arrow had struck his scapula at a downward angle, glanced off, and penetrated his chest. The bloody arrowhead protruded from Shadow's fur. Pine held him down and Gorg tugged on the feathered end. It was still connected, so he clutched the tip and rotated the feathered shaft until it snapped free. Quickly, he pulled the shank out. Shadow squealed and Pine comforted him. The front shaft fell out on its own. Some blood seeped out, but it seemed no organs were hit. Shadow would live. Not wanting to jolt him, they constructed a litter using two lances, the quiver straps, jute, and Pine's shirt. Bru and Pine carried him.

Hurrying to them, Werth and Luca spilled their story of how Grand Moon had suffered his end. For Pine, this meant he could focus on his family and the journey back to Twin Oaks.

At the camp, Zyanya had organized a team to help track Grand. As soon as she saw Shadow was wounded, she called her healer, Axel Reyna.

He came with his kit. The moment he saw the dog, he shook his head.

"Your Highness, I have no experience with animals."

"Treat him as you would a hairy man."

"Yes, Your Highness." Axel frowned and looked over to Pine. Sensing the man's distress, Pine faced Zyanya. "Your Highness. Tell him I will hold Shadow still while he cares for him."

Once Zyanya assured Axel of his safety, Axel showed Pine where to have Shadow lay and brought out the makings for a poultice. He mixed all-heal herb with honey and mashed ginger root. Axel showed Pine a wet sea sponge and pointed to Shadow's chest. Pine held Shadow's head. Occasionally, Shadow whimpered while Axel cleaned his injury, and when he pressed the cure-infused moss against the wound. Axel repeated the treatment to Shadow's side. Then with Pine's help, Axel secured the poultices with jute.

Through Zyanya, Axel told Pine, "Keep him still today. Leave the poultices; I will give him another treatment tonight. Give him no food, but as much water as he will drink. Walk him some tomorrow but also rest."

Pine thanked Axel, and with Bru's help they carried Shadow to the hut they shared. They laid Shadow on a thick stack of furs.

The Era of Herbalists

In tears, Maita Tupac stood in the doorway. He asked Bru, "Is Shadow going to be alright?"

"He will," said Bru. "Today he must rest, but tomorrow he would welcome your company."

Maita wiped his cheeks, bowed his head, and ran home.

CHAPTER 5 5

❦

Fulfilling the Prophecy

THE ENTOURAGE APPROACHED Twin Oaks. Thanks to the observer on the hill, the villagers were well aware of Zyanya's progress. Witt wanted to run ahead, but Chirp explained how the ceremony worked, so he stood beside the road waiting with the rest of the anxious villagers.

Standing beside the Nyte family, Ric and Reba held each other. Many other friends and relatives from Seaside Hill came. A bison horn sounded. Adorned in flowers and feathers, Zyanya strolled at the front of the parade with a sentry on either side. Four litter bearers carrying Lily, Pine, and Shadow followed. Seeing them, the crowd cheered. Behind them, men towed travois filled with trade goods.

Recognizing Chirp, Zyanya strode to him. "By uniting and returning these missing, separated lovers to the kin of their birth, a prophecy will be fulfilled."

Gorg signaled and the four men lowered the litter. First Pine stepped off and he helped Lily. With Pine's help, Shadow made it to his feet. He limped from the litter to Pine's side. Facing Pine and Lily, she muttered a prayer in her tongue. Then she turned. "Who claims this daughter?"

Reba and Ric stepped forward, and Ric said, "We, her father and her mother."

Zyanya took Lily's hand and led her to her parents. They took Lily to the sidelines. Reba trembled and cried as she embraced Lily. Tears ran down Ric's cheeks, but his smile swallowed them.

"Who claims this son?"

Chirp and Gemma moved up. "We, his mother and father," said Chirp.

Zyanya led Pine and Shadow to Chirp and Gemma. "According to the prophecy written in the age of the first people, on this day begins a millennium of peace and prosperity."

The Era of Herbalists

The crowd cheered and drummers, singers, and dancers from both villages made themselves known. Out came the food and drink.

The Nyte family gathered. Neva had been holding back, waiting for the proper time. "Father. The village is too small for two herbalists, and it has been my wish to become a midwife."

"Twin Oaks thrives with you as herbalist. With that thought, then it must be you would be an equally skilled midwife. You have my blessings."

Neva hugged Chirp. "Good, because I am already being schooled."

Witt spoke up. "Father? I have been the herbalist assistant since you were taken. Ask Neva, she will tell you of my worth."

"I can see that with my eyes. You shall stay my assistant, and soon it will be you wanting your own helper."

Among those in the crowd, Pine spotted Falk Moon. Their eyes met and Falk came to Pine. "It was told to me that my son forced you into the waterfall. Is the tale true?"

"Yes. While he stabbed my back, he claimed Lily for his."

"For that I am sorry. I am glad that you both survived. No one knows what became of Grand, but now that you both live, his crimes are not the same."

Pine wanted to tell Falk how Grand had been swept away in a flash flood, but instead he simply nodded and went back to Lily.

Both the Twin Oaks and Seaside Hill council members met with Zyanya. Of all the samples she had brought for trade, bamboo topped the list. Especially when she explained how easily the plant grew and how quickly it matured. The cocos confused them, but they liked mangosteens. Also, with samples of cloth and spun cotton fiber, she had brought a loom and a weaver to teach.

For her people, she collected a basket of maize seeds, fine pelts, tanned skins, salt, and baskets. Also, Zyanya visited the herbalist hut to see Neva's extensive garden of herbs and cures. She left with a basket of seeds and bulbs. A gift from Neva, for saving Lily, her brother, and Shadow.

After the festivities, Twin Oaks offered huts for Zyanya and her people. She took Bru away from his friends and brought him to her hut. To be alone with him, Zyanya ordered her sentries away. "Bru? Do you see me as a woman?"

"Yes, Your High…um, Zyanya."

"Something in me has changed. I no longer wish to be a priestess. I only want to be a woman."

"Can you not be both?"

The question caused her to think. Of course she could do both, but after seeing her father for what he really was and how he had mocked the gods, her own faith weakened. "My father said there are no gods. What if he was right?"

"I do not know of gods. I drink water; it gives me life, so I worship it. The same with fire, the air, and the earth. All she provides gives life. So, to me, she is worthy of worship."

"She?"

"According to my mother, the earth is a woman."

"And what of me as a woman? What would I deserve from you?"

"You deserve more than I can give you."

Zyanya took his hands in hers. "Did you not tell me once you would defend me with your life?"

"True, Zyanya. I would."

Staring in his eyes, she said, "That is more than I need. More than I would ever want from you. All I desire from you, is you."

"Me? A simple pot maker?"

"What I see before me is a strong man with a gentle nature, and the only man to ever stir the womanhood in me."

Everything he heard from her freed his own longing and Bru pulled her close. Tenderly, he cupped her cheek and kissed her lips. Zyanya responded and pressed her mouth against his. Bru's hand found the tie on her dress. He tugged on it, and the cloth fell to her feet.

Naked, Zyanya pulled Bru's loin skin off. Holding her, he lowered them to the furs, and they fondled and kissed each other.

Bru said, "I do not know about gods, but I have found a goddess I wish to worship."

"Make me with child," whispered Zyanya.

"Yes, Your Highness," said Bru. He set off on the task.

Epilogue

In the south, the people of the seven sacred cities settled on the plain, a day away from the sea. The city spread from the blue stream to the south to the green river to the north, and against the hills to the east. Bent on forming their own townships, some clutches of refugees unwilling to dwell in such a large community set off on their own in all four directions.

Missing the sea, Werth joined up with the group going there. Unable to find any of his own kin, Luca went with him.

Erecting a hut near Bru and Zyanya's, Gorg found a woman to keep him company. More than that, she had two young sons and an infant daughter for him to raise.

Since Zyanya had stepped down from her role as leader, the people elected a council to govern. Still, people sought her wisdom, and sometimes she shared what they pursued. These days her main concern was the child thrashing around inside her swollen belly. Bru, too, had his worries. So much so that Zyanya hid the listening cone from him. Still, many times she woke with his warm face pressing on her and his beard tickling her tummy. Gonda Mara was nearly as bad, making her drink bitter concoctions and forcing her to walk when all she wanted to do was eat mangosteens, drink coco juice, and pee.

To the north, in the spring, Twin Oaks celebrated another wedding: Roth Uhl and Neva Nyte. Most of the village attended, and many of their friends from Seaside Hill came.

The introduction of cloth and bamboo gave both Twin Oaks and Seaside Hill new looks. And with the trading came new families, and some of the existing families grew with children.

One evening, a crowd gathered around Pine and Lily's hut. Inside, Neva performed in her new occupation as midwife. Both Reba and Gemma assisted.

Outside, Pine paced among the hopeful assembly. Roth did his best to clear space for him. Chirp and Ric sat by the fire in front of the herbalist hut, sipping spirit juice and telling tales.

Each sound caused Pine to pause and listen. But each time it was nothing. So Pine kept marching, and Roth maintained the space for his seemingly endless journey. Then he heard a wail. Lengthy and noisy. Gemma peeked out the door flap. "Pine! You have a daughter!"

Pine rushed to the doorway and gazed at the child in his mother's arms. Another louder cry sounded, and Reba came to the door with his other child. "Pine. You also have a son."

Even though Pine had heard with his own ears the two heartbeats, the sight of them caused him to faint. Thankfully, Roth caught him, and Witt splashed water in his face.

Satisfying Song's love of the sea, Ash took her to a secluded section, and he built a fire and rolled out their bed nest. Song heated some ginger and honey-coated bison, and peeled some mangosteens. Having learned how, Ash split a coco, poured the juice in gourds, and scraped the white fruit on platters. They ate, drank spirit juice, and laughed. Afterwards, Song and Ash strolled along the shore. Somehow they felt less clumsy walking barefoot in the sand. A beached log gave them a place to sit, and they watched the sunset.

Later, after their third coupling, Song stared at the sky and asked, "Why do some of the stars shoot across the sky and die?"

Having seen one fall in the forest once, he was about to tell her his theory about celestial collisions, but instead he said, "In jest, the gods throw the stars at one another and when they catch them, they eat them."

"Finally, my husband makes some sense."